AT THE
MOUNTAIN'S EDGE

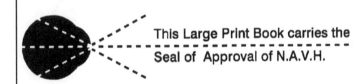

This Large Print Book carries the
Seal of Approval of N.A.V.H.

AT THE MOUNTAIN'S EDGE

GENEVIEVE GRAHAM

KENNEBEC LARGE PRINT
A part of Gale, a Cengage Company

Farmington Hills, Mich • San Francisco • New York • Waterville, Maine
Meriden, Conn • Mason, Ohio • Chicago

Copyright © 2019 by Genevieve Graham.
Kennebec Large Print, a part of Gale, a Cengage Company.

Kennebec Large Print® Superior Collection.
The text of this Large Print edition is unabridged.
Other aspects of the book may vary from the original edition.
Set in 16 pt. Plantin.

LIBRARY OF CONGRESS CIP DATA ON FILE.
CATALOGUING IN PUBLICATION FOR THIS BOOK
IS AVAILABLE FROM THE LIBRARY OF CONGRESS

ISBN-13: 978-1-4328-6508-5 (softcover alk. paper)

Published in 2019 by arrangement with Simon & Schuster, Inc.

Printed in the United States of America
1 2 3 4 5 6 7 23 22 21 20 19

To Dwayne . . .

*You never know who you're going to
meet on the side of a mountain.*

Only those who will risk going too far can possibly find out how far one can go.

T. S. ELIOT

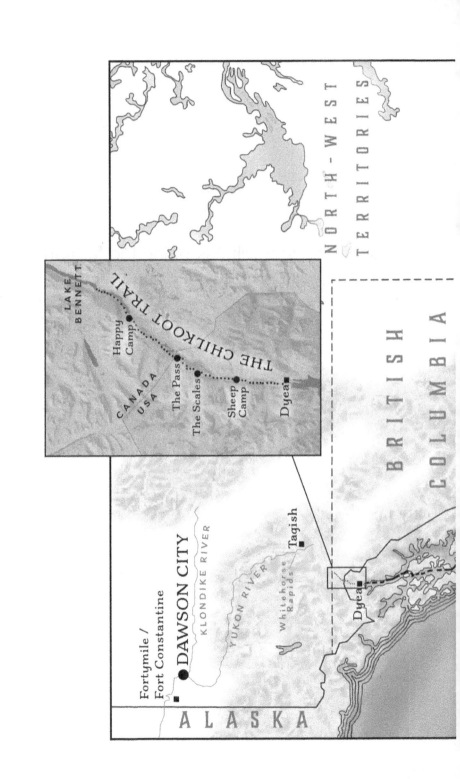

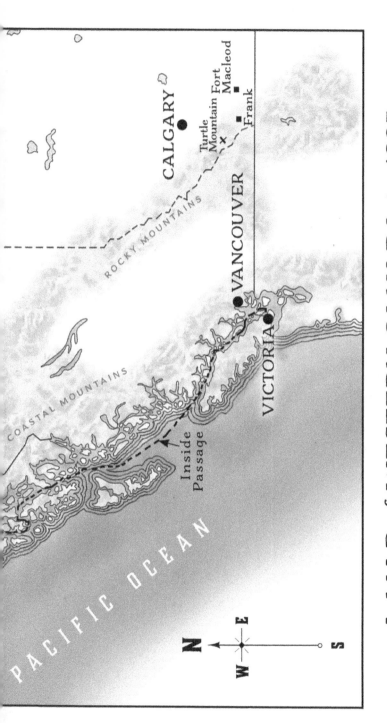

A MAP of WESTERN CANADA in 1897

■ ■ ■ ■

PART ONE:
THE TRAIL

■ ■ ■ ■

ONE:
LIZA

1897

Liza's laugh was out before she could stop it. No one else in the room made a sound. She glanced at her mother, wondering if perhaps she'd misheard her father's words, but she looked as bewildered as Liza felt. Even Stan had been stunned into silence, and that was rare. Her brother usually had something to say about everything. She let her breath out slowly, timing it with the sober tick-tock of the old clock on the mantel behind her, waiting for her father to laugh and assure them he'd been joking.

Up until a minute ago, the evening had been like any other. Liza had been absorbed in *The Adventures of Sherlock Holmes* — though if her brother would stop spouting trivia about the rubber forests of Nicaragua or whatever it was from his latest *National Geographic Magazine* she would have been even more engrossed in it. On the other side of the room, her mother had been quietly

13

sewing in her armchair by the fire while Liza's father set out his pipe and tobacco, the ledgers for the family's general store spread in front of him.

Then, as calmly as one might announce they were going for a walk up the street, her father had declared his intention to move both the family and their business from Vancouver to Dawson City, in the Yukon. That's when Liza had laughed, and the choked sound had fallen flat in the ensuing silence.

"They call it the 'Paris of the North,' " he said.

To Liza's bewilderment, he looked absolutely thrilled about the idea, and he was regarding his family as though they'd leap at the opportunity. Certainly she would, given the chance to see the *real* Paris. But this?

After an uncomfortable pause, Liza's mother spoke. "Arthur, what on earth are you talking about?"

"An adventure the likes of which none of us have ever imagined, my dear." He beamed, drawing out his answer as he drew out the lighting of his pipe. The aromatic smoke began curling above their heads, but its normal ability to soothe Liza was absent tonight. She was as impatient as her mother to know more.

"Just because the rest of the world is taking leave of its senses," her mother said, lips tight, "that does not mean this family must do the same."

"Think of the business, Agatha," Liza's father replied. "The Klondike Gold Rush is the opportunity of a lifetime. We shall build a future in which all our roads are, quite literally, paved in gold."

"No, thank you," she replied. "I am more than satisfied on our present muddy road. As far as the business is concerned, I am quite content. Thanks to this gold phenomenon, the depression is finally lifting, and while I'll admit the past few years have been challenging, our store is already doing much better. The prospectors are buying their supplies from us, so there is no need for us to move to the distant wilds."

As her parents spoke, Liza cast a glance at her brother. He appeared to have recovered from his shock, and from the eager lean of his body Liza could practically see a pick and shovel already clenched in his hands.

"Father, I think this is a marvellous idea," Stan said, sounding more like an excited little boy than a young man of twenty-two. "Besides, I'd love to ride a dogsled."

"Don't be absurd," Liza said. "You don't

know the first thing about dogsledding. You'd end up in a snowdrift."

"No, I wouldn't. There was a dogsled display set up outside the Vancouver Hardware shop today, and the shopkeeper was demonstrating how to drive them. It didn't look all that difficult."

"I saw that display, too. The four raggedy mongrels they'd hitched to it hardly looked as if they were up to that type of journey."

"So now you're an expert?"

Liza closed her eyes. Once Stan had something on his mind, there was no way to get around it.

"Didn't think so. Clubb and Stewart over on Cordova Street call themselves 'Klondike Outfitters,' so I imagine they'd know all about it. I could go ask them."

Their father cleared his throat, interrupting their banter. "No doubt Mr. Clubb would be happy to sell you whatever your heart desires for four times the usual price."

"If supplies are so expensive," her mother interjected, "then I don't see how we can afford this venture."

Liza did. For the past three years, she'd peeked at the store ledgers when her father wasn't looking, fascinated by the columns of figures, the rise and fall of sales. Last year, when the newspapers had announced the discovery of gold in the Yukon, she'd watched as the store's numbers soared to a thrilling new height. But she never told her father she'd done that. Ever since they'd first set up their store in Vancouver, Liza had worked behind the counter. She'd only been ten years old, and her father had quickly noticed the magnetic effect her bright smile had on customers. Now, at twenty, Liza still loved running the cash, but she longed to do more and had asked her father if she could work on the ledgers.

"Your job is to help the customers," he'd replied.

"I can do more than count change," she'd insisted.

"Leave the accounting to me. It's a man's job."

The remark bothered her, but none of her attempts to change his mind worked, so she took matters into her own hands. She figured it wouldn't do anyone any harm if she quietly taught herself how the shop's finances worked, and one of the first things she discovered was that her father was an adept businessman. Now she realized she should have suspected something was brewing. He'd been studying the newspapers with more intensity of late, and she'd noticed him stockpiling snowshoes and other outdoor equipment. She just hadn't imagined any of it might be for their personal use.

"We wouldn't be mining, would we?" she asked. "We know nothing about mining."

"Of course not," her father replied. "We'd be mining the miners. Trust me, Liza. This is an incredible opportunity. We cannot lose."

"But we *could* mine, right?" Stan pressed.

A tiny whistle sang through the room as her father drew on his pipe. "If you can find the time, I don't see why not. But our priority will be in establishing the business, because in order to afford what we will need in Dawson City, I will be selling both the shop and this house."

Liza caught her breath, and her fingers dug into the arms of her chair.

"Arthur," her mother said carefully, "I know your heart is set on this, but it seems . . . irresponsible. To start with, the Yukon is not the place for a young lady."

Liza's thoughts touched on handsome Charles MacGillvray, the young man who stopped by to see her at the store every so often. Charles hadn't done anything more than flirt over the counter, and Liza didn't feel a terrible longing when he wasn't around, but she did feel a tug of regret at being denied the opportunity to see how things might go between the two of them.

"Our daughter is not a dainty flower," her father said, appraising her. "She's made of stronger stuff."

"Am I?" Liza asked.

"Certainly. You've never shied away from hard work. Besides, you and your mother would always be with Stan and me, safe from any possible threats."

"Oh, Stan would protect me, would he?" Liza gave her brother a sideways look.

Stan ignored her and turned to their mother. "Let's go, Mother," he urged. "Think of it! The Klondike Gold Fields! It's a strike like no one has ever seen before, and it's so close!"

"Close?" Liza said. "For someone who reads as much as you do, you might want to brush up on geography."

"I mean as compared to the rest of the world, obviously. People are travelling to the Yukon from all over — America, Europe, England — and all of them are much farther away than we are. After a few weeks up there, they return home with boats full of gold. I read some have more than a hundred thousand dollars of gold with them! Think of that: *a hundred thousand dollars!*"

Her mother studied the three of them.

19

"There will be no more talk of the Yukon. The Petersons are not embarking on another wild goose chase, and that's that."

"*Another* wild goose chase?" Liza's father asked, his smile fading.

"You know what I'm talking about, Arthur. Our life in Toronto was perfectly fine. Because of you, I bid my family goodbye and we uprooted everything so we could move to this rough, rainy place." She kept her eyes on him as she stabbed her sewing needle through the coat she was mending. "Since then we've poured our lives and everything we have into the store — and now that business is finally starting to improve, you want to move us again. It's not fair, Arthur."

Silence descended over the room. Toronto meant little to Liza, since she and Stan had been very young when the family had come to Vancouver. The voyage had seemed like an adventure to them — no one else they knew had ever taken a train! — and they'd both settled in well. But Liza knew her mother still longed for the family she'd left behind. Especially her sister, to whom she still wrote weekly letters. While she did seem happier now that the store was doing well, whenever Liza made any passing mention of Toronto her mother drooped like a wilted flower, speaking wistfully of its bustling streets with their colourful shops and window displays, recalling the dances and parties she had attended regularly before she'd met her husband.

Liza's father rose and crossed the room, surprising them all when he knelt at the side of his wife's chair. He carefully pried her sewing needle from between her fingers, then took her hands in his own.

"You've sacrificed so much for our family, my dear," he said gently, "and yet I am begging for more. Yes, our store is relatively successful, but we are still a small fish and the market here is saturated. Because of that, I fear we may never reach our potential." He kissed her knuckles. "I want more for you, Agatha. I want to give you the life I promised you when we married."

Her expression eased. "Oh, Arthur. You have."

His fingers skimmed along the faded upholstery on the arm of her chair, then paused over the worn patch near her elbow. "No," he said. "This isn't what I promised you. You deserve so much more. Do you remember the day I took you to the Crystal Palace? How you said you would love to see the original in London? I promised I would someday give you the world, and now I can take you to the top of it. From there, the sky is the limit."

"We talked about a lot of things," she replied. "Young people always have dreams they can't fulfil."

"And yet here we are, a quarter of a century later, and I still dream. We have been so busy these past few years with family and work that I fear we have discarded whatever youthful aspirations we once held. I confess this gold fever has lit a fire in my heart, a desire to explore the unexplored, a thirst for adventure, and it is my hope that I have only to ignite this passion within your own heart for you to feel a similar longing."

"Is that right? Am I to be so easily swayed?"

Liza had never heard her father speak this way, of hearts and adventures, of promises and dreams, and though her mother appeared unmoved, her voice had softened.

"I see it not as swaying you so much as reminding you."

After a moment, her mother spoke again. "How would we live, if we were to do this thing? How does it work?"

In that instant, Liza saw herself in the future, and her throat tightened. The Liza in her mind stepped out of her home, suitcase in hand, and the door closed behind her with a terrible click of finality. Travel to the Yukon? She shuddered at the thought. Why, that was thousands of miles away. And wasn't it buried in snow twelve months of the year? Vancouver at its worst was only ever inconvenienced by two inches of the stuff.

Everyone else might be fine with this plan, but Liza did not want to go. Absolutely not. No matter how much gold was buried up there, she had no interest in leaving Vancouver. Everything she knew was here. Of course she'd admired the sun blazing on the distant mountain peaks before, wondering what it might be like to stand up there and look down over the city, but those had never been more than passing, romantic thoughts. Never, *ever* had she dreamed of climbing a mountain. But now . . .

"Will it be a temporary thing?" she asked. "I mean, we would return to Vancouver afterwards, wouldn't we?"

"It would last as long as it needs to." The smile that spread across her father's face was full of wonder. "The world will be stretched out before us, and the opportunities are boundless."

She hesitated. "But we don't have to leave right away, do we?"

"Oh yes," he said, getting to his feet. Now

that the matter was resolved, he had a bounce to his step. "As soon as possible, if we are to stay ahead of the pack."

Liza looked to her mother, who had resumed her mending with new purpose, but she wouldn't meet Liza's eye. She would follow her husband without any further questions, Liza knew.

As her father left the room, Liza leaned back in her chair, her head spinning. How could they possibly travel to the wild frontiers of the Yukon? How would they know what to do? How would they look after themselves? The more she thought about it, the more frightened she became. She had no question that her father was a smart man, that he believed this move was the right thing for all of them, but it sounded more than a little crazy to Liza. She let her breath out slowly, trying to ease the panic that had tightened her chest. Her father would take care of them, she reminded herself. He would do everything he could to prepare them for the road ahead. All Liza had to do was trust him. And she did. With all her heart.

The problem was that she didn't trust the Yukon.

Two:
Ben

Ben Turner knew what kind of man he wanted to be. He'd always known. Every bruise he'd weathered, every cry he'd clenched behind his teeth, and every tear he'd saved for the privacy of the darkness had shown him who he did *not* want to be. He just hadn't figured becoming that man would be this difficult.

"It's a shame, Constable Turner," Sergeant-Major Scott said, cutting through Ben's thoughts.

The Sergeant-Major sat behind his desk, smoothing out his thick black moustache and studying a file while Ben stood at attention, arms locked straight at his sides. With all his heart he wished he could be anywhere but where he was at that precise moment.

Scott continued. "You're top of the class in marksmanship, you've mastered everything from first aid to those tricky questions of the law, and you're the best damn horse-man I've ever seen. You would be a definite asset to the Force if only . . ."

Ben focused on remaining calm, staring straight ahead, keeping his mouth shut. He knew what was coming.

"It's your temper," the Sergeant-Major said, tapping Ben's open folder. "You know that. Listen, Turner, it's simple. If you can't learn to hold it in check, we can't have you in the North-West Mounted Police." He raised an eyebrow, peered across the desk at the cuts on Ben's knuckles. "To your credit, at least you took it out on a fence post this time, not the fellow who upset you. Still, your inability to control your anger is of great concern."

Ben knew Scott was right, and that frus-trated him more than ever. He'd gotten car-ried away again, annoyed by Constable Hill's constant complaints as they'd marched that morning. In the instant Ben had barked at Hill and called him lazy, he had known he'd made a mistake. It wasn't his place to discipline anyone, and he'd already been reminded of that many times. The Sergeant heading up the march had given Ben a tongue-lashing for it, and Ben had been so angry at himself that he'd wheeled around and punched the fence post behind him. It had been a stupid thing to do. And now he was here.

Rage came as naturally to Ben as breathing. It was the only thing he'd ever learned from his father. Had he followed his father's lead, Ben's life would have been much simpler. He could have remained on his father's poor excuse for a farm, lashing out when the need arose, relishing the pain of split knuckles, roaring until he saw red, and no one would have come after him for it.

But he had never considered staying at the farm. After his parents died, Ben had fled the place. He'd lived rough for about five years, squatting between occasional barns and scattered trees, hunting and trapping just enough that he didn't have to beg. He'd lived on and off with the Blackfoot, and he'd worked as a cowboy, doing whatever needed doing. He'd adjusted to life as a tumbleweed, rolling wherever the wind pushed him, and he'd never felt sorry for himself. Because even when the skies opened or the wolves circled too close, nothing could ever be as bad as his life on the farm had been. Out on his own, no one beat him. No one looked at him as if they wished he'd never been born.

"I am well aware," Sergeant-Major Scott said, twisting one edge of his moustache,

27

"that you are hating every second of this interview. And I appreciate the fact that you haven't flown over the desk, intent on murdering me." He leaned back in his chair. "Should I take that as a sign that you're working on controlling that temper of yours?"

"Permission to speak, sir?" Ben asked.

Scott lifted an eyebrow. "I am not a 'sir,' Constable. I work for a living."

Ben had been so tense he'd forgotten. Only commissioned officers were addressed with "sir." "Of course, Sergeant-Major."

"All right. Go ahead."

"I've known anger my whole life. It's what I grew up with, and it's what I've always used to get by. Wasn't 'til I got here that I found out my temper was a problem, and now I'm working to fix it. I am getting better. Just like Mack with his riding. He can stay on a horse a lot longer these days. In my case, I'm sorry for beating on that fence post." His knuckles were still swollen, but he resisted balling them into fists. He wasn't permitted to move when he was at attention. "Even sorrier today. It won't happen again, Sergeant-Major."

Scott nodded. "Depot Division is here to teach men like you how to be a Mountie, but I'll be honest with you. We've been doing this for twenty-five years, and we've learned that not everyone is cut out to be one. Mounties have to be the best they can be, every single day. They are here to earn respect and keep the peace, and they look after people. But if you don't fix this problem of yours, folks aren't gonna feel safe around you. Frankly, we don't need a man like that on the Force."

Ben's stomach was in knots. Being a Mountie was all he had ever wanted. Just a few months ago, he'd finally worked up the courage to wander into the outpost at Fort Macleod, where he'd stopped in front of the poster nailed outside the door. He'd never been a strong reader, but this was important, so he took his time and slowly put the words together in his mind. *Join the North-West Mounted Police!* the bold print had beckoned, and he'd leaned in to make sure he understood the requirements. Yes, he was active and able-bodied. Yes, he could tend and ride a horse. Yes, he was sober. He had no idea what having a "sound constitution" or an "exemplary character" meant, but he had known right away this was the life for him. Now Sergeant-Major Scott was questioning that, and rightfully so.

"You know you're gonna make more mistakes, right?" Scott continued. "Everyone does. It's part of living. What matters is how you handle those mistakes, and what you do the next time a problem comes up." He closed the folder and got to his feet. "Tell you what. You have six weeks left in your training here. Show us we can rely on you."

"Yes, Sergeant-Major. I will."

"But you're on dangerous ground, Constable," he said, reaching for the door. "If you take one more step out of line, you're finished here."

Burning with humiliation, Ben strode from the office to the stables, then stepped inside his horse's stall. The tall black gelding jerked his head up, sensing Ben's dark mood, but a moment later the horse relaxed and huffed out his approval as Ben worked through his frustration with the curry comb. As he brushed, Ben felt the anger drain from his own body, and he breathed more easily, grateful that at least here, with the horse, he could use his strength for good.

Once horse and saddle were gleaming, he mounted and rode to the large paddock where the others were already in formation.

"Ah, Constable Turner." Corporal St. John's nasal sarcasm cut through the air. "Good to see you. We were hoping you would honour us with your presence at

30

some point today."

Ben's retort was on the tip of his tongue, but he bit down on it and joined the others without a word. No time like the present to work on his patience.

Ben had ridden horses for as long as he could remember. Having left Fort Macleod, he'd spent five days in the saddle and arrived in Regina. There he'd stepped into Depot Division, where everything had been new, from the spurs to the saddle. In his cowboying days, he had only ever ridden bareback, and he was used to throwing his body carelessly over a horse before galloping away, then leaping off before the animal had stopped running. A saddle was a completely different thing. It took away the sensation of being connected to the horse — though he had to admit that it did feel a heck of a lot better on his backside. The saddle and the riding drills reined him in, forcing Ben to focus on order and formation rather than give in to his natural tendency to ride hard and fast. Keeping both him and his horse restrained at every step was a slow form of torture for Ben, but he stuck to it, and over time the exercises became more natural.

The hours Ben and the other Constables spent training with the horses were nothing compared to the endless exercises required of them. The men underwent exhausting endurance tests, learned fighting skills, and practised shooting. When they weren't sweating and panting out in the field, they sat at desks and learned the law. Everything was done with a sharp "Yes, Sergeant-Major! No, Sergeant-Major! Whatever you say, Sergeant-Major!" and at night they couldn't wait to fall into their cots. Ben had seen men start to nod off at the supper table before being swiftly reprimanded, and he'd heard more than one muffled "Yes, Sergeant-Major!" in the middle of the night as someone dreamed about training. A couple of weeks in, a few of the Constables quit, but Ben kept on, hoping he was strong enough, fast enough, and smart enough to make it to the end.

I'm almost there, he thought.

"Work *together*! You're a *unit*!" Corporal St. John shouted at the men, breaking Ben's reverie. "You must know the man and the horse beside you like you know yourself."

Ben faced forward, but his eyes darted to the side, checking to make sure the man across the paddock from him was lined up properly. Their paths needed to intersect without forcing either horse to slow or stop. He hoped Mack, who was bumping along behind him, was doing the same, but he knew Mack generally spent more time worrying about staying in the saddle than he did about the drill. Mounties did everything together, so if one man made a mistake they all suffered for it. As the drill continued, Ben watched Mack from the corner of his eye and was glad to see the older man's expression was set in concentration. By the end Ben was impressed. Mack had completed the exercise without any problems.

"Nice work out there today," Ben told him as they walked the horses back to the stable.

Mack smiled. "Thanks. I'm getting there."

Ben nodded. Me too, he thought.

In the final week of Depot, the Constables were informed that they would be individually tested on their ability to use their training in real-life situations. Ben was sitting in the classroom one morning when Sergeant-Major Scott appeared in the doorway.

"Constable Turner," he said, and every head swivelled to look at Ben. "This way."

Nerves rushed through him as he got to his feet. This was it. If he passed this test, he would be a Mountie. Trying to keep his breathing steady, he followed the Sergeant-Major outside and saw that one of the small outbuildings was engulfed in flames. The staff in the area were paying no attention to the inferno, so Ben figured it was part of the test.

Scott led him to a spot about twenty feet away from the fire. "A citizen is trapped inside," he said.

They would have used a dummy for this exercise, Ben knew, but he'd be expected to treat it like a real person.

"You are to find the victim and administer first aid. The victim is your sole responsibility, Constable. In this scenario, I want you to assume there are other Mounties out here with you, even though you cannot see them. They will do their job, and you will do yours. Do you understand?"

"Yes, Sergeant-Major." So this was a team exercise, he realized, even though he was actually alone. This about trusting the other men to do their jobs while he did his. *I can do this.*

"Go ahead."

Ben didn't hesitate. He dashed to the building and leapt through the flames licking at the door frame. It was smoky inside, and the heat was intense, but if he could get this done quickly he'd be all right. In under a couple of minutes, he found the dummy beneath a fallen beam, pulled it from under the debris, and carried it outside. After laying the body on the ground, he followed every lesson he'd been taught while Sergeant-Major Scott watched. It was up to Scott to determine when the victim was "breathing" on its own.

Then a woman screamed, and Ben's focus shattered. He spun in place, instantly on high alert, and scanned the field for the source. There — beyond the fire, by the cookhouse. A man was shaking a woman, and she was flopping around like a rag doll. Ben leapt to his feet and took a step towards them.

"Where are you going?" Scott asked.

"Sergeant-Major, behind you, there's a woman —"

Scott didn't even glance in the direction Ben had indicated. "Your assignment is here," he said.

The woman shrieked again, stumbling backwards as she tried to wrestle out of the man's hands, and Ben's heart raced. She needed help. He knew from experience that if the man started hitting her she might never get up.

"Sergeant-Major, I —"

"If you leave your post," Scott said, "you might as well leave Depot today, Constable. Empty-handed."

The agony of not racing to the woman's aid was like a physical pressure on Ben's chest. He dropped to his knees and continued treating the dummy for its imagined injuries, knowing the sooner he finished this assignment, the sooner he could help the woman. After another minute, Sergeant-Major Scott told him he could stop what he was doing, and Ben jumped to his feet. Before he could set off running, Scott held out his hand.

"What are you doing?" Ben asked, bridling at his interference. "I have to —"

Scott turned towards the couple in the distance, who were now standing apart from each other. "Thank you, Mr. and Mrs. Purcell!" he called. "You both did an excellent job."

Ben gawked at the pair, who were now waving cheerily at them, then looked back at the Sergeant-Major, baffled.

"That was part of the test, Constable Turner."

"What?"

Anger pulsed through Ben as he pieced together what was going on. The woman had never been in danger. She was only there to make a fool out of him. How dare Scott bait him like that? Didn't he know what that would do to Ben? He squeezed his hands into fists, clenching them so hard his nails bit into his palms, and the sting cut through his daze. *No, he didn't know,* Ben realized slowly. Scott couldn't have known how difficult it would be for Ben to stand by while a woman suffered like that. No one would, because Ben kept that part of his life locked deep inside him. All Scott had done today was present a real-life challenge, nothing more than that. One finger at a time, Ben relaxed his hands.

"You did well, Constable," Scott said, studying him. "We've all taken note of how strong you are independently, but what we needed to test you on was how you would react knowing you were backed up by your fellow Mounties. We needed to make sure you could accept being part of a team. As difficult as that test was, you were right to leave the other, seemingly more important incident to one of them." The shadow of a smile curled beneath Scott's thin moustache. "I bet you're angry about the deception, but I had to push you. I had to see if you could control your temper, and you did. Well done."

Ben closed his eyes briefly as the last dredges of anger ebbed from his body. "Heck of a test," he admitted.

"We're proud of how far you've come," Scott said. "Congratulations. You'll make a great Mountie, Constable Turner."

No one had ever said anything like that to Ben before, and the tight grip of emotion he felt in his throat was unfamiliar. "Thank you, Sergeant-Major," he managed.

On the morning of Ben's graduation, he donned his uniform then paused to study his reflection in the barracks's small mirror. Gone was the softness of his cheeks and the childish confusion in his expression. His eyes were clear, his posture strong. Of course some things would never completely disappear, and he leaned closer to examine the faded scar carved beneath his left eye, given to him by his father ten years ago. *Something to remember me by,* the old man had said. As if Ben needed any kind of reminder of what it was like to be hit in the face with a board.

He shook his head to scatter the memory and focused instead on the vivid red of his coat. It was the finest, most sturdy article of clothing Ben had ever seen, let alone worn, and even though he'd worn it many times during his training, he still had to resist the urge to touch every one of the eight brass buttons gleaming against the wool. The coat's collar, cuffs, and hem were edged with a striking yellow cord, and matching stripes ran down the sides of his navy trousers before they disappeared into his black leather boots. That morning Ben had shined those boots until they practically offered a reflection.

"Come on, now," Corporal St. John teased, handing Ben his formal white helmet. "No need to be goggling at the mirror all day like a lady."

Ben adjusted the gilded chain of his formal helmet under his chin and glanced one more time at his reflection. He looked a lot like the Mounties he'd seen at the outpost when he'd dared to enter their building for the first time. That seemed like a lifetime ago.

Inside the hall, Ben took his place in line with his fellow graduates, all of them standing tall and ready to serve. One by one they were called forward and recognized, and as Ben's own name was called he lifted his chin with pride, a new sense of confidence coursing through him.

This, he thought with satisfaction, *is where I belong.*

THREE:
LIZA

Liza leaned over the cold metal rail of the SS *Islander,* scanning the wide expanse of the Inside Passage as the clamour of the ship's engine filled her ears. Stan, standing beside her, didn't seem to mind the noise or the monotony, but the novelty of travelling by ship had quickly worn off for Liza. They had set off from Victoria four days ago, and now they were travelling to Dyea, the entryway to the Yukon and the first stop on their trek to Dawson City. Liza had heard somewhere that the *Islander* was the most luxurious vessel on this route, but for the life of her, she couldn't figure out how it had gotten that sort of reputation. If the *Islander* truly deserved it, Liza had no desire to see the competition.

"Look there!" Stan suddenly yelled. "Killer whale!"

Liza squinted. "Where?"

"Just watch. They have to come up to

breathe."

"Yes. I know that."

It hadn't even been a week and already Stan's constant display of knowledge was wearing on her nerves. Being educated about a subject was all fine and good, and he could be quite useful when she needed information, but what he didn't appear to grasp was that Liza wasn't exactly ignorant. She knew whales —

She gasped with delight as a slender fin cut through the water not twenty yards away. The orca skimmed the surface, giving them a glimpse of its sleek black head and the distinctive patch of white on its cheek, then sank again. Two more fins followed in its wake, cresting for a moment then disappearing, as if the creatures were connected to an underwater wheel.

"Three!" Liza cried, pointing. "I saw three of them! How beautiful!"

She was distracted by a sound beside her, and when she looked over she saw a dirty white dog standing on its hind legs against the rail, tongue lolling from its mouth.

"Did you want to see the whales too?" she asked the dog, who wagged its tail in reply.

A quick peek determined her new friend was female, and pregnant at that. Liza knew to be careful around her, since most of the dogs on board were too ornery for a person to approach, but this one seemed just as delighted by the sight of the whales as Liza had been. She reached out a hand for the dog to sniff, then stroked the grimy fur on her neck, enjoying the friendly contact.

"You're very sweet," she said, scratching behind the dog's perky ears. "You're not like the others, are you?"

Stan scowled. "Sure she is. She's filthy and probably crawling with fleas."

"At least she doesn't want to bite me."

"Someone bit her, though. Look at that front paw."

"Oh dear," Liza murmured. The paw was badly swollen, and its fur was matted with dried blood, drawing flies. If Liza could clean it — but when she reached towards the paw, the dog jerked it away and retreated to lick her wound.

"Nothing I can do if she won't let me. Poor thing. Do you think she'll be okay?"

Stan shrugged. "It'd be a waste of a good dog if she died. I hear sled dogs are pretty valuable out here."

The whales were gone for now and the dog had left as well, so Liza and Stan decided to wander around the ship, detouring to bring their parents toast and tea in their cabin. Their mother had suffered terribly from seasickness ever since they'd boarded the ship. Fortunately, their father was devoted to taking care of her, and today she said she was feeling a little better. She didn't finish her toast, though, so Liza pocketed the crust in case she ran into the dog again. Before she left the cabin she kissed her mother's cheek, then said a silent prayer that she would recover soon. They all needed to be strong for the journey ahead.

The thought made Liza pause, as it always did. Was *she* strong enough? She wasn't sure.

Within a matter of weeks, her old life had ended. The store was gone, the house had been sold, and everything they still owned was stowed in the bowels of the reeking SS *Islander,* her home for forty days or so. Trapped on board with about a hundred and fifty other passengers — only three of whom, she believed, were women — she was constantly bumping elbows with strangers, and she'd learned the hard way to be careful where she stepped. In addition to its regular passengers, the boat carried oxen, cattle, horses, goats, and dogs, none of which worried about where they left their droppings.

At least the weather wasn't overly cold, she mused as she and Stan returned to the deck. They were both dressed warmly, but she'd always imagined that the North would be exceptionally freezing, so this damp but manageable chill they'd been experiencing was somewhat of a relief. Stan had said something about the coastal mountains shielding them from the worst of the weather, just like in Vancouver.

"Sometimes your endless stream of trivia is actually useful," she'd teased.

"Sometimes your endless stream of questions isn't too annoying," he'd replied, smiling.

Not only were they protected from the cold as they floated up the Inside Passage, but they were also sheltered from the ocean's temperament by a chain of islands. That made it a calm waterway, which had been a relief. Before they'd left Vancouver, Liza had made a point of studying the map her father had rolled out on the dining room table. She'd worried about the meandering route the *Islander* would have to take, but the thoroughfares were not nearly as narrow as she'd feared. The map hadn't done justice to how the coastline constantly changed, either. Rich forests along the shore melted into ancient beds of rock before they swelled back into view, harbouring what she imagined must be a world of wildlife. And beyond the endless rocks and trees loomed the distant profiles of mountains, which Liza tried hard not to think about.

As they chugged upstream, she let the monotony take her mind to the week before when she'd met her four closest friends at the Hotel Vancouver. When she'd told the girls that her family was about to embark on a journey to the Yukon, they were understandably stunned. The table had fallen silent for a whole minute before anyone started talking again. Then their exclamations had ranged from sympathetic to disbelieving and even, incredibly, envious, and Liza had found herself feeling obliged to at least play the part of someone who was excited about the voyage. But the whole time she feigned anticipation, she'd been thinking of those distant mountain peaks.

She wouldn't be able to ignore them for much longer. She was about to discover if this was the adventure of a lifetime, as her father called it . . . or if it was all a terrible mistake.

"Are you okay?" Stan asked. "You've been staring into space for five minutes."

She blinked, clearing her thoughts. "Yes, I'm fine." She spotted an open bench and started towards it. "I just need to sit down.

We can watch for more wildlife from there, okay?"

"Sure," he said. "Maybe we'll see more whales. Actually, did you know . . ."

He was off again, chattering about something or other, and Liza tuned him out as she studied the coastline. During these afternoons they often saw herds of deer grazing along the banks, but sometimes they saw shipwrecks, and every time they spotted one of those sunken hulls poking through the surface of the water Stan would study it with a ghoulish curiosity. Liza had to look away from them. The thought of the *Islander* hitting a boulder and sinking, dragging the passengers under that freezing water, absolutely terrified her. Today, thankfully, they saw no rusting metal sticking out of the water, though they did spot a large brown bear at the water's edge. Stan informed her that it was a grizzly hunting salmon, and since he was usually right, she didn't argue.

"There's your friend," he said.

She turned, confused, then smiled as the white dog limped towards them, tail wagging.

"Why, hello there."

She dug in her pocket for the crust she'd saved and dropped it in front of the animal.

46

As the dog crunched loudly on the snack, Liza looked more closely at the injured paw.

"Stan," she said. "Would you mind getting me a glass of water and a cloth?"

"Where am I supposed to get that?"

"I'm sure you'll figure it out," she said, waving him off.

He left with a huff.

"Thank you!" she called absently, then turned back to the dog. "Let's see if I can help you feel better when he gets back with that. Do you have a name? How about I call you Blanche? To go with your pretty white colour." Seeming to approve, Blanche stretched her neck upwards so Liza could scratch her throat. "Does that feel good?"

By the time Stan returned, Blanche was much more at ease, and she didn't complain when Liza dabbed the paw with water.

"I think if I clean it maybe I can see how to mend it," Liza told her brother.

"I went all that way so you could clean a dog?"

"Oh, Stan. Do stop complaining and help me out." She tilted her head, examining the injury. "What do you think?"

He crouched beside her. "I don't know. It looks infected."

If they hadn't been on this wretched ship, Liza could have taken her to a veterinarian, and maybe they could have done something. As it was, she could do nothing but gently wind the cloth around Blanche's paw, making a sort of sock bandage.

"I hope this helps you feel better," she said. "I'm sorry I can't do more."

In the weeks that followed, Liza looked for Blanche, but she only saw her a couple of times in passing. The bandage was gone by then, and her tail hung lower. It was difficult, seeing the sweet dog that way, but there was nothing Liza could do. On the bright side, Liza's mother was improving, though she hadn't ventured out on deck more than a half-dozen times. Ironically, just as she had regained her appetite, the ship's food had become short in supply.

"I can't believe you had to pay for this voyage," Liza muttered to her father. "Food rations? They should pay us to put up with all the inconveniences."

Her father had left her mother sleeping in their cabin to come stand with Liza at the rail, choosing the morning's drizzle over the fetid air indoors. Liza wasn't sure there was much of a choice. Unless they were heading directly into the wind, the cramped steamship smelled so terrible Liza couldn't breathe through her nose.

"These tickets were difficult to acquire,

and they cost an arm and a leg," her father admitted. "Ah, well. It will be worth it in the end. We must believe that."

"You do, don't you? Still believe it?" she asked, sensing a note of uncertainty.

"Of course, my dear." He put a comforting arm around her shoulder. "We shall all be glad when our store opens its doors in Dawson City. But we must take it one step at a time. First stop will be Dyea."

"At least that will be better than this ship!"

He chuckled. "Your mother would definitely agree with you there."

Just then, a boat approached from the opposite direction, catching Liza's attention. It was the first vessel she'd seen travelling south.

"They must be heading home," her father said. "I imagine we'll see more as we get closer to Dyea." He squinted at the men on board. "I would very much like to hear their stories."

As the boat drifted closer, Liza stared, transfixed. All she could see was gold. Open trunks and gaping sacks lay mostly untended on the decks, their contents catching the sunlight. Confused, she took in the ragged appearance of the passengers, their emaciated bodies stooped and draped in worn clothing. They certainly didn't look like they'd struck it rich.

"Look how the boat is weighted down!" Stan exclaimed, squeezing in beside them. "There must be even more gold beneath the deck." He cupped his hands around his mouth. "How's the mining?" he shouted.

"Go back!" they yelled. "There's no food! Turn back now while you still have a chance!"

Apprehension fluttered in Liza's stomach. "What are they talking about?" she asked her father.

"Don't let them bother you," Stan said, logical as always. "Of course they want us to go back. They want to keep the gold for themselves. Just look at what they've already mined."

Their father agreed. "I don't understand why they'd complain. After all, that much gold could buy a man anything he needed."

"But if the mining is that good," Liza asked, "why are they leaving?"

"Maybe there's a limit to how much a boat can carry," Stan suggested. A smug smile played over his lips as they watched the vessel drift past. "I say let them go. All the more for us!"

But Liza couldn't dismiss the strangers' warnings so easily. They still rang in her ears hours later, as she tried to fall asleep. What had happened to them? Were they just not prepared? Her family had packed a whole store's worth of food and provisions, but what if that wasn't enough? What were they getting into?

A week later, Liza's mother emerged onto the deck on her husband's arm. The relatively fresh air brushed colour onto her cheeks, but it was plain to see that the seasickness had taken its toll. She was unsteady, bracing herself against the rail beside Liza, and while she claimed to feel fine, the dark rings beneath her eyes said otherwise.

"Captain says we should reach Dyea any time now," Stan said to their father.

Liza almost cheered. "Thank goodness. I'd give anything for a soft bed and warm meal."

"You're headin' the wrong direction if you want comfort," a male voice drawled, and Liza turned towards it. "I understand folks up this way need to get creative if they're looking for warmth."

The speaker leaned on the rail a few feet away, staring openly at Liza. He spat a lump of tobacco over the side, and she cringed when it plopped noisily into the water. *I am no longer on the civilized streets of Vancouver,* she reminded herself.

"I've seen you around this ship," he went on, his hooded gaze intent on her. "I've been watching."

Alarm skittered up Liza's neck, and she looked to Stan and her father. Stan quickly put himself between her and the stranger and folded his arms.

"Thank you for the advice," he said stiffly. "We'll be fine."

The stranger nodded slowly, though his predatory eyes lingered. Eventually he gave Liza a slow wink, then wandered away, disappearing into the crowd.

Even after the man left, Liza couldn't get him out of her head. There was nowhere she could go on this damn boat where the stranger couldn't follow. An unfamiliar fear swirled through her. Had he been spying on her this whole time? She'd been so focused on her mother and everything else going on that she hadn't even noticed, and now she felt distinctly uneasy. Were other passengers watching her the same way? She scanned the crowd, suddenly wary of every man in sight. For the first time in her life, she felt helpless. What had her father been thinking, bringing her here?

Liza heard her mother let out a long breath. "Arthur," she said quietly, "these men . . . I don't feel at all safe around them. Do you suppose it is just the monotony of this sea journey that is bringing out the brute in them, or is this what we can expect to encounter along our entire journey?"

Liza looked to her father. *Let's go home,* she pleaded silently. *Please take us home.*

He patted his wife's hand but didn't answer her question. "You will both be fine, Agatha. Stan and I are here to protect you."

Before she could respond, the sky opened up and a terrible, sleety rain pelted the deck. Her mother magically produced an umbrella and pulled Liza in close.

"Let's go back to the cabin," she suggested.

But the crew suddenly began to shout, "Dyea! Dyea!" and the whole boat shifted as dozens of men squeezed through the corridors and onto the deck, their travel-weary lethargy having transformed abruptly to impatience. Alarmed, Liza and her mother clung to the rail at the deck's edge, trying to stay upright on the slippery floor.

"Where's the wharf?" Liza's father yelled, squinting through the rain.

"No wharf here," a passing sailor told him. "This beach here is Dyea's welcome mat. When the tide's high, nobody gets in. It's on its way in now, so once we drop you off, you'll want to move as quick as you can." He pointed at a number of small barges bobbing offshore, moving towards the ship. "That's what those boys are there for. Get your money out, folks!"

Everyone was shoved forward as the boat abruptly slowed, then inched as close as it could to the shoreline. From the relative shelter of her mother's umbrella, Liza peered hopelessly through the deluge at the long sandy beach stretched in front of them.

"I don't understand," she said through chattering teeth. "There are no d-docks or buildings. Do they expect us t-to just climb off while we're still sailing? And then where do we go?"

"We're not the first to land here," Stan reminded her, shivering hard himself. "Can't be that difficult, can it?"

"Stan's right," her father said, wiping his arm across his eyes and scanning the ship. "If others have done this, so shall we. We simply must be smart about it." He set off towards a group of sailors, then called back over his shoulder, "Collect as many of our things as you can and bring them to the edge of the boat. I'll take care of the rest."

Liza and Stan looked helplessly at each other. How could they —

"You heard your father," their mother

said, an unexpected determination in her voice. "The sailors are piling cargo over there." She snapped her umbrella closed. "Let's go."

Liza grabbed Stan's sleeve, and the three of them stumbled towards the heaps of baggage, arms extended for balance as they did their best not to collide with other passengers. The whole deck was caught up in a mad rush as men dashed around, finding and claiming their items. The sailors dumped luggage onto smaller, waiting boats, all while trying not to slip on the icy deck. Horses, oxen, dogs, goats, and anything else with four legs were released into the water to fend for themselves. Liza had never seen or heard anything so chaotic in her entire life.

Stan called out when he found the crates labelled Peterson. He heaved one towards Liza, but it was too heavy, and the sides were too wide for her reach. She grabbed a sailor and gestured at what he was carrying. "I need your crowbar!"

He gave it to her without question, and Liza drove the claw into the lid, then pried it off with a grunt, thankful her father had tasked her so many times with unpacking stock at the store. She reached inside for their bags and handed her mother as many as she could handle, then she filled her own arms. Ducking around other passengers, the three of them made their way to the side of the boat and squinted through the storm for Arthur.

"There he is!" her mother cried.

"Agatha!" he called as the barge he rode wobbled closer to the ship. "Get ready to jump on board."

Liza's mother hesitated for just a moment before leaping forward and landing safely in his arms.

"Your turn," Stan said to Liza.

But Liza couldn't move her feet. The whole idea of voluntarily leaping over open water was daunting. Really, the barge where her parents waited was little more than a raft, piloted by one man with a stick, and from the way it rocked, Liza could tell there was nothing sturdy about it.

"Liza, I know," Stan said gently. "I'm scared too. But we have to do it. Let's go. I promise I'll be right behind you the whole way."

"Come on!" her father yelled.

If it weren't for the storm, Liza was sure everyone on the ship would have heard her heart thundering.

"Don't think about it," Stan said beside her. "Just jump."

Liza held her breath and vaulted over the gap, ridiculously pleased with herself when she skidded, upright, across the wet barge. Behind her, Stan yelled a warning, then flew across, but his arms were so full that he lost his balance and slipped. The barge dipped and rocked, and Liza watched helplessly as he slid towards the water feet first. Just in time, her father reached out and dragged him back to safety.

And that was just the first load, Liza realized. Her mother turned to her, the resolve she'd clung to up until that moment draining from her eyes.

"Stay here, Agatha," Liza's father said. "I need you to watch over our things."

Liza was tempted to suggest that perhaps they needed *two* people to watch their things, but she knew she couldn't. In the back of her mind she could still hear the desperation of the men who had been heading home, and if she'd learned anything from them it was that her family would need everything they had brought if they were to survive the journey ahead. But they'd have to move fast if they were going to get it all off this ship.

This time, Liza didn't question the folly of it as she reached for the ship's rail and threw herself over, and her brother and father followed. Every time they brought another load, the barge sank a little lower, until water covered the toes of Liza's boots and her hands and feet grew numb. When everything was finally loaded, her father spoke to their pilot, who shoved off towards shore.

"Ha!" her father exclaimed. "Now *that* was exciting!"

They looked at him in disbelief, then Liza's mother gave an unladylike snort, which set Liza off. One by one they started to laugh, though Liza wobbled on the edge of tears. When they eventually reached the beach, Liza dropped off the raft, stifling a gasp as she sank ankle-deep into the sand. Cold, muddy water seeped through her boot seams.

"Tide's rising fast, folks!" their pilot announced, clearly anxious to go back for another fare.

Everywhere on the beach, men were hauling crates away from the creeping water. Some hollered prices as they went. "Don't want to lose your things now, do you?" they called. "Only fifty dollars! Right here! Fifty dollars is worth it to keep your powder dry!"

Liza's mother pressed up against her. "Fifty dollars? Just to carry our things to the end of the sand?"

"I don't see any other way, Mother," she replied, shivering. "We'll lose everything if we don't get help."

Her father was already down the beach, counting out money to one of the working men. When he looked back at his family and gestured towards a horse and wagon, Liza just about cried with relief. She swept rain-drenched hair off her face, hoisted one of the smaller crates from the sand, and lugged it towards the wagon.

"Quickly, quickly," her father sang in passing, his arms full.

How could he be so cheerful? Liza wondered irritably. After moving so many boxes and bags, her arms ached from the tedium of lift, carry, load, lift, carry, load, and hunger was making her dizzy. She watched with amazement as her mother resolutely picked up yet another bag and slung it over her shoulder. This had been a difficult voyage for her, and yet she wasn't stopping. Nor would she, Liza resolved, as she curled her ice-cold fingers around the edges of the next crate.

A startled horse screamed close by, then Liza heard a giant splash followed by the sound of a man wailing with grief. When she spun towards the noise she spotted the man from the ship — the one who said he had been watching her — slumped at the water's edge, his head in his hands. From what she could tell, the flailing horse nearby had tripped, then panicked, falling over in the water and overturning his barge. It appeared most of the man's supplies had been submerged instantly, and Liza didn't see even one other traveller coming to help him retrieve his things. Their energy was already being spent on avoiding their own near catastrophes. Unnerved, Liza hurried towards her family's wagon. She had never heard a man cry so desperately before.

"Poor fellow," her father said, taking the crate from her. "He will have to return to Victoria now. By the time he replenishes his stores, it will probably be too late."

"Come on, Liza!" her mother called. "One more load!"

After she'd set her final box on the wagon, Liza started up the beach, relieved that the rain was letting up. Of course she was already soaked through, her unwieldy skirts twice as heavy as before, but as the sky cleared she was able to focus her attention on the landscape before her instead. The mountains were no longer a faraway apparition. They were all around, owning the sky and the land beneath. Liza was no longer simply an observer. She was part of this magnificent wilderness, and that fact took her breath away. She was *here.*

From her father's map, she knew their ultimate destination — Dawson City — was hundreds of miles past those forbidding peaks. On paper the trip had seemed arduous but straightforward: sail to Dyea, climb the Chilkoot Trail, proceed down the other side of the mountain, then travel by boat up the Yukon River to Dawson City. Seeing the journey stretching in front of her now, she had no doubt there would be many trials ahead, and yet with every uncomfortable, sloppy step she felt more drawn in by the land's power. It seemed to be infusing her body with its strength. Apprehension made way for an unexpected sense of anticipation.

"I am in the Yukon," she said, loud enough that only she could hear. "And I am going to walk to Dawson City."

FOUR:
BEN

It didn't matter how clean Ben was at the beginning of his rounds, he wasn't going to end up the same way. The cold, late September rains had turned Fort Macleod into a giant, slushy mud bath. The day before, the outpost had received a couple of reports from farms a number of miles away, so Ben and his partner, Constable Bob Miller, had set out early that morning, tugging their Stetson hats low over their brows to shield them from a light but stubborn drizzle. After an hour, both men were soaked through and their boots were caked in mud. Neither had stopped Miller from chattering on beside him.

In the month since Ben had been stationed at the Fort, he and Miller had got along well enough, though on Ben's first night at the Fort Miller had had a little fun, trying to unsettle him as they sat around the supper table.

"You'll see all types out there," Miller had warned, watching for a reaction. "Some of the Blackfoot aren't too friendly with us. That worry you?"

"No." Ben knew the Blackfoot pretty well, but he didn't bring that up.

"Maybe it should." Miller chuckled. "Well, if it's not them, I bet we can find something else that'll give you a fright."

Ben didn't bother to argue. He didn't doubt Miller and the other Mounties had had their share of adventures, even times when they'd been afraid, but he had a feeling Miller didn't know real fear. Not like Ben did, anyway. After his life on the farm, Ben was fairly confident nothing could frighten him anymore.

Still, Miller seemed a good enough fellow, with a headful of brown curls and a hundred-dollar smile. He was from Ontario, with a year's seniority over Ben, and he talked enough for both of them, but that was all right with Ben.

By the time the two of them reached their first stop, the rain had ended and sun was high in the sky. That was a blessing, since the rancher needed help searching the fields for four cows, all of which were set to drop calves any minute. It wasn't the most alluring of missions, but Ben and Miller headed in opposite directions, riding through messy coulees and behind patches of brush. Ben had just about given up hope when he found one of the cows, and he got there just in time to help her tiny calf into the world. In the end, all four cows and a total of six calves — including two sets of twins — were located, and Boyd was so pleased that he insisted the Mounties go away with a package of moose pemmican: dried cranberries, Saskatoon berries, and meat, stuck together with moose fat.

The taste of it took Ben back five years, to when he'd briefly lived with a group of Blackfoot. They had introduced him to this staple, and the greasy snack had kept his belly satisfied when there was nothing else to fill it, which had happened a number of times before he joined the Mounties. He was just finishing off a slice as they approached their next stop: Jerry Barlow's place.

Jerry was a well-known drinker in the area, according to Miller. The day before, Jerry's neighbour had come to the outpost on his way out of town to ask the Mounties if they would check on Jerry and his wife. He was concerned because nobody had heard from the pair for a couple of weeks.

"Do you smell that?" Miller asked.

"I'm glad we're upwind," Ben replied.

The meaty stench of decay clung to the air, and if the day had been any warmer they'd have heard flies. As it was, they tied kerchiefs over their mouths before they opened the door to the Barlow house, and Ben suppressed a gag as he stepped inside. Barlow was lying flat on the floor, dead as a doornail but much messier.

"Drowned in his own vomit," Ben said, taking in the rest of the filthy room. "Based on all these empty bottles, I'd say he never knew what happened."

Behind him, Miller's boots crossed the floor towards the only other room. "Wife's long gone," he reported. "Her things ain't here, and there's a good layer of dust."

That explained Barlow's binge, Ben thought sadly. He'd never met the couple, but the sight of Jerry's dead body in front of him made him wish he had known there was trouble out this way, because maybe then he could have done something to help before it was too late.

Between the two of them, Miller and Ben carried the body outside. When they were far enough away from the house, they dug a grave and buried the man.

"Good day's work, I'd say." Miller leaned on his shovel. "Considering the mud and the calving and this fella, I don't think we could get much dirtier than we are now. Let's get back. Could do with a drink myself."

Ben eyed him. Drinking wasn't an option for members of the North-West Mounted Police except in a few sanctioned cases.

"Joking."

"Sure you were," Ben said wryly, but Miller's comment had managed to lighten the mood and he was grateful for that.

When they finally passed through the gates of Fort Macleod's timber walls, the faint aroma of fresh bread in the air greeted them, and Ben's stomach grumbled. Supper wouldn't be for another couple of hours — the pemmican would have to tide him over.

"I'm off to see Red, get him to take a little off the top," Miller said, reining his horse towards the barbershop. "See you later."

Ben continued on past the Fort's various buildings to the stables. He figured he'd better clean up both the horse and himself before he did anything else. After the general store and the blacksmith, he passed the pristine white house where the Reverend lived, right beside the church. Ben had never had much time for religion. Whenever he saw that place, with its imposing steeple reaching towards the heavens, he thought of his mother and her desperate prayers. When it came down to it, God hadn't seen fit to save her. Pushing memories to the back of his mind, Ben nudged his horse to pick up the pace.

At the stable, Ben cleaned and groomed the horse, then he returned to the barracks to do the same for himself. When he felt presentable, he headed into the dining hall for supper. A dozen of his fellow Mounties were already sitting around the table, and Ben knew all but one: a man with a heavy beard sitting on his own. When the stranger didn't introduce himself, Ben leaned over to Miller and whispered, "Who's that?"

Miller kept his voice low. "Sergeant Eb Thompson. You'll want to stay on his good side."

Ben waited for him to elaborate, but he didn't, which was odd in itself. Miller rarely held his tongue on any subject.

Instead, Miller asked the room, "Inspector joining us tonight?" through a mouthful of stew. "I wanted to speak with him about a run-in I had up at the railway a few days back. Missed him at his desk."

Ben noticed Sergeant Thompson raising his head at the mention of a railway matter.

"Something happen?" someone else asked.

"More of the same," Miller replied, swallowing another bite, "but it's a *lot* more. A whole lot of Americans with guns, liquor, and attitude, all of them heading north with their hearts set on gold."

At this, Ben leaned in, eager to hear more. Ever since he had arrived at Fort Macleod, he'd heard tales about the gold fever that had sent thousands of stampeders to Canada's North, hoping to carve a shiny fortune out of the earth. Ben glanced towards Thompson, who was resolutely rubbing his beard as if he had something to add to the conversation, but after a moment the man's gaze returned to his bowl.

"Gentlemen!" Inspector Wood said as he entered the room, and Ben rose along with the others. "Be seated, please. We are honoured this evening by the presence of 'D' Division's commanding officer, Superintendent Samuel Steele."

Ben hadn't yet met the renowned Superintendent, but he'd heard a lot about him. Steele's name was always spoken with a kind of reverence even though Ben had the impression that some of the Mounties thought the Superintendent demanded too much of his men. He supposed he was about to find out if that was true or not.

"Superintendent Steele's military and

policing reputation spans decades and covers a vast territory within the Dominion," Inspector Wood told them. "He's set the gold standard for the rest of us, having done everything from defeating whisky traders to policing railway construction to keeping the peace. He almost single-handedly defeated Big Bear and snuffed out the Métis Rebellion twelve years ago. The Superintendent deserves our utmost respect, and I expect each of you to make a positive impression."

Tables were immediately cleared and uniforms straightened, and when Steele entered the room Ben jumped back to his feet. He wasn't sure what he'd envisioned, but now that he saw him, Ben thought the tall and barrel-chested Superintendent looked exactly as he should. Before he said a word, Steele regarded the group sharply, holding each man's eyes for a long moment before moving on to the next. When his attention shifted to Ben, the weight of his examination felt like more than a mere observation. It was as if, he thought, he'd been given an order before it was even spoken.

"Good evening, gentlemen," Steele said as they resumed their seats. "I trust that what I have to say tonight will not come as too much of a surprise." He cleared his throat.

"The time has come for me to call for volunteers for the Klondike."

Ben's ears pricked at the night's second mention of the gold rush. He'd wanted to know about it, and no one had more inside information on what was happening in the North than the Superintendent.

"Inspector Constantine and Staff Sergeant Brown are presently in the Yukon with some of our hardiest men," Steele said, "and they are in need of reinforcements now that the gold rush is in full swing." He raised one eyebrow. "I'm not going to lie, gentlemen. This is a tough job. Not only is there a lot of work to be done up there, but it's damn cold. *Damn* cold. And even after we add a couple dozen Mounties to the area, the stampeders will still outnumber us by at least a thousand to one." He paused. "Because of this, I will only be sending men who feel they are hardy enough to be of assistance in an extremely challenging climate. If you choose not to go, you will be neither penalized nor judged."

"You make it sound like fun, sir," joked one of the men in the back of the room.

Steele's piercing eyes were on the clown before Ben even figured out who had spoken. Nobody dared glance back at the offender. Steele didn't react, just stood silent and forbidding as granite for a full minute. When he eventually resumed speaking, there was a collective exhale in the room.

"The Yukon is breathtaking but treacherous," Steele continued, "and the stampeders are an interesting mix of naive greenhorns and hardened criminals who do not take kindly to answering to anyone but themselves. Until the Force took over a few years ago, the miners, with their gambling houses and saloons, ruled themselves. Now we have better control, but the population is swelling exponentially, which means we have to increase our own numbers just to keep up. We will absolutely not allow lynch mobs and gangsters to rule over these people. Not in Canada."

A new sense of purpose swelled in Ben. This was his chance to do some real good and be part of a grand adventure.

"I am sending a contingent of forty Mounties from across the Force to the Klondike, including three men from this post. One of those will be Sergeant Thompson." The Sergeant responded to Steele's address with a respectful nod. "Sergeant Thompson has experience travelling in that part of the country as well as dealing with the people living in those regions. He is well qualified to lead this mission." Steele considered the rest of the men one more time. "So I am looking for two more. If you are inclined to embark on a mission of this magnitude, please see me in the morning."

That night, Ben lay on his cot and contemplated the ceiling for what felt like hours, indifferent to the snores rumbling around him. As a child, he'd slept under a rotted hole in the roof of his childhood home, and when he was too afraid to stay in the house he'd watched spiders working their way across a beam in the barn's loft. At Depot the ceilings had been uniformly white, and here at Fort Macleod he saw sturdy timber. The Yukon's night sky, he imagined, would have no ceiling at all. In his mind it would be an endless black sprinkled with stars, a wide-open opportunity for a new life, and one where he could make a difference. It was exactly what Ben needed.

The next morning he dressed before reveille, determined to be the first at Sam Steele's door.

"You are quite new to the Force," Steele noted, his head bent over a couple of pages. Sergeant Thompson sat at the Superintendent's side, scrutinizing Ben as Steele went through his file. "But you do have an admirable record. I see you've made excellent progress in a very short period of time."

"Thank you, Superintendent."

Sergeant Thompson sat at Steele's side, scrutinizing Ben as Steele went through his file.

"Why do you want to go to the Klondike, Constable Turner?" Steele asked.

"I want to go where I'm needed most, sir. I'm not afraid of hard work."

"You are a strong-looking chap," he agreed. "But you're also quite young. The Yukon will demand a great deal from you. Do you have the discipline?"

"I do, sir," Ben replied, more certain than ever about the challenge that lay ahead.

Steele regarded Thompson. "Questions, Sergeant?"

"Says in your Depot file you got a problem with fighting." It was the first time Ben had heard Thompson speak. His voice was gruff, as if he didn't use it all that often. "That right?"

"Not anymore, Sergeant."

"Saw that too." He hesitated. "What I want to know is, you still got that anger in you?"

Ben wasn't sure how to answer, but win or lose he had to tell the truth. "I reckon it's part of who I am, Sergeant."

When neither of them responded right away, Ben's heart sank. Had he said the wrong thing? The men behind the desk exchanged another quick glance, then Thompson nodded.

"I ride to Calgary tomorrow morning," Thompson said.

Ben hesitated, not sure what he was saying. "Yes, Sergeant. And I'd like to go with you."

Thompson's beard twitched with what Ben would have sworn was amusement. "Good, because you are."

Ben grinned, caught up in a swell of relief and anticipation. "Thank you. You won't regret it."

FIVE:
LIZA

Liza looked out the grimy window of their Dyea hotel room, mesmerized by the river of strangers flowing by. Most, she knew, would be headed to Dawson City, but a fair number showed no immediate signs of continuing on, which baffled her. Why would anyone want to stay in this cold, miserable excuse of a town when the promise of treasure lay ahead? Even with the mountain trek looming before her, Liza couldn't wait to get out of here.

Her father's original plan had been to spend no more than one night in Dyea, where they would rest briefly and prepare for the next leg of the journey. But Liza's mother had fallen ill again, this time with a bad cold she'd caught from being out in the freezing rain the day before, hauling heavy bags around that absurdly long beach.

"I just need a hot cup of tea and I'll be fine," she'd protested, sitting up in bed.

"I admire your determination, Agatha," Liza's father said, easing her back onto her pillow. "But we both know you will need more than that. Get some rest, my dear. The trail can wait a day or two."

"I do apologize for the delay, Arthur."

"Don't give it another thought." He patted her hand. "All shall be well."

Even as her father reassured her, Liza could see he was anxious to get moving, as was Stan. Her brother was not generally a patient person, and any delay in this voyage clearly frustrated him. As they dined that morning on a vastly overpriced breakfast of dry flapjacks, eggs, and fried strips of pork, Liza tried to raise their spirits.

"She will feel better soon," she told them. "Let's look at this in a positive light. I know you will both deny it, but we are all tired after the voyage and the landing. A break will do us good. Why don't you two explore the town today? I shall stay with Mother and make sure she is all right."

Temporarily appeased, the men had set off, and Liza had brought tea with a bit of honey to her mother. Once she was sound asleep, Liza had nothing to do but look out the window. It wasn't until mid-afternoon that her father returned.

"Knock, knock!" he said quietly.

"She fell asleep an hour ago," Liza replied softly, turning from the window. "So she will probably sleep another hour or so."

Liza's father shrugged out of his coat and folded it over a chair. "You must be tired of being cooped up in here. Why don't you go exploring now? Stan's downstairs waiting for you."

Liza didn't wait to be asked twice. She was up and out the door as fast as she could go.

"How is she?" Stan asked, glancing up from a copy of *The Dyea Press.*

"Better. A few more days is all she needs."

"Good. I'm losing my mind in this place."

"*You* are? I've only seen it from the window!" Liza cried. "So now it's up to you to show me around."

He held out his arm. "With pleasure."

The streets were crowded with rough-looking men and wandering animals — most of which were thin as rails — and Liza was aware of eyes on her. She'd known that her presence would draw attention, but the lewd comments of the man on the boat had made her situation feel that much more perilous. She held Stan's arm a bit tighter as they walked along the main street, and she tried to focus on the variety of shop-fronts rather than her own nerves.

Commerce was everywhere, she saw, from banks and real estate brokers to ladies of ill repute crooking fingers of invitation to every man who passed. Lumber was stacked as high as buildings, and men loaded and unloaded wagons all along the wide street. The largest building in town bore a sign saying *Healy & Wilson,* identifying itself as a trading post, hotel, and restaurant. Her father had mentioned Healy before, calling him a trailblazer since he had built the very first shop in Dyea, but when Stan and Liza stepped inside his store and checked around she was unimpressed. Healy had a great deal of stock, but little thought had been spared for presentation, and Liza couldn't get over the unbelievably high prices. In fact, every shop window along the street displayed signs advertising similar ludicrous "bargains."

"How can they ask so much?" she wondered out loud.

"Because they can," Stan replied. "These men already traded their worlds for a dream of gold, so why wouldn't they pay everything they had left to achieve it?" He grinned at her. "Oh, Liza. We're going to be so rich."

One after another, people left Healy's with their arms full of ridiculously priced purchases, and Liza started to believe Stan might be right. The thought buoyed her as they made their way up the muddy street. Dare she hope all this would work out as her father had planned? She squinted up at the mountains, hoping his optimism was well-founded, but it certainly wasn't going to be easy. From what she could see, most of the trail was uphill.

"Who's that up there?" she asked, spotting a dozen or so men in the distance. They were gathered around tipis with their arms crossed, observing the passersby.

"The Tlingit," Stan replied. "I read about them."

Of course he had. "Klinkit?" she said, sounding out the word.

"Yes. They've lived here forever along with the Tagish and the Hän. As a matter of fact, the Hän call this place 'Tr'ondëk,' which the first settlers mistakenly pronounced as 'Klondike.' "

"It's amazing you can remember the day of the week with all that trivia in your head."

"Not trivia. *Information.*"

That made her smile. "So tell me, what are they doing here?"

"Prospectors hire them to help carry their baggage up the pass."

"They don't look very big," she noted.

"Maybe not, but I've been watching them.

They're stronger than you'd think. They have to be. They have a long way to go." He surveyed the snow-capped mountains, shielding his eyes with one hand. "Sixteen miles from here to the peak, they say, and those fellows do it over and over again with every new arrival."

Liza stopped. "Sixteen miles?" She was sure she'd known that before, but now that she stood here it seemed an impossible number. "How long will that take?"

"I guess it depends on the climber," Stan said, pausing beside her. "A man on the boat told me the whole trip from here, past the peak, then down to Dawson City took his brother about three months."

"Three months!"

"Yes, but he also said it was worth every step once he got to the goldfields."

Liza did a quick calculation and realized her father had worked the timing out exactly. By the time her family got over the peak and arrived at Lake Bennett, the Yukon River would be just about ready to thaw, and then they would sail up the river and be among the first to arrive at Dawson City in the spring. As much as she hated the idea of winter travel, she had to admire her father's planning.

Stan nudged her and nodded towards the

Tlingit packers. Two of them had hoisted large packs onto their backs and were headed towards the mountain, followed by a string of travellers.

"They might be small," said Stan, "but I told you, they are mighty."

Over the next couple of days, the family resigned themselves to staying in Dyea a bit longer. Liza spent every morning with her mother and took heart when she saw her improving, but she was more than tired of sitting in that room. She looked forward to the afternoons, when her father would return and spell Liza off.

"Stan should be back any minute to take you out," he told her.

Pulling on her coat, Liza headed downstairs to wait at the front door, but long minutes passed and Stan was nowhere in sight. Probably caught up in a conversation with no idea what time it was. Since they'd landed here, Liza had become convinced that her brother should consider a career in journalism, because he simply couldn't resist approaching strangers and asking them a stream of questions.

She gazed longingly at the street. After days of grey weather, it was finally bathed in sunlight.

"Come on," she muttered, her fingers tapping against her skirt. "Let's go, Stan."

Back in Vancouver she'd been able to walk almost anywhere by herself during the day, and though she was well aware this place was nothing like Vancouver, she couldn't help toying with the idea of setting out on her own. For the most part, the men she saw appeared to be caught up in their own errands. What were the chances anyone would even notice if she walked among them? She'd stay to the side of the street, calling as little attention to herself as possible. She doubted anyone would try anything untoward in broad daylight, and she could ignore any unpleasant comments that came her way. They were only words, after all.

When she pushed the door open, the sunshine reached for her, and its touch felt like heaven on her skin. She took a step, then another, moving cautiously onto the ragged walkway that connected Dyea's false-fronted buildings. As she suspected, she received a few passing glances, but no one seemed particularly interested in her. She would stay vigilant, but for now she felt relatively safe.

A little way down the walkway, she paused outside a shop, curious about an unusual-looking hat for sale, and was about to wander inside when she heard an odd noise. She listened again and realized it was a whimper. Curious, she walked around the side of the shop and came upon a filthy white dog lying in the shadow of the building.

"Blanche!" she cried.

The dog was still, but her eyes opened at Liza's cry. As Liza came closer, Blanche tried without success to raise her head, but she did manage to lift the tip of her tail in recognition. She was panting heavily, and her damaged paw was swollen into a repulsive, unnatural shape.

"Sweet girl," Liza breathed, crouching by the dog. Her fingers brushed over the outline of Blanche's rib cage, clearly visible through her dirty coat. "I am so sorry for you."

That's when she noticed three oddly shaped lumps lying in the mud by Blanche's tail. Tears rushed to her eyes as she recognized the stillborn puppies for what they were.

"Oh no. Poor, poor girl." Liza stroked Blanche's head.

Blanche whimpered again, and a ripple of movement in her abdomen caught Liza's attention. Moments later, a small, wet shape appeared under the dog's tail, and though it wasn't moving, Liza felt a spark of hope.

"You can do this," Liza told Blanche. "I promise I will take care of your baby somehow."

Blanche looked as if she could hardly keep her eyes open.

"Please be strong. Just a little bit longer."

Then, with barely any visible effort, the puppy flushed out of its mother and landed in the muck. Blanche struggled to reach her baby, but she couldn't summon the strength to move far enough. Without a second thought, Liza picked up the newborn and placed it on the ground by Blanche's face. The new mother sniffed it, seeming to gain energy as her tongue swept over the puppy, removing the membrane, cleaning its muzzle and back before rolling the tiny body over. But the puppy — a female, Liza saw — didn't move. She didn't make a sound.

Blanche looked at Liza, a startlingly human expression on her face, and Liza's heart broke for her. Cupping the puppy in the warmth of her hands, she rubbed her thumbs in circles over the small body, willing it back to life.

"Come on, little one," she said, holding the puppy against her throat. "You have to live."

She could feel the puppy's paws pressed

to her neck, small as her baby finger, and the tiny ears tickled her skin. But the little one didn't stir.

"I'm sorry," she said gently to Blanche. "We tried. You did your best."

As if she understood, Blanche's sad brown eyes closed, and moments later she was gone. Liza felt sick to her stomach. Neither Blanche nor her babies had ever stood a chance in a place like this. Liza's hands shook with emotion as she lifted the fourth motionless puppy to her face.

"Oh, you poor dear. I wanted to meet you. I would have taken care of you."

Then Liza froze, startled by a slight quiver of movement between her hands. Had she imagined it? She turned the puppy onto her back and placed one finger on the small chest, her eyes closed in concentration. Beneath her touch, the fragile rib cage lifted and fell, lifted and fell, then one leg stretched out.

Liza let out a cry of delight and clutched the precious little dog to her chest. "Don't worry, little one. I will keep you safe. You're my baby now, and I'll never leave you."

She named the puppy Blue after the vivid shade of the sky on the day she was born, and with the help of the innkeeper and his goat, little Blue got stronger every day. She was mostly white, like her mother, but the floppy triangles of her sweet ears were dark, the bridge of her nose was spattered with spots, and she had a lone black patch on the centre of her chest. Blue fit perfectly inside Liza's coat, just over her heart, and when Liza heard Blue's little sounds or felt her wriggle within the folds of her coat, hope ballooned inside her. If this little creature could survive out here, she decided, then so could she.

Three days later, Liza's mother claimed she felt well enough to leave Dyea. In the early grey morning, the full glory of the sunrise still hid behind the mountains, the family began preparations to leave. Stan finished packing the wagon, and Liza and her mother waited for Liza's father to settle his account with the hotel owner.

"Do you really feel you are up to this?" Liza asked, concerned by her mother's pale complexion. "I mean, are you strong enough?"

"Whether I am or not, I must be." She lifted her chin. "We're on this path, and there's no going back."

Liza reached inside her coat when she felt Blue squirm. "Would you like to carry Blue? She keeps me warm and boosts my spirit. I'm sure she'll do the same for you."

"I would like that very much." Her mother lifted the puppy up to study her more closely. "Hello there, Blue. You're very pretty. I wonder if your eyes will be blue, like your name."

"Blue eyes? On a dog?"

"I understand that's a specialty of the dogs in the North." She pressed Blue's velvety coat to her cheek briefly then wrapped the puppy safely into her coat. "At least she will be comfortable on this journey, even if the rest of us are not."

Liza spotted Stan striding purposefully towards her, all business, and her heart sank. She had seen that expression before. "Uh-oh," she muttered. "You'd better keep her hidden, Mother."

"We're not bringing the dog with us," Stan declared. "She's another mouth to feed, another thing to worry about. We will have more than enough to keep us busy."

"Of course I'm bringing her!" Liza exclaimed. "She's my dog. I would never abandon her."

"It's too much work," he objected.

"Actually," their father said, returning to the wagon, "I see nothing wrong with bringing the pup. In fact, she will most likely grow up to be quite protective of our Liza, and in a place like Dawson City I imagine it might be beneficial for a young woman to have added protection."

Stan fumed, but Liza couldn't help grinning at her victory. As if she'd understood the conversation, Blue chose that moment to poke her muzzle out from inside her mother's coat.

"Come on, Stan," Liza said, gently scratching Blue's ears. "Even you have to admit, she is the cutest thing."

But he kept walking, and he didn't look back.

"She's your responsibility, Liza," her father reminded her. "If you really want to keep her, you must take good care of her."

"Oh, I will, Father. Nothing's going to hurt this sweet angel."

He touched the little head with one finger. "She might be an angel now, but as she gets bigger she's going to keep you busy."

Just then the morning sun burst over the peaks, bathing the world in gold, lighting the trees and the rocks and the path they must follow. As her father headed towards the wagon, Liza took a deep breath, then blew it out slowly, finding a sense of courage in the sun's warmth.

"What is it Father says?" Liza asked her mother. "The greatest part of the reward is knowing how hard you worked to earn it?"

Her mother took Liza's hand. "I imagine we'll have to remember that many times during this trek. At least we will be together," she said, cocking her head towards Stan, "and we can remind each other of that whenever we forget."

Liza's brother stood by the horse's head, a little ways away, and she could see his annoyance in the way he avoided looking at her. She hadn't meant to upset him. The two of them might have their spats, but she adored her brother. She needed him, too.

"Stan," she said as she approached, "I promise Blue won't be a burden. And I'll try not to be one either."

At that, he cracked a smile.

Liza's gaze rose up the face of the mountain, and the eagerness she'd embraced moments before melted away. The negligible slopes of Vancouver's streets were the steepest terrain she'd ever walked, and right now all she could see were impassable forests through which they must hike, and impossible rock walls over which they must climb.

"I'm scared," she said, growing serious. "What if I'm not strong enough for this?"

He turned to her then, his earlier anger gone. "Don't worry. I'll help you," he said.

"I'm really glad to hear you say that," she said, taking a deep breath. "Because to tell you the truth, I'm afraid that every single thing about this journey is going to be very, very difficult. And I know without a shadow of a doubt that I'd never be able to do it on my own."

Six:
Ben

Ben leaned against the blade of the wind, straining to focus on the Constable in front of him, who constantly appeared and disappeared within the twisted corridor of snow and forest. The blizzard was so thick that even when the twenty soaking-wet Mounties finally broke free of the smothering trees and entered a clearing, Ben barely noticed the difference in the view. It wasn't until a gust of wind sheared through, shoving the driving snow to the side, that he caught sight of a flagpole bearing a faded but wildly flapping Union Jack.

It had taken the better part of two months, but Ben, Sergeant Thompson, and Miller had finally made it to Fort Constantine. The three of them had ridden from Fort Macleod to Calgary, then travelled by train to Victoria. Two separate steamships later, they arrived at the town of Fortymile, and from there they'd picked up a number of other Mounties and begun the hike to Fort Constantine, the first North-West Mounted Police outpost established in the Yukon.

As remote as a man can get, Thompson had said before they'd set out. Now that they'd made it, Ben didn't think Thompson had been exaggerating one bit. At least here, they'd been told, they might rest awhile, which was something everyone in their party sorely needed.

A shout cut through the storm, and a bulky shape lumbered towards the men and spoke with Thompson before turning back to the Fort. Stumbling through the snow, the line of Mounties followed their guide, and the dark outline of a building finally emerged from within the blizzard. Dazed with exhaustion, Ben had to blink hard to convince himself it wasn't an illusion. Then the Constable from the Fort yanked the door open, bracing it against the wind, and they filed in, stomping their boots and dripping onto the floor.

It wasn't much warmer inside than it had been outside. Cold air seeped through the dirt floor, and the post stoves burned green wood that didn't put out much heat. Despite his congestion, Ben could smell the stink of pelts softened by humidity and the sweat of unseasoned timber walls. Their wet group wouldn't improve things much, he thought. They'd barely washed in weeks.

At some point along the trail Ben had caught a vicious cold that had drained what was left of his energy, and the last steps of the trail had seemed almost impossible to take. Now, the walls around Ben seemed to sway. Not for the first time, he hoped he had what it took to survive out here, for there was no going back.

But he didn't regret his decision to come. Everything about this voyage was new to Ben. He'd never imagined riding either a train or a boat in his lifetime, and since their Calgary departure he had seen so much that fascinated him, from the bustling port of Victoria to the first signs of gold mining. The scrawny, filthy prospectors had been so absorbed in their work their hungry eyes barely touched on the Mounties passing by. They amazed him, the way they survived by squatting in ragged tents or cutting hollows into the riverbanks for their meager shelter. If all the miners were like those, Ben figured his job would be more about taking care of them than enforcing any laws.

Along the way, Ben and the others had also met some of the Hän, and though their English was practically non-existent and Ben's limited Blackfoot meant nothing to them, they were able to communicate about some things. With the Hän's guidance, the Mounties made woven dip nets to catch spawning Arctic grayling, and Ben learned the hard way that he needed to be cautious of the sharp dorsal fins when he picked one of the fish up. On the bright side, when a grayling was roasted over a fire, it only took a couple of minutes before the soft white flesh was cooked to perfection.

"Like trout," Miller had noted, picking a bone from between his teeth. "Delicious. Brings me back to when I was a boy, fishing with my brothers. I remember a time when . . ."

Throughout the journey, Ben and Miller had shared a tent. In the beginning, his partner's constant chatter had been a kind of comfort on miserable nights, but Ben had quickly tired of it. By the end of the day, when they collapsed into their sleeping bags too weak for conversation, he was grateful for the dull grumble of Miller's snores. Now that they were inside Fort Constantine, Miller was energized and back to his old self: talking out of turn, demanding to know how soon they would eat and what the meal would be, subjecting their guide to the same string of complaints he had made throughout their journey.

Other than Miller, the men were in no mood to speak. They staggered through the corridor to the dining hall, where they sank wearily onto benches, melted snow flowing like streams from their coats to the floor. Ben focused on the table, imagining a plate full of food before him. But even more than food, he craved sleep.

A Sergeant Ben didn't know suddenly shot to his feet and introduced Inspector Constantine just before the big man strode into the room. All the men jumped to attention, and Ben stood as straight as he could manage.

Constantine is a very important man, Thompson had told Ben a few weeks before. *He has three titles now: Commanding Officer of the NWMP in the Yukon Territory, Chief Magistrate, and the Home and Foreign Secretary.*

Ben couldn't fathom what all that meant, but it seemed like a lot of responsibility for one man. *How does he do it?* he had asked.

Admiration lifted Thompson's mouth into a rare smile. *Rumour has it he keeps three separate desks in his office just to keep all his duties straight.*

Like Superintendent Steele, Constantine was a legend. Two years earlier, he and the twenty Mounties under his command had been responsible for the establishment of this very Fort, creating order out of chaos. Now he stood stiffly before his men, wearing a beaver fur cap and a bison coat draped over his red serge. The dim light of the room turned his silver hair a flickering gold.

"Gentlemen, welcome to the Yukon," he said. "I trust your journey was swift and uneventful, but I know you must be tired, so I shall keep this brief." He reached inside his coat and produced a clear bottle as tall as one finger. "This is the cause of all the fuss." He shook the bottle, as economical with his movements as he was with his words, then placed it on the table beside a lantern. The light brought the bottle to life, and the glittering treasure within danced like fire. "This, gentlemen, is Klondike gold."

Constantine passed the bottle to the first man on his left, then waited as it was handed around and examined. Ben handed it to Miller, who turned it in all different angles, enthralled. When Miller reluctantly gave it to Thompson, the Sergeant barely looked at it before handing it off again.

"Gold comes in all shapes and sizes," Constantine continued, "but the currency in the Yukon is mostly the dust, which must be weighed to be evaluated. In every town you visit, the saloons and shops will have scales on their counters for measuring the gold's weight and value. One ounce of gold dust — when it is pure — is worth about sixteen dollars right now. That's also about what most working men in Dawson City are paid in a day."

Ben stared resolutely at the gold, but he could feel Miller's eyes on him. The Constables back at Fort Macleod were paid only fifty cents a day. Since he and Miller had volunteered to go to the Klondike, they were now receiving a full dollar a day. A far cry from sixteen.

"Gold itself has no magnetic properties," the Inspector said, "and yet it draws people just as powerfully. The prospectors you saw along your journey here are only the beginning of the migration. Tens of thousands will follow on their heels." He frowned. "The unfortunate truth is that many of these people are unprepared for the conditions they'll face. Even before we factor in the perils of snow so deep a man could be buried within hours, the terrain itself is harsh and unfamiliar. Starvation, broken bones, and illness are common. But every one of these travellers already has a fever; gold has lit that fire in them, and they are very, very ill from it. The North-West

Mounted Police supplies the medicine they require by maintaining sanity in the middle of madness."

Constantine walked purposefully to the window behind the men, and they all turned to look. Through the foggy panes, Ben could see the blizzard was dwindling, the snow and ice pellets softening to sleet.

"Our laws are not popular with American prospectors, who make up a large percentage of the men coming here for the gold. Many have lived in areas like Skagway in which thievery, assault, even murder are common occurrences. They are desperate men living in desperate times in a desperate place. We must always be on guard."

He faced them, hands behind his back. "Remember the motto of the North-West Mounted Police. *Maintien le Droit.* Uphold the right. And that is what we are here for. We defend the law and protect the people, and we command a great deal of respect in this wild place. I expect you to be proud of that, and I expect you to make me proud."

In that moment, it felt as if Constantine was speaking directly to Ben, and a fresh wave of loyalty rippled through him. Long ago he had recognized his own need to do better in this world, to take his father's example and turn it upside down, but no one in the NWMP had so clearly outlined what was being asked of him until now. The call was invigorating, but when Constantine left the room the last dregs of Ben's energy went with him. Fortunately, the arrival of a hearty caribou stew with a side of fresh bread brought him back, and as the men tucked into their meal a contented hush fell over the room.

By the time they were done eating, the storm had melted into a frozen fog. Ben left the building to set up his tent — there wasn't enough space in the barracks for everyone — then he walked to the river and took a seat on a fallen log, letting his mind wander over what lay ahead.

Ben had been assigned to a detachment that would soon hike the forty-eight miles to Dawson City to build a barracks. According to Constantine, the rough and reckless rabble of Skagway were moving into Dawson, and until the Mounties took control of that town there would be no law. That, Constantine had stated, would be accomplished within a few weeks. After that, two detachments would be sent on to the summits of the Chilkoot Trail and the White Pass. Those men would construct two more outposts from which they would collect customs and monitor the feckless travellers coming to the goldfields. Ben hoped to be in one of those detachments as well.

"How you feeling?"

Ben looked up, surprised to see Thompson standing behind him. He hadn't heard him approach.

"Better. Thanks," Ben replied, though his throat felt as if it were lined by broken glass. "I feel almost human again. Whatever the Hän put in that tea you gave me the other night really helped."

Thompson lowered himself onto a log across from Ben and reached inside his coat for his pipe and tobacco. "Best thing you can do on the trail is get advice from the locals."

"We could have starved if we hadn't met them."

"We'd have been all right, but they did make it easier," Thompson agreed. "They figured out folks like us a long time ago, and I find if you treat them with respect they'll do the same with you." His expression was thoughtful. "The people up here have been trading with the Hudson's Bay Company for about fifty years now, but I don't know." He shook his head. "I have a bad feeling this gold rush and all these travellers are going to change things for them. It'll at least force them to move."

Thompson lit his pipe and squinted at Ben over the puffs of smoke. "You grew up around the Blackfoot, didn't you?"

Ben's stomach sank. He'd forgotten that Thompson had seen his file. Ben purposefully hadn't told the NWMP anything about his father when he'd signed up. He didn't remember mentioning the Blackfoot, either, but he'd been pretty nervous during the interview. He must have, for Thompson to ask. Now that it was out, Ben supposed it didn't matter that he knew, really. He hadn't been with the Blackfoot for all that long, just on and off after his parents had died. But he'd been there long enough to know they had been far better parents than his own. They never judged him, beat him, or pointed a gun in his face. They trained him to hunt, to fight, to ride, to live off the land, and, most important, to believe in his own strength. All things his father had never bothered to teach him.

"Some," Ben replied. "Did some cowboying, too. I kind of went wherever the wind blew me."

Fragrant pipe smoke filtered through Thompson's beard, then veiled his face. "I married a Blackfoot woman. Sinopa was her name." His voice softened as he spoke. "We had a son, Chogan."

101

Ben and Thompson had gotten to know each other a little around campfires along the trail, but he wasn't used to the Sergeant talking about himself.

"Had?" Ben asked tentatively.

"They both got sick with *la grippe* a ways back. Influenza." Thompson let his breath out slowly. "After they died, I joined the Force. Needed something to keep me busy."

"I'm sorry about your family."

Thompson nodded. "What happened to yours? You had no kin on your application."

"They died," Ben said, dismissing the story with a one-shouldered shrug. He didn't want any part of that life messing up the one he was living now.

Thompson frowned. "Yeah, I got that much. They got sick?"

The sound of the river rushing past seemed suddenly louder to Ben, and he unconsciously raised his voice a little. "I don't really like to talk about them."

Thompson tilted his head. From the way he was regarding Ben, he thought the Sergeant was probably taking a good look at his scar. Ben looked away. The man was perceptive. Ben would give him that.

"Apologies," Thompson said. "I didn't mean to pry."

"There's nothing to tell," Ben lied. He

hated being forced into a corner. "It's just —"

"Good evening, gentlemen," Miller announced as he settled onto the log beside Ben. "Constantine says tens of thousands of people are coming. Think he's right?"

For once, Ben was glad of Miller's interruption. "Sure. I believe it," he replied.

"Me too. What about the gold? Think we'll get a chance to dig our own fortunes up there? It'd be a shame to miss out on this opportunity, since we've come all this way."

Ben wondered that himself. He glanced at Thompson, but the Sergeant wasn't offering anything.

"I imagine we will," Ben said. "But who has the money to buy a claim? I sure don't. Maybe a half claim."

Miller grinned. "I reckon I'll do whatever I have to to find the money if it means I'd be making sixteen dollars a day."

"You do realize this ain't all about the gold, right?" Thompson snapped. His tone was almost always harsh when he spoke to Miller, regardless of what he was talking about. "We have to get to Chilkoot first, and that's gonna be the toughest thing you've ever done. Up there, nothing breaks the wind. There's no shelter at all. Up there, *we're* the trees. Don't get cocky, Miller."

Miller's jaw flexed. "Some of the boys are going to visit the saloons across the river," he said, ignoring Thompson's rebuke, "and I hear Constantine's looking the other way tonight. You know, as a kind of welcome. You interested, Turner?"

Despite the pull of sleep, Ben had a feeling there wouldn't be many more chances to enjoy themselves that way once they got back on the trail. "Yeah, I think I am."

Thompson surprised him by heading down the bank with them and climbing into their canoe, but as soon as the three of them stepped inside the first saloon Thompson spotted someone he knew and left them on their own. Ben and Miller edged towards the bar, and when their whiskies arrived, Ben inhaled, letting the alcohol fumes clear his stuffed nose before he took a sip. The liquor burned at first, but the tingling numbness that followed was soothing on his throat.

"I'm looking forward to Dawson," Miller said after he drained his first glass. "I miss civilization. I miss the noise and the women."

"Dawson doesn't sound like civilization to me," Ben replied. "More like a whole bunch of crazy people fighting over a dream."

"A dream? Haven't you read the papers?

People are making boatloads of money up there."

"Sure, but if thousands are already there, why do we only hear about a few lucky ones striking it rich? What happens to the others?"

"That doesn't concern me." Miller held up a finger, and the bartender brought him another whisky.

"You're a Mountie," Ben reminded him. "That means it *is* your concern."

"We'll see," Miller said, appraising a woman as she crossed the floor. "Something tells me things are gonna be a whole lot more exciting in Dawson than they have been so far."

"I guess we'll find out."

Over the next week, they spent their time training in preparation for the next leg of the journey, and by the end Ben could hardly wait to get moving. The drills had grounded him, and his good health had returned.

But on the night before their departure, Ben couldn't sleep. An odd beam of light shone through the ceiling of his tent, and after an hour of tossing and turning he threw open the flap and stepped outside to see what was going on. The sight took his breath away, and he stared in wonder as a thick green ribbon of light curled and swayed across the cloudless sky, winding around flickers of white, pink, indigo, and every shade in between. As he watched, the colours shrank as if they inhaled before rolling back across the heavens like a great, flowing sheet. Ben was hypnotized. Along the route north he had caught glimpses of the aurora borealis, but the magic was so much more tonight, as if the heavens were consoling the isolated men with this gift before they set off again.

"It don't happen all the time. Not like that." Thompson stood a few feet away from his own tent, gazing upwards. "Appears to be putting on a show for us."

"That's quite a show," Ben said.

"Yeah, well, this is quite a place, and you ain't seen half of it." Thompson paused. "Just wait until winter really hits and brings seventy feet of snow with it. I bet you'll wish you'd never come."

Thompson's words of warning hung in the air like the frost on his breath, but they didn't frighten Ben. He wasn't afraid of what might lie in his future. The only thing that ever scared him was his past. Whenever Ben grew even slightly apprehensive about anything, he focused on what he'd already survived. After saying good night to Thompson, he ducked back into his tent and thought about that cold autumn night his mother had died, and the panic he had felt when he'd fled the empty farm. Young and alone, with no idea what he would do next, he had chosen to sleep on the hard prairie grass under the endless stars rather than return to his parents' farm.

Tonight he slept under the same sky, but everything was different. He was no longer alone, and he was no longer a boy. His future stretched before him, its boundaries undefined, rich with promise and adventure.

Seven:
Liza

"Come on, Larry." Liza curled her fingers through the horse's halter, urging him forward. "I'll pull if you pull."

It was Liza's turn to lead the wagon, which wasn't a difficult job, but it was slow. The poor old nag was so worn down that his preference was to sleep, not walk. She'd been struggling with the lazy horse for an hour, and she'd ended up naming Larry after a friend of her father's who rarely got out of his chair.

"Straight on, Liza!" her father called cheerily from behind. "Follow the road."

Despite the hundreds of feet and hooves that had already passed this way, Liza had a lot of trouble calling this path a road. Each step was a lesson in trust. Snow camouflaged uneven rocks, and firm-looking dirt patches often gave way to mud. Just now her right foot sank into a mushy spot.

"At least the sun is out," Stan said, catching up to her.

"True," she replied. "Instead of wretched, I only feel miserable."

"It's not that bad." He chuckled. "You said you wanted off the boat, and you said you hated Dyea. Now you're done with both."

He was right. It did no one any good to gripe. "I'm sorry. I don't mean to be a grouch. I'm just so hungry. I hope there's food in the next town."

"Me too. I could eat a horse."

"You needn't bother with this one," she replied, tilting her head towards Larry. "He doesn't have enough meat on him to feed a barn cat."

Stan leaned towards her. "Father had to pay six hundred dollars for him back at the beach, so try not to complain too loudly."

"Highway robbery," she muttered back. "He's not worth five dollars at home."

"I know. And once we get to the bottom of the steepest part of the mountain we'll have to let him go. Father will sell him off to someone who will take him back to the bottom, where he'll make this trek over and over again."

Liza suddenly found fresh appreciation for Larry. He might not be full of life, but at least he was pulling their things. She patted the horse's dirty brown neck. "I'll miss you when that time comes," she whispered to him.

The string of travellers stretched as far as she could see, both in front and behind them. Not surprisingly, most were men, though once in a while she spotted a skirt. She was intrigued by some of the travellers' unusual luggage, and it made her wonder how much these people knew about living rough. Her family were novices, but at least they hadn't brought along heavy furniture and musical instruments like others she saw. Their obvious poor planning concerned her. How would these people fare when the temperature dropped and endless heaps of snow fell along with it? Who would turn back, and who would stay the entire five-hundred-mile course?

"Look at that." Stan pointed towards the meadow. "Someone left their trunk."

"The owner probably didn't have a wagon," her father said. "Trunks are too awkward to carry. Bags are easier."

Curiosity got the better of Liza and she handed Larry's reins to Stan. "I'm going to see what's in there."

Holding up the hem of her skirt, she crunched through the small drifts of snow dotting the meadow and knelt by the trunk, but when her fingers touched the locks she hesitated. Someone before her had made the difficult decision to abandon their things right here, and she wasn't sure it was her right to pry. Then again, by abandoning his possessions the prospector had made it clear he no longer wanted or valued them. Which meant, Liza decided as she unclasped the locks and opened the lid, that the things in this trunk were now available to the public and she had every right.

A tintype photograph in a tarnished silver frame was the first item to catch her eye. The photograph was of a young woman with dark hair, and a frothy collar bubbled to her chin. It was the frame that interested Liza, because it occurred to her that an item like that would sell well at the new shop. Eager to find more, Liza rummaged further, and half-buried in the folds of a man's smart white shirt she discovered a silver locket on a chain. When she undid the tiny clasp, she recognized the same woman's photo within, and a kind of indignation rose in Liza's chest. Had he not cared for the woman? He must have, since her likeness was in a locket that should be hanging near his heart. And yet here she now lay, abandoned. How difficult had it been for him to exchange the love of his life for the uncertain dream of a fortune? What kind of man chose gold over love?

Liza absently weighed the locket in the palm of her hand as she looked around. The meadow was dotted by similar trunks. *So many,* she thought, struck by the bitter realization that every trunk was filled with personal things so many men had chosen to discard.

Her mother walked carefully through the field towards her. "The owner won't be coming back," she said, practical as ever. She dug Blue out of her coat and set the puppy on the ground to do her business. "If you don't take it, someone else will."

That was all the encouragement Liza needed. She pocketed the necklace then dug through the trunk for more treasures. *Like I'm mining for gold,* she thought wryly, *except most of this is silver.* She unearthed a few more things she could easily manage: a pair of beautiful fountain pens, a Meerschaum pipe in its case — almost brand new — and another, smaller silver picture frame. She decided to remove the photograph and leave it in the trunk, just in case. If the owner ever did come back, the photo would be here, waiting for him.

"Agatha, dear!" Liza's father called from the wagon. He'd stopped on the trail to wait for them, blocking other travellers. "We don't want to fall behind."

"It's time to go," her mother said, reaching for Blue, who had wandered closer to Liza.

"I'll carry her for a while," Liza said, scooping the puppy up and tucking her into her coat. "Go ahead. I'll be there in a minute."

Liza swept her hand along the bottom of the trunk one last time, and a heavy wool garment brushed her fingers. Who on earth would leave warm clothes behind when they were in this place? She pulled the material out from under but was disappointed to see it was only a pair of trousers. She started to fold them back into the trunk, then stopped and held them up again, a scandalous thought crossing her mind. The trousers weren't overly large, and if the gentleman had also packed suspenders . . . She rummaged further. Aha!

"Liza!" her father called again. "We want to make it to Sheep Camp by nightfall!"

"Coming!" Quickly, Liza rolled the little treasures into the trouser pockets, then grabbed a sweater that had been folded underneath. Back at the wagon, it took only a moment for her to covertly pack the new acquisitions into her bag.

"All done," she whispered to Blue as the family set off again.

The rocky path began to slant upwards, and the air grew consistently sharper the higher they went. As her muscles cramped and her lungs burned from exertion, Liza walked closer to the wagon and held on to its side for support. Her family's earlier chatter slowed, and the trail fell quiet until an eclectic mix of tents, huts, and small log buildings appeared in the distance.

Liza grabbed her father's arm. "Is that what I think it is?"

"If you think it's Sheep Camp, then I believe so," he replied, walking with renewed vigour.

Liza's mother was keeping up, but she was breathing hard. "Let's find accommodations right away," she said to her husband, and he nodded and took her arm.

As they entered Sheep Camp, Liza observed her surroundings with disappointment. She wasn't sure what she'd been expecting, but this place was no more than a miniature, even grubbier version of Dyea. The family eyed the dozen or so hotels skeptically, then decided to spend some of their valuable money so they could stay in one for a night. Even though they were no more than one-room buildings, at least they promised more warmth than a tent.

That night, Liza lay beside her mother, between Stan and their father, in an oppressively hot room bursting at the seams with three dozen strange men. The stink of unwashed bodies and wet fur coats was so stifling that Liza had to cover her nose with a scarf, and even with Blue snuggled next to her, she still couldn't fall asleep. She had known it would be rough in the North, but this was different. This was repulsive.

When morning came, they staggered gratefully into the fresh air.

"Promise me we won't sleep there again," her mother said, the circles under her eyes darker than ever.

Liza's father nodded in agreement. "We'll only spend one more night in the camp. And I think a tent would be better."

"Oh, it wasn't so bad," Stan said, stretching his stiff limbs.

His ability to bounce back from even the worst conditions baffled Liza. Like her father, Stan had taken to the journey like a bee to flowers. He was perpetually making friends with other travellers and asking questions about their experiences.

That night, Stan persuaded Liza to go with him to a saloon and listen to old-timers tell their stories. Her mother objected — a lady didn't belong in a saloon! — but Liza's father convinced her that their daughter would be fine. She would have Stan with her, he said, and the world was different out here — it had its own particular rules. It sure was, Liza thought.

She was nervous as she passed through the saloon door, but she was emboldened by the relative indifference paid to her by the crowd inside. Stan had made a beeline for the scruffiest-looking prospector she had ever seen, so she followed close behind and sat beside her brother at the man's wobbly table. The prospector was probably only forty, but he could have passed for twice that. His nose was purple, badly deformed by frostbite, and strings of his hair clung to his neck and hung past his shoulders, barely distinguishable from the massive beard hiding most of his face. Liza tried not to stare when she thought she spotted something moving amid the greasy strands, and she distracted herself by nuzzling Blue against her cheek.

"Nine days?" Stan was saying. "How did you live on that mountain in a blizzard for nine days?"

"Ain't so bad when you know what you're about, but it ain't no business for tenderfoots, boy." He held up a small bottle

116

twinkling with gold dust. "But here it is. Here's what it's all for. Ain't she a beauty?"

A month ago, Liza might have been impressed, but these days they constantly saw gold in some shape or form. Still, Stan was mesmerized by it. "You have no idea how to mine for gold," she'd remind him, but he'd only shrug and ask, "How hard can it be?"

Right now he was leaning across the table, focused on the miner. "What did you eat?"

"I had oats, and I had a couple o' candles."

"Candles?" Liza blurted. "You ate *candles*?"

"Can't say as I recommend neither, but I'm still here, ain't I?"

Stan didn't bat an eyelash. "Could you move around, up there on the mountain? During the storm, I mean."

"Ain't nobody movin' round, boy." The man rolled his red-rimmed eyes towards the ceiling. "Exceptin' ol' Whisky Jimmy, o' course. He had to move round now, didn't he?"

"Why's that?"

"That ol' boy ate his dogs. He'd have to move to catch 'em, I s'pose." The prospector scowled at Blue. "Sure wish I'd had a dog."

Liza tightened her grip, and Blue wriggled in protest. "How could he eat his *dogs*?"

"They was gonna die either way, girl. Some men cut their teams loose, but it's a death sentence up there either way. Dogs'll freeze or starve or get picked off by wolves, same as anyone else." He tapped the table with one grimy finger. "Might as well give them a quick way out, I say."

"How cold does it really get?" Stan asked, sidestepping the issue.

The miner held out a filthy hand, palm side up. "Let's say you're holding a block of ice in your bare hand. Got that in your head, boy? Now keep that ice there 'til your hand freezes. While that's happening, your face freezes. Your belly freezes. Your balls freeze. Everything freezes." He touched the tip of his damaged nose. "Your nose falls off, and your ears, too. You wish you was dead." Liza made a sound of disgust and looked away. "All you can think about is finding a fire," he went on. "Now imagine you're crawling uphill on your frozen hands and knees, and you're lugging fifty pounds of gear on your back." He started laughing, a strange cackle that sounded unnatural to Liza. "How's that, boy? How's that? Cold enough?"

Stan's mouth hung open as he drank in every awful detail, and Liza felt a ripple of concern. Ever since their father had brought up the idea of going to the Yukon, Stan had been keen. When they'd seen the men on the boats with all the gold, drifting away from Dyea, his eagerness had grown. And now, surrounded by prospectors and mountains and the reality of the Yukon, he had become almost obsessive.

Liza looked around the room, and all she could see were ragged men hunched over tables or gathered by the bar, passionately discussing the exact same topic. And when she turned back towards Stan, she saw a similar set to his posture.

"That's enough," she murmured into his ear. "I want to leave now."

Stan held up a hand, ignoring her plea. She felt a brush against her shoulder and glanced up as one of the men raised an eyebrow at her. Heat poured into her cheeks and she grabbed Stan's arm, but he was entirely absorbed in the miner's story.

The stranger moved on, but Liza's heart would not stop pounding. She was trapped in a crowd of strangers, and that crowd was clustered in the middle of nowhere.

I have to get out of here.

Stan didn't notice when she jumped to her feet, pushed through the crowd, and burst through the door. Outside, she sank ankle-deep in mud, but the cold shock of it was a relief. She was free.

Then she looked up and up, following the trail with her eyes until it disappeared within the crevices and curves of the mountain, and the thumping in her chest returned. She wasn't free at all. She was trapped in the North, caught tight in its jaws, and there was no way out.

Eight:
Ben

Winter in the Yukon was like nothing Ben could have imagined. January had carved itself deep into the ground, freezing lakes solid and turning difficult land passages into forbidding trails of sheer ice. Snowdrifts piled on Ben's eyebrows, and icicles hung from his whiskers, sealing his lips together. He could barely see through the slitted goggles he wore to prevent snow blindness, and he'd forgotten what his fingertips felt like. And the wind . . . Thompson had been right — the Mounties were now the trees, bent double against it.

Before their departure from Dawson City two weeks ago, each man had been issued a buffalo robe, a beaver cap with ear flaps, mittens, long woollen stockings, goggles, and moccasins, to which Ben had added a pair of waterproof sealskin mukluks he'd purchased from a local Hän. But the clothing did little to shield them from tempests that threatened to freeze the men to the spot as they made their way to the summit of the Chilkoot Trail.

The world was an uninterrupted vista of black and white, offset by nothing save the blue of the sky on rare days when the storm clouds cleared. Today was one of those days, but just because the sun was out, that did not mean Ben felt any warmth. This morning, a perfect circle surrounded the sun, a razor-thin, frozen rainbow cutting through lacy clouds with bursts of yellow burning at either side. The story the Hän told was that the yellow spots were fiery earmuffs which kept the sun warm when the cold got this extreme. Under its icy glare, tiny tornadoes of snow skimmed across the frozen landscape, danced through the air, and set ice crystals winking from faraway branches.

Ben's detachment had been climbing for days, and the higher they went, the harder breathing became. The only one who didn't seem as affected by the ascent was Thompson, who trudged through the knee-deep snow as if it were no more than a steep set of stairs. Ben assumed that was because the Sergeant had done this trek before, and he tried hard to keep up, but the snow beneath his boots was unreliable, sometimes supporting his steps, sometimes giving way and dropping him hip-deep. Every move was exhausting. He'd lost count of how many times he'd had to wrench his leg free of snow. He was tugging it loose yet again when he stopped, distracted by a small black twig, maybe two inches long. It poked out of the snow by his right hand, which was odd, since there were no trees anywhere near them. Curious, he pulled at it, but the twig broke in his grasp and the surrounding snow collapsed in a heap by his feet.

Ben stumbled backwards with a cry, realizing the twig was not a twig at all. Sticking out of the snow was a frozen hand, three of its blackened fingers and a thumb grasping at the sky.

Thompson turned. "What is it?"

"A body."

Ben scooped more snow away, revealing a coat sleeve frozen stiff and the solid side of a man's torso. He heard Thompson climbing down to him, then he was beside him, helping him dig. The two of them shovelled enough snow away to see the corpse's grey face, its lips black and drawn slightly back in a snarl, as if he had dared to challenge death. Horror rumbled through Ben's chest at the thought of what the man would have suffered out here, waiting for the inevitable end.

"His eyes are still open."

Thompson swept away more snow. "Starved, then froze, looks like. Keep digging."

"Why? What do we do?"

"Can't leave him here."

"We can't bury him. The ground's frozen."

Thompson looked at him from beneath heavy lids. "Listen, this won't be the last corpse we find. We'll take them up top and store them 'til spring, then we will give them a decent burial." He called down to Inspector Belcher, who would be in charge once they made it to the Chilkoot Pass. "We need a sled." Then he frowned at the snow by Ben's feet. "Tuck that finger into his coat, would you?"

Ben stooped to pick it up, but when his mitt closed around it, he gagged.

"Disturbing, ain't it?" Thompson said, and Ben was relieved the Sergeant hadn't laughed at his weak stomach. "It's like seeing ourselves after the Yukon's done with us. We think we're special." He gestured towards the body. "But here we are."

Trying not to think too much about what he was holding in his hand, Ben slid the finger into the dead man's pocket, but his brain wasn't fooled. No matter how far they went, the image wouldn't leave him. All the way up the mountain, over the Chilkoot Pass, then down the steep slope towards Crater Lake, Ben thought of that four-fingered hand clawing out of the snow. When the wind nearly shoved Ben down the mountain, when the ice stole his footing and the pelting crystals of snow blinded him, he saw again that broken finger stuck in the dead man's pocket. *That will not be me,* he told himself over and over again. *I will not die here.*

At the summit, Inspector Belcher directed them to make camp on Crater Lake, which was located just beneath the Chilkoot Pass. From there, they were ordered to set up a larger tent back up top, to serve as the official outpost. Ben supposed that because of its location, Crater Lake would be slightly shielded from the wind, but once they'd established the camp, he had a lot of trouble finding much difference between the two. If there was, it was hard to appreciate when they were shivering around a tiny tent stove or digging themselves out of three feet of snow every single morning.

"This is the worst place on earth," Miller said. "Remind me what we're doing up here?"

Ben saw no reason to waste his breath. They were hundreds of miles and countless hours from any kind of relief.

"Just dig," he replied.

Every morning, he and Miller awoke hours before sunrise to the arrhythmic patter of water dripping on their blankets from the melting frost on their tent ceiling. Shuddering with cold, they rolled from their cots, then got their blood pumping again by shovelling the wall of snow that sealed them within the tent.

When Superintendent Steele arrived a couple of weeks later, he ordered the immediate construction of an actual wooden outpost.

"He must be joking," Miller said to Ben that night. "How can anyone haul building materials up those trails, let alone do construction in this weather? Steele's insane. Where are we supposed to get lumber?"

For the first time in months, the familiar burn of Ben's anger flared in his chest. Where there had once been friendly conversations between him and his partner, now all Ben heard were complaints and arguments. He squeezed his hands into fists, resisting the urge to force Miller into silence.

"We signed up for this," he reminded Miller stiffly. "They told us it was going to be difficult."

"This isn't difficult," Miller huffed. "It's

ridiculous. Can't we wait for spring?"

"Have you seen the thousands of people climbing the Chilkoot?" Ben countered. "They are dying out there. If we're going to help at all, this has to be done right away."

Despite the bitter cold and the constant, punishing snowstorms, Ben and the others hitched themselves to sleds as if they were oxen and dragged timber, canvases, and tools to the summit so they could build a twelve-foot-square building to house a couple of men, their supplies, and a workspace.

When the day was done, Ben fell asleep within seconds of lying down, though he awoke sporadically, disturbed either by winds buffeting the tent or his own convulsive shivering. Firewood was more valuable than gold at the summit, and everyone was forced to be frugal with it. On some nights they made do without any at all, because the hardiest of them would have to trudge through seven miles of snow to get any. Without a reliable source of heat, the men were unable to dry clothing and blankets, and the smell of mildew — the only thing that could still grow — hung over them like a cloud.

"I can't do this anymore," Miller muttered.

They were huddled over the tiny stove while a blizzard raged on around them for the third straight night, and for once, Ben was inclined to agree with his partner. He was fighting another cold, which had settled into a wheezing bark in his chest, and was worried about catching the pneumonia that was already rampant among the men. Every one of them had lost weight and their skin was almost burgundy from the cold. Frostbite took the tips of both of Miller's ears, and even the stalwart Thompson had a painful-sounding cough that plagued him day and night. There was a real likelihood, Ben knew, that some of them would die out here in this forsaken corner of the world. Maybe all of them.

"I mean it," Miller said again, his voice hoarse. "I can't stay here."

"You can't leave," Ben replied wearily. "That's desertion. They'll catch you, and that'd be worse than it is here. Even if they didn't catch you, where would you go? You'd die out there."

Tears squeezed through the corners of Miller's eyes, and Ben felt a prickling in his own.

"It'll get easier," Ben said.

"How do you know?"

"Because it can't get worse." *Please, God.*

Don't let it get worse.

The snowstorm raged uninterrupted, and yet construction of the outpost continued. After the tenth straight day of the blizzard, they returned to their camp after work and discovered the lake water had risen under the weight of all the snow. With almost half a foot of ice water flooding their tents and the wind blasting too hard for them to consider moving camp, the men dragged their sleds inside to hold their bedding out of the water's reach. And still the snow fell.

To Ben's bewilderment, the prospectors kept coming. Sometimes, when the blizzard briefly eased, he could see the town of Dyea at the bottom of the trail on one side. If he looked the other way he saw the trail to Lake Lindeman. Both sides were marked by a steady line of climbers.

"Does no one have the sense to stay inside?" Ben wondered out loud.

Miller shuddered with cold beside him. "Gold fever's keeping them warm."

"Not warm enough." Every few days they found another frozen corpse abandoned in the snow. Ben would never get used to the sight of them.

"We can't stop them from coming," Miller said. "Makes us pretty much useless up here."

We supply the medicine by maintaining sanity in the middle of madness, Inspector Constantine had said.

"We're not here to stop them," Ben reminded him. "Just keep them safe."

"Then we're failing."

Ben knew that. They all knew it, but they were doing all they could.

That afternoon Ben hammered the final one-inch board into place on the outpost, then they roofed the building with a canvas tarpaulin. All that was left to do was install the Maxim machine gun and a Lee Metford carbine. Yukon Commissioner Walsh and Inspector Constantine had ordered them to be hauled up to each summit to serve as visible reminders of the Mounties' authority. Regardless of the weather, the Maxim would be manned at all times.

The next morning, Ben and the nine other men in his detachment stood by the brand new Chilkoot Pass outpost, bundled in their buffalo coats, posing for an official photograph as Inspector Belcher hoisted the Union Jack. Afterwards, they squeezed into the new building and inhaled warm air, fragrant with woodsmoke and coffee. For the first time in a long time, Ben enjoyed the rare luxury of slipping off his mitts. He tucked them under his arm and rubbed his hands together until heat sparked within them.

Inspector Belcher stood at the front of the room, waiting for everyone to settle down.

"Gentlemen, if you haven't already, please pour yourself a cup of coffee," he said, sounding cheerful despite the raging storm outside. "Congratulations on a job well done. Some might have said the construction of this building under these circumstances was impossible, but I am pleased to see that those naysayers underestimated the strength and dedication of the North-West Mounted Police."

His next words were cut off by someone coughing, and that seemed to loosen everyone else's chests as well. The strength of the North-West Mounted Police, Ben thought with regret, had been greatly reduced. He could only hope they might one day recover. After the coughing subsided, Belcher spoke again.

"In addition to congratulating you, I have an important matter to discuss." Belcher paused. "We have all seen bodies on the trail. As you can probably imagine, those are not the only ones. Of the travellers who have managed to complete this journey and reach Dawson City and the goldfields, many succumbed shortly after their arrival. A number of those deaths were a result of illness, but others are dying due to their own negligence. They have come all this way with picks and axes, but they have not thought to bring enough food or provisions to survive."

Belcher reached for an envelope on his desk, then slid a sheet of paper from within. "To prevent more needless deaths, the North-West Mounted Police will now be enforcing the one-tonne rule, recently established by Yukon Commissioner Walsh. Take a look at this, then pass it along, if you please."

After scanning the page, Thompson wordlessly handed it to Ben, who studied the words, then shared it with Miller and the others. On the paper had been typed a long list of items, ranging from a hundred and fifty pounds of bacon to five yards of mosquito netting and a dozen pairs of wool socks.

"What you see on this list is a year's worth of supplies," Belcher explained. "The food is approximately three pounds per man per day. The other items are there because, as we all know, they'll need much more than food to survive out here. Therefore, each prospector is required to bring every item on this list before they can pass this out-post."

"Everything?" Miller blurted. "That's too much! Why, four hundred pounds of flour alone is fifty dollars!"

Inspector Belcher eyed Miller. "Everything."

As much as Ben hated to side with Miller, he had to ask. "How will that work, Inspector?"

"You're familiar with The Scales?" Belcher asked.

The Scales was the last stopover village before the final climb up to the summit. It offered a number of so-called restaurants, a couple of alleged hotels, a saloon, and a few offices and warehouses. It had its share of entertainment and miscreants, just like all these other improvised towns, but overall Ben remembered it as a place of commerce.

"The travellers' freight will be weighed at The Scales before they proceed up the trail," Belcher said. "When they reach the summit, each traveller will be subject to inspection. If they do not have all the required items, they are not permitted to go through. Simple as that. In addition, all goods purchased outside of Canada will be subject to customs duties."

"How can they carry all that?" Miller demanded.

"They'll find a way if they want it bad enough."

"But they can't —"

"Constable Miller, obviously they cannot bring everything at once." Belcher lowered his voice as if he were speaking to a child. "They must learn to pack properly and carry portions at a time. Between climbs they will leave their belongings here at our post for safekeeping until they have brought everything. If they choose to carry fifty pounds, they will climb the trail twenty times. If they choose to carry twenty pounds, they will climb it fifty times." His smile was tight. "Do you understand the arithmetic, Constable?"

"Yes, sir," Miller said, subdued.

"Any other questions?"

The thought of turning all these people around after they'd come so far made Ben feel a little queasy. He knew the climb. Sixteen steep, ice-covered miles each way, all of it done while carrying heavy loads and battling vicious storms and temperatures. But the more Ben thought about it, the more he could see Belcher was right. Shipments of provisions to the Yukon were few and far between.

Miller was still shaking his head. He

pointed at the list. "Yes, sir, but . . . but each man must have *thirty pounds of nails? Eight pounds of baking powder?* It's —"

"That's enough, Constable. You have your orders, and they will be carried out starting tomorrow morning. Thank you, gentlemen. You are all dismissed."

"But —"

Ben grabbed Miller's arm. "They'll die without this rule. We don't have any way of bringing in supplies later on, when they run out. What Belcher's saying is that by enforcing this, we're making sure they'll help themselves. This is the only way we can give them a fighting chance."

Miller pulled out of Ben's grasp. "It's too much," he insisted.

Thompson finally spoke, putting an end to the conversation. "Let's hope it's enough."

NINE:
LIZA

"Get a move on, Liza!" Stan called.

Liza could picture him pacing outside her tent, lips pursed with impatience.

"I'll be out in a minute," she muttered, pulling on her boots. "The mountain's not going anywhere."

Today the climb to the summit began. Up until now, the journey had been relatively easy — the rough conditions had been the worst of it — but no one had any delusions that this next leg would not be every bit as difficult as it looked. Since the mountain was far too steep for any horse and wagon, her father had sold Larry, and now Liza, Stan, and their parents would each pull a sled and carry a pack. Fortunately, her father had also paid a number of Hän packers for their assistance, then he'd spent more money to safely store the family's remaining provisions in a warehouse in Sheep Camp. After they reached the top, they'd have to repeat the climb until they could bring all their things up.

When her father said they might even have to climb it three times to get everything, Liza decided she would not be making the trek in her corset and skirts. Feeling both rebellious and smart, she folded her dirty skirts away and pulled on the appropriated trousers, then twirled with delight. They fit just right.

"What do you think?" she asked Blue, lifting the puppy to her face. Blue's tiny tongue touched Liza's nose, which suggested to Liza that she approved. "I agree. Now let's just tuck you in, then we're ready to go."

When she stepped outside, Stan's eyes bugged out. "What are you *wearing?*"

"Trousers," she replied, basking in the freedom of taking long steps without being dragged down by miles of material. *Men are so fortunate!* she thought.

"Mother's going to —"

"Liza!" her mother gasped, and grabbed her husband's sleeve.

"What on earth?" Liza's father said. "Go back and change your clothes, Liza. This is most unseemly."

"I will not," she replied firmly. "Dressed like this, I will be of much greater use. Not only am I warmer, but I can move more easily and carry more."

"People will stare!" her mother objected, then she pressed a handkerchief against her mouth and turned away, coughing. She still wasn't well enough for the trip, Liza kept thinking, but she was determined not to hold them back even one day more.

"Don't we want that?" Liza countered. "Isn't getting noticed the best advertising for a business? Everyone will be sure to remember the girl who wore trousers on the trail."

"That's what I'm worried about," her mother replied.

She knew her mother was remembering the ship and that awful man's unwanted advances, but the more Liza thought about it, the more she knew she was right to dress this way.

She took her mother's hands in her own. "I will be safe, Mother," she said. "You, Father, and Stan are always with me. Besides, if you think about it, skirts probably draw more of the wrong kind of attention than trousers would."

Her mother didn't look pleased, but she also appeared to consider Liza's point.

"If you're not going to change, I guess there's nothing I can do about it," her father said, though he sounded reluctant. "It's time to go. We shall soon see if your choice in clothing was wise or not."

As Liza picked up her pack, she scanned the camp for Larry, wondering if he'd been taken away yet. She assumed her father had sold the horse to the man who had approached them before, offering a price, and she knew how it went: the buyer would lead a herd of the healthiest animals back down to the beach, then sell them again. It saddened Liza to think of poor Larry repeating the whole trip over and over again, but the horses who could not be sold due to festering injuries or crippling exhaustion would fare even worse. They would be left here to drift, and there was neither food nor shelter for the pitiful creatures.

Stan, who was ready to go, pack on, sled in tow, was staring reverently up the mountain. "The Chilkoot Trail. This is it."

"What trail?" Liza said, slinging her pack on and trying not to groan under the weight. "All I see is a wall of rock."

"Look there! Way, way up there."

She squinted hard, following his finger, but — There! Tiny figures moved ever so slowly towards the summit in a long black line.

"Are those *men*? They look like ants!"

"Let's join the colony, shall we?" her

father said, stepping onto the narrow path.

Once they were underway, Liza had to agree with her parents at least in one aspect: it didn't take long for her to get noticed. Women were rare on the trail — a woman wearing trousers was enough to stop some men in their tracks. She pretended not to see the looks or hear the comments tossed her way, but a few turned her stomach.

"That's what you get for dressing that way," Stan told her.

"Hush. Why don't you put on my skirts sometime and see how you like it?"

He could scold all he wanted, but freeing herself from the confines of her corset and skirts made Liza feel like there wasn't anything she couldn't do. As if she was shedding her old skin to make way for a new, stronger version of herself. She couldn't imagine how her fragile mother could bear all that weight in addition to her awkward, wet skirts, and she felt guilty for not coaxing her into her own pair of trousers. After all, there had been plenty of others left behind in those abandoned trunks.

As the trail rose, the temperature fell, and fur coats which had previously been stowed were put to use. In one aspect, Liza was more fortunate than the others, since she had her own precious little heat source curled up against her chest. But her coat, like all the others, was heavy, and the snow dragged it down even farther.

The snow began later that day. As a child, Liza had stuck her nose to the living room window at the first sign of snowflakes, and even now, as she stood on the side of a mountain, the silent snowfall was hypnotizing. The tiny flakes grew in size and number, piling one on top of the other until they created a soft world of white.

But in under an hour, she realized this snow was not like any she'd seen before. What had started as a placid dance swiftly had become a full-on battle, and she could see no more than three feet in front of her. As if determined to force her and the rest of the travellers back down the mountain, the blizzard doubled its efforts yet again, and Liza had to bow her head and concentrate on each step she took. She could barely see her family anymore; they had become as grey and shapeless as everyone else on this mad trek, and they no longer wasted their breath by offering encouragement.

Nothing could have prepared Liza for this trek. Not the newspapers, not the shouted warnings of men in boats returning from the peak, not even the repugnant stories told by toothless prospectors with mangled noses. She shook her head, trying to clear the water from her face, but the melted snow blurred her vision even worse. Everything was cold and wet and heavy, and each step took more effort than the one before, but she didn't dare stop, because the line would move on without her and she couldn't risk losing her family in the —

"Liza! Watch your step!" Stan called from behind.

"Watch your own step," she muttered under her breath. She turned to yell back at him, but she wobbled sideways and slipped. With a gasp, she spread out her hands just as her knees hit the icy step hard, and she bit back a cry. Blue wriggled, letting her know she was all right, but Liza's heart still raced. One more wrong step and she could have tumbled down to the bottom.

"Get moving!" yelled an unseen climber.

Despair washed over Liza. Everything about this journey was terrible. Had her father imagined this nightmare when he'd told the family this would be the "adventure of a lifetime"? Adventure of a lifetime indeed! She wasn't supposed to be here, clinging to the side of a mountain in the worst snowstorm she'd ever seen. She should be home, working on her father's inventory or dusting shelves, squeezed into her corset, wearing her favourite skirt, laughing easily with customers or friends, perhaps enjoying a sherry later on.

But here she was. She had no choice but to keep climbing. The line of travellers stretched for miles ahead of her, and Liza set her gaze on the hat of a tall man ahead of her. Back at Sheep Camp, she'd spotted him — he was the tallest man she'd ever seen and as slight as a scarecrow — and yet he moved onward with determination. Using the man's hat as her beacon, she took a step, and another, and another. He became a type of destination, though he would always be ahead of her.

When they finally reached the summit, Liza's body was layered in bruises from falling so often on the icy trail. Her eyes burned from the sun, snow, and wind, despite the goggles her father had given them all, and her lips had cracked so badly she could not have smiled if she wanted to — which she didn't. Her parents, silent and grey, slumped into their tent, and seeing them broken like that frightened her even more than the looming clouds overhead. Only Stan appeared intact, though she saw exhaustion even in his laboured movements.

As soon as her brother had assembled their shared tent, she collapsed inside it and opened the top of her coat so Blue could climb out, soft and untouched by the storm. Liza's mind swirled helplessly with fatigue as she cupped her hands around the dear little face and drew her closer, craving the comfort of her warmth against her skin.

The mountain was endless. They had climbed for fourteen hours today. Tomorrow they would do it all over again. And probably the day after that as well. The raging snow and ice would beat them down forever. Was the old prospector right? Would they lose their fingers, toes, and noses before finally collapsing and becoming part of yet another drift for others to pass by? When the puppy nuzzled closer, snuffling by her ear, the precious sound was Liza's undoing, and she gave in to the tears, wishing they could wash away the storm and the mountain and the endlessness of the day. As sleep began to close over her, thick and black and welcome, she hugged Blue a little tighter and whispered a quiet prayer that this mountain would not be the end of them.

TEN:
BEN

Dressed in their buffalo robes, beaver hats, and sealskin mitts, Ben and Miller leaned on their shovels and waited for the day's first prospectors to reach the summit of the Chilkoot Trail. The outpost was complete, the flag waved valiantly on the mountaintop, and the Mounties were about to put the new one-tonne rule into effect. Ben knew deep down it was for the good of everyone, but when he'd woken up that morning, apprehensive about what was ahead for him that day, he started to think the Mounties motto should be changed from *Maintien le Droit* to *Do Things No One Else Wants to Do*.

As the prospectors arrived, some collapsed in heaps. A lot were overcome by coughing fits, and most were too out of breath to speak. The Mounties welcomed the newcomers with cups of water, and when everyone was somewhat settled, Miller bellowed, "Everyone! Gather round! We have an announcement to make."

"I've got this," Ben told him, thinking the news might be easier for the weary travellers to take coming from him rather than Miller.

"Sounds good to me. I'll back you up," Miller replied, smiling wryly.

As Ben explained the new rule, speaking as gently but firmly as he could, he watched the prospectors' expressions of interest change to shock, then anger. At the end of his speech, the crowd erupted in protest.

"This can't be legal!" one man cried, grabbing his friend's arm. "Why, this is . . . What's the word, Smit?"

Smit shook his head. "I'd call it blackmail or something."

Ben held up his hands, trying to soothe the angry travellers. "The rules are for your own safety," he said, echoing Belcher's speech. "Now, no one is saying you have to get up and go right away. Rest a bit. Have some more water."

Miller chimed in. "But keep in mind that every minute you wait, another man is staking a claim." He gave a casual shrug. "Could be your claim. Of course, I'm just reminding you of what you already know."

"What about our things?" one prospector asked.

"Your things will be safe here with us. Make a pile, then raise a flag over it — a tall flag, so you'll be able to find it when the snow buries everything," Ben said. "You can leave a man here if you're uncomfortable with that arrangement, though that'll slow your progress."

Over the course of the next week, Ben lost track of how many times he explained the one-tonne rule. The prospectors kept on coming, day and night, their frozen faces bruised by the elements, their bloodshot eyes dead with exhaustion — and yet as soon as he told them the rule they were able to find the energy to sputter their outrage. It got to the point where Ben could almost predict what kind of reaction he'd get based on how the person was dressed. Expensive, city-style coats usually meant he'd face righteous fury and accusations that the Mounties were infringing on their rights. More practical clothing suggested an experienced traveller. Those men grudgingly called the new rule a dirty deal but backed down with a little more understanding.

One morning, Ben approached a man the size of a grizzly to show him the list of supplies he'd need to bring if he wanted to continue on, and the prospector's face darkened. "I'm not doing that," he growled.

"It's the law," Ben replied, moving towards the next man in line.

But when Ben was about ten feet away, the prospector pulled out a pistol and aimed it at him.

"Ben!" Miller yelled, drawing his own weapon and pointing it at the big man.

"I ain't going back down there," the man roared. "You can't make me do that."

The Yukon wind screamed through the uneasy silence, but of the dozens of people standing around the summit, not one seemed to notice. All eyes were on the showdown between the grizzly man and the Mountie.

Ben didn't reach for his own gun. Instead, he focused straight ahead, past the barrel of the pistol and into the man's eyes. He saw the determination in the prospector's stance and the anger in his expression, but Ben wasn't afraid. It wasn't the first time someone had pointed a gun at him, and this was what he'd been trained for. He gestured for Miller to lower his gun, then he turned back to the prospector.

"Hand it over, sir."

The big man spat to the side. "Ain't gonna happen."

"You are in Canada now," Ben reminded him, "and we are the North-West Mounted

Police. I'll give you the benefit of the doubt and guess you don't yet know that we're the law up here." He tilted his head ever so slightly. "Now give me your weapon."

The man shook his head, his dark eyes on Ben's. "It ain't right what you're doing. Ain't right at all."

Back at Depot, the Constables had been taught that the longer a tense situation continued, the worse it could get. A few feet away, Miller had lowered his gun, but in his periphery Ben could see him shifting from foot to foot, looking for an excuse to fire. He was a stack of dynamite ready to go off. Ben would have to act fast if he was going to protect everyone up here.

No one in their right mind would shoot a Mountie in broad daylight in front of so many witnesses, he told himself, purposefully ignoring the voice in his head that reminded him that no one here actually *was* in their right mind. With his eyes on the angry prospector's face, Ben strode directly up to him and pried the weapon out of his massive hand before he could tell what Ben was doing. Once he had the pistol out of the man's reach, Ben stepped back, relief rushing from his chest to his face. A tiny line of sweat had broken out across his brow, but he maintained his neutral expression as if he'd done this same maneuver a hundred times before.

Miller gave an almost inaudible whistle. "Nicely done," he mumbled.

Ben checked the safety on the pistol, tossed the weapon to Miller, then turned to the man. "Absolutely no revolvers, pistols, rifles, ammunition, or weapons of any kind are allowed past this point. Also, we're collecting duties on anything purchased outside of Canada."

The prospector scowled at the information. "No guns?" he asked. "How are we supposed to defend ourselves?"

"What do you need to defend yourself against?" Ben asked for the thousandth time that week. It still surprised him that weapons were the first objection, not custom duties.

"You know what."

"In Canada we don't allow weapons," Miller said, stepping in. "So that means you won't have to worry about defending yourself against any. Get it?"

"I want to speak with someone in charge!"

"Superintendent Sam Steele will be visiting this outpost tomorrow," Ben said. "You can wait to speak with him, but if you decide not to, we will either accept your surrendered weapons and tariffs right now, or we will accompany you back to the base and out of the Yukon. You'll hear the same thing from the Superintendent."

"How can you do this?" came a muffled yell. A slight traveller stormed up to Ben, covered so completely in goggles, scarf, and furs that Ben couldn't see his face. "Do you have any idea what we just came through?"

"I do," he assured him. "I've been through it myself a few times." He pointed at the Maxim. "We carried that up on my last trip."

The man ignored him. "You want everyone on this mountain to bring an unreasonable amount of supplies up here, then you want to collect duties on it? No, sir. That's robbery. We won't do it."

"Sorry, sir, but you either bring everything on the list or you don't get past me."

Frozen mitts flew to the fellow's face, and he ripped off his scarf and goggles. "Who do you think you are, ordering us around like that?"

At that moment, a noisy gust of wind swept past, stealing Ben's gasp of surprise. The traveller wasn't a man at all, but a woman — though no one could blame him for his mistake. Not only was she bundled up beyond recognition, she wore *trousers*. He would never understand the insanity of this place. Men were crazy to come all this

151

way, but why would a woman choose to do it?

"Sorry, miss, but the rule stands."

Her windburned face reddened further. "My family and I have already done this trip three times just to get our things up here. Now you want us to go back and buy *more* because we don't have all the stuff on your list?" She stomped her boot. "This is ridiculous. What kind of monster are you?"

He met her glare with his own. "If your heart is set on reaching the goldfields, then yes, you will have to go back down there. Probably many times. Until you have satisfied the requirements of the North-West Mounted Police." His frustration bubbled to the surface. "And since you asked, I am Constable Turner, the monster responsible for ensuring you and everyone else up here survive this winter."

"Don't patronize me," she said, her nostrils flaring.

Ben's hands clenched inside his mitts. He was so tired of these people and their arguments. He worked too damn hard to shrug it off every single time. He pointed to an area off the beaten path. "Do you see that big cave we dug in the snow?"

She nodded.

"That is our morgue. A few times every

week we find starved, frozen bodies on the trail. We store them in there until we can send them down to Dyea, where they'll be buried when the ground thaws. Every time we bring in a corpse —" She cringed at the word. Good, he thought. "— we go through their coats and bags to try and find some kind of identification so we can contact their families, but I imagine many of them will never be claimed."

He saw her shudder as she regarded the cave. "When those people were coming up here, we didn't have this one-tonne rule. If they'd brought all the supplies on this list with them, they might still be alive. The truth is, I would rather not store your body in there."

Her eyes met his and his annoyance ebbed away. "My parents are ill."

Over her shoulder Ben noted three people watching her. Two were leaning heavily against the taller one in the middle, and the one on the right hacked noisily before gasping for breath as a coughing fit began. Ben had heard that dangerous sound before and knew she was right. Her parents were in no condition for a return trip just yet.

"We have a hospital tent at Happy Camp. You should take them there."

"This is . . ." She looked away, but not

before he saw tears shining in her eyes.

Reality was settling in for her, he thought. He'd had weeks to get used to this place, and when he'd finally arrived he still hadn't been prepared for it. How could a young woman have any idea what she'd be dealing with up here?

"It's difficult," he finished for her. "And we understand that. But Miss . . . ?"

"Peterson. Liza Peterson."

"Trust me, Miss Peterson. We know it's a lot to ask, but this rule is meant to help you survive."

He turned his attention to the next person in line, but even as he spoke to the new-comer he glanced back at the woman. She was gesturing to her family, passing on the message. He watched them slowly load up again, then trudge away from the pass, following her lead to Happy Camp. That girl has some grit, he thought. I hope she makes it.

Eleven:
Liza

Liza's eyelids warmed against the sunlight, and she dozed a little, dreaming of April in Vancouver. Back then she hadn't been forced to climb mountains in a slow, awkward line, lugging a fifty-pound bag. In Vancouver, there had been flowers and laughter and freedom, good food, friends, and a comfortable bed every night.

Stan's voice broke through her daydream. "Get up, Your Highness. We can't sit around here all day."

If only she could ignore her dear brother, shut him out like she'd almost managed to shut out the exhausting white world around them. She was so tired of him, of the mountain, of the snow — really, she was tired of everything. And she missed her parents terribly. Since they'd left them to recover in the hospital tent at Happy Camp — wasn't *that* an ironic name — over a month ago, she and Stan had made this

155

climb on their own more than thirty times each. Now most of the family's supplies waited outside the Chilkoot Pass Mountie post, buried deep under the snow. She hadn't wanted to leave the last time they were up there, because their father hadn't been doing well at all, but her mother had insisted they return to Sheep Camp.

He'll be disappointed if we aren't ready to go when he is, her mother had said.

This was the last time Liza would ever have to climb this accursed trail, and that's what made it bearable. That and Blue, of course. Playing and snuggling with Blue at the end of each day was a big part of what kept her going. In the last weeks, the puppy had grown so much, though her paws were still far too large for her body. And just as Liza's mother had suspected, she had icy blue eyes. Even Stan had fallen for Blue, throwing snowballs for her to chase and wrestling over sticks. On the last two trips, the puppy had managed to climb most of the trail on her own, with only a little help from Liza.

Unlike Blue, who loved bouncing through drifts, Liza had had more than enough of the snow. For nearly two months the white stuff had come down, and based on the fissures zigzagged across the white and the distant rumblings heard from the ground beneath, Liza thought the mountains were almost as tired of holding it as she was of seeing it.

But today was a gift from God. The snow had let up, the clouds had dispersed, and the sun was out in all its glory. All around Sheep Camp, sled dogs lolled, warming their bellies in the sun's warmth, and the trickle of streams could be heard in the distance. Liza didn't intend to waste such a beautiful morning by climbing an icy staircase. Piling both packs into a stepping stool, she had clambered onto a huge boulder already warmed by the sun, then lain back and let her thoughts drift to happier times.

Stan had objected, of course.

"A lot of other people have the same idea as I do," she said, indicating the dozens of men relaxing among the boulders and around the snowy field. Many had even laid their coats out to dry in the sunlight. That seemed like an open invitation to little Blue, who wandered around the snowy field, sniffing everything and visiting everyone, her tail constantly waving. She was getting more independent every day, but she always came back to Liza.

"Liza," Stan said.

She said nothing. She was convinced she

was growing mould on various parts of her body, and the heat seeping from the boulder into her soggy, clinging clothes was intoxicating.

"Liza! Get up, would you?"

"Stop it, Stan! Give me a little longer. What's the rush?"

He was relentless. The only one pushing them harder on this journey was their father, and he wasn't even there. "So help me, Liza. If, after all this time, we get up there and someone tells me they've sold the last claim while you were indulging in your daydreams —"

"Oh, stop your bellyaching," she said. He stood at the bottom of the boulder, hands on his hips, and the exasperation on his face struck her as funny, but she didn't dare laugh. "It's not like I've been here forever. It's only been an hour or so."

"An hour too long. Come on."

When she didn't make a move, he huffed with annoyance, then turned towards his sled. The bulky, overloaded thing was only about twenty feet away, but the deep holes their boots had left between the sled and the boulder seemed to go on forever.

"I'm going anyway, with or without you," he announced, and she knew he meant it. "I'll see you at The Scales."

"Fine."

"Fine."

He'd left his pack at the base of the boulder, she noticed, right beneath her. Well, she wasn't carrying it for him. She tried to convince herself that she shouldn't feel bad as he headed off, his tall black boots no match for the drifts, but she could practically feel the cold rivers of melted snow sloshing between his toes.

"Wait, Stan." She squinted up the mountain. "What's that sound?"

"What's what? Stop making excuses, Liza. Get down."

"Listen, for once!" She wasn't sure what she'd heard. Like an *oomph,* as if something large had fallen.

He kept walking. "I don't hear anything."

"Close your mouth and open your ears for a change."

He rolled his eyes, but then he cocked his head. "Was that thunder?"

"Do you see any clouds?"

As they listened, an uneasy feeling settled in Liza's stomach. When she got to her feet on top of the boulder, a full person higher than anyone else, she could see the people on the trail were slowing, awakening to the same dull roar. Some had turned back.

"It's getting louder." The lovely warm

surface of the boulder trembled. "I don't like this, Stan. It feels wrong."

"Avalanche!" someone screamed just as a massive cloud of snow exploded up the mountain, far above the camp. "Run! Run for your lives!"

Paralyzed, Liza watched the snow barrel down the slope towards them, becoming a massive, unavoidable wall of white. Climbers scrambled down the trail as fast as they could, and one word became a hot potato, jumping from one man to the next — *Go! Go! Go!* — but go where? The whole field was just a path for the avalanche to consume as it charged towards Sheep Camp at breakneck speed.

"Get down!" Stan yelled at the same time as Liza shouted, "Run!"

She leapt off the boulder and landed in waist-deep snow at its base, right next to the two packs. Afraid to move, she leaned beyond the massive rock's edges, waving frantically at her brother.

"Come here, Stan! *Run!*"

He was moving like a stick man, wrenching one leg at a time from the thick, wet snow, then plunging into it again, his eyes on Liza. Why was he still so far away?

"Faster, Stan! Come *on!*"

She kept screaming, and he kept uselessly

yanking his boots out of the snow, and in an instant the avalanche overwhelmed them, the crushing, almighty vengeance of the mountain stealing their voices, their breath, their heartbeats. Liza pressed herself hard as she could against the side of the boulder, and the vibrations of the mountain rocked and hammered against her cheek. *Please, God, don't let this rock roll over!* The snow flew over her, around her, onto her, its fury endless, its white becoming darker as it blocked out the sun.

Then all at once it stopped.

Stan, was her first thought. *I have to find Stan.*

As her eyes adjusted to the darkness, she saw that the boulder had shaped the cascading snow into a sort of cave. A room with no door. A room she had to escape before it became a tomb. Standing on top of both packs, she reached up and outward, testing the snow where it was farthest from her, afraid with every breath that the roof would collapse on top of her. She had no idea how thick it might be. At first nothing moved, then something gave way, and the area shifted, dropping a few chunks of snow. She tried again, this time using more force, and the ceiling gave way, dumping so much snow she cowered against the face of the boulder to protect herself. When it was done, everything below her knees was stuck, but she could hear men's voices, and the relief of knowing she'd not only survived but wasn't alone was overwhelming.

"Stan!" she yelled. "Stan! I'm okay! I'm coming!"

She climbed to the surface and scanned the area, taken aback to see that all the hotels and saloons stood, relatively untouched by the slide. Then she turned the other way and realized how miraculous that had been.

"Dear God," she whispered.

The field was gone. The level of rock- and branch-riddled snow was higher than any of the two-storey buildings behind her. All the tightly packed tents and the people inside them and the horses and the wagons and the packs were gone, washed away and buried somewhere beneath.

A man stopped beside her. "Looks like ten acres gone. You ever seen anything like it?"

Liza had no time for him. "Stan!" she cried, joining the chorus of men stumbling over the field, calling out names. "Where are you?"

A faint voice came from a few feet away. "Help me!"

She fell to her knees and started to dig. "Stan! Stan! Are you there?"

"I'm here!"

She dug with her hands as hard as she could, and the snow turned pink as her fingernails ripped apart, but none of that mattered. Stan's voice was getting louder. Suddenly a hand broke through and began widening the hole. Then she saw the face below and couldn't breathe.

"You're not Stan!" she cried.

"Don't leave me!" the man pleaded. "Help me out!"

Shaking with exertion, she got to her feet and staggered away. Someone else would have to help him. Somewhere in the back of her mind, she knew she should be pleased — she'd just saved someone's life. But what did it matter if it wasn't Stan's?

"Stan!" she called.

"Here!" The sound was like someone yelling through a pillow, but still she heard his cry.

"Stan? Is it you? Tell me it's you!"

"Liza! I'm here!"

She stopped and pictured him beneath her, encased in tons of solid snow. How deep was he?

"Are you all right?"

"I . . . I can't move. I don't know which

way is up."

"I'm coming! I'll get you!"

She threw off her coat and began digging like mad. She lost track of time, almost forgot where she was, and soon snow was piled in drifts around her. Her hands were like planks, stiff and bleeding, and her lungs screamed for air. But Stan's voice never came any closer.

"Stan? Talk to me!"

"I'm here." He sounded funny, like he was slurring his words. "I'm awfully tired."

"Don't go to sleep!" She'd never know where he was if he did that. She'd never be able to save him. "Talk to me so I know if I'm getting close."

"I don't think I can."

"Excuse me, miss."

A shovel hit the snow beside her and the man wielding it began to dig. Liza stumbled back, out of the way, squinting against the sun until the man's profile came into focus. It was the young Mountie from the top of the Chilkoot Pass, the one who'd forced them to keep carrying things up.

"It's my brother," she said, swallowing a sob. "Please, *please* save my brother."

"What's his name?" he asked, not breaking his rhythm.

"Stan. Stanley Peterson."

Sweat darkened the front and back of the Mountie's grey shirt and his face was flushed, but he kept digging and throwing, digging and throwing, until at last he paused.

"Call him again."

She was on her knees in a heartbeat. "Stan? Stan! Are you okay? We're coming for you!"

Nothing.

"Stan!" she screamed. "Wake up! We're almost there!"

"I'm here." His words were as thick as cold syrup. "But I'm so tired. I can't. It's too much. You . . . you can stop."

"What are you talking about?" she shrieked.

"I love you, Liza."

The finality of his statement terrified her. "What?! No! Stop that! You are *not* going to die here on this bloody mountain." The Mountie — what was his name? Turner? — was leaning over his shovel, catching his breath. "Why did you stop?!"

He shook his head. "I'm sorry."

Sorry? He was *sorry*? "Dig!"

He didn't make any move to start again.

"Give me the shovel," she demanded, scrambling to her feet.

Without a word, he handed it to her, then

stood back, still breathing hard. Liza's muscles screamed. *Dig, toss, dig, toss.* But her arms were failing her. The shovel dropped from her cramped hands, and she fell to the ground beside it, beating the snow with her fists.

"Stan!" she wept. "Stan!"

There was no answer.

She pushed the shovel towards the Mountie. "Please?" she asked, aware that her voice shook. "I just need a break. It's okay. He can go to sleep for a bit, and we can still get to him —"

"I'm sorry, Miss Peterson. It doesn't work that way," he said.

"What are you saying?" she cried. "I can't let him die down there. Not while I'm sitting right here!"

Constable Turner was watching her intently. "It's not a bad way to go, from what I understand. He'll fall asleep slowly. No pain."

His voice was so gentle, but his words cut straight through her.

"But . . ." How could she answer? "He's my brother."

Constable Turner's attention had shifted to another person in need. When he turned back to her, she saw the compassion in his eyes, but it was lost on her.

"I'm sorry, Miss Peterson. Truly I am. We did all we could." He bit down on his lower lip, then moved away. "I'll give you your privacy."

She watched him go, a chaos of emotions rolling through her. How *dare* he leave? Then she recalled how hard he'd dug, how determined he'd been to rescue her brother. And now he was running through the deep snow, shovel in one hand, moving towards something or someone Liza couldn't see. Thirty feet away from her, he started digging. *God, he must be tired,* she thought.

She swayed over the pit she'd dug, ringed by snow that entombed her brother, and the terrible truth of the Mountie's words became real. There was nothing anyone could do. As she stood there, Stan still breathed beneath her, but he was going to die. Her knees gave way, and she dropped onto the snow, wishing she could be under it with him. She laid her cheeks on the ground, feeling as if the whole world pressed down on her.

"Stan?"

"Hey, Liza." His voice was husky, like she'd woken him from a nap.

A sob caught in her throat. "I can't get to you."

He paused. "I know."

God, it hurt. How could she go on without him? "Are you cold?" she managed.

"Not anymore. I can't feel much at all. It feels funny to move my lips."

"Are you scared?"

"Yeah."

"Me too."

Stan didn't say anything.

It was so hard just to lie there. She squeezed her eyes shut. She had no right to cry. She wasn't the one dying.

"Stan, if you hadn't told me to jump off the boulder I'd be buried, too."

At first she thought he wasn't going to answer, then he said, "But you're not. You're safe, and that's good. You gotta get back up top, take care of Mother and Father. Promise me you'll go to them, Liza. I know you want to stop, but they're gonna need you since I'm . . ."

She waited to hear how he'd say it.

"They'll wonder where we are," he said quietly.

The terrible mountain loomed above her, stripped of so much snow, buried under so much more. "There's no trail left. So many people are gone."

"Promise me," he said. "As soon as there's a trail, you'll climb it."

How could she go on without him? The

vastness was already too big for the two of them. It was inconceivable for just her. But she would have to. She would do anything for her big brother. Anything.

"I promise."

The sun beamed down on the murderous snowfield, its light beautiful and blinding. Liza blinked away her tears, thinking how perfect everything had been just minutes before. The sun on the boulder, the warmth on her face . . . Then realization hit her, and she was suddenly bathed in a cold sweat. It was her fault. *It was all her fault.*

"Oh God, Stan. I shouldn't have spent all that time sitting in the sun. Oh, Stan! I'm so, so sorry! I wish —"

What she wished was for him to be right here, right now, hugging her like the big brother he was, but she couldn't say the words.

"I love you, Stan," she managed.

"I love you too, but Liza, you're wrong. I need you to remember something. None of this is your fault. It would have caught us if we'd been climbing, too. Then we'd both be trapped."

"I'd rather be dead than live without you."

"Don't talk like that," he said, then, "Liza?"

"Yes?"

"Can you do one last thing for me?"

One last thing. "Name it."

"Sing me that hymn. You know the one. Help me go to sleep."

God help me.

She took a deep breath, closed her eyes, and did as he asked.

"Lord, with me abide," she began, her voice shaking. "When other helpers fail and comforts flee . . ." It was a pathetic, worthless apology, but it was all she had. "Help of the helpless, O abide with me."

Then she turned her face so her trembling lips touched the snow, and she said farewell.

Twelve:
Ben

Ben's shovel hit the ground, slicing deeper and deeper, but with each cut the level of snow rose, covering his feet and climbing up his legs like a living thing, so thick it locked him in place. The whiteness swept over him like a giant wave, then around him, a whirling, endless tunnel, closing in. The wind screamed, and something black spun within the walls. He grabbed it and saw it was a twig, but the twig cracked open and became a finger, and the finger became a hand, and suddenly the tunnel was spiked by hands stretching out, spinning around and around, and the scream was getting louder. Ben grasped for the hands as fast as he could, but as he touched them they shrank away, swallowed up by snow.

He drove his shovel into the wall. He had to get through. He had to get out or else he would die. They would all die. But his hands were small, like when he was a child, and his shovel lifted only a handful of snow. A spoonful of crystals. Not enough. Never enough.

"You're useless and weak. Everyone will die because of you."

That was his father's voice, but his father wasn't supposed to be here. And yet there he was, standing behind Ben, beside him, in front of him, doubled over with that ugly laugh Ben could never forget.

"Give me the shovel!"

"I can do it!" Ben yelled back, but his father had swelled bigger than their farmhouse, and the shovel was now in his hands. He raised it over Ben's head.

"You better run, boy."

The shovel came down behind him, and the snow flew everywhere, an avalanche snapping at his heels. Ben ran for all he was worth, but he couldn't get through the snow. He couldn't see, couldn't find his way in the dark. He looked down, and the snow cracked apart, tearing the mountain in half, forcing him to leap —

Ben burst from his nightmare, his chest heaving. At first he was lost — the darkness around him smothering and unfamiliar — then he heard men talking beyond the tent and everything came flooding back. The avalanche. He jerked upright, then cried out when his muscles cramped in protest. The digging. The dream was starting to make sense. It had been a while since he'd dreamed of his father, though. All these years later, the bastard still wouldn't leave him alone.

Ben had been fifteen and working at the far end of the field when he'd heard screaming in the distance. So much like the screaming in his dream. He'd sprinted towards the house, knowing he wasn't fast enough but also knowing he couldn't stop. He had to get to the house and to his mother. He had to stop what he knew was coming. What was probably already happening. But the house was so far away, and without a gun the best he could do was distract his father away from her, but maybe, he'd thought, his lungs screaming for want of oxygen, his heart twisting with the awful sounds of her cries, maybe he could do something this time. Maybe he could finally be the man his father said he would never be.

He yanked open the door and stumbled inside, but before he took another step his father's thick fist crashed against his cheek and drove him to the floor. Ben staggered to his feet, managing to shove his mother out of his father's reach, but a second blow snapped his head sideways, launching him across the room. Everything went black.

He awoke to a hot, solid ring of metal pressing against his forehead and the sight of his mother lying dead on the floor. His father was clutching a gun, and he was crying. The gun was shaking.

"Don't kill me, Pa," he pleaded, wondering if the old man could even hear him. "Please don't kill me."

All of a sudden the door slammed open, and a man in a red coat barged inside. Without hesitation, the Mountie pointed a revolver at Ben's father.

"Put the gun down," the Mountie said.

The gun pushed harder against Ben's head. Whisky made his father more than mean; it made him stupid. And now it had made him a murderer. When the Mountie's warning went unheeded, he strode over and pressed the muzzle of his revolver against Ben's father's greasy skull. Ben was trembling so hard he could barely see, but then his father's familiar, bloodshot eyes slid into focus, and — at last — the pistol's barrel left Ben's head. He scuttled to the corner of the room, gagging at the sight of his mother's bloody, sprawled body. The metallic sound of cuffs closing over his father's wrists caught his attention, and he looked up as the Mountie paused in the doorway.

"I heard screams from the road," the policeman said. His eyes drifted to Ben's mother. "I'm sorry I couldn't get here sooner."

"Yeah," Ben grunted.

"I'll take him in, then come back to help with the burial."

"No," Ben replied. "I'll do it myself."

He was the man of the house now. The only man. The only one left.

A week later, the Mountie came back to the farm to tell Ben that his father was going to be hanged.

"Good," Ben replied.

That was seven years ago. Now Ben sat on the edge of his cot, rubbing his brow, trying to erase the last echoes of his father's laugh. All his life, he had done everything in his power to become the opposite of his father. To help people, not hurt them. But how many people had died under his watch? How many had he *let* die?

Those screams in his nightmare, he knew, weren't from his mother. They had belonged to Miss Peterson, and they would haunt him forever. Because today, when her whole world was crumbling and she needed saving, Ben had been the man in red. And he had failed her.

THIRTEEN: LIZA

Liza awoke in an unfamiliar building, alone and confused. As consciousness seeped back into her mind, a vague memory came to her of strong arms lifting her out of the snow, carrying her through the black night to a cot where she had cried herself to sleep. Now daylight glowed through the filthy window, and she slowly sat up, wishing she could stay in the empty room forever. But she had made Stan a promise.

Beyond the cabin, men were still digging, chopping through the frozen ground and uncovering what they could of the dead. Some bodies had been entombed beneath thirty feet of snow, and when they were brought to the surface their limbs were frozen into whatever position the avalanche had forced them into. When Stan was lifted out, Liza hadn't known what to do. She wanted to hold him, to somehow warm him back into existence, but she was too afraid to even touch his hand. She was haunted by his placid grey face, almost unrecognizable as that of the man who had pleaded with her to stop wasting time.

Stan was wrong — she had done this. She had killed him. And she would never forgive herself.

Blue was gone as well. Her heart twisted at the memory of the trust sparkling in those bright eyes and the feel of Blue's downy fur against her fingertips. Hadn't she promised Blanche that she'd keep her puppy safe? She couldn't even find the body. She did ask, but as far as she knew, no one had found her.

After four days, over sixty bodies were uncovered, including Stan's. The Mounties arranged for them to be taken to Dyea, where they would be properly buried, and for Liza there was no question of whether or not she would accompany the procession. She'd watched with horror as the vultures of Sheep Camp descended upon unclaimed corpses, rifling through frozen pockets for personal items before the Mounties could chase them away, and she'd sworn that would never happen to Stan.

Neither of the Mounties travelling to Dyea was Constable Turner, and she was glad about that. Over the last couple of days, she'd seen Turner in the distance, but she'd had to look away. She accepted that none of it was his fault, but she couldn't forgive him for abandoning her and Stan. She hoped she never saw him again.

After the Dyea burial service was over, Liza knelt by Stan's grave to say goodbye one last time, but she had no more tears left. For months she had hiked, climbed, and crawled through hundreds of miles of wilderness, always moving towards uncertain rewards. She had torn her legs and hands on rocks and ice so many times she'd given up on ever healing, and she'd wrapped the blisters on her feet until she'd run out of rags. Hunger had twisted her cramping stomach, and she'd retied the rope around her trousers' waistband a dozen times. Her body begged for sleep and food and some kind of solace, but the only thing she could acknowledge was that she couldn't stop yet. She'd made a promise, and she would not break it. There was nothing for her in Dyea, so she began the trek back up to Sheep Camp, where she'd left her packs, having paid for their guaranteed safety in advance. They were all she had left — both sleds had been lost in the avalanche.

The next morning in Sheep Camp she sat on her packs and scooped the last bite of cold beans from her dented tin cup, watching the activity around the camp and wondering about her next move. After all these trips, she recognized some of the people in the crowd, but she didn't know any by name. Most were getting organized, preparing to continue their climb, and she should be doing the same. She chewed the tasteless beans and forced herself to think hard, because right now she was stuck.

There was no way she could carry both packs up the trail by herself without a sled. If her parents were here, they'd know what to do, but Liza had never had to figure out something this important by herself. Maybe her father had been right to keep her from the store's finances.

After a moment's reflection, Liza decided the smartest thing she could do right now with her limited money was spend it. A cluster of Tlingit packers stood at the base of the trail, talking among themselves and eyeing the exhausted travellers, and Liza pulled a few folded bills from her coat pocket and counted what she had. There wasn't much, but if she could get the last of the family's belongings to the summit she wouldn't have to worry about any of it again. Her father would take the reins after that, and once his new shop opened in Dawson City there would be plenty of money. He always said that no one could guarantee a gold strike, but one could always bet on both need and greed. As long as their shop had what the miners wanted, the Petersons would be just fine. But if she couldn't get these packs to her father, none of that would happen. Taking a breath for courage, she started towards the packers.

"Good afternoon," she said, approaching a group of three men who stood apart from the others.

"Pack-er?" one asked. His voice was deep but soft, the syllables stretched out.

"Yes, please. Those are my bags there."

She presented the extraordinary sum of fifty dollars — a dollar a pound was the going rate, she understood — but two of the packers abruptly turned away. The third said, "Silver. No paper."

At least he spoke a little English, Liza thought, digging out the equivalent amount in silver. She held out the coins, but she could tell from his stance that it still wasn't enough. With no other choice, she fished more coins from her dwindling supply. Even then, the packer seemed a little reluctant, but in the end he took the money. Then, to her surprise, he bound the bags together with a rope, then hoisted both onto his back. To better distribute the weight, he passed a wide leather strap under the bags, then across his forehead like a sling.

"Thank you," Liza said, hardly believing her good fortune. No wonder he had wanted more money! "When do we go?"

In response, the packer strode silently towards the path, his walking stick in hand. He was a short, solid fellow, and he moved with an unexpected speed. Liza dug in, determined to keep pace. Without the weight of her pack, she felt as nimble as a goat even as they climbed. When it got steep enough that she had to crawl on all fours, the lack of baggage made a world of difference.

At The Scales, just like every other packer, Liza's companion raised his rates. She had no choice but to pay, but this time she knew it was well worth the price.

"What's your name?" she asked as he counted her coins.

"Káh," he replied.

"Nice to meet you, Káh. I'm Liza. Does 'Káh' mean something in English?"

He looked up slowly. " 'La-sa' mean something?"

"Uh, no," she said, realizing how silly her question sounded.

He crouched and tightened the rope

around her packs. " 'Káh' is Man. Is all."

Perhaps Man was his name, she thought. Then again, perhaps he was saying he had no interest in talking with her, and she should mind her own business. If Stan were here, he'd most likely know. Then again, if Stan were here, she'd have no need to hire a packer.

She left Káh with the bags and went for a little privacy behind a nearby shack. On her way back, she crossed paths with a young man.

"Beg your pardon," she said absently, moving past him, but he blocked her way.

"Good afternoon, miss. I consider this an opportune time to introduce myself." The man stuck out a grimy hand, which she made no move to touch. "Name's Ezekiel Booth."

She thought she recognized him from Sheep Camp, but he looked like any other traveller, gaunt faced and dreary eyed.

"Nice to meet you," she said. "If you'll excuse me —"

He slid his black cap off and pressed it against his chest. "I'd like to offer my sincere condolences on your recent loss."

She felt her cheeks grow hot. How did he know about Stan? There she was, thinking she knew no one and no one knew her, and now this? Her whole body tensed at the thought that he'd been watching her, like the man on the boat.

"Thank you," she said curtly. "Excuse me, please."

"Your grief is a terrible thing to witness," he said sombrely, reaching out to touch her arm, but she shifted away. "It is a terrible thing when a lovely young woman such as yourself is left without a protector, and so I thought I'd be a gentleman and offer my services. Free of charge, of course." When she didn't respond, he explained by saying, "I'd like to personally accompany you the rest of the way."

She gestured towards her things. "I have a man already helping me."

His face slid closer to hers, and she almost gagged at the tang of rum on his breath. "He hardly seems like good company on such a lonely path."

Her impulse was to shove him out of the way and run, but where could she go? She was alone now, and she'd become very aware that this wasn't going to be the last time this happened.

"That's enough, Mr. Booth," she said, standing her ground.

"I am only suggesting —"

"No, thank you."

"— that a little warm companionship can do wonders for a person."

"I said no." How many times would she have to say it?

He winked as he set his cap back on his head. "Think about it. If you should find yourself in need of such comfort, I am at your beck and call."

When the horrible toad was out of sight, her whole body started shaking as if someone had thrown ice water over her. All along the trail, she'd made fun of the idea that Stan was any kind of protection, but the truth had become alarmingly clear: without him, she was vulnerable. When two men wandered close by, she observed them closely, despising the necessary wariness that had taken root in her.

Káh called from near the line, and she hurried over.

"Ready," she told him.

In truth she felt far from it, and Mr. Booth wasn't the only reason why. It had been two weeks since she'd seen her parents, but it felt like a lifetime. Now Liza was mere hours away from their waiting arms, and as much as she craved their embraces, she knew she was going to break their hearts as soon as she told them about Stan.

She glanced back down the mountain one

more time, her heart heavy with grief. Her brother was there, and there he would stay.

Then, from somewhere in the dusty corners of her mind, a memory rose, as clear as could be. She and Stan had been sitting by the fire in their living room months before her father had even considered moving to the Klondike. Liza had been absently knitting a sweater while her brother went on and on about his latest interest: the different theories about death.

"I'm convinced that even after people die, they're never really gone," he'd said. "In fact, I'm sure of it."

She set her knitting in her lap. "That's ridiculous. We are born, then we die. That's all there is."

"But what comes after that physical death?" he asked. "Everything I read says the soul is immortal, and a soul is what makes us human. So think about it, Liza. If a human soul is immortal, we can never be truly gone."

But he *was* gone — at least from her side.

"If you're there," she said, her gaze lifting to the endless grey sky, "I could really use your help today."

She didn't expect to feel or hear any kind of response, but the idea that he might be watching was a comfort. When a space eventually opened in the line of prospectors, Liza set her worn boot on the first step of the Golden Staircase with a little more certainty.

This section of the trail was the steepest by far, but thanks to the recent work of a couple of energetic prospectors it had become much easier, relatively speaking. Three trips ago Liza and Stan had arrived at The Scales to discover that two men had taken their axes to the top 150 feet of the icy path, carving out three-foot-wide stairs which the travellers had named the Golden Staircase. The men had also put in place a brand new toll, but Stan had proclaimed that was just "smart business," and it was worth every penny. Over time, other climbers constructed more stairs, and someone even installed a rope for the prospectors to grip as they climbed.

Despite the stairs and the rope, the climb was still achingly slow, since every traveller had to wait for the one ahead to take another step. Like now. Liza wasn't sure why they'd stopped, but they had been halted for a few minutes, and the men behind her were starting to yell. She peered around Káh to see a gentleman in a heavy fur coat, on his knees and blocking the trail up ahead. His head was bowed over his pack, and his shoulders shook with sobs that tore at Liza's heart.

"Clear the way!" someone yelled.

"Keep moving!" shouted another.

Before Liza knew what she was doing, she was squeezing past Káh towards the weeping man.

"Sir." She touched his shoulder, and when he raised his sad eyes to hers she recognized him as the tall man whose hat she'd followed for so many days. "I'd like to help you. I haven't been carrying my own pack this trip, so I'm free to carry yours."

"What? No, no!" he protested. "You're a woman. I can't give my load to you! How could I —"

"Only for a little while," she coaxed. "I'm plenty strong enough. And to be honest, I've relied on your own tall figure to be my guide through many of my previous trips, so consider my help as payment of sorts."

"Get a move on!" someone called from behind, and his shout was echoed by an impatient chorus.

The man kneeling on the icy path regarded Liza with disbelief, but he swiftly rose when she reached for his pack. Up close she saw he was even taller than she'd first thought, and slender as a sapling. How did he manage to stand up when the wind thundered past?

"How can I let you do this?" he asked, closing his eyes with shame. "Oh, what would my beloved Olivia say? My dear children would think less of me, I'm certain. No, no. If I could only rest a few minutes. It's my back, you see. It's —"

"Get moving!"

Liza spun around. "You can wait a civil moment, please."

"That's what happens when a woman's on the trail," she heard someone mutter.

She rolled her eyes and turned back to the tall man. "Your family will think nothing of it. You came all this way to ensure their lives would be enriched, and I'm certain they will always love and respect you for that." She held out her hand. "I'm Liza Peterson. Pleased to make your acquaintance, Mr. . . . ?"

"Dexter. George Dexter." He shook her hand. "As much as the very idea horrifies me, at this juncture it appears I have no choice but to surrender to the weaknesses of the body and spirit and gratefully accept your offer, Miss Peterson."

"Think nothing of it," she said. "We can all use a little help once in a while."

She moved in front of him and shouldered his pack, startled by its weight. "Mr. Dexter, have you a strap of some kind? I'd like to . . ." She swept her finger across her brow, indicating the way Káh carried her bags.

His eyes widened with understanding, then he dug through his pack for a strap. After studying Káh for a moment, he wrapped it around the bag and Liza's forehead. The flat leather pressed hard against her brow, but it immediately displaced much of the weight of the bag.

"That's better," she said. "Let's go. It looks like it's about to snow again."

It didn't take long before her back began to ache, but fortunately, the towering George Dexter did a good job of distracting her with an entertaining monologue about his wife and three small children back in New York. His adoration for his family was obvious, and Liza imagined that leaving them behind must have been one of the most difficult things he'd ever done.

"I don't mean to intrude," Mr. Dexter said after a pause. "But you'll admit, it's unusual to see a woman alone on the trail."

"The reason I am alone right now is because my —" She stopped, unsure. It was difficult to say the words even to herself, let alone a stranger. But she wouldn't be able to avoid the subject for much longer. She took a deep breath. "My brother died in the avalanche."

"Oh, I'm so sorry."

"My parents are waiting for me at the summit. They don't know yet." Tears rushed to her eyes, but she couldn't afford to start crying, here on the middle of the mountain. Besides, there would be time enough for tears when she finally saw her parents. "To be honest," she said, "that's one reason why I'm glad to be able to help you. I need to do something to keep my mind off what has happened."

"Anything that you need, please ask," he said.

She gritted her teeth and pushed on as the sky opened again, dropping heavy flakes onto their heads and backs. To her great relief, George's back recovered sufficiently after an hour or so, and he reclaimed his bag. When they finally reached the summit after another hour, he set it down with a groan.

"We made it," Liza announced, her smile weak but present. "The worst part is officially done." That's what Stan had told her. Everything would be downhill from this point on.

A tired grin split George's sagging cheeks. "Miss Peterson, I was lost out there. I'll never be able to repay you."

"You would have done the same for me."

"Still, I am truly grateful. I promise you, Miss Peterson, should we ever meet again and you are in need, I shall be your knight in shining armour."

As Mr. Dexter's hat moved away, bobbing over the other travellers' heads, Liza turned to look for Káh. He was waiting near a stack of provisions, Liza's bags lying on the snow at his side.

He shook his head, his expression bemused. "You carry man's bag. You crazy girl."

She nodded. "Perhaps."

"Good," he said, surprising her with a contagious smile. "You get rich, crazy girl."

She chuckled. "I wish I could hire you again, but from now on my father will be in charge. Besides," she said, reaching into her pocket and pinching the alarmingly thin wad of money within, "I don't think I can afford you anymore."

"Is okay."

He turned and walked back in the direction of the Staircase, and through the falling snow she saw him lower himself to the ground. She knew from experience that the best way to the bottom was to slide straight down the mountain, and when Káh disappeared from view she hoped he enjoyed the ride as much as she had. It certainly had been more fun than the opposite direction.

Dragging her bags behind her, she shuffled towards the Mountie outpost, eager to locate her parents and wondering how on earth her family was ever going to get to Dawson City at this rate. She imagined her father was working on a plan to sell some of the extraneous supplies in order to hire more packers but he'd have no idea how urgent that was. He didn't know they no longer had Stan's strong back to count on. These logistics would be up to her father, not her, and she knew he'd be relieved to take on all those responsibilities again. Still, her mind went to a mental list of everything they'd carried to this place, and she sorted through what might be the smartest items to sell and to keep. Maybe she'd suggest a few things to him when they got to that point if he was still feeling a little weak.

"Welcome to the Chilkoot Pass," said the bearded policeman manning the outpost. "I am Sergeant Thompson. May I have your name, please?"

She was pleased to see that she'd be speaking with a Mountie other than Constable Turner. She told him her name, and he searched for it on his list. After noting that she'd brought all the required items to the summit, he held the page out to her and she reluctantly dug into her dwindling cache of money to pay the tariff she owed. Thank goodness she could count on her parents to buy her a meal when she got to Happy Camp.

"I can tell you've climbed the Chilkoot Trail a number of times, miss. Must feel good to have it all done," the Sergeant said.

"Yes," she said quietly. "This has been a long, horrible trip."

"You weren't affected by the avalanche, were you?"

Devastated was more like it, she thought, but from the sympathetic look on his face, she knew he didn't mean to sound callous.

"I was," she admitted. "We were at Sheep Camp. My brother," she said, just loud enough to be heard over the wind. "I . . . Constable Turner tried to dig him out, but it was too late."

"Please accept my condolences," he said softly. "May he rest in peace."

"Thank you."

"From the contents of your packs," Thompson said, getting back to business, "I imagine you're setting up shop rather than mining."

"Yes," she said, thankful for the change of

topic. "My father is waiting for these last bags so we can continue the journey and he can open a shop in Dawson City."

"Where is your father currently?"

"Happy Camp. When my brother and I left a few weeks ago, he was in the hospital tent with a fever." She remembered the last time she'd seen him there, lying helpless under layers of furs. Her mother's cot had been set up right beside his. "My mother stayed with him — she hasn't been well either."

"We have records of those patients, if you'd like to come inside and check."

She nodded, brightening at the thought of sitting in a clean, warm room.

As soon as he opened the door, she smelled coffee, and that was enough to convince Liza that life was about to take a turn for the better.

Fourteen:
Ben

A strong, hot cup of coffee was exactly what Ben needed after another restless night. As soon as he'd closed his eyes to sleep, he'd seen his father again and heard the screams, and that meant he had barely slept. If he was going to make it through today, he needed coffee, and he knew he could get one at Jake's Hotel. Like so many other places at Sheep Camp, Jake's was little more than a dilapidated cabin marked by a sign someone had painted. The cracks in the log walls were stuffed with moss, and the two windows by the door were made of empty bottles, flat sides out. But they served coffee, and that's all Ben cared about at that moment.

The Mounties had stayed at Sheep Camp for four days, digging and helping to get the tough little camp back on its feet. The injured had been tended, the dead taken to Dyea. Any bodies still beneath the snow would have to wait for the spring melt before they could be put to rest properly. This morning Ben and the others were headed back to the summit. He was glad to be leaving the squalor, though he wasn't looking forward to the final climb. Under the April sun the snow was so much heavier, and the dips and drifts that had existed before the avalanche were now unpredictable trenches of mush.

After he finished his coffee, he went outside to relish the quiet before the rest of the camp awoke. As he breathed in the crisp morning air, he heard a small sound coming from a pile of lumber someone had salvaged from the disaster. He crouched and peered inside the stack of wood, and he spotted a puppy shivering in the shadow of the lumber.

"What are you doing in here?"

Ben took off a mitt and scooped up the little body, which shook in his hand. The little dog couldn't be more than a few months old, Ben thought.

"Where'd you come from?"

He checked her for injuries but found none, though he could feel every one of her ribs.

"Let's find you something to eat."

He tucked her inside his coat to warm her,

and she settled against his chest almost immediately, as if she recognized the spot by his heart. Once he fed her goat's milk and scraps, she came to life, prancing around in the snow and following Ben wherever he went. Her happiness was contagious, and Ben was distracted from the dark thoughts that had hung over him like rain clouds these days. By the time he was ready to depart for the summit that afternoon, Ben had decided to bring her with him.

"Keitl's not gonna stay small for long," a Tlingit man told him.

"What's 'keitl'?" Ben asked.

"It means 'dog,' " the man answered, picking up one of the puppy's wide, white paws. "She's gonna grow."

"Keitl," Ben repeated, and that became her name.

Keitl had energy to spare, and it was obvious to anyone that her size and strength would eventually match those of the mighty huskies that made up most of the sled dog teams. From her markings, Ben was fairly sure one of her parents was not of that breed, but she had a lot of the same characteristics. Her pointed black ears swivelled at every sound, and her ice-blue, almond-shaped eyes sparkled with intelligence, but the black mask worn by so many huskies was incomplete. Instead, her white forehead was dotted by half a dozen spots, like big black freckles. The one feature that Ben figured marked her as unique was a large patch of black in the middle of her broad chest. To him, it looked like the shape of a heart.

FIFTEEN:
LIZA

The inside of the Mounties' post was warm and dry, and Sergeant Thompson's hospitality was more than welcome after Liza had spent so many weeks in tents. She took a bite of toast, then wrapped her hands around the hot cup of coffee while the Sergeant disappeared to fetch the right paperwork. As much as she dreaded telling her parents about Stan, she couldn't wait to see them.

But when the Sergeant returned, his face was drawn. Liza felt her stomach twist.

"Is this him?" the Sergeant asked, setting an open book on the table between them and pointing to a name.

She nodded, dreading what he might say.

He sighed. "Miss Peterson, I'm sorry. Your father, he . . . died of pneumonia two weeks ago."

She stared at him, too stunned to cry. "He *died*?" Her thoughts flew to her mother.

"What about my mother? Where is she?"

Thompson tugged at the collar of his coat. "I'm afraid I do not have good news for you on that front, either."

"What do you mean? Is she still sick? Has she gotten worse?"

"She was on the mend, but after your father died, well, she was distraught, as you can imagine." He exhaled. "Then the news came about the avalanche, and she went downhill. She's alive, but it doesn't look good."

This couldn't be happening. "I came as quickly as I could," she said breathlessly, tears stinging her eyes. "I had to go to Dyea for the funeral, and after that they needed time to clear the trail —"

"I know, but she was feverish and desperate for news of you and your brother," he said. "Also, ever since the avalanche, no one who has come through has mentioned any female survivors."

That stopped her. "But I —"

"Your trousers, Miss Peterson," he reminded her gently.

Liza grabbed her thighs. "They only saw trousers," she whispered, hollow with realization. "They thought that we . . . that I . . ."

"Shall I take you to your mother?" Thompson asked.

"Yes!" She wiped her eyes. "Please. She has to know I'm still here."

Thompson located another Mountie to replace him at the post, then they set out, with Liza walking as fast as she could. When they arrived at the hospital tent, Thompson left, and a nurse led Liza to where her mother lay, covered in heavy furs. *There were two cots here before,* Liza thought as she approached, grief thick in her chest.

She drew close enough to catch a glimpse of her mother, then drew back sharply, not recognizing the grey, shrunken features of the face before her. With her eyes closed and her mouth slightly open, her mother almost looked dead. How could she have transformed so much in only two weeks?

"Mother?" She raised her voice a little. "Mother? It's me. It's Liza."

When she didn't react, Liza dipped her fingers in a cup of cooled tea that had been left on a table next to the cot. She pressed the wetness to her mother's cracked lips, but it took three or four times before she gave any sign of noticing. Then the tip of her tongue appeared, seeking the moisture, and her eyes slowly opened.

Light as a feather, Liza touched her mother's hot cheek. "I'm here, Mother."

"Liza?" Her voice was weak and her eyes unfocused. "I . . . I thought . . ."

"They were wrong," she said. "I'm here." She reached for the cup and held it to her mother's lips.

Her throat moved with effort as she swallowed. "Your father . . ."

"I know," Liza said softly. "I'm so sorry I wasn't here."

Hope bloomed on her mother's face. "Where's Stan?"

Liza wished desperately that she could lie to her, keep the awful truth to herself at least until her mother was recovered. But she couldn't. And she couldn't hide her emotions any longer, either. Tears spilled down her cheeks.

"He got caught by the avalanche," she said. "We both did, but I got out. I dug so hard for him, Mother, but —" She choked on a sob. "I couldn't get to him. He was too deep."

She could hear the grief, guilt, and shame in her own voice, but in the quiet after she spoke she was certain she also heard the faltering of her mother's heart.

"I'm sorry," was all she could say. "Oh, Mother, I'm sorry about so many things. But it's just you and me now. We have to pull through, don't we?"

A lone tear trickled down the side of her mother's face.

"Don't we?" Liza said again.

The slightest of nods, then her mother closed her eyes, pushing out more tears. "It is I who should be sorry, Liza. We never should have come here. I never should have made my children take this horrible journey. Even your father admitted as much to me at the end." She drew her hands from beneath the blankets, and Liza saw her fingers were wrapped around her husband's pocket watch. "Take this with you," she said, then she slid off her wedding ring. "And this as well."

Liza stared at the treasures. "Oh, but Mother. You —"

"Keep them safe."

An eerie sense of calm had settled over her mother's features. It was just like when Stan had spoken through the snow, telling Liza she could stop digging.

"No, no, no. Don't do that. Don't leave me alone out here," she pleaded, gripping her mother's hand. "Please, Mother. You promised we'd stay together. Back in Dyea — you *promised*. I can't do this alone."

"You can." Her mother strained for a breath. "You're strong, just like your father said." She closed her eyes again. "I love you, Liza."

"I love you, Mother," she whispered, her lips salty with tears, her heart racing with panic. Now more than ever, she hoped Stan had been right about no one ever really being gone.

She sat by her mother until nightfall, gripping handfuls of the fur covering her mother and watching the feeble rise and fall of her chest. When it was too dark to see, Liza spread her coat on the floor beside the cot, then she curled up and fell asleep, her parents' cherished items clasped to her chest.

In the morning Liza rose and gently touched her mother's cheek, but it was cold. She was gone. And Liza was utterly alone.

Sixteen:
Ben

At first, Ben couldn't believe what he was seeing, but as he drew closer to his tent and Keitl started sniffing through the items on the ground, he realized he was right. While he'd been out on rounds, Miller had dumped all of Ben's possessions — including his cot and blanket, his extra shirts and socks, even his hat press — into the melting snow outside their shared tent. This was pushing their already fragile partnership too far. Annoyance flared. Anger coursed through his veins, and he squeezed his fingers into fists, fighting to maintain control. Ever since he had returned from Sheep Camp, it felt to Ben like it took almost nothing to set him off. He needed to be careful. Jaw clenched, he carried his pack into the tent, set it down, then rounded on Miller.

"What's going on?" he demanded.

"You're leaving, ain't you?" Miller said. "Might as well get packed up."

"Don't be an idiot." Ben strode outside and grabbed his cot, brushing off a dusting of snow as he came back into the tent. "I'm not leaving for a week. I'll sleep inside until then, if you don't mind."

Miller lay back on his cot, arms crossed. "Suit yourself. Don't matter to me."

"Uh-huh." Ben grabbed more of his ousted belongings and brought them back inside, Keitl trotting at his heels. "I can see that."

A week before, Inspector Belcher had read the men a report from Superintendent Steele which said the ice on Lake Lindeman and Lake Bennett was beginning to soften. The Mounties at the summit had been waiting for the update for a while, because it signalled that they were about to get very busy. All winter long, huge crowds of prospectors had been stripping the land around those two lakes so they could build rafts and boats because as soon as the ice was gone, they planned to sail down the Yukon River to Dawson City and the goldfields. The trouble was that the Yukon River was not nearly as accommodating a thoroughfare as these prospectors seemed to think it would be, and based on experience, the Mounties had no illusions about how well these naive travellers might do on the water. In preparation for the thaw, Steele had ordered posts to be set up all along the route, each one flying the Union Jack, but he needed more men to patrol the area. Belcher appointed both Ben and Sergeant Thompson to go, but he'd decided to keep Miller at the summit.

For Ben, the assignment couldn't have come at a better time. He wanted to leave the mountain and its vivid reminder of the murderous avalanche, and he couldn't wait to get away from Miller, who was grinding on his last nerve.

When all his things were back inside the tent, Ben sat on his cot and took out his rifle kit, hoping the routine of cleaning his weapon would calm his nerves. Keitl curled up by his feet with a contented sigh.

"Don't see why I can't go with you and Thompson," Miller said, watching Ben.

Ben ignored him, sliding the cleaning rod in and out of the barrel of his rifle, clearing out the old powder as Miller yammered on.

"Belcher don't need me here," he grumbled. "He needs me at Lake Bennett. You know what? I might just go anyway."

"That's his call, not yours," Ben said. "I reckon you doing that would be considered insubordination. You don't want to tempt Belcher."

"You don't want to tempt Belcher," Miller mimicked. He started picking his teeth with a thin piece of wood. "He don't know what he's talking about."

Ben cocked the lever open, peered inside the chamber, then swabbed the barrel a couple more times. When he was satisfied, he got to work cleaning out the chamber.

"Why you and not me?" Miller demanded.

Ben finally met his gaze. "You know why."

"No, I don't. What, is your Sergeant buddy giving you inside information?"

Ben set the gun aside with a little more force than was needed. "They're looking for men who aren't afraid to work hard," he said, holding Miller's glare.

Miller sat up straight. "What's that supposed to mean?"

When Ben didn't respond, Miller threw his feet over the side of the cot and leaned in so his face was right in Ben's. Keitl gave a yelp and scrambled to her feet.

"You and your damn dog. I've had enough of both of you."

Ben gritted his teeth. "We're leaving soon."

"I ain't afraid to work hard, and you know it."

That was almost laughable. "Really?"

For a moment, it looked like Miller might

admit Ben was right, but that would be too much to ask for. Instead, he asked, "Speak to Belcher for me?"

In Ben's eyes, Miller did just enough to get by, and in most cases he was the one asking for help as opposed to offering it. Ben would never call himself perfect, but at least he could honestly say he'd done his best. That's what being a Mountie was all about.

"I can't," Ben replied. "It's not up to me. Look, things are changing. Just stay here, do the job, and they'll send you down soon enough."

Miller's expression hardened again. "You know, if we were in opposite positions, I'd stand up for you."

The tension in the air was like a string he could pluck.

"Well," Ben said. "We aren't."

Miller shoved him, and they both jumped to their feet, going nose to nose as Keitl darted out of the way, barking. All winter long, Ben had put his pent-up rage to good use behind hammer, shovel, and axe, but that work was finished. There were no more physical demands distracting him from showing Miller what he really thought of him.

"What is your problem?" he growled.

"Right now I guess it's you," Miller replied, shoving him again.

Keitl's barks picked up, louder and sharper, and Miller snapped, "Shut up, dog!"

Before Ben could stop him, Miller kicked the dog. Keitl cried out, and all Ben saw was red. He lunged at Miller, sending them both through the tent flap and onto the snow. Ben landed on top, and as his fist smashed into Miller's face he felt the pressure of holding back for so long lift away. He struck him again, and Miller snarled back through blood-coated teeth, rolling Ben onto his back so he could take a swing at him. He only got in one punch before Keitl jumped on top of both of them.

"Gentlemen," Thompson said, appearing out of nowhere.

Ben and Miller froze.

"On your feet."

They jumped to attention, staring straight ahead, neither of them wiping at his bloody face. Keitl cowered behind Ben as Thompson came in close.

"Been a long winter, hasn't it?" he asked, hands behind his back. "I bet that felt good."

From the corner of his eye, Ben saw Miller flash a brief smile, but Ben didn't move a muscle.

"Are you children done fighting now?"

"Yes, Sergeant," they replied.

Thompson shook his head. "I doubt that."

Regret closed over Ben like a cloak. What had he done? All that work. All those months. All the discipline it had taken to get to this point, and in the end he was no more than when he'd started: a brawler with a quick temper.

Keitl pressed her muzzle between Ben's knees, peeking out at Thompson and whining softly.

"Tell you what," Thompson said. "We're all worn down. I'll let this one go. But you only get one warning. No fighting within the ranks. You both know that."

"Yes, Sergeant."

"I do have a suggestion," Thompson said brightly, taking a step back. "We got a week left up here. How about neither one of you says a word to the other until then." His beard lifted at the corners. "Except maybe at the end, when you can admit how much you're gonna miss each other."

They didn't move until after Thompson had left. When they faced each other again, Miller's resentment was easy for Ben to see. It smouldered beneath the surface, and Ben could tell it would only take one spark to set him off again. Ben knew that feeling well, but now all he felt was shame. He'd been right to protect Keitl, but he shouldn't have given in to his rage. Doing that made him no better than his father.

SEVENTEEN:
LIZA

A pearl of water ran down the tent's canvas seam, then plopped into the growing puddle at the bottom of Liza's cot. As one fell, another appeared, then the next, and the next, hypnotizing her. For the last three nights, she'd lain in her tent and stared at the ceiling, wishing she could disappear. With her family dead, there would be no one left to miss her. So many times she considered walking outside, lying in the snow, and slowly falling asleep. Just like Stan. If she walked far enough, no one but a Mountie would ever find her body.

Sergeant Thompson had promised they would bury her parents properly, side by side in the spring. Right now, their frozen bodies were stacked with the others in that bleak morgue Constable Turner had shown her the first time they'd met.

George Dexter had been very supportive. The day her mother died, he'd come upon her, weeping outside the hospital tent. He'd consoled her, brought her food, and kept her company.

"It's my turn to help you, Miss Peterson," he'd insisted, "in whatever way I can. What can I do? Shall I arrange to have your things sent back to Vancouver for you?"

She couldn't bring herself to answer him. For two days, he had done what he could to draw her from her miserable state, but Liza was numb with sorrow and guilt. She heard him now, settling outside her tent flap as he often did.

There was a brief scratch as he lit a match for his pipe, and longing rose from Liza's chest to the tips of her ears. She knew that sound so well. As the pipe's soft white smoke scented the air, she closed her eyes and imagined her father sitting in his favourite armchair with the worn uphol-stery. She saw again the brief glow of his tobacco leaves and the smoke dwindling from between his lips as he pored over the store ledgers. "A good day's work, a good day's work," he would mumble to himself.

"I thought I might speak to you philosoph-ically today. About the reason we are all here," George said, breaking into her thoughts.

"I'm here because I survived when my

family did not," she replied shortly.

"My dear, that is not a *reason,* that is a *result,*" he said patiently. "A reason is like a purpose, whereas a result is an outcome. I believe God has a purpose for us all, and in my case, well, I believe something in His plan requires me to be right here, right now."

"There's a *reason* you are sitting outside the tent of a girl with no family and no future in this godforsaken place?" She knew she sounded bitter, but she was past the point of caring.

"Yes, I believe so."

She rolled onto her side, resting her cheek on her arm. "What reason could there possibly be for that?"

"Perhaps so I can be here for you in your time of need. Just like you were there for me that day on the trail."

"If it hadn't been for that day on the trail, our paths might never have crossed," she countered. "What would have been your reason then?"

"Ah, but they did."

"But what about —"

"I do not think in what-ifs, Miss Peterson. What I know is that because of you, I still have a chance to make something of myself and return to my family a prosperous man."

She heard him draw gently on his pipe as he considered that point. "At least that is my hope, anyway."

She let his words sink in, then said, "I'm only here because my family dragged me along. Look how well that turned out."

"Give yourself a gift, Miss Peterson. Let the knowledge that God has brought you here for a reason comfort you in this difficult time."

She sighed. "Well, I wish God would tell me if my path should be forward or back."

"That, my dear, is up to you, and you alone."

Through the wall of the tent she saw him get to his feet, then move the chair back to the side as he always did. Before he left, he paused by the entrance.

"Miss Peterson, I understand your grief and your indecision. I cannot imagine how I would choose were I in your position." He exhaled slowly. "But I must leave this place tomorrow. It is time for me to continue my journey. I wish I could help you with the next step, but that is up to you."

George's boots crunched away into the distance, and Liza stared straight ahead, feeling defeated. She was so tired of indecision. Of the crippling grief that made it difficult for her to breathe, let alone imagine leaving the tent.

He was so certain, she thought enviously, that there was a divine reason she was here. Just like Stan, who had been convinced that no one was ever really gone. But how did any of that help her escape this horrible place in her life? Why *was* she here? Why was she the only one in her family to have survived? And what if she left this place and continued on? What could she do in Dawson City? Run the store on her own? The very idea made her laugh. She knew very well what her father would say about that.

All her life, she'd been told not to worry. She need not concern herself over the business of the store. She need not worry about the journey north. All would be well, and her parents and brother would look after her. But they were all dead. Even Blue, who had given her so much joy in such a short amount of time, was gone. Liza was alone at the mountain's edge, and she had to make the most important decision of her life.

The simplest choice would be to slide down the mountain the way she'd come, back to Dyea. From there she could board a ship to Victoria after the ice broke in the spring. She could go back to Vancouver and civilization. Back to friendships and laughter and the real world. Except . . . everything she'd known was gone. She could never have her old life back. And if she returned to Vancouver, she feared the pain of having to face all those memories without her family by her side would be unbearable.

She had a vague idea of what lay ahead if she kept to her father's original plan: the crowded banks of Lake Lindeman and Lake Bennett, the dangerous expanse of the Yukon River, then Dawson City, a town she'd heard was wild and unpredictable. The "Paris of the North," her father had called it. That's where his shop was meant to be and where they were supposed to make their fortune. But even if Liza did make it to Dawson City, there was no way she could open a store of her own.

Except . . .

She rolled onto her back, wondering. What *did* she know about running a store? She had been her father's enthusiastic shadow for years. Why had he discouraged her? Did he really feel she wouldn't be able to do it, or was that simply his old-fashioned thinking?

Was there any reason she *couldn't* do it?

The afternoon sun was baking the canvas of the tent, and the suffocating heat forced her outside for air. All around her, winter was gasping its last breaths, its icy power humbled beneath the warmth of sixteen hours of sunshine a day. The mountain peaks were melting, and streams gurgled and danced under shrinking sheets of ice, thirsty for their own share of warmth. Nearby, a group of men were standing around a fire, sharing stories and drinking coffee from tin cups. On her other side a couple of men were packing their sleds, doing business with the Tlingit, getting ready to move on.

Other than George, everyone here was a stranger, but it came to her that they all had something in common. Each one of them was weary, bruised, and underfed, but they were also survivors, limping relentlessly towards a shared goal. No one could guarantee what lay ahead, Liza thought, and it was terrifying to choose a path when you couldn't see its end. And yet every one of these strangers was obliged to follow the same blind hope.

Including me.

Liza stretched her arms as wide as she could, easing the stiffness from her muscles.

Her gaze lifted past the mountains and up to the endless blue sky. Was her family watching, waiting to see which way she chose? The memory of her father's face, his joyful anticipation of their success, came to her then. She took a deep breath of cold, bracing Yukon air and she made another promise.

"I will make you proud."

EIGHTEEN:
BEN

Thompson made Ben's last week at Chilkoot bearable by sending word that he needed his help at Happy Camp. It was obvious that Thompson's motive was to put some distance between him and Miller, and Ben was grateful for that.

"What do you need me to do?" he asked when he arrived.

"I was just heading over to talk with Josef Olenev about his dogs," Thompson said. "They attacked a couple of other teams this morning and hurt three dogs. You want to handle that?"

"I can do that."

"I'll keep Keitl with me," Thompson offered, and Ben resisted the urge to grin. Keitl had been with Ben for about five weeks, and, with the exception of Miller, she'd worked her way into just about everyone's soft spot. Even the gruff Sergeant's.

"Safer here," Thompson explained. "Oh,

and don't let Olenev tell you he don't speak English."

Right away Ben saw what Thompson was referring to. The tethered dogs in question were rangy and mean, scrutinizing him with hungry eyes as he spoke to their master. He could see they were hungry, but then again, who wasn't? A good master took care of his team before he took care of himself, and that didn't seem to be happening here. Olenev held up his hands and feigned confusion at Ben's words, but when Ben calmly informed him that he'd be removing the dogs from his care, the Russian got the message. Ben watched him tie the dogs better, then the Russian assured Ben — in excellent English — that he and the team would be gone the next morning.

After that was settled, Ben wandered around the other tents, checking that everyone was doing all right. The mood at Happy Camp was, in general, more cheerful than over at the Chilkoot Pass, since most of the travellers thought the worst of their journey was behind them.

Whenever they asked him if the road ahead was easier, he'd say, "Nothing about this journey is easy, but you've made it this far, so you're probably stronger than you thought you were before."

He knew that was true for him. Physically he was leaner than ever due to the hard work and limited food, and working in the snow had hardened his muscles to iron. But it was more than that. With the exception of time spent with Miller, Ben's temper had been almost non-existent up here, and when it did rear its ugly head, he had easily funnelled it into whatever work needed doing. He felt more confident around the prospectors these days, and he could see how they relied on him, which only made him more confident in what he was doing. Every day it got easier to put past mistakes behind him.

"Good afternoon, Constable," said an older man in a tired hat. He stood smoking by a fire with some other men. "Care for a cup of coffee?"

"No, thanks," Ben said. "I just filled up at the post. How are you gentlemen doing? All rested up, ready to go?"

"Sure, sure. We was just saying what a fine day it is to get a move on."

One of his buddies said, "A fine day to get rich!"

"Have a safe journey," Ben said, moving on to the next tent. "Good afternoon, sir. I —"

He stopped in his tracks and removed his

hat at the sight of Liza Peterson standing a few feet away. Her eyes were closed, her face upturned to the sun as she drank in its warmth. She looked thin, he thought. He could tell she hadn't heard or seen him yet, and he briefly considered moving on before she did, but that would be cowardly of him. He couldn't avoid her.

The last time he'd seen her was the night after the avalanche, when he'd found her asleep and half-frozen on the snow above her brother. She'd barely stirred when he'd carried her inside and set her in a safe bed. That was the night his nightmares had started again. Over the last week or so he'd started sleeping a little better. But seeing her now brought a heavy swirl of guilt back to his gut.

"Good afternoon, Miss Peterson."

She turned away from the sun, her open expression closing as she recognized him. "Oh, hello, Constable Turner."

Ben wasn't afraid of much, but something about this woman made him nervous. "I was hoping I'd see you again," he said, walking towards her. "I wanted to say again how sorry I am about the last time we met."

"You tried," she said dismissively. "You did all anyone could do."

He was surprised to hear her say that. "I

wish I could have done more," he said. "I imagine your parents are relieved to have you with them again."

She looked away. "They died."

"What?" He must have misheard.

"They died," she repeated, facing him again.

"I . . ." What should he say? What *could* he say? He had seen a lot of loss on this trail, but her hardships seemed to outweigh them all. He cleared his throat. "I am so sorry. I can't imagine how you're feeling right now."

An uncomfortable pause stretched between them. He was about to go when she said, "I'm leaving soon."

"You are? Can I help you send your things back to your home?"

"No, thank you," she replied, raising her chin with determination. "I've decided to go on to Dawson City."

He'd seen that look before, back at the summit when she'd charged up to him and challenged the one-tonne rule. Back then he'd thought she had grit. After everything that had happened to her since, he hoped she still had that fight in her. He scratched his cheek, wondering how to tell her what he was thinking.

"You should know, Miss Peterson, that the

journey ahead is —"

"Difficult. Yes, I imagine it is. But it can hardly be worse than what we just survived." She started to turn back to her tent, then stopped as if she'd just remembered something. "Constable Turner," she said, her voice softening slightly, "there may be something that you can help me with, if you have a moment."

"Of course," he said without thinking. "How can I help?"

"I'm wondering if you might be able to help me sell some of my things. I'll still bring most with me, but since I'm on my own now, I need money to pay for packers."

He was impressed by her plan. She might be young, but from the sounds of it, she was quite experienced. That made him wonder who she'd been in her life before all this.

"We can't sell them for you," he replied, "but we can let people know you are looking for buyers."

"Do you think that will take very long?"

"It depends upon what you are selling, but I'll start making enquiries right away."

"Thank you."

Her face broke into the loveliest smile Ben had ever seen. Captivated, he started to return it, then realized her greeting wasn't for him. She was focused on someone behind him. Ben turned and saw a tall, slender man approaching.

"Hello, Mr. Dexter," Miss Peterson said, then she gestured towards Ben. "May I introduce you to Constable Turner?"

"Ah!" Mr. Dexter held out a hand. "A member of the venerable North-West Mounted Police. An honour to meet you, Constable. Keeping the public safe, are you?"

"I do what I can," he said, shaking Mr. Dexter's hand and studying his face. It had become second nature to Ben, trying to figure out the character of a man through his eyes.

"Mr. Dexter and I met on the climb up here," Miss Peterson explained, "and I'm indebted to him for all his patience of late."

"I was indebted to her first," the man replied amiably.

The comment piqued Ben's curiosity, but he didn't ask. For the first time since he had met her, Miss Peterson seemed almost happy now that she was chatting with Mr. Dexter. There was an easiness to their conversation that Ben envied.

"I thought you'd like to know that I've made a decision," she was saying now.

"I was hoping as much, seeing you out

here in the sunshine. Will I be continuing my journey with or without your company?"

"With," she said.

Dexter's narrow face split into a grin. "Wonderful! We shall have a time of it, Miss Peterson. You'll see. This part of the journey will be entirely different." He glanced cheerily at Ben. "At least we won't feel as if our lives are in danger this time."

Ben opened his mouth to offer a warning, but Miss Peterson spoke first. "I hope not. But I'm afraid I must ask you for a little more time, if that's possible." She filled him in on her plan to sell some of her things. "Constable Turner has graciously agreed to help get the word out."

"Very pragmatic," Dexter agreed. "Certainly I can wait. And I shall help as well, of course."

He seemed genuine, Ben thought, stepping back. Miss Peterson clearly trusted the man, and from what he'd seen, she appeared to have good instincts.

"I will let you know if I hear of any buyers, Miss Peterson," he said, then he nodded at her travelling companion. "Nice to meet you. I'm glad you'll be with her on this trail."

"As am I," Miss Peterson said. "I cannot imagine making the rest of this journey all by myself."

Ben flinched inwardly. She hadn't been looking at him when she said it, but he couldn't help wondering if that had been a pointed remark aimed at him, about what had happened to her brother. Whether she'd meant it that way or not, Ben burned with shame as he walked back to the outpost. No matter how hard he tried, Liza Peterson would always remind him of how he had failed. As he trudged through the snow, he heard his father's voice in his head, reminding him that he would never amount to anything. If only he could be sure the man was wrong. He flexed his fists, wishing there were a nearby fence post he could hit.

Nineteen:
Liza

Liza crouched by a stream, filling her canteen for the second time in a row. The water was so cold it hurt her teeth to drink it, but it was clear and clean and felt wonderful on her throat. She drank all she could, then filled the canister again and headed back towards George, who was sitting on a log a few feet away. Despite taking slow, cautious steps, she still managed to slip on the muddy riverbank and fall completely into the muck with an inelegant splash.

She struggled upright with a groan. "I am surrounded by water, but I keep getting dirtier. I beg you, Mr. Dexter, please tell me that at some point in my life I will be able to properly bathe. I cannot stand my own filth."

"Soon," he said, and she could see he was trying to contain a laugh. "For both of our sakes, I truly hope it is soon."

A burly young man tromped through the grass behind them, covered head to toe — and beard — in mud, and George gave her a wink. "You and I are not the dirtiest here, but I'll allow we are not much better."

George, Liza, and her hired packers had come a good distance, journeying down the mountain towards Lake Lindeman. The spring warmth played wicked tricks, making untrodden paths hazardous and deep, and the frozen lakes were unpredictable, but at least the snow had given way to grass and thick forests had sprung up around them. With each step, the sadness that had threatened to crush Liza became less of a burden, and her grief gave way to a new sense of purpose.

With a groan, George slung his bag onto his shoulder, and Liza gave him a sympathetic smile.

"I've been meaning to ask," she said as they returned to the trail. "What's in there that's so heavy?"

"My camera," he admitted, "though I shouldn't complain. It is more cumbersome than heavy. You see, I had promised my darlings I would take photographs of my experience and send them along with my first gold nugget."

"What a lovely idea," she said.

With a pang of self-pity, she realized that she would probably never have need of a camera. No one was left to ask for photographs of her.

"It was, wasn't it? Although I must admit it is somewhat awkward to carry all this way." He gestured towards the discarded trunks and bags that still lined the trail. "I imagine all these things seemed necessary at first to every traveller."

Liza glanced blankly over the field but felt no urge to search the bags for treasure. Since Happy Camp, her heart just wasn't in it anymore.

"But there must have come a point when they decided they could carry them no farther." He seemed to consider the option, but then he shook his head. "I cannot cast this aside. I couldn't bear to let Olivia down."

"Of course not," Liza replied, and though the mere mention of family hurt, she was sympathetic. "I'm sure Olivia and the children would love to see those photographs. But might I make a suggestion?"

"Certainly."

"You and I have both seen photographers along the trail. Why not ask one of them to take your photo? Or you could simply purchase photographs of the area when we get to Dawson."

"Yes, yes. You're right, of course. It's just that my dear Olivia gave the camera to me as a gift before I left, and I told her it would be safe with me."

"Do you think she'd mind terribly if you left the camera here?" Liza asked. "I imagine she would be happy just to have you home again. That is how I would feel, anyway."

"I suppose you're right." He squatted by his pack and removed a leather-wrapped box camera from within. He set it reluctantly beside the path, then lifted the pack again. "Much better."

Liza picked up the camera, sorry for him. She knew what it felt like to leave things behind. "I have another idea. Before we go, I shall take your photograph. How would that be? Then we can send the film to Olivia along with your first nugget, just as you'd planned."

"That is an excellent solution!" George scouted their location, more animated than she'd seen him in some time. "All right," he said, pointing. "If I stand there, you will be able to photograph the mountain behind me."

"You'll have to show me how."

"Of course. Come, we'll use a tree to stabilize the camera." He led her off the path, and once he figured out where he wanted her to stand, he peered down through the top of the camera. "Yes, this will do just fine. All right, Miss Peterson. Beside the handle here you can see three things. This is the hole through which you will look at me." He tapped a small silver key beside the hole. "You don't need to worry about this bit. That is what I will use afterwards, to wind the film and prepare the camera for any photographs yet to be taken. Now, this small lever in front of the winder key is what you will use to actually trip the shutter and take the photograph. Look down that hole, do you see?"

"Yes, but . . ." She glanced up and studied the mountain again. "It's backwards."

"Yes. It works with the mechanics of a mirror. The photograph itself will not be backwards."

She'd heard about that before somewhere — probably Stan — but had never seen it for herself. "Fascinating. All right, Mr. Dexter. I am ready. You go stand over there."

After she had taken the photo, she held the camera out for him. "There you go. Now what?"

"These Kodaks make it so much easier," he said almost to himself, striding towards her. He examined a window in the camera's back, then said, "I see there is only one exposure left on the film. Wait here a moment, would you, please?"

Camera in hand, George approached a passing traveller, and the two carried on a brief conversation. After a moment, the other man took the camera and George sauntered back to Liza.

"Now I shall be able to send my family a likeness of me with my closest friend from this adventure," he said.

"Oh no. I can't — I'm in trousers, for heaven's sake!"

He chuckled. "Come, come, Miss Peterson. That makes it even more unique. Let us show them a lady in trousers, shall we? My wife has surely never seen the like."

"Well, if we're going to do that, let's make it even more interesting for her," she suggested, hoping to take the focus off her. She waved at the half-dozen packers waiting nearby, and they took up position behind George and her.

"Excellent idea, Miss Peterson," George said.

Once the photo was taken, the prospector returned George's camera, and the packers moved back to their loads. George carefully removed the spool of film then placed the empty camera on the side of the trail.

"You know," he said, picking up his own pack, "I believe Olivia would be in complete agreement with my decision. I feel lighter in every way."

"I am happy for you."

"I can see that. I must say, it is a true pleasure to see you smile again."

Guilt tingled through Liza. "I never thought I would be able to do that ever again, but it is getting a little easier."

"They would want you to be happy," George said gently.

She nodded, knowing it was true. Somewhere along the route towards Dawson, a spark of hope had ignited within the ashes of Liza's heart, and though it was weak, it was keeping her warm. This journey had worn her down in every imaginable way, but it had not killed her. And though it had taken so much, it had also given back by making her more resilient than she'd ever thought she could be. The closer she got to her destination, the more she dared believe that maybe, just maybe, her father's dream could become hers.

The Earth, she knew — even without Stan's lessons — was forever spinning on its axis, its place in the universe set. But within those boundaries, nothing ever remained the same. Running water cut a continuously changing path; the seeds of flowers rode winds to populate new ground. She, too, felt herself changing, growing, adjusting. And as long as she could bend and grow like the feather-soft heads of grass dancing in the breeze all around her, she would thrive. And even flourish.

TWENTY:
BEN

Ben stopped short, astonished by the sight of Lake Lindeman's long, narrow banks. What had once been thick acres of dense forest was now stripped of trees, replaced by a crowded city of stained canvas tents rippling under a smoky sky, and the air reverberated with the crack of axes, the banging of hammers, and the songs of hundreds of saws. Thousands of prospectors who had been stranded there before the deep freeze were building boats and rafts, readying themselves for when the ice broke — which would be soon. Already Ben could see a number of large, dark patches showing through the lake's thinning surface.

Thompson, Ben, and Keitl followed the beaten trail towards the strange new shipyard, making no attempt to be heard over the noise. Ben was struck dumb by the mayhem going on around them, and the more he saw, the less confident he felt.

Thousands of prospectors were living here, and there were only a handful of Mounties.

"How are we supposed to do anything about this?" he asked Thompson. "Won't matter how many of us come, it'll never be enough to manage them all."

Thompson said, "Steele will have a plan. Mark my word."

They continued towards Lake Bennett, where they discovered a slightly smaller but still overcrowded version of the camp at Lindeman. At least there was a Mountie outpost at Bennett and, subsequently, some semblance of order.

They were greeted by the enthusiastic, mustachioed Constable Cassius Baxter, who had been examining the partial skeleton of a boat before Ben and Thompson arrived. Spotting them, he clapped Ben on the shoulder. "You got here just in time, boys."

Ben and Thompson introduced themselves, then listened to Baxter's overview of the ragged shipyard. When he led them to a nearby raft, Ben ran his hand carefully over its rough planks, hesitating over the uneven joists. He knew nothing about boats, but he'd seen enough boards hammered together to know when it hadn't been done right.

"The builder's a bank clerk from Boston,"

Baxter confided. "Him and his son came up here together. The man can barely lift a hammer, he's so slight. Never built a thing in his life before now."

The sense of helplessness Ben had felt at Lindeman swept through him again. Spring would open the floodgates both metaphorically and physically, and from what he could see, most of these gold seekers would cast off in vessels that barely floated. If the rapids ahead were as bad as the ones they just passed, the prospectors would never make it.

Baxter chuckled. "You call those ones rapids? You ain't seen nothing yet. Just wait a bit and we'll introduce you to some real whitewater. Last year we lost over two hundred crafts, and there wasn't nearly as many people then as there are now." He gave Ben a sympathetic smile. "I know what you're thinking, but don't let it get to you. We do what we can out here, and that's all anyone can ask. Come on inside. Superintendent Steele is expecting you, and we'll get some chow soon."

They met others in the dining hall, and everyone straightened at Steele's entrance. Just like the last time Ben had seen him, the Superintendent studied every face in the room before he began to speak, his expression strong, solid, and confident. Considering the chaos Ben had just left outside, he couldn't help but wonder if Steele ever got worried. At a time like this, it seemed the fate of the entire Yukon depended upon this one man.

Steele got right down to business and outlined the plan of action. Before any of the travellers could set sail, the Mounties would have to approve and register every single watercraft, and that included jotting down the names of everyone on board — as well as their next of kin. They had to move quickly, because the ice was due to break up any day now.

"With God's help and the new rules I am imposing," Steele finished, "I believe we will not experience as unfortunate a season as the last one."

Thompson jabbed his elbow into Ben's side. "I told you he'd have a plan."

Steele's plan entailed a lot of detail work, but every man did his part, and when the ice finally cracked at the end of May the resounding noise was followed by eager shouts along the banks of the lake. Still, the mighty Yukon River would not be rushed. Solid sheets of ice followed the current, twisting in a slow, gradual dance, then colliding and smashing again, their bulk both lethal and unpredictable. Ben shook his head ruefully at the prospectors who hadn't been patient enough to wait for the river to be completely clear before setting sail. There was nothing anyone could do when the powerful plates of ice swung around and crushed their fragile crafts.

By the time the ice had fully melted and the bulk of the boats had set sail, Ben, Thompson, Baxter, and most of the other Mounties had already begun hiking the banks of the river towards Dawson City. From their path along the shore, they monitored the advancement of the boats, noting the obligatory serial numbers Steele had ordered be painted on each craft.

After a few hours they reached the ad hoc town of Canyon City, the last stopover point before the thirty-foot walls of unforgiving basalt rock on either side of the river began to narrow, creating two major sets of white-water rapids. A contingent of Mounties had been stationed at the top, where they warned travellers about the danger below and recommended that women, children, and less adventurous prospectors take the safer and much longer trail instead. Anyone who chose to risk the rapids had to go through the Mounties, who checked each vessel and tried to ensure an experienced pilot was at the helm. In some cases, the Mounties themselves took over and piloted the boats.

Ben heard the water's frothing power before he saw it, and the force of it rolled through his chest like a locomotive, but he also heard an unexpected metallic jingling, and when they rounded a bend he was surprised to see a couple of horses pulling something that resembled a large wagon.

"What's that?" he asked Baxter, who had proved to be a great guide along the trail.

"Oh, why, that's Macaulay's tramway," Baxter explained. "Feel like resting your feet?"

"Always."

"Macaulay can take a man and his freight — even a small boat if he wants — five miles along that track he laid out in the forest. Pretty major undertaking, but he's finding it lucrative."

"Sounds like a great idea," Ben replied.

"Sure, sure. If you got twenty-five dollars to spare, it is. At this point, that's a pretty steep fee for most folks." Baxter meandered close to the edge of the rock wall. "And if you take the tram, you don't get as good of a view. Come see."

Ben's breath caught in his chest when he glimpsed the whitewater thirty feet below, curling and twisting up from the riverbed's rocky bottom, and he had to turn away from the edge. It wasn't the height that got to him; it was the water and how it grabbed at the crafts, spinning them without mercy, dragging them under when it could.

"I don't like feeling useless up here," Ben told him. "I mean, all we can do is watch."

"It's a little better farther on," Baxter reassured him, "at the bottom of the White Horse Rapids. At least we're closer to them there. Even so, there's not much we can do."

"It's incredible, watching these fools," Thompson mused as they walked. "They got no idea what they're doing or where they're headed, but they're fine with gambling everything just to get there quicker."

"We could save them all a whole lotta trouble," Baxter said.

"How's that?" Ben asked.

"Poor fools think there are still gold claims available."

Ben frowned at him. "So did I. Aren't there?"

"A lot of 'em have already been snapped up. Plenty of these fellas are gonna find themselves working for other miners who came last fall, or else they'll be making their money some other way."

"Hardly seems right," Ben thought out

loud, "letting them even try."

Baxter shrugged. "We warn them all before they set sail, but they got some kinda deafness when it comes to the idea of giving up."

Ben's sense of futility didn't ease when they reached the wide base of the White Horse Rapids. When panicked voices bounced down the canyon, he still couldn't reach them. Thompson stood beside Ben, humming nervously as he watched a raft come down, and Keitl whined softly between the two of them.

"What do you think?" Ben asked.

"Pretty close to the side," Thompson muttered. "Looks like you gotta stay in the middle so it doesn't pull you, but you gotta stay clear of that big rock, too. Takes some skill to get through."

After the raft safely completed its run, it drifted towards the landing spot where Ben waited, and the four passengers hopped from the raft to the water to the sand. Most were too shocked to speak, but one man was grinning from ear to ear.

"Wooey! Wasn't that the greatest thing I've ever done!" He slapped his friend on the back. "Why, I'm moved to climb back up and do it all over again!"

"You can do it on your own, then," his

friend replied, then he staggered to the side of the landing and threw up.

"Here comes Constable Dixon!" Baxter yelled, grinning. "That boy knows what he's doing. He was raised on the water, and my, oh my. Just look at him go! He's the best pilot we got. He's done this dozens of times, but he always makes it look exciting."

"How many's he got on board?" Thompson asked, sounding awed. "Eight?"

Constable Dixon's boat shot down the rapids, and Ben couldn't take his eyes off it. A commanding shout echoed off the rock walls, and the passengers shifted on cue before the boat moved to the centre of the river, rolling over and under the waves, disappearing, then flying into the open in great bursts of spray. After Thompson's earlier observation, Ben's concern was about the massive rock in the centre, but Dixon's raft swept effortlessly past, and his passengers let out shouts of excitement rather than fear. Before two minutes had passed, the barge slipped out of the waves and coasted freely towards the calmer waters. Constable Dixon lifted his hat and waved it at his fellow Mounties, a wide grin on his wet face.

Thompson chuckled. "Cheeky bastard."

"Uh-oh." Baxter was looking upriver

again, and this time he wasn't laughing.

Everyone's attention went to a raft floundering at the top, spinning towards the rock in the middle. The passengers were paddling hard, but they were caught by the water and everyone could see it.

Ben put up a hand to shield his eyes, trying to make out the passengers. "Look at that one fella. How's someone that tall supposed to balance?"

The man in question was teetering wildly, lurching forward when a wave crashed up from behind, stumbling back when the bow lifted again. He had an oar, but as he lost control, it flailed uselessly. One of the other passengers spotted the problem and staggered over to grab him, but before he could get there the tall man's arms windmilled, the oar flew like a bird, and the man disappeared.

"George!" someone screamed.

Ben knew that voice. He took off up the trail, running towards the scene as fast as he could, with Keitl bounding just ahead of him.

Back on the landing, he heard Thompson yell, "There's a woman on that raft!"

"What's she doing on there?" Baxter shouted. "Women aren't supposed to ride down!"

Halfway up the rapids, Ben's heart sank. It didn't matter how close he got, there was no way he'd be able to help. The boat would inevitably land at the bottom in either one or many pieces before he could get to Miss Peterson.

"Can you see him?" Thompson called up to him.

Ben scouted the foamy water for George Dexter. "No."

His attention returned to the struggling raft, and he saw with relief that the pilot and passengers had regained control. Right away he made out Miss Peterson, soaked from head to toe. Her face was set with determination as she plunged her oar in again and again, following whatever instructions she could hear over the roar of the water. They were almost through, so Ben scrambled back down to the landing point, and Keitl thundered past, reaching the placid little cove before him. She stood at the edge of the water, barking madly at the approaching raft and shifting nervously from paw to paw.

"That man —" Ben said to Thompson.

The Sergeant's expression was grim. "Yeah. I recognized him too."

Miss Peterson was the first off the raft. Without hesitation, she dropped into the knee-deep, frigid water and sloshed to the shore, where she started making her way back up the canyon. Her face was as pale as snow, her long brown hair wet and hanging loose.

Ben stepped in front of her. "Miss Peterson . . ."

"D-did you f-find him?" she stammered through cold, blue lips. Ben wasn't even sure she'd seen him — all her attention was on the water. "Where's Mr. Dexter?"

From up the bank came a whistle, and Ben turned to see two Mounties haul a dripping body from the water. They squatted beside it, checking for a pulse, then one of them shook his head.

Ben turned back to Miss Peterson, but she was gaping up at the two Mounties, swaying and shivering uncontrollably. Ben quickly removed his coat and draped it over her shoulders, wishing there was something more he could do. Only when she clutched the lapels and pulled them together did she blink up at Ben.

"I . . . your friend —" he tried.

Maybe he was wrong. Maybe she wasn't looking at him. Her eyes seemed to have lost their focus.

"P-poor George," she whispered, tears streaming down her face. "Oh, George! It's so unfair!"

It *was* unfair, Ben thought. He faced the water, hands clenched. What was the point of having Mounties down here when there was no way to prevent something like this from happening?

Just then, Keitl reached up and put a filthy paw on Miss Peterson's knee. Startled, she glanced down, and Ben heard her catch her breath. She dropped to her knees and touched Keitl's muddy fur, examining the black patch on her chest. To Ben's surprise, Keitl seemed to be just as curious. She sniffed the woman, then licked her face, her tail wagging madly.

"This dog —"

"I'm sorry about that," he said. "She thinks she's helping. Keitl, come here. You're filthy."

Miss Peterson's brow creased with confusion as she watched the dog return to Ben. "She's yours?"

"Miss Peterson, I am very sorry about George Dexter. I know he was your friend," he said gently. Once again, words seemed meaningless. "It will only be a small comfort, but we do have a record of all the men on your barge, so we'll be able to contact Mr. Dexter's family directly. At least you won't need to worry over that aspect of this tragedy."

She was still staring at the dog.

"Miss Peterson? Is there anything I can do?"

"No." Her eyes shifted abruptly to Ben, and in that moment he saw a different woman altogether. The sadness in Liza Peterson's expression had hardened to stone.

"If there's anything —"

She peeled off his red coat and handed it back. "Here. Take this. There's no need to worry about me. I'm used to surviving on my own."

He watched her walk away without a backwards glance, then he looked down at the rejected coat hanging off his fingers, a heavy reminder that he was responsible for these people. And he had failed them again.

"This journey isn't over yet, Miss Peterson," he said softly, lifting his gaze. "The next time you need me, I will not let you down."

■ ■ ■ ■

PART TWO:
DAWSON CITY

■ ■ ■ ■

Twenty-One:
Liza

"What was I thinking?" Liza muttered to herself as she stomped up the hill towards her tent.

She and the Tlingit packers had finally arrived outside the sprawling tableau of Dawson City that morning and had quickly set up camp in a sheltered spot out of sight of other travellers, a quarter mile from the town. The camp was temporary — her next step was to rent a permanent storefront. After bidding farewell to her packers, Liza had made straight for the busy streets of Dawson. She hadn't gotten far before she noticed the men of the town ogling her, whistling, and offering her the chance to make "easy money." Her face had burned with embarrassment when she realized the reason: she'd neglected to change into her corset and skirts. She'd gotten used to the convenience and comfort of wearing men's clothing on the trail, but here, where men's minds were no longer on the climb, they were definitely the wrong thing to wear.

I might need money, she thought as she searched through her things for her best dress, a cake of soap, and a cloth, *but I'll never be that desperate.*

Down at the river, she dipped the cloth into the cold water and washed her face and hands. She scrubbed patches of dirt off her dress, polished her boots, and combed through the mess of tangles in her long, dark hair, gritting her teeth against the pain. After she'd woven it into braids, she pinned them under a hat she had moulded back into shape, tucking in the ends as neatly as she could. She wished she had a mirror, but that extravagance was packed away, hopefully not broken from the trek.

More than that, she wished her father were here. Ever since Dyea she'd been shocked by the outlandish cost of goods and services, and during her hasty trip into Dawson she'd noticed with dismay that the signs in those windows advertised startlingly higher prices. She couldn't even imagine what rent might cost, but she had a pretty good idea it was well beyond what she could afford, given that she'd had to spend most of her cash on packers and tolls.

Liza fingered her small supply of money.

If her father were here, he would cross his arms and let the well-oiled wheels in his mind work out a solution as he'd done so many times before. If only he'd let her in on his secret back then.

"What should I do?" she whispered.

A memory of her father crystallized before her. It was a moment four years before, when she'd asked for a beautiful illustrated edition of *Pride and Prejudice* — the illustrated one with the magnificent gilt peacock on the front and spine. She'd seen it in the catalogue and wanted it from first glance, but when she begged her father to buy it for her he had shaken his head.

If you want something, you must decide how to get it, he'd said. *Not if, but how. Just like when you were just a toddler, learning how to walk. You couldn't stand knowing your Stan could walk and you could only crawl. You watched him like a hawk, then all at once you stood up, grabbed the table's edge, and refused to fall no matter how much you wobbled.*

And the very next day you walked on your own, her mother had finished for him. *You saw your doll across the room, and you simply went and got her. That's all there was to it.*

She'd smiled at their words, but they hadn't helped her with the challenge of acquiring the book. If her father would let her do more in the store, then she'd be able to make more money, but until then she'd be stuck. She'd scanned her bookshelves, imagining the copy of *Pride and Prejudice* joining her existing collection of treasured books, and it came to her that she didn't need the ones she'd already read. When she went to him, her father proudly approved her plan to sell off some of her older books, and in time she bought the beautiful new edition.

Liza closed her purse and went to the pack where she'd tucked away the little treasures she'd found along the trail. She didn't need to look at her father's ledger to know that if she was to survive here she would have to sell something to make something. Tucking the jewellery into her coat pocket, she headed back down to Dawson's busy streets, more wary this time, but obscene suggestions and catcalls no longer chased her down the street.

At the first pawnshop on Front Street, Liza peered in the window and spotted a typewriter, a fiddle, a set of gold-rimmed teacups alongside a box of slightly tarnished silverware, a stunning candelabra — which made her wonder what the owner had imagined the Klondike might be like — and a lady's elegant gold gown, among other things. Her treasures would fit in nicely here, she thought. Chin raised, shoulders back, she pulled open the pawnshop's door and strode directly to the counter.

A sombre-looking clerk rubbed his thick brown mutton chops with speculation as she walked towards him. "Can I help you?" he drawled.

"I hope so." She pulled out one of the necklaces from the trail and placed it on a velvet square already laid on the counter.

Without a word the pawnbroker pulled out a loupe to inspect the chain and locket. "Loan or sell?"

"Loan." She could get more from loaning now, and she planned to sell it herself when she had her own place.

"I'll give you five dollars. Interest's twenty-five percent."

The offer was low, but she'd expected to bargain — she'd learned along the way that was how it went in the North. "It's worth a great deal more than that," she said coolly. "We both know that."

"Perhaps, but this is Dawson City."

She frowned at the necklace. Apparently she would have to loan the pawnbroker much more of her stock if she was going to raise enough money for rent.

"It isn't enough for what I need," she admitted.

"What about that?" He pointed at her waist, where her father's pocket watch hung just inside the folds of her coat. Then he switched his gaze to her mother's ring on her finger. "Or that?"

The idea of parting with the last tokens of her family sent a wave of panic through her, and she cupped her hand protectively around the watch. "Those aren't for sale."

Unconcerned, he crossed his arms. "Five dollars for the necklace. Take it or leave it."

She scooped up the necklace and dropped it back into her pocket. "This is absurd. I shall bring my business elsewhere."

"No one will offer more. Especially to a woman. You're a bad risk."

Heat flared in her cheeks at the suggestion. A necklace was a necklace. Pawning items had nothing to do with whether she was a woman or not. She would prove him wrong.

"You don't know anything about me. Good day, sir."

But an hour later, as she slumped out of the last pawnshop on the street, she had to admit that he'd been right.

As she passed a general store, her stomach grumbled at the sight of a barrel of apples, and she peered into her purse, counting what she had left. The apples were soft and a dollar each, but she hadn't eaten since morning, and she was starting to feel dizzy with hunger. With no other choice, she handed over the money.

Outside on the boardwalk, she took small, economical bites of the apple, watching people wander by. Her stomach cramped, but the pain was more from anxiety than hunger. Had she made the wrong decision by coming here? Her eyes fell to her hand, to the gleaming band of gold her mother had worn for so many years. If she couldn't find a store to rent, it wouldn't matter if she had the ring or not; she'd have no livelihood. The image of those lecherous men with their disgusting propositions came back to her, but she pushed it away. She wasn't that desperate yet.

"Quite a city, ain't it?"

A young man had quietly approached and now stood beside her, observing the traffic. He was pleasant looking and fairly well dressed, though the edges of his sleeves were worn. Not rich, not poor, she thought, aware that's how she appeared as well.

"It certainly is," she replied. "Though I don't know if I'd call it a city. More of a sophisticated camp."

"A camp in the process of becoming a city," he said pleasantly. "Construction and commerce from all over the world meeting right here. It's an exciting place to be." He flashed a roguish smile and extended a hand in greeting. "Maxwell Somers. Pleasure to meet you."

"Miss Elizabeth Peterson," she said. "Have you been in Dawson City long?"

"I arrived a few weeks ago from Boston."

"You speak from experience, then. This is my first day, and I am just getting my bearings."

The corners of his mouth dipped. "Pardon my impertinence, but I'm curious why such a lovely young lady is alone on this crowded street. Have you a husband nearby? Perhaps a brother or father?"

"I am on my own," she said, leaving it at that. He might be friendly, but Stan had told her enough stories about swindlers for her to know she couldn't trust strangers.

"Surely you're not planning to mine, Miss Peterson."

She laughed despite herself. "No, no. I have laboured hard enough just getting here. I'm opening a shop. That is my family's business."

"Excellent! I am in the supply business, so perhaps we shall be partners at some point. In any case, I shall look forward to frequenting your store. Where is it?"

If only she had an answer. "I actually don't have one yet. That's the trouble. I am embarrassed to admit that I was unprepared for the high cost of rentals here. I have sought out funds from pawnbrokers, but they don't pay well enough for what I need. And their interest rates are shameful."

"Ah, yes. The generous nature of Dawson City." He scratched his throat thoughtfully. "I might know of a place that would suit you."

Her heart flipped. "Oh?"

"It isn't much, but still." He paused. "It might be good enough for starting out."

That's all she needed, she thought, daring to hope. A place to start from, then once the business was underway, well, the sky was the limit. Only —

"I imagine it would be far too expensive for me to afford," she said.

"That's the best part, Miss Peterson." His face broke into a wide grin. "I own the building, and I'm sure you and I . . . You have collateral, I assume?"

"I have a full inventory, I just don't have shelves to put it on."

"Let me show you the place, then you can show me what you have. After that, I am certain we can work out some sort of deal that will be agreeable to both of us. Do you have time to see it now?"

"Yes, of course," she replied, trying not to appear too excited. But how serendipitous this was!

She glanced eagerly from side to side as she walked down the street beside Mr. Somers. Soon her shop would match these flashy, painted window displays — no, she decided, her shop would have much brighter windows.

"I think you're going to like this place," Mr. Somers said, filling the silence. "It has a little surprise that will make it even more worth your while."

Liza nodded, but she was starting to feel a niggling of doubt. The farther they went from the city's core, the dingier the buildings became.

"And here we are!"

The lopsided little building he was indicating stood as far from the hub of downtown as it could, but when he swung open the door, she saw that it was, as he'd said, a good place to start. Though the space was small, it had shelves and a counter already installed. With a little ingenuity, she could make it work. She was delighted to learn Mr. Somers's "surprise" was a small alcove off to the side, and hidden behind its curtain was a cot. This would be more than just a shop, it would be her home, and the best part was that her things would never be out of her sight.

In a gallant gesture, Mr. Somers agreed to accept the necklace she'd offered the pawnbroker as a first instalment, as well as a few more small items. He gave her two weeks to make up the balance, then provided her with a wagon and an extra pair of arms to help her transport her things. It took them the bulk of the afternoon to unload all the boxes, and when they'd finished she turned to her new landlord with a smile.

"Mr. Somers, I can't thank you enough for this. Is there a lease I should sign?"

"Dear Miss Peterson, you will soon learn that Dawson City does not work that way. Everything here is done with a handshake."

She hesitated, wondering what her father might have thought of this arrangement, but she didn't have much choice other than to accept. Ignoring the voice of caution in her head, Liza shook Mr. Somers's hand and thanked him for his generosity.

The moment the door closed behind him, Liza began to unpack everything she had. Too excited to sleep, she kept working late into the evening, using the light of the northern sun beaming through her crooked doorway to finish. Besides her front counter, the store had plenty of shelves — they had needed only a little hammering to make them level — and there was a good, sturdy table in the middle of the room. When she'd run out of shelves, she'd used her travelling crates to hold and display more items. Finally, all the wares they'd lugged up the mountain were in their rightful place, and she stood back to admire the shop. *Her* shop.

Yawning, she hung up her apron, and as she leaned down to untie her boots a small package landed at her feet with a dull thud.

"Oh, George," she murmured, clutching the parcel to her chest.

A few days before the river disaster, George had written a letter to his family and wrapped it in a package along with his camera film. He'd given it all to Liza, asking her to post the package when she made it to Dawson, as he would be going straight to the goldfields. Or so he'd thought.

She traced his neat printing, picturing his long fingers curled around the pen. Of course she would mail it as he'd asked, but after all that had happened, that hardly seemed like enough. After all, he had been her only friend. With a sigh, she pulled out a piece of paper and tried to think of what to write. She knew the Mounties would have notified Olivia immediately by telegraph, so what she would write now would be the words of a friend, something that might help George's family smile again. She owed him that at the very least. After a moment of thoughtful reflection, she let her pen glide over the paper writing about George's indomitable and inspiring spirit on the trail and how he had helped her through a very dark time. When she was done, she tucked the letter inside the package and set it aside to take to the post office. After that, she briefly considered taking the time to write to her friends in Vancouver, but she decided to put the paper away instead. No looking back, she told herself.

She lay down on her cot and pulled an old blanket to her chin. In the quiet, her thoughts unspooled. After months of struggle and grief, she'd established her very own shop in the middle of the Yukon, a place where her father had declared anything was possible. She should feel happy, even celebratory, but a heavy sense of loneliness had descended on her instead. What was the point of all this hardship when no one else was here to share in the rewards? She didn't even have her dog anymore — though it was comforting to know that Blue was alive. Her mind flitted back to the day at the rapids and the wrenching betrayal that had twisted her heart when she'd seen the black, heart-shaped patch on the dog's chest. How on earth had Blue survived the avalanche then ended up with Constable Turner, of all people? Why *him*? Every time trouble found Liza, he had been there as well. A terrible coincidence, of course, but a fact she couldn't easily navigate around.

She took a deep breath then let it out, needing to clear her mind. Because against all odds, she had made it to Dawson at last. Here she had a chance at a fresh start. She hoped, and not for the first time, that she'd seen the last of Constable Ben Turner.

Twenty-Two: Ben

At the crest of the hill, Ben reined in his horse and dropped off the saddle. From here he had a view of the junction of the Klondike and Yukon rivers, as well as the creeks and valleys of the goldfields. The echoes of men's voices drifted up to where he stood, broken only by the hammering of picks and shovels.

It was hard to imagine what this place had once looked like. From what the old-timers at the mines said, where Ben was now standing, there had once been a forest of willow, birch, and pine, all of it unaware of the thick vein of gold that had solidified far beneath its roots. Since the discovery of gold, the forest no longer existed. Its timber had been chopped and used, its ground hacked and cut, until it was no more than a bald wall of rock streaked with white paths of panned gravel.

The valley below Ben had served as a

small fishing camp for generations of the Hän, but like the hillside, the camp had been stripped for use and was unrecognizable now. Gold mining required water, so streams had been bridged or dammed, and the creeks which had once brought fish to the people had been forever altered. Nothing about the clean, clear water at the top was recognizable in the mines' murky runoff.

The men of the Klondike existed here in the thousands, having traded the predictability and comfort of the lives they'd known for a cold, muddy dream of gold. They had struggled to get here from all over the world, and now they staggered daily across a tightrope stretched between misery and euphoria. To Ben, it didn't seem much more than that — an existence. He sure didn't think he could call it a life.

Ben and Keitl headed down to the claims, leaving his mount up top where the ground was more stable. A good horse was worth hundreds of dollars around here, but no one would ever think about stealing a Mountie's animal, and everyone knew this big boy was Ben's. He rode this way every few days to check on folks and pass out mail when he could — though most of the time there wasn't much of that. This morning he was tasked with an extra assignment from Thompson.

Pay close attention to the men's packs, he had said. *Steele thinks someone might be smuggling guns in, and I think he's right.*

Who? Ben had asked.

We don't know for certain. Listen and watch for now. If I hear anything I'll pass it along.

By the end of his rounds, Ben hadn't seen anything that might suggest crooked deals or guns, but he had helped out a few of the miners and ordered some of the sick ones to head into town and seek medical help. Typhoid was rampant these days, as well as a long list of other illnesses, and they were in a constant race to cut back on contagion. The miners gave Ben an easy greeting as he rode past, and he recognized their eager expressions. They were headed to Dawson City. Time to cash in.

The trail from the mines to Dawson City was like a river: all the gold dug out of the ground flowed directly into the city, then its tributaries branched off between saloons, dance halls, hotels, and banks. If a man came into town without gold, he had to search hard to find work, because nothing in this town came for free. But if his packs were loaded with dust and nuggets, the tantalizing doors of Dawson swung wide open in welcome.

Ben figured Dawson City was as different from the Chilkoot Pass as a rainbow was to dirt. The vast whiteness of Chilkoot had echoed with silence. Impersonal, necessary interactions between Mounties, the travellers, and the dogs were the social limit. But here in Dawson, a growing boomtown with over fourteen thousand people, the noise never stopped. Working women with plunging necklines and negligible skirts leaned over balconies, jeering and flirting without shame, and every day new people arrived, keen to start this new chapter in their adventures. *Cheechakas,* those folks were called — as opposed to the "sourdoughs" who had been there awhile — and they were easy to spot. They were the ones stumbling through the crowds with their mouths hanging open, awed by the sights.

It had become second nature for Ben to scan the street as he walked through the town on his rounds. Dawson's citizens hung tight to their belongings, aware that professional thieves and con men slithered among them. Many of those had learned their trades on the often violent streets of Skagway under the tutelage of the infamous Soapy Smith. But Dawson City was nothing like Skagway, in large part because of the Mounties' enforcement of the gun laws at the summit. That wasn't to say Dawson was squeaky clean, though.

"Hey there, Constable Turner."

"Good afternoon, Daisy," Ben replied, tipping his hat to the young prostitute.

Daisy crouched to give Keitl a scratch on the head and Ben a front-row seat to her impressive cleavage. She blinked up at him from under her lashes.

"Looking for something to pass the time?"

Daisy lived in one of the tents on Paradise Alley, which had sprung up almost overnight in an area between Front Street and Second Avenue. Each one had a girl's name painted on the front. It was part of Ben's job to check on the area, make sure everyone was all right, but the sight of those tents always made him feel sick. He hated to see girls living and working in such a filthy slum.

"Daisy, you're a beautiful woman, but you know you're talking to the wrong man."

"Can't blame a girl for trying."

"You be careful out here, Daisy. And keep an eye on the water."

The last week had been rainy, and with the snow melting, the river had risen to an alarming level. Steele predicted they would soon be relocating the townsfolk due to flooding.

"Oh, I'll be fine," Daisy purred. "It's Ralph Stevens's wife you need to worry about."

"What do you mean?"

"I heard she's in hospital tonight, and that her husband put her there. It's not the first time."

Ben didn't hesitate. "I'll take care of it."

"She won't charge him with anything."

"I understand." More than Daisy would ever know. "I'll talk to him."

Ben immediately headed to Stevens's home: a big house on Sixth Avenue, away from the downtown noise. He'd never met the man, but Ben knew a little about him from the chatter around Fort Herchmer. Stevens was in his early forties, wealthy from his claims and the roulette wheel, but a couple of times Thompson had wondered aloud if he might have another side business that kept him flush.

As Ben strode up to the house, hot under the collar at the thought of what this man had done to his wife, he reminded himself to keep his temper under control, but when Ralph Stevens answered his knock, a crystal tumbler in one hand and cuts on his knuckles, Ben's hands reflexively clenched at his sides.

"Ralph Stevens?" he asked.

"Yes?" Stevens's voice was low and gravelly, hardened by whatever was in his glass. "Who are you?"

"Constable Ben Turner from the North-West Mounted Police. I'm here to charge you with assault."

Ben hadn't planned to say that, but the words were out of his mouth before he could stop them. Stevens's nonchalant arrogance cut through Ben's calm, and he knew he had to do something, not just make threats. He was tired of people getting hurt on his watch.

Stevens crossed his arms. "I have no idea what you are talking about." He studied Ben's uniform. "*Constable*, is it?"

He'd noticed Ben's lack of officer chevrons, then, but that didn't deter Ben. "Mr. Stevens, most men worth a rat's ass give their wives gifts and respect. You, on the other hand, gave your wife such a beating she's in the hospital for at least a couple of days. And from what I understand, this ain't the first time. That's assault, and assault is illegal."

Stevens tugged at his collar. "You got proof?"

"I do," Ben bluffed. "You'll have to come with me."

"I see." Stevens held up a finger. "Hold

your horses, Constable. I'll be right back."

Ben heard him shuffling around in the next room, and he unclipped his holster just in case. But when Ralph reappeared, he carried a couple of small moosehide sacks, not a pistol. The sacks were called "pokes," and Ben knew each one was filled with about sixteen dollars' worth of gold dust.

Stevens offered the bags with a knowing smile. "Let's forget all about this. Let bygones be bygones, as they say."

In his hands was more money than Ben could make in a month as a Mountie, but the idea of accepting a bribe sent bile up his throat. He held out his cuffs. "I suggest you tuck those pokes back in your pocket before I charge you for attempting to bribe a policeman — in addition to assault."

"Those won't be necessary," Stevens said. "I'm sure we can come to some sort of agreement."

"We can talk all you want at the jail, Mr. Stevens."

"Do you have any idea who I am?" he demanded, his face flushing. "You're harassing the wrong man, boy."

"As far as I'm concerned, you're someone who's broken the law, and that's all I need to know."

"You're making a mistake."

"Turn around now, Mr. Stevens. Hands behind your back."

The cuffs made a satisfactory *click!* as they were fastened, and Stevens's large wrists bulged against the restraints. As they walked towards Fort Herchmer, neither man said a word. Only when Stevens slouched miserably on the small bench within his cell did Ben break the silence.

"I need to know one thing," he said, locking the door behind him. "When you're out of here, will your wife be safe with you? Because if the answer's no, I'm gonna find her someplace else to go."

A fleeting expression of annoyance passed over Stevens's face. "Yeah, yeah. She'll be safe."

"Good, because if I hear that you so much as give your wife a headache, you're gonna end up back in here, you understand?"

"She'll be fine," he grumbled, "but you might live to regret this."

"Keep talking," Ben said, sitting behind a desk and getting started on the paperwork. "You might get out of here in a month or so at that rate."

Ben had neither evidence nor a witness, so in place of a report, he wrote a note to Thompson, explaining why Ralph Stevens was in the cell. What he'd done wasn't official by any means, and he knew he could get a slap on the wrist for doing it, but it was worth it. This way Stevens would know he meant business in the future. Besides, he might have made an enemy out of Stevens, but by doing so he might have saved a woman's life. The first he could handle. The second felt really good.

Twenty-Three: Liza

Liza nearly jumped out of her skin at the sound of her door opening. "Come in!" she called, patting her hair into place.

At the sight of Mr. Somers in the doorway, her heart sank a little. For three long, rainy days she'd been staring at the empty scales she'd bought for weighing gold dust, waiting for her first customer. Until this moment, the only person Liza had seen in the shop during those three days was a waif-like man in rags who had pried open the door in the middle of her second night. Fortunately, Liza had been unable to fall asleep, and the creaking door had given her intruder away. She'd sprung to her feet with a blade in hand, and the man had taken one look at her, then fled. Now she slept with a knife under her pillow.

Despite the knife, she had trouble sleeping at night. She couldn't stop thinking of her impeding rent and she was plagued with regret at taking this place so quickly. The shop was too far from the centre of town, and on closer inspection she'd discovered the floor was uneven and splintered in places. The ceiling, she was certain, would have leaked if it didn't also serve as the floor of the upstairs brothel. From the clipping of heels, she could tell the ladies overhead were doing a whole lot more business than she was. She hated the idea that her father might be right about her not being able to manage a store, but it was starting to feel that way.

"Miss Peterson!" Mr. Somers was grinning broadly. "I've brought you something." With a flourish, he presented her with a large white sign with *Open for Business* painted on it in bold black lettering.

"How thoughtful of you," Liza said, trying to sound cheerful. "Did you paint it yourself?"

"I did. I apologize for the messy letters." He glanced around. "I know you don't have a window to display it in, but I thought you could at least have it set up outside. No one has been in this place for a while, so people aren't used to shopping here. With the help of the sign, your success is practically guaranteed."

Maybe this was all she needed to grab the

attention of passersby, Liza thought. "How can I thank you?"

His smile faltered. "Oh, I must not have been clear. It's not a gift. Since you are an experienced merchant, you understand the value of advertising, and I am sure five dollars won't bother you overmuch."

She tried very hard not to flinch at the cost. "I don't have cash right now, Mr. Somers —"

The twinkle returned to his eyes. "That is a small matter. Have you more of those rubber boots? Perhaps a pair of those could serve as payment?"

"I can manage that," she said.

She brought out the boots, and he graciously set the sign up outside before heading back to the centre of town. Perhaps he'd been right, because by the afternoon she'd had her first three customers. Two were ladies from upstairs, and the third was an older gentleman who had come from the same direction. Any paying customer was a good customer, she kept telling herself. Even better, she couldn't help feeling a bit smug about their purchases. When her family had first begun to place orders for this voyage, she had been adamant that her father buy luxury items like silk fabric.

"They're hardly practical, Liza," he'd said.

"These men will be mining in the dirt, not going to dances."

"But there will be women there. You said so yourself. The silks may take up space," she'd coaxed, "but they weigh very little."

He'd done the figures in his head, factoring in space, weight, possible profits, and eventually given in. "All right. But not too much."

"And silk underthings . . ." she had persuaded.

As she'd predicted, she'd sold a bit of both to the women who had come into the shop. Her father would have been surprised, she thought. And proud. She couldn't resist looking up at that pathetic ceiling and hoping he was watching.

Slowly but surely, more customers began trickling in, and soon her rubber boots' worth of advertising had paid for itself.

One afternoon a woman wearing a peculiar feathered hat and grey kid gloves stepped into the shop, and from the uncertainty in her expression, Liza could tell she already regretted having entered the sad little building.

"Good morning," Liza said brightly, determined to make up for appearances. "What a lovely hat."

The woman's eyes shone with gratitude.

"Do you think? My husband is not fond of it, but I think it's cheerful. One never knows what to wear in a place like this, do they?" She took in Liza's display, then moved on to the varied items on the shelves. "We've only just arrived, you see."

"Welcome to Dawson City," Liza said. "And you can tell your husband that hat is exactly what you should wear around here. You'll see all kinds of people wearing different things. That's part of the charm of this place."

Her customer went directly to the shelf where Liza had stacked the various bolts of silks, but Liza could tell from the way her gaze wandered that she wasn't going to buy any of it. She was clearly interested in style, though, and Liza thought she might like to see the jewellery she kept behind the counter for safekeeping. She pulled out the small wooden box that she'd lined with a square of black velvet to showcase the baubles she'd picked up along the trail.

The jewellery acted like a magnet, and the woman honed in on a silver bracelet. "This is lovely," she said. "Though I wonder where I would wear such an item. I don't mean to cause offense, but this city is filthy. The streets are mud, and the floors are dirt. I'm sure there are nice places here, but I am just so tired of feeling dirty. I've tried dusting, you know, but once it's gone there's always more."

"It's a continuous struggle," Liza commiserated. "I can barely keep up. I sweep three times a day on some days —"

"You sweep? You have a broom?"

"Well, yes. I have this." Liza fetched it from behind her bedroom curtain.

The woman dug inside her bag. "May I buy it from you?"

"My broom?"

"Yes! No one has any to sell! I have asked around, and one of the shopkeepers down the street told me he just sold his last one for twenty-five dollars. Twenty-five dollars for a broom! Can you imagine? I know that scarcity breeds demand, but my floor is simply . . ." She offered Liza a handful of bills. "Would you accept seventeen dollars? It's all I brought with me today."

"Of course," Liza said, making the exchange with a smile. "I can easily make another."

"Thank you," her customer replied, elated. "You're a lifesaver. And I'll be back another time. Your jewellery is lovely."

Once the woman left, Liza looked thoughtfully at the money in her hand. Out of necessity, she had woven that broom together in less than an hour — Stan had seen instructions in a book and taught her how to do it when they were young. If she could make and sell a few more brooms, she would be able to pay her rent.

"What do you think, Father?" she said out loud. "Everyone around here has boots, rope, and shovels, but I am the only one with a broom!"

What else were the citizens of Dawson missing? she wondered, tapping her pencil against her cheek.

"Hairbrushes," she mused. "Tooth-brushes, soap . . ."

This might work out after all.

Twenty-Four: Ben

Dawson City was buzzing during the day, but it was at night that she really hummed. That was Ben's favourite time to make his rounds. Despite the rain that had been melting Dawson's streets to mud over the past couple of days, a dozen steamships were docked down at the waterfront, complete with waving flags, battling pianos, and dancing girls leaning over the sides, waving bottles of champagne in invitation. Nothing to worry about there, he thought to himself, just a whole lot of people having fun.

The wildest action could always be found farther into town, behind the sparkling signs and plate-glass windows of Dawson's saloons. Anyone with money or something to prove — or both — felt the same binding pull that mercury had on gold when they approached the wide-open doors of a pulsing saloon. Every night but Sunday — Steele had decreed absolutely no business was to be open on that day of the week — hundreds of people crowded into the bars, trying to forget the gloom of the goldfields and fool themselves into believing they could overcome the constant ache of loneliness with music or dancing or gambling, if only for a little while.

Ben slid beneath the Monte Carlo Saloon's intricately carved archway and wandered into its smoky den, sensing the mood of the room. A couple of girls had taken up positions on either side of the piano, and Fingers McMahon was playing up a storm, flanked by a fiddler Ben didn't recognize. In Ben's opinion, Fingers wasn't as good as the Rag Time Kid down at the Dominion, but he wasn't bad, and the crowd wasn't complaining. The tables around the room were full and the bartenders were busy, but Ben didn't sense any potential issues, so he headed towards the gambling hall at the back. Beyond the hall was the Monte Carlo theatre, complete with stage, seating, and balcony with box seats. Taking up the entire second floor of the building, above all the noise, were a dozen bedrooms available to rent by the hour.

"Everything in order, Constable Turner?"

Ben turned to see "Diamond Tooth" Gertie Lovejoy flash him her famous smile.

"Good evening, Miss Lovejoy. You're looking ravishing tonight."

The diamond planted between her front
teeth glittered. "Given the understanding
that you offer that compliment purely out
of the good of your heart and not a desire
for something more carnal, I am flattered."

Just like everyone else, the dance hall girls
had dreams to chase and bills to pay. Many
of them were prostitutes as well as perform-
ers. Some mined for husbands, or at least
benefactors, but there were rare determined
women, like Gertie, who were dancing their
way all the way up the ladder to fame and
fortune.

"Good crowd tonight," she said.

Ben nodded, his eyes always scanning the
crowd. "Quiet day in the fields, so I expect
there won't be much dust thrown around
tonight."

"Except the regulars. Those boys can't
stand to hold on to their money for more
than a few minutes," she said. "Have you
met Sailor Bill yet?"

"Who?"

" 'Sailor Bill' Partridge. Over there by the
mirror, in the navy suit. Sitting with Shorty."

If gossip was a commodity, Diamond
Tooth Gertie was a vein of gold, and every
time Ben came in she tried to impress him

with at least three new pieces of information. Ben was happy to play along. In his
line of work, insider's knowledge could be
extremely helpful.

He squinted through the smoke. "The
gentleman with the girls on either shoulder?"

"That's him. Australian lad. You'll want to
get a good look at his face, because you'll
never see him in that suit again. Legend has
it he never wears the same thing twice, and
I believe it. I know I saw him in something
different earlier today."

"Where's his money from? Here?"

"I heard he made it in gold in Queens-
land. Not sure how he's doing here." Another of the dance hall girls joined Sailor
Bill's party, and Gertie shrugged. "Doesn't
matter, I suppose. He has enough."

"Seems so."

"Do you know that stubby little person
over there?" Gertie casually waved a couple
of manicured fingers towards the corner of
the room, avoiding the vulgarity of a direct
point.

"You'll need to be a little more specific. I
see a bunch of — Oh. That one?"

"Did you know that's a *woman*? They call
her Calamity Jane."

"I've heard of her," he said, but what he'd

heard wasn't all good. Rumour was she'd killed some men. "Didn't know she was here, though."

"Other than that . . ." Gertie trailed off. "The Moose bought another claim."

Ben clicked his tongue. "I'm disappointed. That ain't news."

"Maybe this town isn't as exciting as it used to be." She tapped her fingertips together. "Let's see."

"You work on that, would you?" he teased. "I'll try to come back later."

"You can't say I lost this round! I just need a few more minutes to find something."

"Let's call it a draw."

He went to leave, then stopped, spotting Ralph Stevens at a table near the bar. Ben hadn't spoken to him since he'd let him out of jail the week before, and now the man was leaning back in his chair, his gold watch and chain sparkling blatantly from within the pocket of his gold-threaded waistcoat. A few other well-dressed men were sitting with him, talking and sipping on whisky, and women leaned over them like ravens ogling shiny treasures. Evidently Stevens had forgotten he had a wife at home.

A soft arm brushed against Ben's. "Ooh. There's a nice big lap," Daisy said as she walked by. "Good to see you, Constable Turner."

"Daisy, wait." Ben caught hold of her arm before he could stop himself. She blinked at him in surprise, then circled around and drew a line down his shirt front with one finger.

"Is this the night?" she asked. "You and me?"

"No," he said, gently removing her hand from his chest. "What are you doing, Daisy? You know that Ralph Stevens ain't a nice guy."

She laughed. "There are no nice guys around here, except maybe Mounties. But the Mounties don't want nothing to do with me."

Stevens glanced up, and, seeing them both, he crooked one finger at Daisy.

"Good night, Constable," Daisy said, moving away.

The noise and action of the Monte Carlo vibrated around Ben, but his attention remained on Stevens. The man wasn't breaking any laws by just sitting in a saloon, but Daisy was soft and young and vulnerable, and the thought of Stevens lifting a hand to her set the familiar tingle of rage burning in Ben's knuckles. Tilting his head slightly, Ben summoned the fury that perpetually simmered deep within him and let it rise from his heart to his eyes. *I see you, Stevens. I'm watching.*

Stevens's slow, arrogant smile slid from Ben to Daisy, and Gertie leaned forward. "Big game going on in the back," she purred in his ear.

He turned to her, grateful for the distraction, though he was reluctant to abandon Daisy. When his anger filled him with fire, he needed to either hit something or make himself scarce.

"Who's playing?" he asked.

"Straight Sam, Mousy Wickers, and a few others. I think some are out of money, though."

Voices rose from the back room, so Ben headed over and stood in the doorway, watching the poker game taking place under a cloud of cigar smoke. Six men huddled around the cards, but only three were still playing.

"Don't know what you think you're doing, Wickers," Straight Sam drawled, chewing on the stub of a cigar that hung out the side of his mouth.

"You ought to be more worried about your own cards, Sam," Wickers said, but he was sweating hard, patting the sides of his neck with a tired cloth.

The third player, a young man Ben didn't recognize, feigned a loud, drawn-out yawn. "Y'all had best play or fold afore I fall asleep."

"Who's that?" Ben asked Gertie.

"Maxwell Somers. From Boston, I understand. Handsome devil, ain't he? All I've heard about him so far is that he's in deep," she said. "He needs to win this hand."

Ben eyed the pile in the centre of the table. A variety of gold nuggets were mixed with an impressive number of pokes and a sparkling silver timepiece. "What's the pot?"

"A grand," someone replied. "Could be the last hand. Somers went all in."

Wickers, lips pinched white with anger, finally flipped his cards over and folded.

"I *knew* it!" Somers slapped the table. "Smart move, old man. Sorry I can't say the same for you, Sam."

Sam didn't seem concerned. "Let's see 'em."

At sight of the young man's cards, the crowd around the table let out a cheer, and Ben could see why he'd been so confident: full house, tens over queens.

Sam waited for the noise to die down, then plucked the cigar from his mouth. "Well, that's a pretty hand, boy. Thing is, it just so happens I got a sister to those

293

queens." Somers winced as Sam laid down the queen of hearts, then fanned out his other cards. "And I got the rest of her beautiful family, too."

Royal flush.

The crowd exploded with whoops and applause, but Somers stared in disbelief at the cards.

"I was bettin' you didn't have —"

"I know 'zactly what you was betting," Sam replied, sweeping his winnings into a bag. "Better luck next time." He pushed his chair back and got to his feet, then he touched the brim of his hat and turned to go.

Somers leapt up. "Hold on! You can't just take all our money and go!"

"Why, sure I can."

Without warning, Somers lunged for Sam's collar, slamming the smaller man down on the table, which splintered and fell under their weight. Wickers joined in, holding a sputtering Sam down as Somers let him have it.

Ben watched the fight closely. The Mounties tended to let these tussles go for a bit so the men could blow off steam, but when another man rushed drunkenly towards the scene, chair held over his head like a weapon, Ben knew he had to intervene. He seized the chair-wielding man by his collar.

"If you wanna stay out of jail tonight," he said, "I suggest you put that down and walk away."

The man did as he was told, then Ben turned back to the ruined poker table and grabbed the top man on the pile — Somers. The young man spun around and tried to slug Ben in the face, but Ben was ready, deflecting the blow and twisting Somers's arm behind his back.

"I wouldn't fight it if I were you," Ben said.

Somers ignored him and tried to wriggle out of his grip, so Ben pulled up on his arm. When Somers cried out, the fighting stopped, and Sam got up with a groan, pressing a cloth against his bloody nose.

"Bastard cheated," Somers muttered through gritted teeth. Sweat glistened on his face. "Should be my pot."

"Looked like a fair hand to me," Ben said. "Can't beat a royal flush. That's just the way it goes."

"Ain't right he gets to leave like that. I'm outta money. I need to win it back."

"That's your problem. Sounds like you should have quit a while ago." Ben released his arm, and Somers rubbed his shoulder.

"You don't understand," Somers told him.

"I gotta have that money."

"Maybe get a job," Ben suggested wryly. "Go on home now. I don't want any more trouble tonight."

Ben stood at the door watching Somers slouch outside then turn up his collar against the solid onslaught of rain, his boots slopping through the mud. The storm had picked up since Ben had arrived, and from the looks of it, he thought it might even be strong enough to shut down the parties on the steamships, at least for a while. Maybe the rain would cool Somers's temper, he mused, but then again, the constant wet was getting to all of them.

TWENTY-FIVE:
LIZA

Liza heaved a box of umbrellas on top of a crate, out of the path of the growing puddles underfoot. Her uneven floor had surrendered to all the rain they'd had recently, and she was nervous about the fact that the Yukon River was still rising. Having swallowed every drop of the spring thaw, the water had licked higher and higher, devouring the crumbling banks until it had spilled over the sides. Now that water was making its way to Dawson City.

Liza stared anxiously at her inventory. How on earth was she supposed to outrace the river? Even if she could get all her stock back into crates, where could she put it all? Even if she could find a space, how was she going to get it all there?

Just then the door burst open, and Mr. Somers strode in, dripping wet and looking far less composed than he had the last time she'd seen him. It struck her that since he seemed to know so much, maybe he could help her with moving her things somewhere.

"Good evening, Mr. Somers," she said. "Nice weather for ducks, isn't it?"

"Do you have the rent?" he asked brusquely.

"I do indeed."

She reached into her drawer for the envelope she'd set aside for him. She'd felt like celebrating two days ago when she'd finally made enough profit to afford her rent. As of today, she even had a little left over.

Mr. Somers held out his hand. "I need it right away."

"Of course. Here you go. Mr. Somers, I was wondering if you had any advice . . ." she trailed off as she watched him count the money. His hands were shaking badly.

"I assure you, it's all there," she said, taken aback that he was checking. He'd always been so genial, so informal about their arrangement, before now.

"What about the interest?"

She blinked. "What?"

"You are two weeks late with your rent, Miss Peterson. There is a penalty for that."

She felt her face grow hot. He had never mentioned interest payments before. "Mr. Somers, we agreed that I would pay you the balance of my rent at the end of two weeks and I would pay you monthly after that."

"You misunderstood me. Interest rates are high in Dawson, and property space is at a premium. Our interest rate is fifty-five percent, which means I will require an extra two hundred and twenty dollars immediately."

Her stomach dropped. "I don't have that kind of money."

"Give me whatever you do have."

"Mr. Somers!"

He put out his hand again. What could she do? She put some — though not all — of her profit in his palm, making sure he didn't see what she kept.

Muttering to himself, he counted the rest of the bills, then slammed the counter. "It's not enough!"

Before she could respond, he'd stomped across the floor and begun scanning her shelves. Sweat dribbled from his brow as he rifled through her things, making a mess of her orderly rows of items. Was he in some kind of trouble? Whatever it was, he was making Liza nervous.

"You gotta be hiding something worthwhile in here," he said.

When he swept his arms across a shelf, smashing a row of jam jars to the floor, she rushed forward and grabbed his arm.

"Mr. Somers, stop!" she said, but he shoved her back, intent on his search.

Liza backed away towards the door — this was an entirely different man from the one she'd met on the boardwalk. "Mr. Somers, I must ask you to leave now," she said, in the firmest voice she could muster.

He stormed over to her. "I'm not going anywhere without your rent."

"I paid what we agreed upon. There was no talk of interest, no talk of penalties, and I have paid —"

"What's this?" His hand went to her waist and closed around her father's watch before she could move away. With a snap of his wrist, he jerked it off its chain.

She lunged for the watch, trying to twist it from his grip. "That's mine!"

"Let go!"

"Never!" She would absolutely not give up this fight. She couldn't. The very thought set her blood boiling, and she dug her nails into his arm. "I would rather live in the street than give you this."

He winced but didn't let go of the watch. "Miss Peterson, be reasonable," he said. "I'll take this, then you won't have to worry about rent until next month."

"No! You cannot have this!" she shouted, and slapped him hard across the face before she knew what she was doing.

He staggered back, his cheek a seething red, then lurched forward. Before she could get out of the way, his fist smashed into the side of her head and she dropped to the floor, pinpricks of light spinning in her head. *He* hit *me!* she thought incredulously, touching her face. Through a woozy fog she saw him coming at her again, and she turned, starting to crawl away, but he caught her and heaved her to her feet.

"Stop!" she screamed, trying to push him away, but his arm wrapped around her waist like an iron bar, and he dragged her to the door and threw her outside. She splashed down in the middle of the flooded street, and her head hit the ground hard.

"Live in the street, then!" he yelled, rushing towards her. "Good riddance!"

"Give me my watch!"

She rose unsteadily to her feet, but he slipped his boot behind her knees and shoved her down. She landed flat on her back and clawed for air as the wind was knocked out of her. When she opened her eyes, Somers was standing over her, and she raised her hands over her head, afraid he might strike her again. Then she felt his fingers grip hers. To her horror, she realized he was trying to wrench her mother's ring off her hand.

"Please! Stop!"

She yanked her fist back, but he dropped on top of her, shouting and grasping for the ring.

"Get off! Help! Somebody help!"

"Give it —"

Then the weight of Mr. Somers was gone, his cries drowned out by a writhing, noisy mass of wet fur. *Is that a bear?* she thought, panicking. She was dragging herself backwards through the mud and slop when a flash of red caught her attention. *Thank God!* She almost wept with relief at the sight of two Mounties splashing through the downpour towards the struggle.

"Keitl!" she heard. "Keitl! Get off!"

"Get him off me!" Somers wailed.

"Keitl!"

She recognized that voice: Constable Turner. That meant the beast bathed in mud, she realized with relief, must be Blue. But this dog, growling and snapping at the terrified Max Somers, was not the sweet, tiny puppy Liza had once held against her heart. At the moment, the dog stood almost shoulder-deep in the muddy water, her head hovering low, practically vibrating with the strength of her snarl. No, this wasn't Blue. This was Keitl, and she was a force to be

302

reckoned with.

Constable Turner crouched beside Somers, rainwater streaming off the brim of his Stetson. "You again?" He glanced over at Liza, then back at Somers. "I see you've moved on from starting barroom brawls to beating up women. Classy."

"Miss Peterson?" said another voice. "What are you doing out here?"

She recognized the other Mountie's beard as he came to her side. "Sergeant Thompson?"

"You all right?" he asked.

Liza was shaking so hard she felt frozen in place. "I . . . I can't . . . move," she managed.

"It's all right," he said, kneeling. "Catch your breath. You've had a good scare."

Across from them, Turner had flipped Somers face down in the muck and snapped handcuffs over his wrists. "You're under arrest," he said, yanking Somers to his feet.

"She owes me!" Somers bellowed. "And that dog should be shot."

"I should have locked you up a week ago at the Monte Carlo." Turner shoved him against the wall and poked a commanding finger in his face. "Stay here."

"I got him," Thompson said, moving away.

With Keitl at his side, Turner sloshed

303

towards Liza. "Are you all right, Miss Peterson?"

But Liza barely heard him. Her mind was spinning with terrible thoughts. What would happen to her now? What would she do? Where would she go?

She winced when Turner pressed his fingers gently against her temple. "It's bruised," he said. "Miss Peterson?"

"I . . ." She covered her face with her hands. "Oh, I'm ruined!"

"She's a liar!" Somers yelled, struggling against the cuffs. "I never —"

"Shut your bone box," Thompson grumbled.

"No! No, I didn't mean *that*," Liza quickly corrected herself. Constable Turner's pale blue eyes were taking in every word, and she let them be her anchor. "I'm sorry. It's just . . . he's —" The words began pouring out. "He's my landlord, and I didn't know about the interest, and I didn't have it, so he threw me out, but I need this place, and he took my father's watch, and I —"

Thompson glared at Somers. "You got her father's watch, you pigeon-livered numbskull?"

Somers jerked his chin towards the middle of the road, and Thompson went out and scooped the watch from the mud.

"Nice timepiece," he said, wiping it clean with his thumbs before handing it to Liza.

She clutched the little treasure to her chest. "Thank you."

"Happy to help," he said, then he spoke to Turner. "I'll take our friend to the post, get the paperwork started. Come see me when you're done here."

"I will." Turner got to his feet, then held out a hand to Liza. "Do you feel well enough to stand?"

"A little dizzy," she replied. The weight of the mud and water on her skirt pulled her off balance and she floundered, but Turner was there to steady her.

"I can take you to the hospital," he offered, "get that cheek looked at properly, if you'd like."

She touched her face and grimaced again. "I'll be all right. I can't leave the shop."

"You might have a black eye."

"There isn't much a doctor can do about that."

"True enough. You wanna tell me what happened?" he asked. "Maybe out of the rain?"

Inside the shop, she dropped into the only chair. "Sorry about the mess," she said.

Keitl positioned herself at Liza's feet, but when she licked Liza's fingers, she pulled her hand away. The last thing Liza needed at this point was to get emotional over a dog.

"Keitl," Turner said, and she returned to his side. His gaze swept over the smashed jars, the brooms, and other items tossed aside. "Why don't you start from the beginning?"

It didn't take long to relay the story, and by the time she was done her hands had almost stopped shaking.

"He won't bother you again."

This was where Liza was uncertain. "But that's a problem," she admitted, hoping she wasn't making a mistake by taking him into her confidence. "Without Mr. Somers I don't have a landlord." She held her arms towards the shelves. "What if he makes me leave? How will I get another building? I can't afford to start all over again."

"I actually don't think that's a problem," Turner said. "The thing is, Mr. Somers — if that's his real name — doesn't own this shop."

That stopped her. "What?"

"This place has been empty awhile, but it's not his."

"But how do you know that?"

"Because the owner doesn't live in Dawson. I think he's gone back to Charleston or someplace." Turner took off his hat, scratched behind his ear. "It was leased, but . . . well, I saw the man who leased this place a while back."

Liza was confused. Somers had never mentioned a partner. "Where did you see him?"

"The morgue."

"The morgue?" she echoed, then the pieces began to fall into place. *No contract,* he'd said. Of course there was no contract — he was a swindler! She should have listened to that voice of warning in her head. She would next time, she vowed. If there *was* a next time.

She looked up at Turner. "Where should I go?"

"I would suggest you just stay here, but things being what they are, well, what are your plans for the evacuation?"

"Evacuation? Because of the flood?"

He nodded, then gestured to her things. "I'm guessing this can't be left here."

"No, this is my livelihood. I cannot afford to lose any of it. I've already lost far too much."

His fingers rubbed his jawline thoughtfully, and she wondered if he was going to simply shake his head and tell her that it couldn't be done. She wouldn't blame him if he did. There were thousands of people in this town who needed help, and most of them didn't have a storeful of stuff to move.

"I will be back for you by noon tomorrow," Turner finally said. "Will that give you enough time to pack everything up?"

Relief washed over her. "I will make sure it's done."

"Get some sleep tonight, all right?" He put his hat back on and moved towards the door, Keitl at his heels. "Oh, and not that I think anything might happen, but you'll feel better if you lock the door behind me."

She didn't have to be told twice. As soon as he was outside, she secured the lock and slumped against the door, bathed in a fresh, sticky sweat. She could have been killed today, and nobody would have known she was gone. Other than maybe Constable Turner, she thought, and wasn't that ironic? She kept remembering how she'd lashed out at him, blamed him cruelly, though none of her tragedies had been his fault. And yet he hadn't let her chase him away. He'd come back. And this time he'd saved her life.

She wasn't surprised to discover that he was as good as his word. The next day at noon he returned with a wagon, two horses, and two more pairs of arms to help.

"Good afternoon, Miss Peterson," he said,

regarding her with concern. "How are you feeling?"

"I'll be all right." She'd glanced in the mirror that morning to see the bruise on her face had bloomed. It was ugly, but it could have been much worse, she reminded herself.

"A good day for a move, wouldn't you say?" he asked, a twinkle in his eye. The water in the road reached past the horses' knees, and the mud sucked at their legs. "Even Fort Herchmer, our outpost, is underwater. This morning Inspector Harper had to use a canoe to get to the officers' quarters."

She started to smile, but the movement sent a sharp pain to her temple.

He peered past her shoulder. "All ready to go?"

"I am. How can I help?"

"You don't have to do a thing."

She watched gratefully as the three men set up boards from her doorway to the wagon bed, then one by one carried her things out. When everything was loaded, the struggling horses tried to drag the wagon forward, but the wheels were stuck under the weight of all her crates. One of the men went to the horses' heads and grabbed their bridles while Constable Turner moved to the back of the wagon with the other man.

"On three!" Turner yelled.

When the wagon finally broke free and lurched forward, all three men went with it, falling face first into the muck as the horses sloshed past. Pain shot to Liza's eye as she stifled a laugh, but it felt good to find something funny after so much loss, and when the men scrambled to their feet, looking like clay figures under all the mud, they were laughing, too, their eyes and teeth shining white through the mess. Eventually the wagon rolled out, and Turner returned for Liza, attempting and failing to wipe all the mud from his face before he walked back through her door.

"Ready?"

"Yes, thank you." She turned to grab her coat. "Oh no."

"What is it?"

"I packed my rubber boots in one of those boxes."

They both studied her short black leather boots. "Well, there's an easy solution, but it's up to you." He took off his coat, revealing a relatively clean grey shirt beneath, then held out his arms. "Miss Peterson, you and I are about to get better acquainted."

She eyed the brown water flowing down

the street behind him. "Okay," she said, since there was no other choice, and she took his heavy coat.

He lifted her, cradling her against his chest. "If you wrap your arms around my neck, it'll make it easier to balance."

Heat rushed to her cheeks, but she did as he suggested. "I hope I'm not too heavy."

"Miss Peterson, compared to everything else I lug around this town, I could happily carry you all day long."

They were closer than they ever had been before, and Liza found herself studying him. For the first time, she noticed a faded scar running from under his left eye to the bottom of his ear. She obviously wasn't the only one with hardship in her past. But as strong and commanding as Constable Turner was, his lips looked very soft from this angle. When he returned her gaze, she looked down, but she had a terrible feeling he'd read her mind. She adjusted her hands behind his neck and it struck her that this very scenario felt oddly familiar, as if his arms, wrapped securely around her, had been there before. Bewildered by the sensation, she blinked away the impossible idea and kept quiet as he carried her through the water.

After he'd placed her safely on the wagon

bench and taken a spot beside her, she asked, "Where are we going?"

"To see a friend of mine," he replied.

Liza spared one last look at her store, resigned. The place likely wouldn't survive the rising flood, but at least she'd saved her things, so she could begin again. When that might be she had no idea.

"Thank you, Constable. I don't know what I would have done without you."

He turned to face her, and instead of a smile, she saw apology in his eyes. "I'm just glad I could do something this time."

TWENTY-SIX:
BEN

As Ben turned down Princess Street and headed towards the Fairview Hotel, Miss Peterson gave out a cry beside him.

"I can't stay in a hotel! Especially not this one!"

"You'd rather stay in a tent?"

"If I knew my things were safe, then yes. A tent would be fine," she insisted. "There's no way I can afford a hotel room, and there's even less of a chance I can afford rent for my things. Please, I really would prefer a tent."

"I think you'll like this better." He reined in the horses, then hopped down from the wagon. "Just wait here a minute."

"Oh, really, Constable Turner." She put a hand over her black eye, as if to hide it. "This is not the place for me. This is —"

"I'll be right back," he said.

All last night, Ben had thought about how he could best help Miss Peterson. There was no way he could ever make up for all the ways he'd let her down, but fate had given him a chance to do some good, and he knew just the person to enlist in his plan. Belinda Mulrooney, the owner of the Fairview Hotel, was a shrewd business person, but Ben knew she also had a generous soul. Right now, Ben was counting on that part of her personality.

He knocked on the side door of the Fairview, and within a few seconds it swung open, bringing Ben face to face with the wealthiest woman in the Klondike. Belinda studied Ben through a pair of thick spectacles while Nero — who Ben thought might possibly be the biggest dog in the world — stood panting at her side.

"May I help you?"

"Hey, Belinda," he said.

Her jaw dropped. "Ben! Why, I hardly recognized you through all that mud. You must have been helping to clear people out downtown. Come in, come in! Let's clean you up a bit."

When Ben had first come to Dawson, he'd been called to Belinda's glamorous hotel to help her with a guest who refused to pay his bill. Then a few months ago, he and Thompson had put a stop to a party that had gotten out of control there, rescuing Belinda from thousands of dollars' worth of damage. A week or so after that, he'd done an emergency patch on her roof after her guests were surprised by a complimentary shower during their supper. Since then, he and Belinda had been friends, and she encouraged him to make himself comfortable in her hotel.

"Actually, I've come to ask a favour," he said, hoping his smile would win her over. Yes, they were friends, but everyone knew that here in Dawson City everything was a business transaction. Even favours.

"Of course, Ben. You have only to ask. You know I can never resist a handsome policeman."

"We got a lot of folks settled," he said, "but there's a young woman in the wagon behind me who is in need of a place to stay."

Belinda's eyes went to Miss Peterson. "I see. I'm sure I can arrange —"

"She doesn't have enough money for one of your rooms, Belinda."

He rubbed the side of his neck and mud peeled off in chunks. Then, as calmly as he could, he explained what had happened the night before between Miss Peterson and Somers. Even now, the thought of that man hitting her made his blood boil.

"She's alone out here. Her brother, her

parents, and her friend all perished on the trail. But she's tough, and she's smart. She figured out how to run a profitable business even in a lousy location. But the truth is she's coming in from behind and it's hard for her to get ahead." He took a breath and played a little to Belinda's ego. "I know it's a lot to ask, but she needs a place to stay, and I also thought she might learn a lot from someone like you. With the business, I mean."

Belinda's expression softened. "Bring her in, Ben."

He couldn't help smiling as he returned to the wagon, but Miss Peterson did not share his happiness.

"I don't think this is appropriate. I can't afford —"

"Do you trust me?" he asked, wanting her to say yes despite everything.

After a long moment, she nodded.

"Good. Come with me."

Belinda was waiting at the door. "Welcome!"

"I present Miss Liza Peterson," Ben said. "Miss Peterson, this is Miss Belinda Mulrooney, the owner of this fine establishment and a friend of mine."

"It's an honour to meet you," Miss Peterson said timidly, extending a hand.

Belinda shook her hand, then hung on, pulling her inside. "Come in! Come in, dear! Don't worry about those boots. I'll just —" She turned, called out for someone who came running with towels. "Nero! Get out of the way, dog. Yes, yes, I know you must smell everyone, but do let them in first, please."

Ben noticed Miss Peterson edging close to the wall, away from the mayhem, and remembered how intimidated he'd felt his first time in the hotel. He'd been reluctant to tread on the plush Persian carpets or touch the smooth mahogany furniture, and he'd stood off to the side, beneath the crystal chandeliers, admiring the gilded frames lining the walls and the oil renderings of nude women within them from a safe distance.

Belinda must have seen her concern as well. "Miss Peterson," she said kindly, "I understand your reluctance, but Constable Turner has brought you to the right place. You are safe here, and I will personally see to the storage of your goods until such time as you are ready to resituate."

"I'm very grateful for your kindness," Miss Peterson said softly.

"It's my pleasure," Belinda said. "Now, shall we get you two cleaned up?"

"Thank you," Ben replied, "but I have things to do, and I'll wash up at Herchmer when I can."

"Of course. Would you care to join us for supper this evening?"

"I'd love to." The prospect of a fine meal at the hotel made the thought of going back out in the rain a little easier to take.

"Excellent." Belinda turned, hearing her name called from within, then said, "Wait here a minute, would you? I shall be right back."

When she was gone, Ben faced Miss Peterson. "I would not leave you with anyone but Miss Mulrooney. Truly. She has nothing to gain by abusing your trust."

She nodded, but he could tell from her expression that she was still apprehensive. She had every right to be after her misplaced trust in Somers, but he knew Belinda would win her over.

"There's one more thing," he said. "I'll be right back." He dashed out to the wagon and returned with an envelope, which he handed to her. "Sergeant Thompson got all your money back from Somers."

For the first time he saw a glimmer of hope in her eyes. "I don't know how to thank you," she said. "This is all I have left, besides my stock."

"I'll be sure to pass your thanks along to Sergeant Thompson." He hesitated. "And Miss Peterson, I hope you don't mind my saying so, but I'd say you have a whole lot more than that money and your stock."

"What do you mean?" she asked.

It had come to him last night in his sleep. Instead of his usual nightmares, he'd dreamed of the first time they'd met.

"You've got a toughness in you, Miss Peterson."

She looked away, but he kept talking, thinking it would do her some good to remember her own strength.

"I noticed it way back when we met at the summit," he insisted. "And in my experience sometimes that's even more important than money. You've come out on top after everything that's happened to you. I got a feeling that if you hang on to that, you'll do just fine. And if you accept a little help from your friends, you might just do better than fine."

She sucked in her cheeks as if she was trying not to cry. "Thank you, Constable. I hope you're right."

She still sounded uncertain, but he detected a touch of resolve in her voice. *Hang on to that grit and I'll be there to help,* he thought.

Belinda returned then, and he turned to go, tipping his hat to them both before heading out into the wet streets.

Twenty-Seven:
Liza

Liza dipped her fingers into the bath to test the temperature — steaming hot — then she climbed in and shivered with bliss as the heat eased the stiffness in her bones. It had been months since she'd had a real bath. Taking a deep breath, she slipped all the way under and delighted in the silent feeling of being completely submerged. When she resurfaced, she took the cake of soap from the ledge and scrubbed her skin and hair as hard as she could, as if she could scrape away all the tragedies of the past few months.

Once she'd finished, Liza stepped out of the tub, wrapped herself in the luxurious fluffy towel, and went to the mirror — where she stopped and stared. She leaned in, hardly believing it was her own reflection looking back at her. It wasn't just the bruise that circled her eye, either. This Liza was all angles. Her face had lost its soft edges, her jaw and the ridge of her collarbone were sharp and defined, and lines had gathered at the corners of her eyes from squinting through the wind. Despite the wondrous gift of the bath, she had not been able to clear away the dark rings of exhaustion beneath them. The woman looking back at her was not strong, Liza saw. This woman had lost heart.

But her body told a different story. As she brushed and braided her hair, Liza noticed a new outline of muscle flexing in her arms. Her back and her legs were similarly defined. Was that what Constable Turner had meant when he'd said she was tough? she wondered, slipping into the clean, emerald-green dress Miss Mulrooney's maid had laid out for her.

She was just fastening the last button when the same maid called her for dinner, and when Liza stepped into the corridor she felt like a new person. At the entrance to the dining room, she paused, astonished by the spectacle before her. The room was warm with conversation and laughter, the sterling silver place settings and crystal chandeliers sparkled like stars, and the delicious aroma of roast beef hung in the air.

"It's something, isn't it?" Miss Mulrooney said, coming in beside her.

"It really is," Liza breathed.

As Liza and Miss Mulrooney settled in at their table, Constable Turner appeared in the doorway, though at first Liza didn't recognize him. He was out of uniform, having traded in his serge for a black coat, his dark hair was swept back, and he had shaved off the short beard she'd seen on him earlier that day. He stood with his hands behind his back, surveying the room until his eyes met hers, then he approached the table.

"Good evening, ladies," he said. "I apologize for being late."

"We only just arrived ourselves," Miss Mulrooney assured him. "Have you seen our lovely Miss Peterson? I swear she is reborn after this afternoon's luxuries."

"You're looking much better," Turner said, then quickly added, "Not to say you weren't lovely before, it's just that —"

"You're very kind," she said, flushing under his gaze. "And you too, Miss Mulrooney. Both of you have been so generous."

"Please, I insist that you call me Belinda."

"Only if you'll call me Liza. You too, Constable Turner."

"It's Ben," he said, looking pleased.

"Wonderful," Belinda said. She held up a wine glass, but when the waiter arrived Ben

323

laid a hand over his.

"Just water for me, please."

"You don't drink?" Liza asked as the waiter poured.

"Very rarely. It's part of the job."

"Poor Constable Ben," Belinda teased. "Well, you and I can still toast the evening, can't we, Liza? To new friends."

Liza lifted her glass, thinking how long it had been since she'd held the slender stem of a crystal glass between her fingertips, then she took a sip. "Oh, that's delicious."

"I'm glad you like it," Belinda said as another waiter appeared, a young boy trailing behind him. "I hope you don't mind, but I ordered ahead for us."

Liza felt tears gather in her eyes as the waiter served each of them a plate of decadent oysters on the half shell. Right behind him, the boy set down their two-pronged oyster forks and filled their glasses with water.

"What is it?" Belinda asked. "Is there something wrong?"

"No, nothing's wrong." She managed a laugh. "I feel like I'm in a dream. The fanciest food I've had in months is tinned meat and potatoes. I had almost forgotten that such luxuries still existed."

"You must miss Vancouver," Ben said softly.

She nodded, swallowing the lump in her throat. "I do, but I'm thankful to have made it here. A lot of people can't say that."

"How long have you been in Dawson City?" Belinda asked.

"About a month. The journey to get here took much, much longer, of course." Liza brought an oyster to her lips, then closed her eyes, savouring the smooth taste of the sea. Just enough lemon juice, she thought. Her mother would have loved it.

"Oh, I do know about that," Belinda assured her, tossing back an oyster as if it was as common as a glass of water.

"Belinda got here a year ago," Ben explained. "She was on her own, too."

"I had barely a cent to my name when I arrived, you know."

"Really?" Considering all this extravagance, Liza had assumed Belinda had arrived wealthy. "I hope you don't think me rude, but how did all this happen? You didn't strike gold, did you?"

Belinda took a sip of her wine. "In a way, I suppose. But I have always been more of an entrepreneur than a labourer . . ." She trailed off, looking at Ben, who was studying his plate with concern. "Is this your first oyster?"

He nodded, holding one up. Liza couldn't help smiling at how his expression softened from caution to interest as he chewed.

He leaned in to fish for his next one, then seemed to remember what they had been speaking about. "Tell Liza about the World's Fair in Chicago, Belinda."

"You were there?" Liza asked. "My brother read all about it in the newspaper. It sounded spectacular."

"Oh, it certainly was. I saw and heard everything," Belinda said. "But I wasn't there as a guest. I ran a sandwich bar there, then an ice cream parlour in San Francisco. When that burned down, I took a job as a stewardess for a steamship company, making extra money by selling furs in various ports." She smiled. "Once you start making money, it becomes quite addictive."

The waiters came by again, topping their glasses and replacing their empty plates with steaming salmon smothered in hollandaise sauce, with green peas and a lettuce salad on the side. Beside her, Ben dove into his plate with gusto, but Liza took a small bite, enjoying the rich flavours. Even in Vancouver, a meal this extravagant was a rarity for Liza — how had Belinda brought such class to the Yukon?

"How did you come to be way up here?" she asked.

"To a girl like me, the word 'gold' is an invitation." Belinda tilted her head. "I thought about what people might like up here and what they might be missing, then I spent all my money buying up those things and bringing them here to sell."

Liza sat a little straighter, thinking of her jewellery cache and the brooms. It gave her a thrill to hear she was on the same track as Belinda. "Like what?"

"Oh, it feels like so long ago! Let's see. Silk underwear was popular. Oh, and hot water bottles. People really did want things like that. I made a killing — enough to open a little restaurant, which did well enough, but that made me think about what might do better." She tapped her finger earnestly on the table. "You know who needs to eat? Miners. And unless they are planning a night on the town, they rarely want to leave their claims. So I built a roadhouse out there — a big, two-storey roadhouse at the junction of the Bonanza and El Dorado creeks. Called it —" She held her hands up as if she were framing a sign on a wall. " 'The Grand Forks Hotel and Restaurant.' Miners came from all around when they'd had enough of living in tents."

"That's where Nero's from, right?" Ben asked. He was leaning back in his seat, his plate scraped clean.

Liza blinked. "Who?"

"Her massive dog."

"Yes! A miner gave dear Nero to me because he couldn't keep him while he was working. He said that at the end of the season we'd see which one of us the dog chose. Well, since you've seen him, you know that dog has more refined tastes than the miner could offer."

Liza laughed along with them, but more out of politeness than joy. Nero's story reminded her of little Blue, and that was a whole other problem. Clearly Ben had no idea his dog used to be hers. How would he? What he would do if she told him?

As if he'd felt her gaze, Ben glanced at Liza, and she looked away, embarrassed.

"I'll tell you one of the secrets I learned when I was running The Grand Forks," Belinda was saying.

"Oh?"

"Never close your eyes."

"Because of thieves?" Liza asked.

"No, though that can be a problem. What I mean is that when you are in our business, you need to quite literally keep your eyes open for opportunities no one else sees.

What I saw at The Grand Forks wasn't just the money coming in. I saw how the dust on the floor glittered! Gold was practically falling out of the miners' pockets and rolling off their clothes, then it was being swept into the trash. Can you imagine?" She threw her head back, remembering. "So I had the floor sweepings passed through a sluice every night. I netted almost a hundred dollars every night!"

Liza's jaw dropped. The story was like a fairy tale. "Did you buy any claims with that?"

"Of course. Five. When the miners came to eat, I heard all the scuttlebutt, and I knew where to buy."

"You never actually worked a mine, did you?" Ben asked.

"No, but I managed them. My father was a miner, so I knew all about it, but the truth is that it looks better if a man is running a mine. Besides, why would I want to do all that dirty work?"

With every word Liza became more of an admirer. Belinda was everything she wanted to be. "You have an amazing story."

Memory and wine had softened Belinda's expression. "So much has happened since I arrived here in Dawson with no money at all. In fact, the first thing I did when I got here was toss my last twenty-five-cent piece into the river for good luck. Best investment I ever made."

She signalled the waiters once more for dessert, and they brought preserved pears and cheese, as well as a plate of bonbons. Liza hadn't eaten anything as magical as candy in so long, and though she longed to scoop one up, she reminded herself that a lady must always mind her manners. Ben had no such reservations. He claimed one right away, popping it nonchalantly into his mouth.

Liza stifled a laugh.

"Men have a different set of rules, don't they?" Belinda said.

Ben's cheeks reddened in the most charming way. "Sorry. The rest are for you."

"No, no, go ahead. We need to keep our Mounties well-fed and happy, don't we?" She turned to Liza. "Your turn, Liza. Tell me your story."

"I'm from Vancouver," she said, "and I learned the business from watching my father. You would have liked him, Belinda. He was quite innovative in his own way, and I think you would have approved of his choice in stock. I hope you'll see it all when I can finally put everything back on shelves. Then you can judge for yourself."

"You enjoy working in a store?"

"I do. I've done it all my life. My father built me a special stool when I was too little to reach the counter so I could speak with customers." She could still recall his expression back then, proud as could be. "He was the one who wanted to come here. He knew it would be like nothing we'd ever seen before, and he was right about that." She dropped her chin. "I think one of the worst things about everything that happened was that he never got to see this place. Really, this was his dream, not mine."

Belinda reached over and put her hand over Liza's. "He's here with you," she said softly.

"I bet you'll make him proud," Ben said.

"Thank you," she said, blinking hard.

After a moment, Belinda spoke. "Liza, I have a thought I'd like to pass by you. I know we've only just met, but I like what I see. And I trust Ben's high opinion of you."

Liza felt her cheeks grow hot, but no one seemed to notice.

"I imagine your poor little shop is drowning as we enjoy our dessert," Belinda continued. "As you think about what you'd like to do next, would you be interested in working for me? I have opened a store myself recently and I'm in need of an experienced manager. It's nearby, only a couple of blocks down from the hotel."

Liza couldn't believe what she was hearing. "You are offering me a job?"

"I have a couple of girls working in there, but they are hardly experienced. To be honest, I view our meeting today as serendipitous, and I would consider it a favour if you would accept the position. Also, since you and your stock will need a place to stay during this time, you are welcome to stay in the hotel for a reduced rate until you get back on your feet."

It might not be running her own store, but Belinda was presenting her with a wonderful opportunity. A second chance. The trouble was, the last time someone had offered her a great deal, things had gone terribly wrong. She was still uneasy after Mr. Somers's deception.

"Belinda, I wish I could accept that invitation, but I am not sure I can afford even the reduced rate at this point. Perhaps I could rent storage space from you and find a less lavish place to stay."

Belinda waved a hand, dismissing her concerns. "Oh, don't worry about that. You'll be an employee of mine, which means you will be able to afford it."

"You'd be wise to accept the offer," Ben

said, setting his napkin by his plate as the busboy slid in for a final collection. "No one is a better employer than Belinda."

Liza hesitated. On one hand, she had absolutely no question that she wanted this. Belinda could teach her so much — things even her father hadn't known, perhaps. She would be an absolute fool to say no. But on the other hand . . .

"I really do hate to ask," she said, "but do you think we might sign some sort of contract? Ben told you about the episode in the street with my former landlord, and that was all based on a lack of signatures —"

"And the fact that your landlord was a con," Ben put in.

Belinda beamed. "I *love* that you asked for a contract, my dear. Yes, yes. Let's make it official. I shall have it all written up and brought to your room tonight. Does that mean you are taking the job?"

Liza took a deep, fortifying breath. For so long she'd come up against nothing but obstacles, and in the last few hours she'd begun to hope that her life might be turning around.

"Yes," she said. "Belinda, I will do my very best not to disappoint you."

"Well, this is something to celebrate." Ben raised his freshly filled water glass in salute.

"I almost wish I could have a little champagne."

"We wouldn't tell," Belinda said, but he only laughed.

"Thank you for a fun evening," he said. "And the best meal I've ever had."

"Oh yes. Me too," Liza said. "A wonderful evening of delicious food and even better company. And your young busboys did a wonderful job. I barely noticed them all night."

"They're good boys and good at their job," Belinda agreed. "My hope is that their training here will mean they will be able to acquire increasingly better jobs when all this is over."

"All this?" Liza echoed.

"The gold rush. It won't last forever, and then we'll all need to make new plans."

Liza had only just arrived here. The thought that the gold rush might be over sooner rather than later sent a shiver of alarm up her neck. "How long will it last, do you think?"

"No one knows that, but take my word for it: a new gold strike will happen within the next year, maybe sooner. The miners will abandon this one for that, and whoever is left in this town will follow them. Miners are fickle. But then again, so are we. We must all follow opportunities."

"It's good of you to teach the boys," Ben said. "Prepare them."

"I do what I can," she replied. A waiter approached Belinda and whispered in her ear. "I'm so sorry, but I'm going to have to leave you. I hope to see you both very soon."

Then it was just the two of them. Despite the comfortable conversation they'd shared over the meal, the silence that fell over Liza and Ben felt slightly awkward. All their shared memories were wrought with pain and heartache, and while Liza wanted badly to apologize for how she'd treated him before, maybe even explain about Blue, she didn't feel like opening those wounds again. She just wanted to move forward.

"I really don't know how to thank you for today," she said finally. "For bringing me here and introducing me to Belinda. I feel as if I have a new lease on life."

"You deserve it. You had a rocky start, that's all."

An idea sparked in her mind. "Would you mind walking me to the river?" she asked suddenly. "I mean to a spot that's not flooded."

"Now?"

She nodded. "I have something I want to do. It will only take a minute."

"Of course."

"Wait here. I'll be right back." She ran up to her room for her purse, then met him at the door.

Ben didn't ask any questions as they walked to the banks of the Yukon River. For a few minutes, they stood quietly watching the nut-brown water flow by, and when she was ready Liza dug in her bag. She produced her last twenty-five cents, took a deep breath for courage, then offered it to the river. It had worked for Belinda. Maybe it would work for her.

Twenty-Eight:
Ben

Despite the flood and the damage it had caused, investors, government folks, and, inevitably, con artists, arrived in Dawson City on a daily basis, and it seemed to Ben that there was a new energy in the town. The men were stirred up, and he found himself stepping in on more brawls as well as following up on more reports of gun smuggling. There was no mistaking that the Mounties needed more men in Dawson — Ben just wished they had found someone other than Constable Bob Miller.

"You two gotta put your differences behind you," Thompson said the day Miller arrived. "We're here to do a job, not make trouble. Keep that in mind."

At least for now, Miller seemed too pleased with the change of pace to start anything with Ben.

"My transfer has been a long time coming, that's for sure," he said. "You remember those nights at Chilkoot when all you could hear was your heartbeat?"

Ben did, and sometimes he missed that silence badly. For him, finding absolute stillness and peace in the wildest of lands had been a kind of magic.

"Well, I got to the point where I didn't even want to hear that heartbeat anymore. And this place . . ." Miller threw up his hands, grinning. "Wow. It's better than I thought it'd be. There's so much going on here! I hardly know where to begin." He chuckled. "Actually, I do. Went and got myself a half claim this morning. I'm gonna make a fortune."

"You said before that you were planning to do that," Ben said, half-wondering where Miller had gotten the cash for the investment. He'd been thinking of buying his own for a while, but there was no way he could afford it yet.

"Took out a loan to get started."

There were plenty of places to get loans around Dawson, some more trustworthy than others. Ben was about to say as much to Miller, but then he reminded himself that Miller's gold claim wasn't his business. The man could figure out the town's inner workings on his own.

And he did, in short order. With Miller's

chatty nature, it didn't take him more than a month to acquaint himself with the town and get to know the key players. During that time, Ben could see he'd be less than helpful as far as maintaining the law went. The man spent more time in the saloons and on the goldfields than he did on patrol, and some of the men he hung around with weren't exactly model citizens.

"It might be all right," Thompson said to Ben one night as they left the outpost. "He might get inside information since he's so close to it. We'll keep an eye on him just in case."

"He's gotta be good for something," Ben allowed, reaching down to pet Keitl. "I'm heading to the Monte Carlo. Join me?"

"Can't. Got a tip about Stevens. I'm heading out to see what the ol' boy's up to."

In a way, Ben wished he could skip his rounds and join him. Ralph Stevens's name kept popping up in their enquiries about the recent increase of handguns around Dawson, and Ben suspected that he still mistreated his wife, but he had no proof. He wanted nothing more than to see that man behind bars.

"Why don't you take Miller?" Thompson suggested.

Ben gave him a sour look.

"Do it. Make him earn his pay."

Inside the Fort, Ben found Miller lying on his bunk, studying the insides of his eyelids.

"Let's go," he said.

Miller cracked open one eye. "Where are you working?"

"The regular spots: saloons, dance halls, you know."

"I'm coming." Miller swung his legs over the side of his bed, pulled on his boots, then reached for his coat and hat. "I'm bored in here. Besides, seems like a nice, warm night."

"And maybe you'd like to do some work for a change," Ben muttered, then he remembered Thompson's advice. As they stepped outside, he put in an effort to start up a conversation. "How's the claim coming?"

Miller screwed up his face. "Nothing yet. I'm panning a lot of the dirt from the last fellow, and he left me his sluice, which I share with a couple of others, but so far I'm getting nothing but rock and more rock." He glowered. "If I find out he sold me a bum claim —"

"What? You gonna go hunt him down? If he duped you, you're out of luck. Nothing you can do about it."

"That's true enough. But I have to pay off

my debt, so I can't quit."

"Where'd you get your loan from?"

Miller snorted. "Wouldn't you like to know? I know you're watchin' me, Turner. Trying to find an excuse to write me up."

Maybe he was. He glanced down at Keitl, trotting at his heels. "I was just asking."

"Did you get your claim?"

"Not yet. I'm figuring out some things." He glanced sideways at Miller. "Don't wanna get duped."

"We all do things our own way, don't we, Turner?"

They continued in a tense silence. From a distance they could see Front Street was crowded and a tussle was going on outside the Dominion, but by the time Ben and Miller walked by, it was dying down. Seeing the Mounties' red coats always took some of the bluster out of the men, which was why Steele insisted the coats be worn at all times when they were on duty — though on a warm night like tonight Ben envied the local men with their loose shirts and trousers. Still, the coats worked: a lot of problems were solved with a simple warning, and any serious fighting and minor misdemeanours were punished by sending the men to the woodpile. Occasionally there were worse infractions, like thieving or possessing a firearm, and those offenders received a "Blue Ticket": a one-way ticket out of the Yukon.

As they crossed the road, Ben spotted Liza down the other street, closing up the store for the night.

"I'll meet you at the Red Feather Saloon," he told Miller, turning towards the shop.

Miller saw where he was looking and grinned. "I'll come with you," he offered. "That there's a woman I'd happily visit any time, though I'd prefer later on in the evenings, if you know what I mean."

Ben put a hand against Miller's chest, resisting the urge to shove him back. "I said I was going. I'll meet you at the saloon."

"Well, now."

"There's no 'well, now.' She's a friend of mine, and I'm checking on her."

"I see." He lifted an eyebrow. "I think I'd like to be her friend too."

"She ain't your type."

"Hello, Constable Turner!" Liza called from her doorway. "Can I speak with you a moment?"

Ben gave Miller a satisfied smile, then called back, "I'll be right over!"

Miller looked impressed. "I reckon I'll meet you at the Red Feather."

"Good idea."

342

As Ben headed towards the store he glanced back at Miller, a sinking feeling in his gut. Maybe he shouldn't have been so insistent. Miller always wanted what he didn't have, and the last thing Ben needed was for Miller to start pestering Liza.

When he reached the walkway that led to the shop, he remembered Liza's earlier reaction to the dog and told Keitl to stay. As always, she did exactly as he'd said, though her bright eyes followed him.

"Hi, Ben," Liza said, coming down the steps. "Hello, Keitl."

Keitl jumped to her feet but didn't leave her spot.

"Do you think I could pet her?" Liza asked.

"Uh, sure," Ben said. "Come here, Keitl."

Keitl trotted over and stood quietly in front of Liza, her tail sweeping from side to side.

"She's so pretty," Liza said softly, scratching behind the dog's ears.

Ben rubbed the back of his own head, puzzled. "She is. I'm glad you think so, but I gotta say, you had me fooled about that."

"Really? Why?"

"You seem to get upset whenever she's around."

"Oh." She sighed and crouched in front

of the dog. "It's not that I don't like her. She just reminds me of things I'd rather not think about." She rubbed Keitl's neck, and the dog gave Liza a gentle lick. "You know what I'm talking about, don't you, Keitl?"

Ben watched as Liza pressed her forehead against the dog's. "What am I missing?" he asked.

Liza stood and took a deep breath. "The thing is, she used to be mine."

"Keitl? She's been with me since she was a pup."

"Where'd you get her?"

"I found her at Sheep Camp." He waited for more, but she just stared pointedly at him, a reluctant smile on her face. Then it hit him like a punch. "After the avalanche," he said slowly, heat rising up his neck. "Liza, I am so sorry. I had no idea."

"You couldn't have known." She looked down at Keitl, sitting at their feet. "Until that day I saw her at the White Horse Rapids, I'd given up on her. I'd assumed she was killed by the avalanche." She sighed. "I'll be honest, I was so lost after Stan died that I barely looked for her. You saved her life by taking her."

No wonder she'd been upset with him at the rapids. "Why didn't you say anything?" he asked cautiously.

"I should have, but it never seemed like the right time." Liza scratched the top of Keitl's head. "I called her Blue because of the sky the day she was born. It was clear and sunny for the first time in so long, and I'd been so unhappy in Dyea. I guess she kind of symbolized hope for me."

He nodded, remembering when he'd found the little dog. He'd felt the same way about her. After all the misery and loss, she'd been like a light at the end of a tunnel.

"You can come visit her any time. I know she'd love to see you," he said, but the offer hardly seemed like enough. "You know, if there's anything you ever need, Liza, all you gotta do is ask."

The corners of her mouth twitched. "Has there ever been a time when you didn't offer to help someone?"

Miller came to mind. "Uh, yeah."

Her laugh was as sweet as honey. "Well, not around me. You've always tried to help me."

The smile faded from his lips. "I'm afraid I wasn't very successful. I'm sorry I couldn't save your brother. I —"

He wanted to tell her how her cries still haunted him when he slept, how the knowledge that men had died under his watch would never leave him alone. Every part of him wished he could go back in time so he could dig until her brother emerged, healthy and whole.

But she surprised him. She reached for his hand and took it between both of hers. Her fingers were cool and soft, but the way she cupped them around his much larger hand felt strangely reassuring.

"Thank you, Ben," she said.

"Liza —"

"No. No. Let me say this, please. I need to thank you for doing all you could that day. I know how hard you worked, and I know you didn't want to leave us. I was cruel to you." She bit her lip. "I blamed you for all my grief, for my family, for George, and even for Blue. And none of it was your fault."

A strange, almost panicked sensation swept over Ben at her words. No one had ever spoken that way to him, as if it mattered what he thought or how he felt.

"It's been months," Liza said, talking almost to herself, "but I still can't get them out of my mind. I try to bury them, let them go in peace, and for a while I feel almost normal. But when I see Keitl, and when I see you . . . it's like you're a tremor in the earth, and you bring them back to the surface so I have to face them again." She swallowed. "And that's when I remember how alone I am."

He hated to see her suffer. Ben knew how to stop a fight, how to disarm a man, how to keep a great many things under control, but how could he ease her heartache? He turned his hand over so he was holding hers. "The truth is we're *all* alone up here. The reason the saloons and the dining halls and the shops are so busy is that everyone's trying not to get too lonely. But Liza, you're not really on your own. You have Belinda. And Keitl." He looked into her eyes, and for the first time in his life he realized he wasn't alone, either. "I'm here too."

Liza opened her mouth to say something, but a loud *crack!* sounded, followed by a scream. Keitl took off like lightning.

"What was that?" Liza cried.

"Gunshot. Gotta go," Ben said, turning towards the noise.

"Be safe!" he heard her call as he ran.

There were at least eighty saloons in Dawson City, so Ben ran to the thick of them. A small crowd gathering outside the Red Feather Saloon caught his eye, and he edged through to see what was attracting their attention. His heart dropped at the sight of a body lying in the street, and as he got closer he saw there wasn't much left of the man's head. Where was Miller? he wondered, stooping to pick up the still-hot Colt .45 lying next to the body. He slid the gun into the back of his waistband. Another illegal handgun to investigate.

"Anybody see anything?" Ben asked the onlookers.

"Thomas never did know when to walk away from the wheel," said a short, bald man, staring down at the deceased. "Shame. Nice enough fella."

"You knew him?"

"Yeah. Thomas Wiedemann. From Missouri, I think he said." The man lifted his hat, scratched his head. "I never seen nothing like what he did in there just now. He just kept putting down thousand-dollar bills on red. Ten times he did that. And ten times black came up. After that he told the bartender he was broke, threw back a whisky, then came out here and did this."

"Where'd he get the pistol?"

The man's hands plunged into his pockets, and he looked away. "Don't know 'bout that."

Ben scouted for anyone whose face might tell a different story, but he didn't see a guilty expression in the whole crowd. But there was Miller hurrying towards him.

"Where you been?" Ben demanded.

Miller ignored him, just stopped by the body, hands on his hips. "Is it true?" he asked. "Is that Thomas Wiedemann?"

"It was."

Miller snorted with disgust, then turned away. "Man owed me a hundred dollars."

Twenty-Nine:
Liza

Ever since Belinda had mentioned that the Klondike Gold Rush might not last that long, Liza had kept her eyes open for opportunities, just as Belinda had advised. After working in the store for a few weeks, Liza had started to see how some of her stock might make a nice addition to Belinda's. After all, it was just sitting in storage. Belinda agreed, and over a cup of tea they negotiated the percentage of profits she would take from the sale of Liza's merchandise.

The venture filled Liza with a kind of energy she hadn't felt in a long time. This morning she was up early, sifting through her boxes in the storage room, trying to decide what to bring to the store, when Belinda suddenly rushed in. Liza had never seen her so upset.

"Belinda, what's the matter?"

"Oh, Liza, you must come with me." She

caught her hand, waving off her boxes. "Never mind those. Someone broke into the shop last night!"

Liza caught her breath. "What?"

"Sergeant Thompson was just here," she explained as they hurried out the door and down the street. "Apparently a man happened by the store about an hour ago, and he heard so much noise he knew something was going on. He didn't dare look, just ran to the Fort and got the police. They caught the bastards before they could steal anything."

"Thank God," Liza said. She'd been imagining their shelves emptied of everything, all their hard work for nothing, but as they got close her relief turned to dread. The beautiful plate-glass window had been smashed to pieces. Nothing was left but ugly jagged shards sticking out of the frame.

"Watch your step," Thompson warned them at the entrance, taking Belinda's arm.

Liza almost cried at the destruction, and she saw the same horror on Belinda's face. It looked like a giant had picked up the store and turned it upside down, then stepped on every item they could find. The thieves might not have taken anything, but they'd ruined most of the stock. It would take days to go over the inventory lists, weeks to replace everything.

Liza felt a tear roll down her cheek and she quickly wiped it away. She knew it was only a store, but it had become Liza's place in a way, and that made the attack feel personal. As if she were cursed. Every time things seemed to improve, something bad happened.

Belinda wandered over, broken glass crunching under her boots. "I have to get back to the hotel," she was muttering, lips tight. "Oh, I'm so angry I could —"

"Leave this to me, Belinda," Liza said firmly. "If anything comes up, I will let you know right away."

"You are a blessing." Her eyes went to the men at the front. "Tell them when they're done to come for a good breakfast, would you?"

"Of course."

Belinda hurried off, and Liza picked her way cautiously across the room, searching for anything salvageable. One of her favourite wool coats lay bunched up on the floor, the right sleeve almost entirely torn off. She was relieved to see that it was only a ripped seam — she could fix that easily — but the slivers of glass embedded in the material would be hard to get rid of. After hanging up the coat, she discovered a box of candles just beyond, lying beneath a can of turpentine. Fortunately, the can hadn't been opened, and at least six of the ten candles were still all right. She carried the items over to the counter — the only table had been broken — where half a dozen tobacco tins had been emptied, and the tiny shreds of dried leaves had been purposefully spilled in a pile. Why on earth would anyone have done something like this?

After she had gathered the unbroken and repairable items on the counter — including a shockingly intact Tiffany lamp — she grabbed a broom from the back and spent the next half hour sweeping. She was just starting the inventory when Ben walked through the door and went directly to Sergeant Thompson.

"They're feeling more than a little foolish now that the drink's wearing off," she heard him say.

"Constable Turner," she said, approaching the Mounties.

"Miss Peterson," he said, sounding equally official. "Are you all right?"

"Just a little shaken, I suppose," she replied. "Who were the thieves?"

"A couple of idiots with more whisky in their heads than brains. They'll be regretting last night for a very long time."

"The woodpile was getting low," Thompson said, jotting something in his book. "Good work getting new recruits."

"But why did they make such a mess?" Liza asked.

"They said they were looking for your cash box," Ben said. "They owe one of the local loan sharks a lot of money."

"Then they *are* idiots. I don't keep a cash box here. Not at night."

"What about a safe?"

"The safe is with Miss Mulrooney. Nobody would think of breaking into the Fairview fortress, so we keep it all there. All I ever have is a float and the profits from the day."

Thompson tucked his notebook inside his coat. "I think that's all we can do for now, Miss Peterson," he said. "I'll give a copy of the report to Miss Mulrooney, and if you can put together some kind of list of what you find missing or broken —"

"That's going to take a while," she warned, feeling a sense of hopelessness returning.

"Whenever you can get it to me is fine. Then we can work on getting Miss Mulrooney some kind of restitution."

"I'll come back later, help fix things up," Ben said. "I'll bring some boards for the window right off. That okay with you?"

"That would be more than okay," she replied, grateful for his offer. "I would love the help. And the company."

She knew the assault was over, the criminals locked up and most likely getting a Blue Ticket home, and yet the thought of being alone in the store still made her nervous. But if Ben was at her side, she wouldn't have any reason to be afraid.

THIRTY:
BEN

Ben eyed the splintered board in his hand.
He didn't have a lot of supplies for building
new shelves, and he'd already had to use
some of the longer ones to block off the
window. Maybe if he sanded this one down
and made it a little shorter . . .

"Nope," he muttered, tossing it aside and
pulling out another.

Keitl set her head on her paws, giving him
a moony look. He knew she'd be happier
outside, chasing rabbits, but he had a feeling Liza might like to see her if she stopped
by.

"So, you remember her?" he asked. "From
when you were little?"

Keitl lifted her head, tapped the floor with
her tail, and to Ben that was a "yes."

"Huh."

He held up the next board, then dug
through looking for one that matched.

"Do you suppose she's gone for her dinner?" he asked Keitl.

Keitl yawned.

He fastened the lumber together with a couple of nails, then wiped the sweat that had gathered on his forehead. After a few moments he looked back at Keitl. "I thought she'd be here. You think I'm on my own?"

She didn't even bother to open her eyes.

When the unit was done, he stepped back. "Where does this go?"

"Over there." Liza's voice felt like a cool breeze on the back of his neck.

"Hey there," he said, eyeing the tray of food in her hands. "I wondered if you were coming."

"I went back for lunch." She hesitated. "I wasn't sure you'd be here —"

"I said I would be."

"Oh, I knew you would," she said cheerily. "You're that kind of person. I just didn't know *when.*"

Her smile brought back a memory from up at Happy Camp, when she'd given that same warm look to her friend, George. It was a beautiful smile. Lit up her whole face.

"That kind of person?" he asked.

"You do what you say you're going to do. It's an excellent quality."

"I try."

"Hungry?" she asked, setting the tray

down on the table he'd fixed earlier.

"Always." He dropped his tools, and when he saw her pull out two china plates he went to the back room to bring out chairs. "This is great," he said.

"It's the least I could do." She reached up, tested a sturdy new shelf. "You're very good at this."

"Policeman, farmer, cowboy, carpenter . . . a man should be handy, I reckon."

As Liza doled out hot chicken and mushrooms, Ben poured the lemonade she'd brought, and Keitl scurried between the two of them.

"You're hungry too, aren't you?" Liza asked, and Keitl dropped to the floor with her most pleading expression. "Don't worry. I have something for you."

Keitl went straight for the ham bone Liza offered, forgetting all about the picnic on the table above her.

"Smells delicious," Ben said, hoping he didn't sound impatient.

After Liza took her first bite, he dug in. The chicken melted in his mouth, and when he looked over she was watching him, amusement in her eyes.

"This is so good," he said.

"I'm glad you like it."

"You know, I could have done with a

sausage or something."

That made her laugh. "You think Belinda's chef would send you a plain old sausage after today's adventure? Not even if I asked for it," she said, cutting a small piece of chicken.

Ben had already eaten everything on his plate, mopped up the mushroom sauce with a soft piece of bread Liza had put on the side, and now he found himself observing everything she did, fascinated by her delicate manners. He'd noticed them that first night when they'd had supper with Belinda at the Fairview. Until that point, he'd seen a beautiful, fiery woman in trousers battling her way to the Klondike, running a business on her own, fighting off loan sharks. He knew she was tough as nails, but when she stirred sugar into her lemonade her spoon never even touched the sides of her cup.

"What?" she asked, catching him.

"Sorry. You know, I don't believe I've ever met anyone like you before."

"How's that?"

Before he could stop himself, he said, "Courageous and stubborn, but delicate as a rose."

Her cheeks reddened.

"Sorry. I didn't mean to embarrass you."

"It's all right." She shook her head. "My

parents used to say when I was little that all they had to do was tell me I couldn't accomplish something and that would set me on the path to doing it."

"I can see that."

She raised her chin. "I'm not going to let this stop me either. Fortunately, most of my stock was still in storage, so we'll be able to start over using that."

"Your parents would be very proud."

Her eyes went to her plate, and she concentrated on finishing her meal. When she was done, she reached for his plate, but before she could he took the empty dishes back to the tray. No need for her to do all that work. She had enough to do.

"Thank you." She looked around the store with a sigh. "Poor Belinda."

"It'll be all right," he said. "You had this place in fine shape before, and I know you're gonna get it up and running again real soon."

"Sure I will." She wrinkled her nose. "I don't know. I feel like whenever something goes wrong, it's the people close to me who suffer the most. Sometimes I think I'd be better off on my own. I'd do less harm." She paused. "Have you ever felt that way?"

A glimpse came to him of a wide-open sky, a wild, unsaddled horse galloping underneath him, a memory of freedom that he'd forgotten all about.

"I used to want that," he admitted, "when I was a kid. But it wasn't about not hurting anyone else. It was more about not getting hurt."

"What do you mean?"

But Ben didn't want to get into that. "It's nothing. All in the past."

Something had changed in the way she was looking at him. Her eyes searched his face, then slid to his scar. He turned his head to the side so she couldn't see it.

"When you were a kid, were you always helping people, like you are now?"

"No," he said softly, the urge to flee bubbling up in his chest.

"Why not?"

"That's something I don't like to think about."

She folded her arms. He recognized the posture.

"You're not going to let me off easy, are you?" he asked.

"I'm just curious," she said lightly, but he could tell she was asking in earnest, too. "How did you get to be all the way out here? Where are you from?"

He picked at one of his nails. "A tiny farm outside of Fort Macleod. Pretty much in the middle of nowhere."

"I travelled across the Prairies when I was a little girl. The landscape is beautiful," she offered. "What did your family farm?"

"Not much of anything. We were supposed to be farming wheat, but my father was more interested in whisky than wheat." He tried hard to keep the bitterness out of his voice. If she asked what he meant by that, he didn't want to have to say.

She leaned forward. "And your mother?"

"My mother was . . . never very healthy."

"They're gone, aren't they?" she asked quietly.

Ben felt a spark of fire in his gut. How had this conversation arrived at this point? He'd kept his past buried and rotting away where no one could see it, knowing it was better that way for everyone. But there was something about Liza that made him open up. She spoke to him as if his feelings mattered, which was a strange notion that he figured he could get used to. But he couldn't let her in any further. There was too much ugliness hidden inside, and telling her about it could only do damage. Besides, what would she think of him if she knew the truth?

"I'm sorry," Liza said, filling the silence. "I shouldn't pry. It's just that you know so much about me —"

"I'm just not . . . I don't want to talk about that." He reached partway across the table and opened his hand in clear invitation, sorry he couldn't give her what she wanted. When she laid her soft fingers on his, a rush of warmth filled him. It suddenly felt so important that he say the right things, that he earn this fragile trust she'd just placed in his hand.

"My past doesn't matter, Liza. I'm making sure that my life right now is a good one." Now he'd come so close to the edge that his boots were hanging over, he took a deep breath and kept on going. "I'm sorry you feel you are better off on your own, but the truth is, Liza, you can't keep me away."

Her eyes were serious, but the corner of her mouth twitched. "Don't you understand? I'm trying to warn you, Ben."

He let himself smile. "Liza, you don't scare me. Heck, I'm a Mountie. I live for danger."

Thirty-One:
Liza

Liza scratched her nails over the frozen windowpane, daunted. The blizzard had started two hours ago and had quickly covered the dirt streets of Dawson in white, but it showed no signs of letting up. At this rate, the snow would be over their knees by the afternoon.

"Think they'll still come?" she asked Belinda as her friend blustered past, making sure all the chairs were set in position, all the cushions fluffed.

"Of course, dear. It's Christmas Eve. Everyone wants to be together."

Liza turned to face the room, decorated in red and gold, and hoped the weather wouldn't keep anyone away. This would be her first Christmas without her family. Her last real Christmas with them felt like it had happened a thousand years ago. She couldn't remember the weather or the gifts, but she remembered the warm, happy comfort of sitting by the fireplace with her family at home playing board games and building puzzles. When she'd told Belinda about their tradition, a spark had lit in Belinda's eyes.

"This town could use a little quiet comfort," she'd said. "I'm sure many people are missing their families back home."

As Liza watched Belinda, she was reminded of Stan when he got an idea in his head.

"We can bring tables and chairs to the lobby, then set out all the puzzles and board games we can find. I'll hire some musicians, and we'll make a day of it." Belinda beamed. "This is exactly the excuse I've been looking for to test out my latest purchase."

"Which is?" Liza had asked.

"Hot chocolate."

Now the smell of hot chocolate and baked goods permeated the Fairview lobby, and Belinda was right, as usual. Within the hour, the place was crowded with guests both rich and poor. As a string quartet played quietly in the corner and people chatted amiably with each other, Belinda gave her busboys little notes to drop on each table which read: *In the Christmas spirit, buy someone less fortunate a hot chocolate.*

Around one o'clock, Ben and Thompson

arrived, looking Christmasy in their bright red coats dusted with snow. Liza felt a flutter in her chest when Ben met her gaze and gave her a slow, lopsided smile. Ever since the break-in, he'd come to see her more and more, and they spent enough time together that even Belinda had raised a teasing eyebrow.

"I saw you both at the masquerade last night," Liza said, walking towards them. "Your costumes were not very good."

"You know us." Ben brushed the snow off his coat. "We love these uniforms so much we practically never take them off." He reached into his pack. "I have a letter for you, Liza."

"Who on earth would be writing to me?" she wondered, studying the envelope, then she looked up. "I hope you haven't come just to deliver the mail."

"Would that be so bad?"

"No, it's just that I have a little Christmas gift for you."

"A gift?" he said. "Why, I can't remember if I've ever been given a gift for Christmas."

He said it nonchalantly, but Liza was taken aback. He didn't often speak of his childhood, but when he said things like that she couldn't help but wonder about his past. Maybe one day he'd trust her enough to tell her about it. Maybe he'd even let her help him for a change.

"That's not true," Thompson intervened. "We gave all the Constables new buttons last year."

"Ah, yes," Ben replied, pleased. "I stand corrected."

"He'll stay," Thompson told her. "He's got nothing else to do today, and I'm wondering if he's smart enough to complete a puzzle. Let me know how he does with that, would you?"

Laughing, Liza assured the Sergeant she would, then she led Ben to a small table she'd reserved for them. As soon as they sat, a waiter appeared with a tray.

"Hot chocolate?" Liza asked Ben.

"Sure, I'll try it."

She nodded at the waiter, who put out two steaming cups and left them with a plate of cookies. She chuckled, watching Ben's obvious attempt at restraint. No dessert was safe around Constable Ben Turner.

"Don't wait for me," she said. "I'm going to open this letter first, but you should help yourself. Oh, and be careful —"

He gasped and put the cup back down.

"It's very hot," she said, a little too late. She held up the plate. "Maybe a cookie will help."

As he munched away, she turned to the letter. She didn't recognize the return address on the envelope or the handwriting. She slipped the card out and her eyes went to the signature at the bottom.

"Oh, Ben! It's from Olivia, George's widow." She read a little, giving him bits and pieces as she went. "She's apologizing for taking so long, as if she didn't have enough to worry about. She also —"

Her fingers shook a little as she pulled out another, thicker piece of paper: a photograph of a group of Tlingit packers, George, and a girl Liza barely recognized as herself. The Liza in the photo was small and filthy, wearing a man's bulky sweater and oversized trousers. The picture had been taken a little over seven months ago, and yet it felt like another lifetime. A different life, a different existence, a different place altogether from where she was now.

"Ben, look." She handed the photo to him. "George had another traveller take this when we were on the trail."

He studied the photo, a small smile playing at his lips. "You both look happy."

"We were, I suppose," she said softly. She'd forgotten how tall George was. Oh, but he was such a gentle giant, she thought, remembering his kind features and even kinder words. "He used to quote Yeats to me," she told Ben. " ' "There are no strangers here," dear Miss Peterson,' he'd say. ' "Only friends you haven't yet met." ' "

"I suppose he was right," Ben said, looking at her thoughtfully.

Liza set the photograph aside, then reached beneath her chair.

"This is for you," she said, placing a tissue paper–wrapped package in Ben's hand.

His eyes lit up. "Really?"

For someone who hadn't received a real Christmas gift before, he took his time unwrapping the present. He looked up at her, confused.

"Thank you?" he said, more of a question.

She reached over, laughing at his puzzled reaction. "They're special mitts I had made for you." She put one on and held her hand up for him to see. "Everyone knows that mittens are warmer than gloves, but they're also harder to work in. Well, this fixes that. There's a spot for your thumb, another one for your first finger, and the other three fit in the last section. Try it!"

She'd first seen the mitts when a Newfoundland fisherman came into the shop wearing them. It was the perfect thing for Ben and she'd asked the local tailor to make them with the strongest, softest black leather he could find and line them with rabbit fur and wool. They had been an extravagance, but she wanted Ben to have the best.

It took Ben a moment to slide his hand in and figure out where everything went, but once he did, he tested it by spreading his fingers.

"These are wonderful. Thank you," he said, and she knew he meant it this time. He twisted his mouth to the side, looking sheepish. "I have something for you, too."

"You do?" Ben was generous with his time, but she knew Mounties barely made any money at all. "Ben, you shouldn't have."

He ignored her, reaching into his pack and handing her a small package wrapped in brown paper. She pulled the twine loose, then carefully opened the paper, revealing a single brass button. On its face was the NWMP crest with a raised image of a bison, a crown, and the word *Canada*. On its back had been soldered a neat brass pin. She traced the design with her finger.

"They call it a 'sweetheart pin,' " Ben said shyly. "I know it's not much, but it's all I —"

"It's perfect, Ben," she said. "It's the loveliest gift anyone has ever given me."

The genuine relief in his expression set

her whole body tingling with an unfamiliar energy, and she glanced down so as not to let him see. Her gaze landed on the photo of her with George, and her old friend's words from Happy Camp came back to her in that moment. The ones about how he believed they were all there for a purpose. Her eyes rose to meet his again, and it struck her that maybe her purpose was Ben.

Thirty-Two:
Ben

Ben strode down Front Street, enjoying the warmth of the sun on his face and the smiles of the folks he greeted along the way. It was cold enough that the river remained frozen solid, but springtime was on its way, and change was in the air. New merchants had sprung up along the boardwalk, well-furnished, classy little hotels had replaced the tiny cabins from the winter before, and where tree stumps had once stuck out of the road, now the street was straight and clear. The city was becoming a home to so many.

Being around Liza this winter had made the cold season enjoyable for once. He could still bring back that sweet smile she'd given him after she'd pinned his button to her scarf, and he didn't think he'd ever seen her without it after that day.

Even Thompson's mood had improved, though that was due to the major progress he'd been making on his gun-smuggling case over the past couple of months, not a blossoming romance. After investigating a lot of dead ends, he'd linked the gun Thomas Wiedemann had used to blow his head off outside the Red Feather to a middleman in the operation, and they had confiscated two dozen firearms. The discovery had prompted a few people to talk, and now all lines of enquiry focused solely on Ralph Stevens. Ben couldn't wait until Thompson had the last pieces of evidence to arrest the man.

From the street Ben heard tinkling piano notes coming from the Monte Carlo, and he turned towards the saloon. He nodded to Henry the bartender as he walked in and asked for a cup of coffee. When it arrived, Ben noted that Henry's fingernails were longer than usual, and that was saying something, because they were usually pretty impressive to begin with. Henry had explained to Ben a long time ago that he used his nails to scoop gold dust off the bar as the night went on, running them through his heavily greased hair every once in a while to keep his stash safe. After everyone left, he panned his own hair and nails for gold.

The Mounties were well aware of the

ingenious methods of making money going on in Dawson City, but most of the time they looked the other way. They understood the difference between keeping the place clean and keeping the parts well oiled.

Diamond Tooth Gertie slid up to him, flashed her smile. "Good evening, Constable Handsome."

"Hi there, Gertie."

"One of these days," she said, "you're going to buy me a whisky and we'll sit down and enjoy it together. How would that be?"

Ben laughed. "Sounds like fun. How's everything going tonight?"

"I'm surprised you don't already know." She clicked her tongue.

He knew that look. "What is it?"

She nodded towards a table where a few men were being entertained by dance hall girls. "You'll wanna watch that one," she told Ben.

"Which one?"

"The one who ain't wearing his bright red coat at the moment."

Ben squinted through the smoke. "Constable Miller."

"He's been sneaking around, offering 'protection' services to the girls. I think some of them have bought in, but only because they're scared of him," she said.

"He hit Daisy the other night, you know."

Ben bristled. "No, I didn't know that." Twice he'd seen Miller coming out of a woman's hut, but he'd let it go. He never would have if he'd known there was violence. "Is she okay?"

"Sure she is. Tough little flower. But he's using his uniform to keep her quiet."

Miller was chatting with one of the girls, his lips close to her ear, and from what Ben could see, their conversation was nothing like the one he and Gertie were having. Miller's hands were nowhere near where they should be.

"Thanks, Gertie," he said, sliding off his bar stool. "You have a good night."

"You too."

He could tell she was watching him as he strode towards Miller and pried the whisky glass from his partner's fingers.

"What are you doing?" Miller asked.

"Come with me," Ben replied, taking his arm. "Now."

Miller objected, but he reluctantly gave in, and Ben half-dragged him into the street, out of earshot.

"What are you thinking?" Ben demanded.

"I'm thinking it's Friday night and I ain't on duty. So it's none of your business."

"Sure is my business. Folks still watch us

when we're off duty."

"Hey, hey, it's fine." In a blink, Miller's scowl had melted into a wheedling smile. "Can I borrow some money, partner? I'll pay you back. It's just that I owe a guy."

Ben had been right. Sounded like Miller had borrowed money from the wrong kind of lender.

"How deep are you in?" Ben asked. "Is this why you're offering 'protection' services?"

Miller started to turn away, but Ben yanked him back and held his lapels so they stood face to face.

"I wanna talk to you about another thing. I hear you hit Daisy."

"She's a prostitute," Miller replied, condescension thick in his tone. "Nothing wrong with hitting someone if she's already breaking the law."

Ben's jaw dropped. "What in God's name is happening to you? You know the law. You also know common decency — or you used to."

Miller shoved Ben away. "I don't need to hear any of this from you, Turner. I've been a good policeman for a long time, but I was living in hell while you were living the easy life out here," he said. "I've done all they said to do and I have frozen every piece of me without complaining."

"You *always* complained."

Miller continued on as if he hadn't heard. "I'm back in the land of the living now, and I intend to live a little. I have a few irons in the fire, so to speak, and no one's gonna get in my way. Especially not you."

"Irons in the fire?"

"Picking up the odd job here and there, you know. And sure, the protection service helps."

"What kind of odd jobs?"

"You don't need to know about that." He leered at Ben. "Not unless you intend to arrest me."

Which was impossible, because Ben had nothing to charge him with. No evidence — really, no crime. But there was something in Miller's belligerence that screamed trouble.

"You're gonna get called out if you're doing something stupid."

Miller leaned towards him. "Who's gonna do that? You gonna report me, *partner*?"

Miller was a whole different man from the bellyacher Ben had left at the Chilkoot Pass. This was a man with no emotion in his eyes, as if something had died in him. Something in the Yukon had killed it.

Ben didn't budge. "You hit Daisy," he said. "So yeah, I am."

Miller's nostrils flared. "I ain't the only one, you know. Lots of gambling and drinking going on with the other men."

"Yeah, but you're the one everyone's talking about."

"Oh, really? And you with that pretty little shopgirl? Everyone sees you. She can't be as innocent as she looks."

That's when Ben punched him. He'd trained so hard to let insults and insinuations roll off him, but this was different. This was about Liza.

Miller lay on his back in the crusty lumps of snow, glaring up at Ben and wiping blood from his nose. "Watch yourself, Turner."

"I'd advise you to do the same." Ben's blood sang through his veins. It had been so long since he'd let his temper loose, and the sensation was energizing. "You want to try that again?"

Miller sat up and sniffed, but he didn't stand.

"Wise move," Ben said.

"Watch your back, Turner. You don't wanna underestimate me."

Ben turned away as if Miller's threat meant nothing, but he wasn't a fool. As he walked to Fort Herchmer to report his partner, he felt the heat of Miller's glare burning into his back. With every step, the man's warning rang in Ben's head. Like every other Mountie, Miller carried a holstered pistol at his hip. What were the chances he'd use it?

THIRTY-THREE:
LIZA

Cape Nome, Alaska. That was the place Liza kept hearing about. As she checked and ordered stock, dusted, changed the window display, tended customers, and did whatever else needed doing, she was always listening to her customers. She hadn't forgotten what Belinda had said about the gold rush, and even though she was doing well with the shop — well enough that she'd recently moved into her own small house — she'd learned that things could change in an instant, and they already were. She'd seen more than a few wagons load up and leave town already. Permanently.

"I guess we'll know for sure when the steamships come in June," her customer was saying as Liza reached behind her for a canister of tobacco. "But from what the papers say, Nome's the next big one."

"Are you going?" she asked, setting it in front of him.

"Nah. My wife is tired of travelling. We've set up a nice little spot, and the children are enjoying the school. I think we'll stick it out here."

She smiled. It was nice to know that not everyone was going to desert Dawson. "Anything else today, Mr. Watson?"

"I'll take a copy of *The Nugget,* too. That's the latest, is it?"

"Of course."

At Liza's suggestion, Belinda had taken out a number of subscriptions to the local paper. Each cost twenty-four dollars a year, but it was worth the investment. Everyone here was hungry for news.

After Mr. Watson had paid and left, Liza returned to her ledgers. Her inventory was going to need closer attention over the next little while, she decided, because the prospect of Nome was already eating away at her profits column. After another half hour of tweaking numbers, she pulled on her coat, locked up the shop, and headed home. It was colder outside than she'd expected, and it was a relief to reach her house and slip into bed.

Her sheets were cool and soft, her pillow fresh, and she felt the day's worries drain from her body as she snuggled in and let her mind wander. This month marked an anniversary of sorts. Almost one year ago she had staggered into the chaotic metropolis of Dawson City, and somehow she'd managed to build a life out of nothing. She had a store that was every bit as prosperous as her father had once dreamed it would be, she was healthy and happy, and she had friends. And, of course, there was Ben.

She hadn't seen him that day, but they'd gone for a nice walk the night before, and he'd even told her a little about his cowboying days before he'd joined the Mounties. Slowly he seemed to be opening up, though he never talked about his family. As she drifted off, she thought about the way Ben kept those memories to himself. It was almost as if he wanted to protect her from whatever had happened to him.

Hours later, she awoke to a pounding on the door.

"Liza!" More pounding. "Liza! Wake up!"

She threw her robe on, lit her lantern, then stopped short when she peered through the window and saw Ben standing there. What time was it? What was he doing there? She opened the door, and the sight of a blazing golden sky made her take a step back.

"Fire!" Ben was filthy, smeared head to toe in grime, and his eyes were bloodshot.

Flickering in their depths was a fear she'd never seen before. "Big one."

She could smell it, the bitter, choking stink of smoke riding a strong northeast wind. The night sky jumped with gold and red and the noise was deafening. How had she slept through all this? Panic rose inside her.

"Where?"

"Started near the saloon by McDonald's theatre, but it's spreading like a monster. It's everywhere. The buildings are dried out and burning like paper. Most of the waterfront is already on fire, and the Opera House just lit up."

"But . . ." Through the crackling of the flames, she heard voices shouting madly at each other. "What about the fire department? Can they not —"

"They brought the new truck down and they're trying, but they can't cut through the ice fast enough to get to the river." He glanced behind him, then back at her. "Your house should be fine, but downtown might be gone by morning."

"How . . . what about the shop? My things?"

Ben whistled, and a grey- and black-smudged Keitl appeared, harnessed to a small wagon.

"You have a little time before the fire reaches the shop, but not a lot," Ben said. "You'll have to be fast. Grab what'll fit on the wagon, and bring it back here. If you have any gold, bring it all. People are losing their entire fortunes tonight. I'll find you when I'm done." He stepped back, dropped his gaze to Keitl. "And keep her with you, okay? She'll get hurt if she comes with me."

Then he was gone, and Liza's heart beat so fast she could hardly breathe. She ran back to her bedroom and pulled on her trousers and a warm sweater, then wrapped a kerchief over her face against the smoke. She headed directly to the shop with Keitl at her side, ducking through the noisy, panicked crowds as the heat grew more and more intense. Men sprinted past with water buckets and sloshed what they could over the buildings, but she could see they were fighting a losing battle. When she got to the store, she began collecting everything she thought Keitl could haul, then she filled her own arms.

"Okay, Keitl. Let's go."

With her tail unusually low, Keitl trotted beside Liza towards the house. By the time they reached it and had emptied the wagon, Liza figured they had time for one more trip. It was harder to get back this time, because people were throwing clothes and furniture into the streets, hoping to save what they could, but their efforts only blocked the bucket brigade.

"Come on, Keitl. We can do it."

As Liza loaded her wagon, smoke started creeping through the shop's door, seeking out the ceiling, and the walls were getting hot. Liza grabbed the last bundles and ran into the street as the saloon a few doors down began to burn in earnest.

"Liza!"

Liza turned towards the voice. "Oh, Belinda!" she cried, running towards her friend. Belinda had obviously been out for a while — her face, hands, and clothes were covered in soot. "Are you all right?"

"I'm fine. I think the hotel will be all right, too. We had a couple of sparks catch up top, but the boys put them out."

Liza noticed men throwing buckets of mud and water all over the hotel's beautiful walls, hoping to discourage the fire, and more volunteers were laying mud-covered blankets on the roof.

"I have coffee on in the kitchen," Belinda said, "and I dumped a lot of rum or brandy into it for the men fighting the fire. After they tasted it, they all wanted to save the Fairview. Though I'll tell you: I took a cup myself and it nearly knocked me silly." Her eyes grew sad. "The dance hall girls — there must have been fifty of them — were all running around in bare feet or slippers, and not enough clothes on to wad a shotgun. They've lost everything. But at least they're warm now, and they've had something to drink to take the edge off."

"I've just come from the shop," Liza said. "I don't think it will make it. I've managed to save a few things, but not much."

Belinda squeezed her hand. "We'll be okay," she said, then something caught her attention and she called to the men, "More mud over there, please!"

Liza told Belinda she would be back, then set off with Keitl again. Once she'd unpacked the wagon, she undid the harness and returned with Keitl to the Fairview, where Belinda had set up a soup kitchen of sorts.

"Steele just declared Martial Law because of all the looting going on," Belinda said, her arms full of blankets. "The miners, gamblers, shopkeepers, and saloon men will have no place to go. We'll take care of them here."

"All right," Liza said. "I'll start with —"

A sharp blast cut through the air, louder than a hundred gunshots going off at once.

It shook the building, rattling the dishes, and they ran outside to see. A massive smoke cloud plumed from the other end of town. Another *boom!* rocked the ground, then another, and even from where they stood on Front Street, they could see planks and windows shooting through the thick grey smoke like huge bullets. Metal sheets flew end over end, crashing onto the burning town and the frozen surface of the Klondike River.

"What on earth?" Belinda cried.

A man tore by the hotel's veranda, and Belinda stopped him, demanding to know what had happened.

"A bunch of miners' cabins exploded down around Eighth and Hanson," he gasped. "Mounties lit 'em up to give the fire less fuel, but some of the cabins had dynamite in them."

Ben, Liza thought. "Is everyone all right?"

"Dunno. Bunch of Mounties down there. Someone said something about a Constable trapped inside." He stepped back. "I'm sorry, Miss Mulrooney, but I gotta get more water."

Without thinking, Liza darted down the street, Keitl by her side. She ran for blocks, not stopping despite the burn in her lungs, racing towards the site where thick black smoke still rolled like liquid tar. She barely saw all the people she passed, barely knew where she was anymore. All she could think about was the feel of Ben's hand in hers, and his steady blue gaze watching her. She couldn't lose that. She couldn't lose him.

When she reached the devastated cabins, men were passing buckets and water was flying, but the fire still raged. She spotted a nurse tending to a soot-blackened body and ran towards them before stopping short at the terrible realization that the body was that of Sergeant Thompson. Blood covered half his face, and what Liza could see of it looked badly damaged. She grabbed a second wet cloth to help the nurse cool Thompson's face while Keitl licked his other cheek clean.

Liza searched the nurse's face. "What happened to him?"

"He and Constable Turner went into those two cabins when they heard a miner had been sleeping it off inside one of them." She pointed. "But the back wall of this one fell in and started burning. A beam collapsed on the Sergeant, but he was near enough to the entrance that he crawled out."

Liza's heart stopped. "But . . . but what about the other cabin? Where's Constable Turner? Has no one gone in to save him?"

The nurse didn't answer, or if she did, Liza didn't hear her. She'd already stepped away from Thompson and was staring in horror at the burning building before her. *Ben is in there.*

She took one of the wet cloths from the ground, wrapped it around her face and head, then sprinted towards the inferno, ignoring the nurse's protests and Keitl's frantic barking. The heat scorched her skin as she raced around the building, looking for an opening. *There!* she thought, spotting a section of the wall that had fallen in.

She tossed a desperate prayer to the heavens, then plunged through the fire. For all the flames lighting the darkness outside, it was black as night in the cabin, congested by all the smoke. Using the bursts of fire beside and above her as guides, Liza moved farther into the building. Her throat burned with every breath she took, and her eyes streamed with tears from the smoke. When a rafter crashed to the floor beside her, she jumped, but its bright orange embers lit up the far wall where a number of timbers had already collapsed. She squinted through the darkness and spotted a shape lying beneath them.

Heart racing, she ran over and tried to kick the lumber out of the way, but the wood was too heavy. She pushed with her foot as hard as she could, rocking it back and forth until the timbers finally shifted. Sparks shot out, and she dropped to the floor, right beside Ben.

He lay face down, unmoving. She knew the black sheen of his hair, though it was thick with ash. She knew the strength of his shoulders, though he lay helpless before her. Another rafter anchored his leg, but from somewhere within her she found an unexpected strength, and she moved it and rolled Ben onto his back. His eyes were closed, his face slack and bloodied. Was he breathing? Was she too late?

She couldn't worry about that now. Standing unsteadily, she grabbed him under his arms and shuffled backwards, dragging his dead weight through the cabin, towards the burning exit. Her breaths came quicker now, shallow, and she wasn't sure if the stars swirling through her vision came from the fire or her own desperate need for air. Was she going in the right direction? The world was spinning, shifting above and below, and she couldn't see anymore. She tightened her hold on Ben, and when she thought she was close enough to the edge of the building she threw herself backwards. Then everything went black.

Thirty-Four: Ben

"Sure helps you believe, don't it?" An unfamiliar voice cut through the fog in Ben's head.

"What's that?" someone asked.

"Miracles. That nurse is calling it a miracle."

"Maybe. Maybe just dumb luck."

"Move aside," a woman demanded.

I know that voice.

"What he needs is air, and I don't mean all your heavy breathing. Back up, boys. Get back to work on the fire. You know Steele's arresting men who aren't pitching in, right?"

A cool hand slid under Ben's neck, dragging him out of the murk, and something cold pressed to his lips.

"That's it, Ben," Belinda said. "You need water. Open up. Let's get you going again."

She poured a few sips into his mouth.

Thank you, he tried to say, but all that came out was a whistle. He wanted —

needed — to open his eyes, but they felt burned shut.

"Hush now. Save your strength. And keep your eyes closed. There's nothing to see."

Something warm pushed against him.

"Keitl! Back up, dog. He doesn't need you licking him."

Ben drifted off, coming to again when a cool cloth pressed against his cheeks, his brow, his eyes. The water trickling down the sides of his face seemed to come straight from heaven.

Where am I?

He remembered voices ringing out, a chaotic choir in the midst of a burning madness.

The fire.

"Liza," he croaked.

"Hush, Ben. You need to rest," Belinda said, but he heard a catch in her throat, and Ben was suddenly alert. What had happened? What could make the indomitable Belinda Mulrooney cry?

Tell me, he mouthed.

He heard her sob. "Oh, that girl."

"What?" he demanded again, though his voice made such a pathetic sound he wondered if she'd even heard it.

"Liza went into the building, Ben. She went in for you." She sniffed. "Everyone was standing around, staring at the fire, and she just —" She caught her breath. "She found you in there, and didn't she pull your carcass to the door? Didn't she get you out?"

"She. Is —" It hurt to breathe. Oh, it hurt so much.

"Fine, Ben. She is fine. She's in the hospital, and she's faring better than you, but only just."

Liza.

He faded in and out of consciousness, losing track of hours and days, brought back intermittently by Keitl, water, and caring voices, sometimes Belinda, sometimes nurses. By the time Superintendent Sam Steele came to his bedside, Ben was able to sit and open his eyes, though they burned so badly he was forced to squint.

"Thank you for coming," Ben said carefully, a hint of his voice returning.

"I'm glad to see you recovering well, Constable. Quite a fire. Quite a fire indeed. Biggest Dawson City has ever seen." The Superintendent inhaled deeply through his nose. "We were fortunate in that we had no loss of life; however, I do have unpleasant news to share with you."

"Miss . . . Miss Peterson?"

"No, no. It isn't her. She is doing well," Steele said, and Ben's relief was immediate.

"I visited her this morning, and the nurses are having difficulty keeping her in bed. Keeps talking about you, wanting to come up here to the outpost. I told her to rest, that you were in no condition to visit, but that you would appreciate it eventually."

"But if she's all right, then what . . . ?"

"I'm afraid the trouble is with Sergeant Thompson." He cleared his throat, dropping his gaze briefly before looking back at Ben. "He was injured quite badly in the fire. A beam fell on him, and it split his face. But he did get out. He will survive. Unfortunately, the doctor had no choice but to remove Thompson's left eye this morning."

Ben gasped, which caused him to cough.

"Steady there," Steele said, handing him a glass of water. "The Sergeant will be all right, given time. It appears that he got out quickly and took in less smoke than you."

Ben knew what Steele was going to say next, and it tore him in half.

"Of course, Thompson will no longer be medically fit to be an active member of the Force, but because of his seniority and exemplary service, he will retain a diminished role. It has yet to be decided where and what that will be."

The Thompson Ben knew would bristle at a "diminished role." "Does he know?"

"Of course." Steele turned and Ben knew he was just pretending to look out the window. "He has requested that I allow him to continue working the case focused around Ralph Stevens. He says he's close to cracking it. So at least for now he will be doing that."

Ben didn't notice Steele leaving. He was staring straight ahead, tears burning his bloodshot eyes. *Thompson is all right,* he kept trying to tell himself. *He will live.* And Ben was alive, thanks to Liza. He supposed they should all count themselves as lucky, but it was awfully hard to see it that way.

Thompson came to see Ben two days later, and Ben did his best to lighten the situation. He admired the new eye patch, suggesting his friend might consider a career among pirates instead. Thompson took the teasing well, but Ben heard the bitterness in his voice.

When Ben was finally allowed to leave his bed, he had to lean on a cane due to a bad knee strain, but things could have been a lot worse. With Keitl by his side, Ben limped towards the door, but when he opened it, he stopped mid-step, paralyzed by the excruciating pain of sunlight cutting into his eyes. He took a moment to breathe through the shock and adjust to the light, then he crossed the threshold and joined Thompson and Steele, who were already outside.

When he could see well enough, he was stunned by the changed landscape. Almost the entire town had been flattened, and what buildings remained at least partially intact were black and grey, either from smoke or from the mud thrown on the walls to discourage fire. They teetered like charred skeletons, looming over mountains of ruined furniture and clothing that had been thrown from windows. The slumped shapes of men wandered through what was left, and he saw them kicking at cinders, searching for anything of value. A few even squatted in the ashes and burnt-out doorways, stubbornly panning for gold.

"Looks like a hundred and ten buildings gone," Thompson said. "Hundreds of tonnes of provisions burned up. Next shipment's not for five more weeks, so everyone's gonna have to cut back."

"Is that the Fairview?" Ben asked, pointing, then he brought his hand back to his head. It was pounding fiercely.

"Yep. Still standing, beautiful as ever," Steele said. "For that we must be grateful."

"Miss Peterson's shop is gone," Thompson said.

But Liza was all right. That's all Ben could think about.

"Speak of the devil." Thompson shielded his one eye from the sun. "Is that who I think it is?"

A woman was walking towards Fort Herchmer, and though she moved slowly, Ben recognized Liza's stride. Evidently Keitl did, too, because she galloped towards her, yowling with joy. Liza leaned down, rubbed the dog's head, and Keitl started running circles around her, not quite underfoot. Ben felt a ridiculous urge to toss aside his cane and run to her, too.

"What is she up to now?" Ben asked.

Thompson chuckled. "As if you don't know. She's as stubborn as you."

"One of us should behave like a gentleman," Steele muttered. He sauntered towards Liza and offered her his arm. "Dawson City's newest hero," he called her. "I'm pleased to see you up and about, Miss Peterson."

"As am I," Ben said when she and Steele had reached them. "Hero indeed."

They could all see that Liza only had eyes for Ben. He couldn't stop staring at her, either. This woman had saved his life. How could he ever show her his gratitude?

"Are you okay?" she asked.

"Yes. Thanks to you."

Satisfied, she faced the rest of them. "Sergeant Thompson? Is that you?"

He gave a little bow. "At your service."

"You shaved!"

"Not by choice. Doctor did it during surgery."

She tilted her head. "I'm very sorry to hear what happened to you. How are you feeling? Does it hurt?"

"Don't hurt at all. I get dizzy, but I guess that'll get better."

Steele took a step back. "Sergeant Thompson, let's you and I go inside, talk over some things."

It was an obvious excuse to leave them alone, and Ben appreciated it. There was so much he wanted to say to Liza.

As they were leaving, Thompson turned back to Liza. "Bravest thing I've ever heard," he said. "I don't know that any woman has ever done anything like that before."

She blushed under his attention, then her gaze returned to Ben. "I'd do it again if I had to."

"Thompson?" Steele called.

"Yes, sir," he replied. "Here, Keitl. Come with me."

Then it was just the two of them, and Ben felt the strangest urge to weep. He took a breath, steadying himself before he spoke. "I never thought I'd be so happy to see someone as I am right now," he said. "Are you feeling all right?"

"I'm getting there," she said. "At least I don't have to go back to the hospital. How's your head?"

He touched the bandage. "It'll be a few days before my hat fits right again. They say part of the roof fell on me. I never saw it coming."

"You should be in bed."

"I wanted to see."

She sighed. "Oh, the town's a terrible thing to look at."

"Not that," he replied softly. "I wanted to see you."

She drew her arms around herself. "*I'm* not much to look at."

"That's not true." He took a step towards her. "Liza, whenever I was awake I thought of you. I'm still in shock, thinking of what you did for me. No one else was going to charge into a burning building, but you —"

"You could have died," she said, her voice breaking. "I couldn't let that happen. I couldn't —"

He dropped his cane, pulled her into his arms, and held her as she sobbed into his chest.

"Liza." He loosened his grip so he could look at her, brushed a tear off her cheek with his bandaged thumb. "You could have been killed."

Her chin quivered. "That didn't matter, Ben. I couldn't imagine living without you."

His hands cradled her face, and he marvelled at the smoothness of her skin, at the way her eyes drifted closed when he leaned towards her. Their lips touched, and it was like nothing he could have imagined, like a hundred candles had lit in his veins, like he was sliding down the icy Chilkoot Trail with nothing to stop him. As if he'd lost control.

It was this last thought that made him stop.

"What is it?" she asked, not moving. "What's wrong, Ben?"

"I'm sorry, Liza." He dropped his arms and stepped back, afraid to even touch her. The longing was an unexpected physical ache. "You deserve better. You don't even know me."

"But I do."

"I'm no good for you."

"You're a good man, Ben. Everything you do —"

"There's a reason I don't talk about my family, Liza." The words poured out of his mouth as if they'd been waiting for a chance to escape. "My father killed my mother."

He saw the emotion swimming in her eyes: the shock, the fear, the disbelief.

"When?" she asked, her voice hollow. "When did this happen?"

"About eight years back."

Her features softened. "But you were just a child."

She was watching him, waiting for more. He knew she wouldn't leave without an explanation.

"You sure you want to hear this?"

"I am."

He picked up the cane he'd dropped and she followed him as he hobbled towards a bench nearby. Slowly, his eyes on the flattened town of Dawson City, he told her everything. How his father was a drunk, how he beat Ben and his mother, how Ben had tried and failed to protect his mother all those years. Then, finally, he told her about that last day. About the screaming he'd heard from across the field, about his mother's lifeless body, about the hot, hard truth of his father's gun pressed against his head, about the Mountie who had saved him.

"All my life I was determined not to be like my father. Everything I did I asked myself if it was something he'd do. Because if it was, I'd go the other way." He hesitated. "But I'm his son, and I always will be. Ain't nothing I can do to change that. I have a short fuse and it catches fire at the littlest things." His fists tightened. "Every day, I fight to keep it under control, but violence is in my blood, and I can't risk you getting hurt."

For the first time in a long while he let his fingers skim over the jagged scar on his face.

"Did your father do that?" Her voice carried no blame, no judgment, and all he could do was nod once. "Ben, listen to me. You were a little boy, raised by a terrible man. No one should have to grow up that way. But everything's different now. You have become a man who saves lives, who keeps people safe." She touched his cheek. "That scared little boy has become a hero. And I love you."

He'd never wanted to hurt her, but he'd never meant to fall in love with her, either. With one had come the other.

He pushed her hands away and the smile on her lips faltered. "You shouldn't have saved me, Liza."

THIRTY-FIVE:
LIZA

Belinda tucked her arm through Liza's and led her through the crowd. "Weren't they marvellous, Liza? There is nothing quite so splendid as watching men in uniform marching in formation!" She glanced sideways. "I don't suppose you noticed how terribly handsome Ben was looking."

Liza kept her tone even. "They all looked very nice."

It was Queen Victoria's birthday and the whole town was celebrating. Playing a bittersweet tune on his bagpipes, one of the local saloonkeepers had led a parade down Front Street. Behind him, the North-West Mounted Police, their red serge spotless, their black boots and brass buttons shining in the sunlight, marched in perfect unison with Steele at their helm. When they reached the centre of town, Steele called the company to a halt and Ben joined two other men to fire a .303-calibre Maxim gun over the Yukon River.

Liza had stood back, wanting to see but not be seen, as the red coats marched past. These days she and Ben were civil towards each other when they crossed paths, but she couldn't manage much more than that. In fact, Ben acted like nothing had happened, which Liza couldn't understand, but from the way he'd kept his secrets from her so well, she figured he was used to bottling up his feelings. Still, things could never be the same between them. Not because of what he'd told her, but because Ben couldn't forgive himself for what he'd had to say — and that didn't lessen the heartache Liza felt.

She'd wanted to stay at home today, but Belinda had insisted they go out, promising that they'd have a wonderful time, sipping champagne, eating ice cream, and gawking at poor fashion choices.

Belinda was pointing out one such instance now. "Look at that lady's elaborate gown. Hardly practical at an outdoor event during the day! I swear, Dawson City really is taking on airs these days. It's just not like it used to be, is it?"

"No," Liza agreed. "Everything's different."

Belinda made a good show of not letting

Liza's mood affect her. "I suppose everything must change over time, and our town's no exception. It will be interesting to see who stays and who goes now that Nome is in full swing."

Despite herself, Liza could feel a sense of optimism in the air, and it wasn't just the games and music filling the streets for the holiday. After the fire, Dawson City had been quickly rebuilt, and the downtown district's pale new timber walls, combined with the clean new paint on the shops' false fronts, gave the town a friendly feel. Even the prostitutes had been cleaned up — or rather relocated. After the fire and because of a particularly nasty outbreak of syphilis, Steele had demanded the town set up a new location for them, across the Yukon River. It was called Louse Town, but the girls preferred to call it Klondike City, claiming that sounded better.

A loud *thwack* rang out nearby, followed by more. "What's that sound?" Liza asked.

Belinda grabbed a young man as he walked the other way. "What's going on over there?"

The young man glanced back. "Firewood-chopping contest."

"Oh! Let's go watch," Belinda said.

Liza held on tight as Belinda led, but she

stopped moving when they got close. Some of the younger men had stepped up with their axes, challenging each other to the contest, and Ben was one of four Mounties who'd peeled off their coats and joined in. He'd rolled up his sleeves and was laughing at something one of the others was saying, loose black curls tumbling over his brow. His smile was the most beautiful thing she'd ever seen. As if he'd heard her thoughts, Ben looked over and gave her a friendly wave.

"Smile, Liza," Belinda quietly urged. "Laugh a little. Let him see what he's missing."

But she couldn't summon much.

The starter pistol fired, axes swung, and sweat flew among the wood chips. Men grunted with effort and some paused to catch their breath, but Ben kept going despite the sweat rolling down his brow and dripping into his eyes. Since he couldn't look her way, Liza felt safe enough to watch him, to appreciate the man she could never have, to accept the ache that came with that understanding. In the end he tied for the win, and the other man seemed quite pleased to be sharing the prize with a Mountie.

When Ben ambled over after the contest,

Keitl by his side, Belinda congratulated him, then hopped onto her toes and waved at someone, casting apologies over her shoulder as she left Liza and Ben behind. Liza doubted she'd actually spotted anyone in particular. It was more likely that she was leaving the "cheering up" duties to Ben, poor man.

Liza rubbed Keitl's neck. "Hello, you beautiful girl. I miss seeing you."

Keitl gave her a lick.

"How are you?" Ben asked.

"I'm well." She answered as if she were speaking to anyone at all, not a man to whom she had offered her heart, then been rejected. How confusing, having to remain calm despite her mind still being furious. Was this how it felt for him, trying to hold in all his anger while protecting everyone around him? "Lovely day, isn't it? Superintendent Steele looked pleased."

"I think he was."

"Are you on duty?"

"Not officially." He shrugged. "But you know. Always watching."

She didn't answer.

"Liza —"

"How is Sergeant Thompson?"

"He's all right. I think he's getting used to doing less, but I don't know how long he'll be able to put up with it. I don't think he's been inactive even one day in ten years before now."

"I'm so sorry for him. Please tell him hello for me."

"Why don't you tell him yourself? You can come to the outpost. They'd be glad to see you."

He was right, of course, but she couldn't visit. And it annoyed her that he thought she could, that he didn't realize the very act of being close to him ripped her heart to shreds.

"You can go see them tomorrow, if you want. I'm going to Tagish for a couple of weeks."

"Oh?"

"Superintendent needs me to pick up some things for him."

So strange, how even now she felt a pang, imagining him gone for two weeks. "By yourself?"

"Well, me and Keitl."

"Excuse me, Constable, Miss Peterson!" They both looked over as a young man strode towards them in a light blue coat, a camera bouncing around his neck. "Riley Cook from the *Dawson Daily News*. Can I get your photograph for the paper? We're taking a whole bunch of photos so everyone can see them next issue."

Ben held out a hand. "Come on, Miss Peterson. Let's give them a smile."

She wanted to say no, but she was flattered someone even wanted to take her photo.

"All right. Just one." Was it wrong that she stood closer to Ben than she needed to?

"You're looking lovely, by the way," Ben said softly as they waited for Riley to get organized.

"Don't say that, Ben."

"I can't compliment you?"

"Ben, it's cruel. You know how I feel about you, and you made it quite clear that you do not feel the same way." She called out to Riley, "Are we done yet?"

He gave them a thumbs-up, and she turned away, blinking hard. Ben followed her. Why couldn't he leave her alone?

"Miller's done," he said. "Did you know that? He's a civilian now."

That was interesting. Ben had never had a complimentary thing to say about Bob Miller, so she was certain this was a good thing.

"He and I had a fight," he explained.

"What?" She whirled to face him, almost forgetting that she was mad at him. "You're not supposed to be fighting!"

"Don't I know it. But he was in the

wrong, and the Superintendent knew it."

"Well, that's good, right?" she said, letting the now-easy flow of conversation soothe her. She had to admit it was nice, talking like this. She missed these moments with him.

"Yeah," he said, sounding unsure. "It's just, Steele didn't give him a Blue Ticket. He let Miller stay in Dawson City, and having him here gets on my nerves. It's like a shadow hanging over me. He's in the stockade for now, but he'll be out in the next week or so."

"Then what will you do? When he gets out, I mean."

"Well, I'll still be in Tagish. When I'm back I'm going to do my best to ignore him." His jaw flexed. "But if he causes trouble again, I'll be ready with cuffs."

"Constable Turner." Steele's voice came out of nowhere, startling Liza.

"Hello, Superintendent."

"Nice to see you, Miss Peterson," Steele said. "Turner, I know you're not on duty, but might I borrow you for a while? It's about Tagish."

"Of course, sir." Ben turned to Liza apologetically. "I'm sorry I can't stay and talk with you."

If she was being honest, she was glad for

the interruption. She couldn't trust herself around Ben. Even now, as he held her gaze, she thought she felt that magnetic draw between them. That gave her hope that maybe someday he'd trust her enough to believe what she'd said. And if he learned to believe in himself, he might just come back to her.

Thirty-Six:
Ben

The Tagish outpost was empty other than Ben and Keitl, and Ben was glad of it. Once he'd made sure he had everything Steele needed, he settled in as comfortably as he could. It was nice to get away from Dawson and the crowds, the constant vigilance and responsibilities that came with being a Mountie. Except for the noise he and Keitl made splashing in the lake or shooting partridge, the only sounds around Tagish Lake were birds — and the ravenous awakening of mosquitoes for the season. Ben covered up as best he could, even draping mosquito netting between his hat and his head to cover his face, but at night it took a while to get past the itchiness and fall asleep.

If he was being honest with himself, it wasn't just the bugs that kept him awake. Liza was never far from his mind. He hadn't been able to take his eyes off her at the Victoria Day celebrations, but he could tell she wanted to be rid of him. And he couldn't blame her.

"I'm an idiot," he said out loud, and he heard Keitl groan.

He closed his eyes, cleared his mind, and imagined himself melting into the land as he'd done when he was a boy. A breeze shushed through the trees, and he breathed it in. This was all the serenity a man could ever need, he thought. Was this what he wanted? Could he live like this? Just him and the dog?

Liza's face returned to him, almost talking him out of it, but he banished the vision of her. If he went back to her, what could he do? What could he even offer her? He'd been a fool to have ever entertained any idea of anything in the first place. Mounties could only marry under very specific circumstances, and though he knew a few men who had done it, he couldn't let himself think about that. In his heart, he was certain he would somehow end up hurting them both.

Maybe he should put in for a transfer, leave the Yukon. Ben felt a brief pang of guilt at the thought of taking Keitl away from Liza yet again, but hadn't she said that Keitl was his now? She belonged with Ben. They both had agreed.

He'd talk to Steele when he got back, he decided. It was the right thing to do. It would be easier on both of them.

Ben and Keitl headed out the next morning, reaching Dawson before noon. Before he could lose his nerve, Ben went to Steele's office and put in his request.

"I'm surprised to hear this," Steele said. "But of course I will send you with the highest of recommendations. You've been a hard-working and dependable asset up here, Turner. You should be proud." He tapped his desk, thinking. "We'll send you to Fort Macleod for now. You'll leave in a couple of weeks, if that's convenient."

Ben tightened his jaw against any hint of emotion. "Thank you, sir."

"Now that that is out of the way, I wonder if you might head to Louse Town," Steele said. "I may have made an error in judgment with our former Constable Miller. Ever since we released him a few days ago, there have been reports of violence around the ladies."

Ben was already up and out of his seat. "I'll take care of it," he said.

"Thompson's aware too, but he left here in a hurry a while ago, took a couple of Constables with him. Sounds like he's finally going to bring Stevens in."

It was near to noon when Ben reached Louse Town. Keitl had been upset at being left back at the outpost, but a couple of the ladies were nervous around dogs and he didn't want anyone more upset than she might already be. When he knocked on Daisy's door, he saw right away that she'd been crying. A fresh bruise bloomed on the side of her neck.

"Miller?" he asked, clenching his fists.

"You just missed him." She hesitated, then said, "Constable Turner, he wanted me to give you a message. He said you underestimated him."

A gear shifted within Ben, and clear as day he saw Liza in his mind and remembered those words coming from Miller's mouth. Dizzy with adrenaline, he stumbled away from Louse Town and raced towards her shop, checking his stride only briefly at the sight of a crowd gathered outside the store. He burst through the door and all he saw was Liza backed against the corner, her chin lifted over the muzzle of Miller's pistol.

"Hey! There he is," Miller announced, madness blazing in his eyes. "Hello, old friend. I've been waiting for you. Look what I found: something you actually care about. I'm glad you got here in time to see me blow her pretty little head off."

Ben didn't slow; he didn't reach for his gun — a bullet was too good for this snake. Ben closed off his mind, pretending he didn't see Liza's terror, didn't see the circle of white pressed against her throat, didn't see the gun. What he saw was Miller.

"You might wanna slow down, cowboy," Miller warned. "Maybe you didn't notice, I —"

Ben let his fist fly, driving Miller sideways with so much strength the pistol rattled to the floor. Just as Ben kicked it out of reach, Miller came back at him with a wicked right hook, and Ben staggered to the side. He shook his head, dazed by the unexpected blow, then he set his feet in a fighting stance, rocking in place.

"Walk away," Miller growled. "I'm in no mood to play nice."

"I ain't going nowhere."

Miller spat blood to the side, his narrowed eyes intent on Ben. "I've been waiting a long time to knock you down."

Ben knew he should call for backup, should hang back and wait for Miller to run at him, act on defence instead of offense. He should read Miller's body language, then strike. He should use his head, not just his fists.

So many shoulds.

He ploughed into Miller like a freight train, ignoring the fists beating down on his back. When Miller spun sideways, Ben went with him, but he was a fraction too slow and Miller used his momentum to bring Ben to the floor. Miller's boot slammed into Ben's side — once, twice — and Ben curled into a ball, gasping for air. Over the pounding of his heartbeat and Liza's faraway sobs, he heard the same gloating sound that his father had made when Ben had been no more than a scared little boy.

Miller was *laughing*.

He thought he'd won. But Liza was right, Ben was no longer a beaten child. Ignoring the agony knifing through his side, Ben reached out quick as a whip and grabbed Miller's leg before it could kick him again. He twisted the boot, straining against ribs that were probably broken, and Miller fell with a crash. Ben climbed on top of him, punching for all he was worth.

"Stop!" A woman's voice, somewhere out there, miles away. "Ben! Stop!"

He slugged Miller again, then flipped him face down, smashing Miller's broken face again and again onto the sweat- and blood-speckled floor.

"Congratulations, partner," Ben hissed, blood spraying with his spit. As he snapped the cuffs shut, Miller's eyes rolled back towards Ben, gleaming white in a mask of red. "You are under arrest. And this time you'll get a Blue Ticket."

A small sound caught Ben's attention. As the room came into focus, he spotted Liza, curled tightly into herself in the corner, staring at him with terrified eyes. Clutching his side, Ben rose to his knees and staggered towards her.

"You okay?" His voice was hoarse, and his heartbeat pounded in his ears like a bass drum. "You okay, Liza?"

But Liza had shrunk away from him, tears streaming down her face.

"Dammit, Liza!" he yelled. "Are you all right!"

She nodded dumbly but otherwise didn't move.

"Ben?"

He turned to see Belinda at the doorway, a crowd peering over her at the scene before them. Her eyes were wide, her body tense . . . and he realized she was afraid of him.

"Help her," he grunted, then backed away, suddenly aware of how he appeared. What he'd done. What they'd all seen him do.

Belinda ran to Liza's side, rocking her in her arms while Liza cried.

She's all right, Ben told himself.

He needed to get out. He hauled Miller to his feet and dragged him through the horrified crowd and back to the Fort. As he shoved the bastard into a cell, the outpost door swung open and Thompson entered, pushing a cuffed Ralph Stevens ahead of him. Stevens gave Ben a sneer as he stepped behind the bars and sat on the floor, and Ben smiled despite his swelling lip. Maybe Stevens was about to get what he deserved. Miller sure was.

"You've looked better," Thompson said, frowning at Ben's face.

Ben closed his eyes, feeling the floor move beneath his boots. He'd have to sit soon and take inventory of what Miller had broken on him. His nose for sure. Rib, too, he thought.

"Not a great day," he admitted.

"What happened?"

He started to give Thompson a rundown of the events that had led him here, but he didn't get very far before the door burst open again and Superintendent Steele strode into the office.

"Constable Turner," Steele boomed. "Situate yourself within the other cell."

"Superintendent?" Ben's voice was strained. His chest stabbed him every time he breathed.

"Now."

Confused, Ben entered the third cell and watched Steele's fingers work the lock to seal him in.

"Constable Miller will be given a Blue Ticket immediately and will be taken into custody as soon as he is outside the Yukon," Steele informed Ben. "You, Constable Turner, are more fortunate. I am assigning you fourteen days in the stockade before you're transferred out of here."

Ben's body was still pulsing from the fight, his head filled with noise. Maybe he was hearing the Superintendent wrong. He glanced at Thompson for support, but his friend could only give him a half-hearted shrug. It wasn't as if he hadn't warned Ben about fighting in the past.

"I don't understand."

Stevens and Miller both snickered, and Steele spun towards them. "Mr. Stevens," he said. "As a member of our fine community, you are a grave disappointment. Your flagrant disregard for both authority and morality has earned you a Blue Ticket from the Yukon. We have no room in this town for low-lifes like you." He turned on Miller, his lip lifted with disgust. "And you have absolutely nothing to gloat about. You are no better than a pathetic common criminal. An embarrassment to the red serge. Miss Peterson has made a full report of tonight's events, and I shall ensure you are punished to the full extent of the law."

Steele turned back to Ben, his keen eyes hard with disappointment. "And you. It was made clear to you in the beginning that brawling was unacceptable among the Mounties. I will not allow our reputation to be tarnished by such irresponsible behaviour. It is only because you have proved yourself to be a commendable member of the Force in the past that I am not relieving you of duty."

A wave of relief washed over Ben then. His job was the one thing he had left — he couldn't lose that.

Steele put one hand on the bars of Ben's cell. "I must say that while I understand the reason, I am aggrieved to see you in this position, Constable Turner. Perhaps this place simply wore you down. God knows we've seen terrible things here." He took a deep breath, let it out again. "I hope your time in here will restore your good sense."

Mind reeling, Ben sank to the floor and he lowered his face into his swollen hands. All he could see was the broken terror in Liza's face as she cowered in the corner, the dread he knew so well. He opened his eyes and stared straight ahead, between the bars of his prison.

I am no better than he was.

Thirty-Seven: Liza

Thompson stood outside Liza's door, hat in his hands. "Ben asked me to bring Keitl to you. He's hoping you'll keep her for now."

She glanced at Keitl. "Why?"

"He's in the stockade. He'll be in there for two weeks."

Liza's stomach sank. She wasn't particularly surprised that he was being punished, but it still hurt to think of him in there.

Thompson shuffled in place. "I think we both know that he went way beyond doing his job. Trouble is, most of the town knows it too. You know how important it is that the Mounties maintain the respect of the community. He could have lost his post over this." His eyes slid sideways. "It's not the first time his fists have got him into trouble, if you want to know the truth."

Liza hadn't been able to get the scene out of her mind. Miller had barged in so fast, threatening her, yelling that she was going to pay for what Ben had done, pulling out his gun and pointing it at her, but Ben had been faster. The heat of his anger had been a tangible force she could feel all the way across the store. Once the fight began, she could see Miller never had a chance. Ben had become a wolf, consumed by blood lust, beating on Miller until she couldn't watch anymore.

Still, she couldn't help but ask, "Is he hurt?"

"Some. Couple of ribs broke, and his face has some healing to do." He turned to go. "Mostly what he's feeling ain't physical, if you know what I mean. He's disgraced, and that's about killing him."

That sounded like the Ben she knew, she thought, watching Thompson walk away.

Liza was glad to have Keitl there, but at the same time she wasn't sure she could bear it. Every time she looked at the dog, she was reminded of Ben. A part of her longed to comfort him; another part wasn't sure she wanted to see him at all.

The truth was, she had been terrified by his rage and his brutal, unforgiving strength. It had come as so much of a shock, since she knew what a gentle man he could be. But now she understood: that fury was exactly what Ben had warned her about.

That was the violence he'd held in check for so long. She remembered the pale anguish in his expression on that day after the fire when he'd finally told her what kind of man lurked within him. At the time, she hadn't understood why he was so adamant that he didn't trust that man around her. Now she did. But she also knew, deep down, that Ben would never hurt her. His anger had been directed at Miller, not her. Ben despised that part of himself, and the only reason he had allowed it to come out was to keep her safe.

As the end of Ben's incarceration neared, she couldn't stay away any longer. When no one came to greet her at the stockade, she wandered in and found his cell by the back wall. He was lying on his side on a cot, a rough grey blanket tossed carelessly over himself.

She moved closer — she'd never seen him asleep before. He looked so young, so completely at peace, and she longed to touch him, to sweep back the black curls falling over his brow, touch the dark beard that had grown in. One of his hands rested on top of the blanket. He could be so gentle, she thought, remembering the warmth of that hand when it had held hers. But she couldn't look away from the healing cuts on

his knuckles. He could also be very powerful.

"Ben?" she whispered.

"Liza?" He sat up, wincing with pain.
Couple of ribs broke, Thompson had said.

"Hi."

He combed his fingers through his messy
hair as he got to his feet. "How are you?"
he asked, approaching the bars.

She almost took a step back, but after
everything, his first concern was her welfare.

"I'm all right," she assured him. "And
Keitl is fine, though she misses you."

"Thanks for keeping her."

"I love having her around." It was so hard
to see him like this. "Are you all right?"

"I will be." He closed his eyes briefly.
"Listen, Liza, there's something I need to
tell you. I'm leaving Dawson. I'm transfer-
ring out."

Her mind raced to catch up. He was leaving? Because of the fight? Surely Steele
wouldn't — No, she realized then, her
stomach curdling. He was leaving Dawson
City because of *her.*

"I've made the Force look bad," he was
saying. "It'll be better anyway. I've had
enough of this place."

She didn't think he really meant that.
"Oh?"

"Yeah. It's time I moved on."

She had to say something. If this was the last time they ever spoke, she needed him to know. She stepped a little closer to the bars.

"Ben, I need to thank you for saving me. From Miller, I mean."

"No. I —"

"I'm not going to lie. You scared me that day, but all this time that I've known you, the only time I've ever seen you get angry was when my life was threatened." She searched his eyes, seeking that connection they'd once shared. "You have protected thousands of us." She paused. "You saved my life, Ben."

"I just did my job."

"Was that all I was?" she asked softly. "Your job?"

His fingers curled around the bars until his knuckles whitened, and he held her gaze for what felt like forever. Then he blinked slowly, and she knew the answer before he said it.

"Yes," he said, turning from her. "Good-bye, Liza."

She couldn't breathe. Somehow she forced herself to back away, to find the door, to walk outside into a world that felt suddenly empty, but she couldn't bring herself to utter the word goodbye.

■ ■ ■ ■

PART THREE:
FRANK

■ ■ ■ ■

Thirty-Eight: Ben

1902

There was no road leading to Ben's childhood home. No clear trails or paths, no sign that anyone had come this direction in a very long time, but Ben knew the way. His horse waded through the long grass, flicking her tail as insects rose in clouds around them, and Keitl trotted contentedly beside them.

In the almost three years he'd spent at Fort Macleod, Ben had never been tempted to ride out this way. The posting had been good for him, the long rides out to the Prairie homesteads a healing salve for the hurt and regret of Dawson City. The hardest wound to close was Liza, but he managed to put her out of his mind. Most of the time, anyway. Every once in a while he'd hear the melody of feminine laughter or catch a glimpse of a woman with a profile like Liza's. When that happened, he'd instinctively move towards her just in case it was Liza. Then he'd remind himself that it couldn't be. He'd given her up, left her in the Far North.

He scanned the empty fields, seeking some kind of landmark from years ago. The idea to visit his childhood home had come to him last week after he was notified that he was being transferred again. He knew nothing about where he was headed other than the place was called Frank — an odd name for a town — and the industry there was coal mining. That was fine with him. He'd had enough gold in his lifetime already. Coal was much more practical — it kept people warm, and they didn't go crazy over it. But after he heard he was going to Frank, his father's farm had gotten into his head and stuck there like a burr. If he was going to start a new chapter of his life, he figured he should probably come out here, see if he could maybe let an old one go.

Eventually Ben spotted the house, sticking out like a wart in the middle of the field. Grass had crept up to the foundation and grown through holes in the walls, and the timbers were splintered with rot. The lone tree in front leaned over the yard, dead as the rest of the place, and the barn, where Ben had sought refuge on so many cold, lonely nights, had almost entirely fallen in on itself.

His mare dropped her head into the grass as Ben slid off her back and walked up to the front door. The old hinges still partially held, and when he tugged they creaked open. He stepped inside, prepared for . . . well, he really didn't know. But other than the natural decay and a thick layer of dust, it was like Ben had never left.

What a bleak place this had been. Of all the times Ben had ached with loneliness, it was here, with his family, that the pain had been the worst. He tried to remember his mother smiling or his dad sober, but their ghosts were as unyielding as they had been in life.

Ben backed out of the house into the fresh air and sunlight, trying to see the place through different eyes. Had his parents ever been happy here? They must have loved each other at one time. Why else would they have gotten married? If that was true, then what had happened to make it all go so horribly wrong?

Keitl dropped a dried-out stick at Ben's feet, then she backed away expectantly. He threw it somewhere in the tall grasses where she couldn't possibly find it, but he wasn't surprised when she loped right back with it in her mouth. He threw it again, and as she ran off, a long-forgotten memory came to him. His father had stood in this same spot all those years ago, he recalled, looking over the field just as Ben was now. Ben would have been five, maybe six, but he remembered that his father's eyes had been a bright blue and lit with promise.

When had that hope faded? What had taken the light from those eyes? Life was hard, Ben allowed. The Yukon had shown him just how difficult it could be, and what it could do to a man. Scraping out a livelihood here hadn't been much easier, he realized. Water was scarce, and the cracked prairie dirt had refused to yield any but the most pathetic of crops. Their labour fruitless, his parents had worn frustration like a second skin, and it had grown on Ben as well. Was that what had driven his father to the bottom of a bottle? Because when he thought of it that way, Ben could almost understand what had happened. He knew what anger felt like, and he knew whisky would only have fuelled it. None of that excused what his father had done, but it did make him more human than demon.

Standing now where his father had once stood, Ben was struck by a sense of sympathy for the man. He could never forgive his father for what he had done, the pain he'd inflicted, but he understood how easy it was to give in to the fury inside of him. He exhaled, and something released inside of Ben and he felt neither fear nor anger, not at his father, and not at himself — for his failings as a boy and as a man. It was as if a weight had been lifted off his chest and he could breathe deeply for the first time.

"Come on, Keitl," he said, pulling himself onto the saddle. "Time to move on."

As he rode, a cold front pushed in, tasting of rain. He'd seen it coming, pressed the horse and Keitl a little faster so they could reach one of the small outposts he'd been told about, but the hills blurred with the approaching curtains of rain before he could get to shelter, and when they finally found the outpost all three of them were drenched and cold.

At least he wasn't in Dawson City, he thought as he coaxed a small fire to life. There the cold never left your bones, drunks were always brawling, and the same old piano music played night after night. At least he wasn't there.

Except if he was there, he'd be near Liza.

He reached down from his cot to scratch Keitl's ears, remembering the stubborn girl who had broken through his walls. He could still picture the very first time he'd met her at the summit, standing up to him, unafraid and intelligent, demanding to know what was going on. Then she'd pulled her scarf down and he'd seen her eyes . . .

Where was she tonight? Had she met someone new? Had she married? He couldn't deny the spike of jealousy he felt at the thought, but he knew he had no right. It had been his choice to leave her behind, abandon her in the Yukon, and there was no going back.

He rolled over, hoping to knock loose the dull ache in his chest, but it never quite went away. Maybe moving on would help with that. Tomorrow he would make for his new home.

THIRTY-NINE:
LIZA

Liza sat behind the counter, chin in her hand, staring at the empty store. As Dawson gradually turned into a ghost town, her days of rushing around had ended. Even Eb Thompson, who had retired from the Force after he'd seen Ralph Stevens put behind bars, had set out, looking for a fresh start. The only thing worse than her loneliness was the boredom that came with it. Belinda's most recent letter lay before her, a reminder that it hadn't always been this way.

Dear Charles is exactly who I want in my life, Belinda had written. *He is an entertaining travel partner, he is energetic in his thinking, and he is not intimidated by me, which was always a challenge in the past.*

He's also a liar and an opportunist, Liza thought. An actual gold digger, though he'd never think of getting his white gloves dirty. She'd said as much to Eb Thompson before he'd left.

The fella's a con man, he'd said, confirming her suspicions. *From what I've heard, he's a barber out of Montreal, not a Count like he says.*

But who was Liza to question her friend's heart? After all, it wasn't as if Liza's knew what it was doing.

She pulled out a paper and pen and started writing back to Belinda.

Since you ask, I am no longer seeing Mr. Sulley. It didn't last long, to be honest. His ego left very little space in the room for me.

As her pen glided over the page, Liza felt the loneliness lift, though she knew it was a temporary relief.

I am trying to come up with something happy to tell you about our little city, but in truth, that task is quite a challenge. There's been another gold discovery in the Tanana Hills, in Alaska, so "little" has become an understatement. When I last spoke with Inspector Cartwright, he told me Dawson's present population is no more than five thousand. If my math is correct, that is about one-sixth the size of when you were here. I must tell you, it is nothing like the town you left.

438

The last time Belinda had been there, they'd sat outside the hotel, enjoying a sherry. She remembered so clearly the moment when Belinda had raised her glass in a toast.

To the old days, she had said.

To the old days indeed, Liza thought. To the snow and ice and mud and hunger, to swindlers and thieves and desperate miners. The old days were the most miserable anyone could ever have known, and yet she missed them terribly.

For as much as the Klondike had taken from her, it had been the most incredible, unexpected adventure of her life. Financially, she had struck it rich, as they say, but just like the fortunes of so many of the men who had come here, it had begun to slip through her fingers like sand. But of course the best parts of her Klondike adventure had had little to do with money.

She reached into her pocket and pulled out the aging photograph of her and Ben, taken at the Victoria Day celebrations. She'd clipped it from the pages of *The Klondike Nugget* and saved it, even though it brought her sadness every time she looked at it. She remembered how she'd leaned towards him that day, but even that closeness hadn't taken away the pain she saw in her own eyes. At the time she hadn't realized he had been looking at her, not the camera. His expression had been tinged by hurt as well.

I know you are wondering about my next steps, as am I. You will no doubt be relieved to hear that I do not believe I can stay here much longer. I have not made up my mind where I will go — though I do not think I shall return to Vancouver. I must have some of my father's intrepid spirit in me, because I feel the nagging urge to search out a new adventure. I am leaning towards reopening the shop somewhere else, which I know you would applaud. There are a number of little towns opening up, and they're hungry for new citizens and merchants. They're all quite a ways from here, though. But I'm hopeful that wherever life takes me, and you, we will see each other again.

Now she'd done it, made herself cry and probably done the same to Belinda. Drying her eyes, she signed her name at the bottom of the page, folded the paper into an envelope, then stepped outside, not at all concerned about closing up early. Who would notice? On a nice, sunny day, Liza could sit outside her store all afternoon and see no more than a dozen people wandering by. When she remembered the noisy crowds and the thrill of being among them, then compared it to this, well, it just made her sad. Why, then, did she hang on so tight?

She should have left months, even years, before, but she'd been weak. The truth was that a small part of Liza still hoped that someday Ben would come back for her, though she knew that would never happen. But if he *did*, well, she had to be here. What if she left and he couldn't find her?

But he wasn't coming back. There was no need for her to stay here, and if she did she feared it would do more harm than good. She would go somewhere else, start a new life.

She stopped in at the post office to mail Belinda's letter, and she was surprised when the postmaster went to the back and returned with an envelope addressed to her. She didn't recognize the rough, scrawling hand, but inside she found two pages. The first was a very short letter suggesting she take a look at the enclosed newspaper article, which she did.

Then her heart began to race.

FORTY:
BEN

The familiar whistle of the mine echoed across the valley as Ben returned from his rounds, signalling one of three daily shift changes. It was four o'clock, the end of the day for many and the beginning for the graveyard crew. Time to turn his horse away from the mountain and towards downtown Frank.

The tiny town had impressed Ben from the very beginning. It amazed him how, in little over a year, a mountain of coal had sparked a town and turned it into a popular stop along the new Canadian Pacific rail line. Stretching from the base of Turtle Mountain, past the Old Man River, and down to the rail line, Frank had everything anyone might ever need: a post office, a two-storey school, a couple of doctors, hotels aplenty, and about six hundred citizens, most of them well-mannered family folks.

It was all because of Turtle Mountain and

its vast stores of coal. The funny thing about the mountain, Ben had discovered, was that it did some of the mining on its own. Sometimes the miners found chunks of coal lying on the ground, as if the mountain had shifted, dropping bits and pieces as it did so. Ben wasn't the only one to find the phenomenon eerie. The local Blackfoot and Kutenai called it "the mountain that moves" and took longer routes to avoid being in its shadow.

For the past couple of years, Ben had been exchanging letters with Eb Thompson. Going by his stories, it seemed as Frank's fortunes rose, Dawson City's fell, so when Ben had suggested that Thompson might come to Frank and take a job in the mine, he'd been interested. In his letter the month before he'd told Ben he was on his way. Ben was looking forward to having Thompson's gruff but easy personality around again, and he wanted to introduce him to his new partner. Constable Robert Leard was a good, steady Mountie who rarely let anything faze him. Of course, after Dawson there wasn't much in Frank that Ben couldn't handle on his own. The difference was that here, Ben had to keep in mind that most men wore pistols on their hips. A small fight on payday could escalate quickly.

Like now, he thought, hearing raised voices coming from the Frank Saloon. He spurred his horse towards the crowd gathering outside the building, then jumped down and cut through to see what was going on. Right away he spotted Vinny Stein, a tall young banker in an expensively cut suit, standing about ten feet away from Joe Britten, one of the foremen from the construction camp, known for his brawling.

"What's the problem?" Ben asked, stepping between the men, catching the strong smell of alcohol on their breaths.

"He robbed me!" Vinny yelled, pushing forward like a bull.

Ben held him back. "Stay here, and don't touch that pistol if you want to keep it."

"I'm gonna get that louse!" the man said. "If you want me to stay here, you're gonna have to make me."

Ben obligingly cuffed the sputtering man to the railing outside the saloon, then turned to Joe. "What happened?"

"Nothing. He's just a drunk fool bent on stirring up trouble with respectable folk." Joe sounded less intoxicated, but he wouldn't meet Ben's eyes. "Why don't you sit him down, Constable? Read him a page from the Good Book?"

"Difficult to do that without knowing the

truth of the matter. Come along, Joe. The sooner we do this, the sooner you can leave."

"I ain't going with you," he snapped.

"You know the rules. If the two of you can't talk this out, the North-West Mounted Police will be happy to provide you both with a couple of nice, neat cells for the evening."

As Ben was speaking, he saw Joe go for his holster and instantly reacted, throwing him on the ground.

"Why'd you have to do that, Joe? Now I got no choice."

He dragged the miner to his feet, but Joe jerked backwards, slamming his skull against Ben's nose. Ben saw stars, but he kept his grip.

"Really? You're gonna hit a Mountie?" Ben said, tasting blood. He cuffed Joe to the other railing, then wiped his face with the back of his hand. Getting hit was par for the course when it came to being a Mountie, but it never got less painful.

"Now, one of you better tell me what's going on here," he said.

Vinny spoke first. "He's got twenty dollars of mine he took cheating at cards."

"Is that right?" Ben clucked his tongue at Joe. "Am I charging you with cheating as well as assault?"

"Check his inside right pocket."

Ben dug in Joe's pocket and pulled out the money, counted out twenty dollars, then handed it to Vinny. The rest he tucked back into Joe's coat. The immediate problem was solved, but from the look on their faces, Ben sensed the fight wasn't quite over. Cheating at cards was more than wrong; it was embarrassing to both sides. He'd have to separate the two men further before things got any worse.

"Need a hand?" a voice asked, and Ben turned to see Thompson striding towards him.

"Am I glad to see you, Sergeant," Ben replied, grinning.

"Been a while since anyone's called me that," his friend said, studying Ben's bloody nose. "Why do I always seem to find you in a tussle? At least it wasn't you throwing the punches this time."

Ben chuckled. "Help me out with them, would you? Then I'll show you around."

After Vinny and Joe were safely locked in separate cells and left under Leard's supervision, Ben and Thompson set out on a tour of the area. Ben couldn't get over how good it felt to be riding with Thompson by his side once more, and today was a perfect day to show off Frank. The flatlands and lower slopes had bristled into a dry golden brown, and the mountain peaks, with that familiar stark grey hovering over the tree line, were beginning to shine white with snow.

"Pretty little town you got here," Thompson said as they turned back. "I bet you don't miss the Klondike."

"I don't miss the cold," he said. "But I have some good memories of the place."

"Me too," Thompson admitted. "I doubt the world's ever gonna see another Klondike Gold Rush."

"You think that's true?"

He nodded. "That mountain's still got gold, but she's keeping it, I reckon. Nobody's gonna bother with the Chilkoot or anything that crazy ever again. I guess we learned our lessons."

"I sure did," Ben said, his mind going to Liza. "How are folks holding up there?"

"A lot have left. Miss Daisy sends her regards."

"Ah. How is she?"

"She's Belinda's personal maid now. She's travelling the world."

Warmth filled Ben's chest. "Now that *is* good news."

"She's a good girl. I was glad to see her get out of the life."

"What about Gertie? She still there?"

447

"Nah. She's living in Portland now, I heard. Married a big-time lawyer."

"That girl always got what she wanted."

The rooftops of Frank were coming into view, clinging to the late sunshine as long as they could.

"How is —" Ben started, but he stopped himself. They rode a little farther. "Is she married too?"

"No, Liza's not married," Thompson said. "She's got admirers, but she ain't interested, seems like."

Hope sparked inside Ben. He'd been so sure she would have moved on by then.

"You ever write to her?"

Ben shook his head. "No. Her life's changed, and so has mine. She's probably forgotten all about me."

Thompson's gaze rose up the side of the mountain. "Not so sure about that," he mused.

"Even still. I bet she wishes she could."

Thompson didn't know about the last time Ben had seen Liza. About how he had turned his back on her after tossing that flippant, thoughtless remark her way. Even as he'd said it, Ben had known that was the cruelest thing he could have said to her. It was also the biggest lie. He had no right to write to her now, invite himself back into her life. He'd hurt her so badly before. He didn't deserve a chance to do it again.

FORTY-ONE:
LIZA

Liza took a deep breath for courage, which seemed ironic in a way. She had climbed mountains, ridden whitewater rapids, fought a man in a flooded street, and been held at gunpoint, but none of that scared her as much as this moment when she stepped onto the railway platform in Frank.

Ben. There he was, standing open-mouthed just a few feet away, staring at her as if she were a ghost. He hadn't changed in four years, and the sight of him sent her heart racing. Beside him, Thompson was grinning from ear to ear.

"I knew we'd surprise him," he said, moving towards her.

She squeezed his arm gratefully. After all, if it hadn't been for his letter, she never would have come here. She never would have known where to look.

"Constable Turner," Thompson said cordially. "May I present —"

"What are you doing here?" Ben asked, his voice hoarse. Then he turned to Thompson. "This had to come from you."

"Show him what I mailed you, Liza. It'll give him a pretty good idea of what happened."

She pulled the paper from her coat pocket and handed it to Ben, but he just kept staring at her. She'd practised what she wanted to say all the way down here on the train, and now was the time to do it. She preferred the other script she'd come up with, the one where Ben rushed to greet her, lifted her into the air, and covered her with kisses, but she would have to work with this one.

"I've been a fool," she confessed. "I hung on to Dawson for far too long. After Belinda left she kept writing to me, asking why I was still in Dawson, why I hadn't looked for you, and I —" Her words came too quickly, but there was no way to slow them down. "And of course she was right. I've always been so stubborn, and so much time had passed, and I didn't have any idea how to find you." She gestured towards the paper he still held. "Then that arrived."

Ben tore his gaze from her face to his hands, and she watched him unfold the clipping from *The Nugget* that Thompson had sent her. She had memorized every word.

451

GRAND OPENING CELEBRATION!
COME VISIT FRANK, THE GREATEST NEW
TOWN IN CANADA!
FREE TOURS, FREE FOOD!
FANTASTIC BUSINESS OPPORTUNITIES!
CHEAP TRAIN TICKETS ONE DAY ONLY!

"I know it's a couple of years old," Thompson explained. "But when I heard you were transferred here to Frank, it caught my eye. Don't know why I kept it at the time, but I'm glad I did."

Ben looked up. "I don't understand."

Liza held out her arm, indicating the mountain of boxes and bags behind her on the platform. "I'm opening a shop here. I wrote to Henry Frank, the founder of this town, and he set aside a perfect space for me. It even has a room on the second floor where I can live."

"Fourth Street. Between Dominion and Manitoba," Thompson informed him.

"That's . . . that's a great location," Ben said slowly. "But Liza —"

A rush of emotions filled her. "You don't want me here," she whispered.

"I'm just having trouble —"

"I shouldn't have come," she said, stumbling back. What a fool she was! How could she ever have thought he might want her

452

after what he'd said back in Dawson? After so many years without a word?

Then his callused hands were cupping her face as gently as if she were a baby bird. "Liza," he said quietly. "Have you come here to be with me?"

Oh, those eyes! The way he looked at her, the way his steady blue gaze held her safely in place. A tear trickled down the side of her nose as she nodded, then she relaxed into his hands, relishing his warm strength. He drew closer, his face so close to hers she could feel his breath. When he kissed her, the rest of the world disappeared, and though his lips were salty with their shared tears, she had never tasted anything sweeter.

"God, Liza. I thought I'd never . . ."

He was staring so intensely into her eyes that she saw the moment when he gave up fighting, when he surrendered his heart and soul and finally believed.

"Liza, I swear to you, I will never leave you again."

Forty-Two:
Ben

Ben's thoughts kept returning to Liza as he rode into Frank at the end of the day. The whole place seemed different to him now that she was there. It was more than just a town now: it was a home. Even the workers camping in tents on the east end seemed happier, though he supposed that could have been his imagination, or it might have been just their gratitude for the blankets he'd passed out the night before — the usually mild temperature had dropped unexpectedly.

In the two short months that Liza had been in Frank, she had been a whirlwind, and Ben could only stand back and watch with admiration. From what he could see, she was even more efficient than she had been when he'd left Dawson. Despite that city's downward spiral, she'd managed her inventory and her savings perfectly, allowing her to start her new store off on the right foot. He wished her family, especially her father, could see her accomplishments.

Together they had repainted the inside of the store a brilliant white, and then he'd carried in glass-covered display cases and stock while she'd fluttered around the space, assembling everything just so.

"I have one last heavy thing I need help with," she said, pointing to the last crate.

He grabbed a crowbar to open the box, then he heaved out a beautifully detailed gold-plated cash register.

"It was a gift from Belinda," she told him, touching it fondly. "She said it was so I'd never forget the gold of the Klondike. As if I ever could."

To prove it, Liza had added one special feature to her stock: a bucket full of gold nuggets. "For anyone who didn't make it up there," she explained. "Everyone wants Klondike gold!"

"Have you thought about what you'll call this place?" he asked.

She smiled. "Of course. The Klondike Gold General Store."

"Frank's a lot different from Dawson," Ben told her the night before she opened. "There's not as much greed, and there's not as much danger. You can trust these folks." He wrapped his arms around her, and she pressed her head against his chest. "Besides, it's my job to look after you, make sure you're safe."

"I'm glad of that," she said. "I'm counting on you."

Now her store was established and popular, and the cheery bell over her door was always ringing. As Ben rode past, heading towards the outpost, he saw she had closed for the day, but he saw a light on on the second floor. She was probably going over her accounts after a busy day. Since opening, her shop had become the most popular store in town.

Ben had no idea how good life could feel until now. If Liza believed in him enough to come to Frank for him, then he was ready and determined to earn her love this time, not fight it. Life was too short to avoid happiness just because he feared what might happen, he thought as he settled into his cot for the night. He blew out the lamp, then grinned to himself. Tomorrow he would show her just how ready he was.

Hours later, Keitl's bark broke through his sleep and he bolted upright, staring into the darkness, his heart beating a mile a minute. Keitl never sounded the alarm like that.

"What is it, girl?" he asked, already getting dressed. He thought about waking Leard, then recalled that his partner had stayed at Blairmore that night, visiting friends. Ben was on his own. "Okay, Keitl. Let's go see."

He staggered back as dozens of deafening cracks split the night air and the whole building shook as a violent, crashing roar thundered outside. What had happened? When Ben yanked open the door, the noise stopped and a swirling dust storm engulfed him. He squinted as best he could, but the air was so thick with dust it was impossible to see anything other than the static electricity in the air, flashing like small bolts of lightning.

He grabbed a lantern, a plan coming together in his mind as he moved. He had to assume there'd been an explosion at the mine. All that earth — it had to be that. He would organize a party of the off-shift miners to get up there and dig the others out. They'd have to work quickly, but those men would know what they were doing better than he would. How long did oxygen last in a blocked mine? he wondered. Thompson would know.

Thompson. Ben's stomach rolled at the thought of his friend. Thompson was on the graveyard shift all April. Was he still alive?

Was *anyone* in the mine still alive?

Ben pulled out his binoculars to try to see through the curtain of dust cloaking the town. When shapes began to emerge, dread filled him. The streets and houses directly below the outpost were fine, but beyond those were nothing but rocks stretching out forever. Rocks the size of houses. Rocks . . . that had replaced houses. This was more than an explosion in the mine, he realized. An enormous rock slide had consumed the town. How far had it gone? How many people had been in its path?

Oh God. Liza.

He had to get down there.

"Come on, Keitl."

They raced down the slope, Ben's chest burning as dust filled his lungs. As they ran along Fourth Street, Ben was heartened to see how many buildings were still standing. Incredibly, the bunkhouse, with maybe a hundred men in it, showed no sign of damage. All over town, people began to pour into the street, stopping him with questions, but he had no answers.

Please, God. Let her be all right, he prayed as he got closer to the disaster.

But when he reached Dominion Avenue, his heart stopped cold. Where buildings had once stood there now loomed a mountain of uneven, sharp-edged boulders. The rock slide had completely swept away the miners' cottages, as well as some of the family homes he'd walked past just this afternoon, the livery stable . . . and Liza's store.

"Liza!" he yelled into the dust, and Keitl joined in, barking. "Liza! Can you hear me?"

He tried to picture where the shop should have been standing, but the slide appeared to have carried everything about thirty feet to the northeast. Keitl hopped from boulder to boulder, focused on the area where the miners' cabins had been, nose to the ground, but Ben doubted she could smell anything through the rubble. Lanterns emerged, bobbing through the darkness like disembodied orange balls as rescuers ran from town, and twenty feet away Ben saw Sam Ennis on his hands and knees on what appeared to be the peak of a roof.

"Help! It's my wife! She's here!"

Reluctantly, Ben put off his search for Liza and went to him.

"I've almost got you, Lucy!" Sam cried. He turned to Ben, pointing with his chin. "It's that beam. It's pinning her. Can we haul it off?"

Together they heaved the timber to the side and began throwing rocks out of the way, then they dug through the underlying stew of cold, wet mud anchoring Sam's wife there. When they finally reached her, she could barely hold her head up, but she did hand a small, screaming bundle to her husband.

"Gladys!" Sam cried, folding back the blanket to examine his mud-smeared baby. "She's fine," he told Lucy through his tears. After kissing the baby's cheek, he handed her to someone so he could get back to work on freeing his wife.

"Constable Turner!" another woman cried from her window. "We can't get out! There are rocks blocking the door!"

"Has anyone seen my children?" a man called desperately. "I haven't found my three children. Please help me!"

"I need help over here!"

It was too much. Too many voices crying out, too many shapes wandering aimlessly in the thick fog of dust. Too many people counting on Ben to solve it all. His mind returned briefly to Sheep Camp, where another mountain had smothered dozens of people, and he fought back a bout of nausea.

Pay attention. Think. These people need a leader. Medicine against the madness.

He climbed onto one of the boulders, pulled the scarf off his mouth, and yelled, "May I have everyone's attention, please?"

At his call, they turned, streaming eyes staring up from dust-coated faces.

"For all of you asking, I have no idea how this rock slide happened —"

Someone called out an idea, but Ben held up his hand.

"— and it doesn't matter right now. We have to prioritize, not stand around thinking. First, we need to set up a field hospital of sorts so we can get the most seriously injured some help." His thoughts were coming together more quickly now. Where could he put the victims? Clearly the two doctors' houses couldn't handle this many casualties. "We'll use the sanatorium for the injured. Can someone look after that? Find Dr. Malcolmson?"

A group at the back conferred and agreed, then headed off.

"We'll need to set up a temporary morgue." He hoped it wouldn't have to be too large, but they'd have to be prepared. One of the women was staring intently at him, seeming to understand, so he spoke directly to her. "The schoolhouse. We'll use the schoolhouse for that. Can you locate Father John? If he's all right, he can advise on how to set that up."

She turned and pulled another woman with her, and they ran off to do what he'd ordered.

"The construction camp's gone," someone reported, "and both ranches."

The extent of the damage was worse than he'd thought. Up until now, he'd been focusing on the downtown area, but there was so much more. He turned and his heart dropped. The air had finally cleared enough that Ben could make out Turtle Mountain's profile — or what was left of it. The entire northeast face had broken off as if the mountain had simply shed unwanted weight, sending millions of tonnes of limestone thundering onto the town, crushing it.

There was no sign of the mine, and any possible routes to reach the miners trapped inside had been destroyed: the bridge to the mine had been knocked out, and boulders now dammed Gold Creek and the Oldman River, swelling both rivers into lakes on either side.

Scanning the faces around him, Ben spotted the mining engineer, who was already poring over a map. "Can you find the entrance?" Ben asked, leaning in.

The engineer nodded. "Yeah. Or close to it. But from the entrance to where they are, well, that'll be anywhere between sixty and three hundred feet thick. We'll never get through that. Not before they run out of oxygen."

"We have to try. We all have friends in there. Let me know when you have it figured out." He turned back towards the other men. "We have to get across the river and be ready to dig. I need you to build a raft, and when we find the entrance we'll string up a rope. We'll ferry back and forth with as many men and tools as we have. Once that's done, we'll dig out the men."

"That's impossible!" someone yelled.

"That's our only chance," he replied.

As the men turned to their work, Ben faced the bewildered townspeople again, and he took a deep breath for all their sakes. "Do what you can and let's pray the mountain's done."

As people scattered to find their loved ones, Ben returned to his search for Liza. *God, please let her be all right.* He stumbled across the rocky landscape, yelling her name until his voice cracked and failed, and still he called. He pictured her lying somewhere underneath him, crushed and broken, and he lost track of time, digging until his hands bled.

"God, Liza," he whispered, wishing his thoughts could reach her. "Give me some kind of clue, and I swear I will find you."

Keitl barked ten feet away from him, then started digging as hard as she could.

Ben stumbled towards her, squinting at a shiny piece of metal winking through the rock — Liza's cash register. A surge of energy flowed through him, and he began throwing rocks and timber aside, calling to her again and again. He was down about three feet when his fingers brushed some soft fabric, and he almost wept with relief. He put out a hand, stopping Keitl's powerful claws, then he used his own fingers to clear the rest of the rock. Had he gotten to her in time?

He touched her skin — it was cold. "No, no, no," he muttered, moving faster. At last he revealed her neck, then the thick cord of her braid. In the next instant, he saw her sleeping face covered in dust.

"Liza!" he said gently. "Liza! Wake up!"

She didn't move. Heart racing, he held his palm in front of her nose, crying out when he felt the soft promise of her breath tickle his skin. After that he couldn't dig fast enough. She had a wound on the back of her head — something had struck her there, knocked her unconscious — but other than that she seemed all right. Trying not to jar her, he slid the scarf off his neck, then softly wiped her face with the clean side.

Her eyes fluttered open. "Ben?"

"Hello, beautiful."

She frowned lightly, confused. "You're dirty."

He laughed through his tears. "You're alive."

"What happened?" she asked, blinking at her surroundings.

"The mountain collapsed," he explained. "I need to get you somewhere safe," he said, lifting her in his arms. He would take her to the Mountie outpost.

"Don't leave me!"

"Never. But Liza, the men are trapped inside the mine. I need to get them out before it's too late."

Forty-Three: Liza

Liza clung to Ben's neck as he carried her over the rock field, stunned by the devastation around her. So much more had been destroyed than what she could see, Ben told her, including her shop. As they passed where it had stood, she buried her face in his shirt, overwhelmed by the thought of rebuilding.

"You okay?" he asked.

"I'll have to start all over again."

He kissed her brow. "*We* will, Liza. I'll be right beside you every step of the way."

When they reached the Mountie outpost, he set her carefully down, tucking a blanket over her nightgown, then kissed her once more before turning back towards the mountain.

"Please be safe," she whispered to his receding back.

Woozy with pain, she fell onto his cot, her cheek on the comfort of his pillow, and slept for a few hours. When she awoke, she couldn't sit still. The waiting was too much. Restless, she moved into the Miners Hotel and helped provide water, food, and encouragement to the searchers and those they had found. Conversations were hushed, tears were shed, and consoling embraces held everyone up. She heard the same dazed exclamations over and over again, and other people's memories filled in what Liza did not know. Like the heroic story of Sid Choquette, the train brakeman who had climbed through the dark over a mile of shifting, jagged boulders the size of a railcar, in time to flag down and stop the passenger train on its way in from Lethbridge.

Sometime near dusk, Liza spotted Ben through the hotel's grimy window, though it took a moment for her to recognize him. His face and hands were black with coal, dirt, and dust, and his shoulders sagged. She'd never seen him look so defeated. Keitl plodded beside him, filthy and tired.

"Are you all right?" Liza asked. "Any news?"

He led her to the window, away from other ears.

"I couldn't do it, Liza," he said softly, and anguish broke his voice. He paused, gathering strength. "It's like that day at Sheep

467

Camp. I did all I could — everyone did — but the mountain was against us. Even with the whole town digging, we couldn't get there. We couldn't even break through. And now, well, it's been too long." He pushed his fingertips hard against his forehead and closed his eyes. "If they were still alive, they will have run out of air by now."

Thompson's rare but heartfelt smile, his black eye patch rising with the motion, came to Liza and grief swept through her, but she had to be strong for Ben.

She touched his cheek. "There was nothing more you could do. You know that, don't you?"

"Thompson would have known they were running out of air. He and the others would have been digging for all they were worth, but there would have come a point when they stopped, and I —"

He faltered, and she pulled him against her, felt his sobs against her chest even as tears streamed down her own face. "Their deaths are not your fault." This was a staggering loss to them both, and to the rest of the town, but she needed him to believe what she was saying, to forgive himself, just as she had after the deaths of her brother, her parents, and George. She tightened her hold on him. "We will get through this," she said. "I swear we will. The town will get back on its feet, and we will be all right. We can do it."

"Yeah." He didn't sound convinced.

"Everyone will be watching, Ben. They believe in you, and they'll follow your lead."

He rested his forehead against hers. The world had changed again, and they would have to change with it. For now, all they could do was breathe.

Then someone shouted.

Liza leaned out the window. "Maybe they found someone."

Ben nodded listlessly.

The questioning voices outside grew louder, then a woman yelled again.

Ben moved towards the door. "I'd better go see what's happening."

"I'm coming with you." Liza pulled on her coat, and they ran outside with the crowd.

A group of men was walking towards them from the far end of the town, right down the middle of the street.

"I thought the rest of the rescue party came back from the mine when you did," Liza said.

He peered down the street. "They did."

"Then who . . . ?"

He grabbed her hand. "Liza . . ." Then he

began to run, pulling her along with him. "It's them!"

Someone cheered, and people emerged from buildings, crowding both sides of Dominion Avenue as seventeen coal-smeared men stumbled towards them like apparitions. Two carried a third man on a stretcher. For a moment, no one said a word. It was almost as if they were afraid to speak, to disrupt the miracle unfolding before them.

Liza's heart was beating out of her chest. "Where are they coming from? How did they get here?"

Like a wave, the families descended upon the exhausted miners, weeping and laughing and wrapping themselves in one another's arms. Ben went to each man, shaking his hand, checking that he was okay. Then Liza heard Ben laugh out loud and saw him pull one of the miners into a hug.

"Eb!" she cried, running over and throwing her arms around them both.

"Thought I'd seen the last of you, old man," Ben mumbled into Thompson's coat.

"I'm hard to kill," Thompson said.

"Thank God for that," Liza said, smiling through her tears.

Forty-Four:
Ben

"How on earth did you get out?" Ben asked Thompson.

They were sitting in the hotel's saloon, each with a soothing whisky in hand.

"We mined our way out," Thompson said simply. "When it started, I was in a tunnel farther back. I was just standing there when a gust of warm air like I've never felt before lifted me like I was paper and smashed me against the far wall. Happened to Dan McKenzie, too, and he cut his head pretty bad. The others came with their lanterns, and it took a minute for us to see straight after that, but then we all headed towards the entrance."

"But it was gone," Ben said.

He nodded. "Dan and a couple others went up to the air shafts, but they'd been sealed off as well." He took a slow sip, remembering. "So things weren't looking good."

Ben listened in awe, imagining the scene as Thompson told him how they'd tried and failed to dig out the entrance until someone suggested the impossibly simple solution that they mine their way out.

"The coal seam is vertical," he explained. "It was slow going, and hot as Hades, but that was our only way. About thirty-five feet straight up. Then all of a sudden, Dan's pick cut through, and we all breathed fresh air again." He grinned. "Nothing ever tasted that good, I'll tell you."

"You were in there thirteen hours," Ben reminded him. "You shouldn't have made it."

Thompson raised his eyebrows. "Well, from what we saw after we climbed out and looked down on the town, *you* shouldn't have made it."

But they had. They all had. As incredible as it seemed, Thompson, Liza, and Ben had walked away with no more than a few bumps and scratches.

It was enough to make a man think long and hard about what could have happened and what he could have lost. As the sun rose, glowing eerily through the dust that hung in the air around the altered profile of Turtle Mountain, it came to him how much he had been shaped by the land, from the flat stretches of prairies to the peaks of the world. Liza, too. He went to her then and led her to a quiet place on the hill outside the outpost.

"Here," he said, reaching into his coat pocket and pulling out an envelope. "It's from Superintendent Steele."

"The Superintendent?" She raised a brow. "You want me to read it?"

"Out loud," he said, hoping his smile wouldn't give him away, "if you don't mind."

"Okay, but this is . . ."

"Please?"

" 'Constable Ben Turner,

" 'I am in receipt of your letter and am pleased to provide you with my response.

" 'Firstly, congratulations on your exemplary — for the most part — years serving the North-West Mounted Police and your commitment to continue with the Force for another five years. It has been my pleasure to watch you mature from an eager, albeit inexperienced, young man to a Mountie who has earned the respect of a great number of people, including the large and often unruly population of the now world-famous Dawson City. You also served the Mounties extraordinarily well during your time spent at the Chilkoot Pass, dealing with extremes and

473

inconveniences few men have ever imagined. Despite all this, you were always professional and served the people well.'

"This is a wonderful letter of commendation from him." Liza looked up. "I didn't know you had committed to five more years, but I'm glad of it."

"Thank you. Keep reading, please."

" *'Now on to your second point. As you are aware, your request mandates that I should do some investigative work into the person you indicated, and though I am already quite well acquainted with her I did complete the necessary requirements. During her stay in Dawson City, Miss Elizabeth Peterson —'* "

She frowned. "Why am I in this letter?"

"Maybe you should keep reading."

She cleared her throat.

" *'Miss Elizabeth Peterson was a fine, upstanding member of our population.'*

"Oh! Well, that's nice of him."

"Go on."

"Okay, okay.

" '. . . *a fine, upstanding member of our population with honest and exemplary business practices, and who generously and selflessly contributed when it came to those in need — and in that I include her daring rescue of a certain Constable during a terrible fire. I'm certain we both remember that quite*

474

clearly. *Miss Elizabeth Peterson has an excellent character and no past criminal record.'*

"Criminal record?" she cried.

He couldn't help but laugh. "You're almost there."

She exhaled, clearly disturbed by seeing her name included in a sentence along with the words *criminal record.*

" '*Constable Turner, I also commend you on your ability to maintain an adequate amount of savings in your bank account. As you know, that is the final requirement in order for me to fulfil your request.*

" '*So, as all of the above are acceptable to me as your Commanding Officer, I am now pleased to accept your petition and grant your request.'* "

Ben watched as Liza stole a glance at the bottom of the letter, and her cheeks suddenly reddened. Ben knelt before her.

"What does it say, Liza?" he asked.

She read the final words, tears spilling down her face.

" '*I wish you and Miss Peterson — should she decide to accept your proposal — a lifetime of wedded bliss. On behalf of the North-West Mounted Police, please accept my congratulations to you both.*

" '*Superintendent Sam Steele*

" '*North-West Mounted Police.'* "

He wiped a tear from her cheek, then took a breath.

"When I was just starting out with the Mounties, I told a whole roomful of men that not too many things in this world scared me," he said. "But you do, Liza. You scare me and thrill me," he said, hoping he could get through this without breaking down, "and you make me a better man. You are my own personal Yukon. The only thing I'm afraid of in this whole world is that I'll lose you again."

He opened the small box in his hands and revealed a gold ring.

Her hand was pressed to her lips, her eyes streaming.

"I've never stopped loving you." He lifted the ring a little higher. "Liza Peterson, would you do me the honour of becoming my wife?"

"Yes, Ben," she cried. "Yes."

She held out her hand, and he slipped the ring over her finger, then he got to his feet and took her in his arms.

"Good thing you passed the Superintendent's evaluation," he murmured against her lips.

Forty-Five:
Liza

"You've done enough," Liza said, her thumb touching the inside of her finger, brushing her thumb over the now-familiar gold ring. She knew she was being selfish, but she hated to see him leave. "Stay with me, Ben."

At their feet, Keitl gave a little bark.

"Keitl agrees with me," Liza said.

Ben gave her an adorable sideways look that reminded her: *this is my job,* and she knew he was right. Frank was being evacuated, and Ben had ridden with her to Blairmore that morning, since she was to billet with a family there while the Mounties and other volunteers cleared the rubble and ensured — as well as they could, anyway — that the mountain was stable.

"Hey, mister!" a young voice called, and they turned to see a little boy run from the house. "Are you a real Mountie? My dad says you're a Mountie."

"I am," Ben replied.

"I like your coat. And your hat," he told Ben. "Dad says Mounties are the law. Maybe I could be a Mountie someday."

"Are you brave?" Liza asked, walking towards him. "You have to be very brave to be a Mountie, you know."

The boy scowled. "Well, sure I am. I ain't scared of nothing!"

"Are you smart?"

He glanced over his shoulder at his mother, who was standing in the doorway. "Yeah, I am. I can read almost as good as my sister."

Liza squatted beside him. "If you are a Mountie, you have to give up everything just to take care of other people. That's what makes Mounties into heroes."

The boy's eyes swept over Ben, taking in everything from his Stetson to his black leather boots. "You don't look like you gave up everything, mister. You look like you *have* everything."

She glanced up with a smile, and Ben was already looking at her, his eyes shining with trust. Her heart swelled, filled with the knowledge of how hard he'd worked to give that vital gift to her. How she loved this man, this courageous hero who had knelt before her, offering her everything he had.

"You're right about that," he said, taking

Liza's hands in his own and raising the left one to his lips. "I can't think of one thing I don't have."

"Nor can I," she said, lost in his eyes.

She knew they had a lot of work ahead of them. The slide had stolen everything she owned: her clothes, her home, her store . . . everything. And yet it was true: everything she needed stood right in front of her, tall and strong and promising to love her for the rest of her life.

Liza could still remember the uncertainty she'd felt when she'd stepped out of the security of her childhood home, suitcase in hand, unprepared for the journey ahead. Now here she stood with not one thing left in her name, and she could hardly wait to step into the unknown. Because after all the danger, all the heartbreak and loss, she finally had the only piece of gold that would ever really matter.

A NOTE TO READERS

Every time I begin working on a new book about a moment in Canadian history, I am embarrassed by the fact that when I was younger I thought history was boring, because through the years of cumulative research I've done for all my books I don't believe I have been bored even once. Every time I dig up a new fact I am drawn in, and the most difficult part for me is not including every single bit of it in the finished book.

My stories are inspired by important chapters in Canadian history that I believe may be in danger of being forgotten. And I have found so many. How could I ever have thought Canadian history was dull when our past is filled with things like the Halifax Explosion, the Acadian Expulsion, German U-boats landing on our coastline during World War II, the Klondike Gold Rush, and the Frank Slide? Can you imagine the real people behind these stories? Because that's what I do. I put myself into those situations with my characters, and I learn the history well enough that I don't just see what happened. I feel it.

I had wanted to write something about the early Mounties for a while, but I hadn't started to really dig into their history until after *Promises to Keep* had been put to bed. Back in 2015, when I had the great honour of touring Canada for the first time with the wonderful Susanna Kearsley, I happened to see a banner outside the Royal BC Museum in Victoria advertising an upcoming exhibit about the Klondike Gold Rush. And guess who I discovered kept the peace and did so much more during that time? Mounties. It was perfect.

So I started to dig. My local library is always the first to know what I am about to work on for my next novel because I usually start off with armloads of non-fiction books, but I do love the internet. When I am intrigued by something not fully explained in a book, or explained in some way that I don't connect to it, I go online and I surf like mad. I search out the usual websites for particular subjects or places or people, but then I go deeper, finding historians whose passion it is to delve into these things. Sometimes I'm able to locate historical reenactment groups, and those people are gems, emphatic and dedicated to every single piece of information, and I can count on them to ensure I get every aspect right. When it came to the Mounties, I was writing about a part of history that continues today, and I wanted to make sure I dug deep. Well, I found treasure this time.

I have a theory that works with my books as well as it does in my personal life, and that is that if something is meant to happen it won't be impossibly difficult to get it done. Things tend to fall into place if I'm on the right track. And the most wonderful thing happened to me at the beginning of this book. It was voting day in Nova Scotia, and I'd gone in to cast my vote at our local polling station. One of the ladies behind the desk recognized me from when she was the librarian at my daughters' elementary school, and we started chatting. After she asked what I was working on, she told me she had an RCMP contact for me who was very interested in Mountie history. So thank you, Elizabeth Sullivan, for introducing me to . . .

Assistant Commissioner of the RCMP, Commanding Officer Brian Brennan! Brian has been outstanding in his support for this book, starting with his loaning me a

Mountie boot box full of journals, photos, articles, and more from the 1800s and early 1900s. What a treasure trove! Included in there was the handwritten diary of Constable R. Brackett from 1923 to 1928 at the RCMP Great Slave Lake subdistrict in the Northwest Territories. I decided to transcribe his diary as a means of learning more, and I thoroughly enjoyed the process. Based on the number of days in which Constable Brackett recalled nothing but the weather and his personal budget, I can see how lonely that life would have been, but then there were moments of excitement and a quiet kind of levity, which I can imagine would be much needed out there in the middle of nowhere. Here are some examples:

Oct 6 1926

Snowed and blowed hard all night and still snowing & blowing like . . . I didn't say it. About four or five inches fell and drifts some places four & five ft high. The only way out is still floating. We put skids under her and had her tied nice to the bank, and today the water has come up high enough to float her. So we still have to put her in winter quarters . . . . But she looks pretty setting there like a duck tied to the bank.

He finishes some of his entries with adorable little jokes:

Give me a sentence with the word fiddle
If de bed ain't long enough my fiddle stick
   out.

But according to *The Klondike Nugget,* things could get more exciting. Especially in the Yukon. In January 1899, it was reported:

COURT NEWS

Robert Russell got 18 months on the woodpile and really deserved more. When he was broke and sick he was nursed back to health in the police hospital and afterwards given employment in the officers' mess room. He responded by stealing everything in sight after but four days. The woodpile at temperatures of 50 below may work reformation.

In addition to the journals, Assistant Commissioner Brian Brennan welcomed me to his office a few times, giving me guided tours down the RCMP Headquarters' hallway of Mountie history and mementos, including the only known gold ring made from an NWMP shoulder title — made in Dawson City, of all places — and classic artwork by Arnold Friberg. Now I know where Dudley Do-Right got his famous cleft chin! When I mentioned to him about my characters needing Christmas gifts for one another, he invited me to see his collection of Mountie button pins, cap badges, and shoulder titles. When Sergeant Thompson mentions in the story that Ben had received a new set of buttons, that is based on fact. The uniform buttons were occasionally replaced — the men sewed the new ones on themselves — and sometimes they took the old ones to jewellers to make them into "sweetheart pins" or hatpins. This helped me imagine the future Mrs. Turner's sweetheart pin from Christmas 1899!

Speaking of the name Turner . . . One day, when I was already deep into creating the story, I got caught up in watching videos about the Klondike Gold Rush and I came across a TED Talk by award-winning author Chris Turner called "Why Canadian History Isn't as Boring as You Think It Is." I was rapt. Every word thrilled me — here was a man speaking my own thoughts, and his words were both exciting and inspiring. At the time that I saw the video I was working on finding the right name for Ben, and Chris's talk felt so familiar to me that I thought his surname suited Ben perfectly.

Every author knows the fever that burns

when a story takes root and begins to grow. I had a wonderful time researching this book — in fact, I took a couple of weeks and travelled around Alberta and visited almost twenty museums. As I walked through the museums — most of them dusty and generally carrying the sense of having been forgotten despite the dedicated museum staff and volunteers — the smell of must in the air, my characters were already there ahead of me, nudging me towards certain exhibits, pointing out details in hundred-year-old photographs.

Ben was with me from the start, always keen to show off the red serge. Every time I saw an outpost I admired the sparse accommodations of the NWMP and orderly arrangement of the few things they had out there in the Canadian wilds, and I thought about what discipline and determination those young men had, having to make sense of a chaotic place and time with very few tools at their disposal. I took pictures of everything from the Stetson hat press — which reminded me of an early tennis racket press — to the Mounties' guns and cuffs, and yes, I even have a couple photos of me dressed in actual retired red serge coats. The North-West Mounted Police (later the Royal North-West Mounted Police and then the Royal Canadian Mounted Police) set up dozens of outposts in out-of-the-way places, often only manned by one or two constables at a time, and I visited a few, like the big Fort Macleod museum of the NWMP and First Nations Interpretive Centre, where they still perform the Musical Ride for tourists, the outpost in Canmore, and the one in the Kootenai Brown Pioneer Village.

During my extended museum tour, I did a lot of research on trains, among other things. At the time, I was sure those would be central to the story — now I know everything I learned will most likely be put to use in a future novel — and I soaked up old maps featuring the meandering tracks of the blossoming Canadian railways and I sat in old train stations just to imagine what it would have been like, waiting there in my corset and skirts, watching hordes of excited prospectors board the trains and travel to the North. At Heritage Park in Calgary — where they had not only a working steam train but also a 1905 wooden CPR Sleeper Car in the process of being lovingly restored — I recorded the train's whistle as it roared by, letting the screech of brakes and shushing of the engine blend in my head so I could imagine them melding with the beating of the excited passengers' hearts. The only way to really write about those things is to take it all in.

One tour that summer that I will never forget took place 150 feet underground, in the Bellevue coal mine. Since I'd determined the Frank Slide was going to be featured in the book, I figured I should experience a taste of the miners' lives, so I put on my warmest hoodie (the temperature inside is usually below 0 °C) and my rented helmet with lamp and I trudged into the dark. As I walked in, I reminded myself how much my research tour inside a submarine for *Come from Away* had terrified me and how claustrophobic I can get, but there was no turning back. Let me tell you, after that tour I suddenly had so much respect for the fortitude of miners. That place was cold and dark and seemed far too unpredictable to me, though I know it was perfectly safe and has been for over a hundred years. When our guide told us to shut off our lamps for a minute, I was blown away. I mean, she said it would be dark, but I quite literally couldn't see my hand one inch from my eye. That was more than a little unnerving, and though it was one of those experiences I shall only do once, I'm glad I did it. Now I know the courage it took for those men to trudge into the always-moving Turtle Mountain every single day.

I like to think that I write in a cinematic way, because that's how I see my stories, and while every place in Canada has striking scenery, it's been incredibly exciting for me to write about the Klondike. The intensity of the North in all its glory astounds me, as do the people who lived there both then and now. If you look for images about the Chilkoot Trail and the Klondike Gold Rush (I will be posting some on my website), you will see black and white photographs that feel almost fictitious. As if no one could *really* live through all that. But they did. And it was the most colourful of those characters who pulled me into the reality of the situation: "Diamond Tooth" Gertie Lovejoy, Belinda Mulrooney, Superintendent Sam Steele, author Jack London, and so many more. The real-life Belinda Mulrooney did indeed marry Monsieur Le Comte Charles Carbonneau in 1900. He had arrived in Dawson City claiming to be a champagne salesman representing interests in Bordeaux, France, but in reality Monsieur Carbonneau was no more than a barber from Rue St. Denis in Montreal.

We often think of the men making their way over the Chilkoot Pass and down to the scrambling city of Dawson, but at least a thousand women (about one out of every ten stampeders) and some children took that same trek. A very small percentage of those women might have been relatively hardened travellers, but the majority would have been faced with an unimaginable challenge. Liza never intended to go to the Yukon. Leaving her comfortable life in Vancouver was the furthest thing from her mind. From the first sentence I saw myself in her, and it was inspiring for me to witness her growing from a quiet, refined young lady to a woman of business who knew what she wanted and went for it.

In addition to all the other challenges of the Trail, women in 1898 also had to contend with the repressive social customs of the late Victorian age. Liza wasn't the only one to trade in her corset, skirts, bloomers, and leg-of-mutton sleeves for men's clothes, and some women even pretended to be men in order to avoid unwanted attention. The women came for all different reasons and they had limited skills, but they had dreams that needed to be paid for. Yes, there were dance hall girls and prostitutes, but there were also female prospectors, hotel owners, photographers, saloon owners, and more like Belinda Mulrooney. Some came to find adventure and gold, some came to find a husband, and some continued to raise their children in a world unlike anywhere else on earth.

One of my favourite stories is about seventy-six-year-old "Barbara," who never gave her last name when she arrived in Skagway and applied for a job as a newspaper seller. She told the boss that "all my life I've wondered what it would be like to go out among complete strangers and make my own way. I always wanted to try it and never got the chance. When the chance came I took it. And here I am!" Probably out of sympathy for the tiny woman, the boss gave her the job, and she amazed them all by becoming the top paper-seller in the town. When she made enough money, she paid two dollars for a piano box, where she lived for six months. She returned to her daughter in Seattle for the summer, but only after making the boss promise her job would still be open for her the following spring and the piano box would still be hers.

Another major character in the Dawson City adventure was Father William Judge, and though he didn't make it into the final novel, he has stayed with me. A slight man with fragile health and dogged determination, Judge — also known as the Saint of Dawson City — drove his one-dog sled, loaded with medical supplies and food, through fifty miles of deep snow between Fortymile and Dawson in March 1897. He adopted the town as his parish, ran a small hospital in a tent, and later built a church. In my research I came across this quote by him, which I think perfectly encapsulates the gold fever that burned in so many prospectors: "One would think that gold is the one thing necessary for happiness in time and eternity to see the way in which men seek it even in these frozen regions, and how they are willing to sacrifice soul and body to get it."

But if one was to truly look for the heroes of the Klondike, I would suggest they start with the Mounties. Imagine these young men, paid only a dollar a day, battling −60 °C temperatures under a continuous bombardment of snow and threat of death, not for fame and fortune, but for the honour of serving the people. Everything I read and learned about the Mounties in my research only confirmed and built upon the respect I have for these heroes of both yesterday and today.

I feel incredibly blessed to do what I do. I never planned to be an author, and I never thought I'd ever have any interest in history, let alone ours. But writing has become my life, and I couldn't be happier. There are so many important stories in our past, and I plan to get to the core of as many as I can. I love to travel back in time and breathe life back into Canadian history, and I want to bring you with me.

ACKNOWLEDGEMENTS

An epic adventure story requires an epic list of sources, and I'd like to publicly thank some of them here — I hope I'm not forgetting anyone, but sometimes the information comes so fast and furious I forget to write sources down.

First of all, I would like to thank Assistant Commissioner of the RCMP, Commanding Officer Brian Brennan for his invaluable personal and professional input on the final manuscript. I am so honoured by his praise for the book. Along the way he connected me to retired RCMP Corporal Tim Popp, who filled my head and inbox with the most wonderful facts about the early Mounties. Without these two men, I couldn't possibly have included such an in-depth look into Constable Ben Turner. I would also like to thank Tom Long (Fort Edmonton Park), Kristine Nygren and Erica Tsui (Fort Heritage Precinct, Fort Saskatchewan), and

Ashley Hardwick (Collections Manager: The Fort Museum of the NWMP) for helping me with my research into the NWMP.

For insight into the Klondike and Dawson City, thank you to the very patient Dylan Meyerhoffer (Collections Specialist: Parks Canada Agency), Alex Somerville (Executive Director: Dawson City Museum), Eilysh Zurock (Archive Assistant: Klondike History Library), Vivian Belik (Reference Assistant: Yukon Archives), Angharad Wenz (Curator: Dawson City Museum), and BC Archives. Thank you also to Charlotte Gray for her excellent work in *The Promise of Canada,* and of course to the late, great Pierre Berton.

For research on the Frank Slide, huge thanks to Joey Ambrosi (Interpretation-Education Officer: Frank Slide Interpretive Centre) and the amazing Monica Field (Manager: Frank Slide Interpretive Centre). Their Interpretive Centre is a fascinating experience, and I would love to go again any time.

When George and Liza were on their way towards Lake Lindeman and were discussing photography, I needed to understand what that entailed in 1898. So I reached out to the very professional and enthusiastic Kevin Murray of www.historiccamera.com

and got a terrific lesson on the Kodak of the day. Thank you, Kevin!

Again, thank you to Leah Belter and her daughter, Christine Watson, for leaving my husband's family reunion just so you could drive the forty-five minutes home and back with your personal scrapbook of your family's journey along the Chilkoot Trail. What an incredible experience!

The scariest part of writing is submitting a manuscript. No matter how many books I've written, I still find that to be the most intimidating part. But from the very beginning of my partnership with them, the team at Simon & Schuster Canada has been incredible, and I'd like to thank my friend and mentor, Susanna Kearsley, for introducing me to them. Also for all the time she spent with me online, on the plane, in the hotels, in the restaurants, in the local fish & chips place, on the beach, in my backyard with Murphy and the chickens, and sharing her wonderfully practical and eye-opening lessons. You are teaching me how to make my dreams come true, my friend! I value every minute I spend with you. Thank you for your generosity, warmth, and support.

Now back to the team at Simon & Schuster Canada, who are encouraging and determined, who always have my back, and who are always looking forward. I am so honoured and proud to be in your amazing stable of authors! I promise to fill the shelves with more Canadian historical fiction for as long as you'll have me. Thank you to Simon & Schuster Canada's fearless leader, President Kevin Hanson, thank you to the gracious and insightful VP Editorial Director, Nita Provonost, and Senior Editor Laurie Grassi, thank you to my busy, busy babysitter, Associate Director of Publicity Rita Silva, thank you to smiling Sales Rep extraordinaire Sherry Lee, thank you to my Promo Queen, Jacquelynne Lennard, and thank you to anyone I carelessly forgot to put on this list.

But there is no one I want to thank more than my guardian angel, my editor, and my friend, Simon & Schuster Canada's editor Sarah St. Pierre. She sees through my often-overwhelming explosions of words and ideas and brilliantly helps me see what I was actually talking about before I got lost, she picks me up when I throw myself on the floor in a self-defeating tantrum, she unabashedly shares my incredible taste in superhero movie versions of my characters (Max = Rudi, Henry = Ben), she holds me in place when new ideas are spinning in ever-expanding circles in my head, and she inspires my wanderlust with her fantastic Instagram travels. So much brilliance and talent and insight in one sweet, smiling woman. Thank you, Sarah.

To my agent, Jacques de Spoelberch, thank you for your tireless efforts on my behalf. I was elated when you took me on back in 2010 (I have your contract framed in my office) and I continue to be honoured by your belief in me and by your representation. I aim to make you proud and keep you busy!

Thank you to my mom, Jane, and her dear husband, Don, for letting me hang out at your place and borrow "the G" when we came for my extended museum tour. I wish I'd remembered to take a picture of the bearskin coat. Mom, the love and encouragement you gave me throughout my life helped me believe I could actually do this author thing, and look at me now!

The support of family is everything to a writer, and I'm fortunate to always be able to count on mine. We're empty nesters now, so I don't see our girls nearly as often as I would like, but when I do they are subjected to my latest book updates (probably repeated many times), my occasional staring off into the distance (inspiration often strikes at the most inopportune times), and both my frustrations and exaltations, and they actually encourage me to do more of all of the above around them. Emily and Piper, I love you with all my heart. You make me proud every day.

I should probably admit right here that while I'm writing a book I fall head over heels in love with every one of my lead male characters. Like . . . maybe to the point of obsession. Early on in the process I see an actor somewhere whose presence fits perfectly with my character's and I end up watching hours and hours of movies and/or TV shows featuring that actor. Henry Cavill, for me, became Ben Turner right away. My husband doesn't mind my crushes, and he patiently watches the movies with me — he actually enjoys most of them, I think — because he knows he's the only real lead in my life. He's also one of my go-to research experts. Danny, Rudi, Connor, and Ben are wonderful, heroic men, and that's because they all have some of my husband's traits, and often they share aspects of his past. Those men are made so real because of Dwayne's willingness to participate in my impromptu interrogations.

I couldn't do what I do without Dwayne's unwavering support, encouragement, and patience. And cooking. And laughter. And love.

Last, but never least, thank you to everyone out there who has chosen to invest both precious money and time on one or more of my books. When you write a review online, I am truly grateful, and when you send me a personal note, I am often moved to tears. As I've said so many times, I feel incredibly fortunate to do what I do, and I love that I have the opportunity to tell Canada's stories. But knowing you're out there, patiently waiting for the next installment, telling your friends about my books, well, it is humbling and beyond wonderful. Thank you from the bottom of my heart.

ABOUT THE AUTHOR

Genevieve Graham is the bestselling author of *Tides of Honour, Promises to Keep,* and *Come from Away.* She is passionate about breathing life back into Canadian history through tales of love and adventure. She lives near Halifax, Nova Scotia. Visit her at GenevieveGraham.com or on Twitter @GenGrahamAuthor.

The employees of Thorndike Press hope you have enjoyed this Large Print book. All our Thorndike, Wheeler, and Kennebec Large Print titles are designed for easy reading, and all our books are made to last. Other Thorndike Press Large Print books are available at your library, through selected bookstores, or directly from us.

For information about titles, please call:
(800) 223-1244

or visit our website at:
gale.com/thorndike

To share your comments, please write:
Publisher
Thorndike Press
10 Water St., Suite 310
Waterville, ME 04901